THE
KINDNESS OF
STRANGERS

"If you wish someone still wrote classic, hard-boiled detective novels, Andy Weinberger does! Every installment in this series is a pure pleasure to read, and *The Kindness of Strangers* is no exception. Amos Parisman is a cantankerous but large-hearted old man pursuing wrongdoers for all the right reasons. His voice is pitch-perfect, and the Los Angeles he inhabits is instantly familiar. Any fan of authentic detective fiction will adore this novel."

—Amy Stewart, bestselling author of the *Kopp Sisters* Series

"*The Kindness of Strangers* combines an engrossing mystery with a vivid feeling of humanity. The *Amos Parisman* series is equal parts suspenseful and soulful, witty and worldly wise, entertaining and heart-breaking. And he's Jewish, too! What's not to like?"

—Elliott Kalan, co-host of *The Flop House* podcast

"Down in L.A., Andy Weinberger's detective Amos Parisman is a Talmudic gumshoe—he's ethically motivated, and often in his investigations, life is really more about asking the right questions than assuming you will actually find the right answers. (I daydream Parisman meeting Eddie Muller, the host of *Noir Alley* for TCM, in a dive near the Chateau Marmont and talking all night.) Since Weinberger 'started late' as a writer, it's only fair to his loyal readers that he finds a way to continue writing about Amos Parisman and Lieutenant Malloy well into the afterlife. Weinberger is an astonishingly gifted and big-hearted storyteller."

—Howard Norman, author of *Next Life Might Be Kinder*

THE
KINDNESS OF
STRANGERS

More Amos Parisman Mysteries
by Andy Weinberger

An Old Man's Game
Reason to Kill

THE
KINDNESS OF
STRANGERS

An Amos Parisman Mystery

ANDY WEINBERGER

PROSPECT
·PARK·
BOOKS

Prospect Park Books
an imprint of Turner Publishing Company
Nashville, Tennessee

www.turnerpublishing.com

The Kindness of Strangers

Cover design by Mimi Bark

Cover illustration by Ben Perini

Book design by Erin Seaward-Hiatt

Library of Congress Cataloging-in-Publication Data

Names: Weinberger, Andy, author.
Title: The kindness of strangers / by Andy Weinberger.
Description: Nashville, Tennessee : Turner Publishing, [2022] |
Identifiers: LCCN 2021028298 (print) | LCCN 2021028299 (ebook) | ISBN
    9781684428175 (hardcover) | ISBN 9781684428168 (paperback) | ISBN
    9781684428182 (ebook)
Subjects: LCGFT: Detective and mystery fiction. | Novels.
Classification: LCC PS3623.E4324234 K56 2022 (print) | LCC PS3623.
    E4324234
    (ebook) | DDC 813/.6—dc23
LC record available at https://lccn.loc.gov/2021028298
LC ebook record available at https://lccn.loc.gov/2021028299

Printed in the United States of America

For Lilla, and for The Jews Who Eat (you know who you are)

"I have always depended on the kindness of strangers."

—BLANCHE DUBOIS, in *A Streetcar Named Desire*

PROLOGUE

It was my cousin Shelly who talked me into joining the Marines, even though he couldn't go on account of his flaming ulcer. *I would,* he said, *you know I would, boychik, but since they won't take me, you need to go instead. You're the only person I'd trust to fill my shoes. You don't realize how much you owe this country, Amos. Think about it. All the blessings.* Shelly was always a great talker. Student body president three years in a row. Head of the debate team. He could talk the skin off a banana if he wanted to back then. And I was young and stupid and sick of being a Hollywood teenager. I believed every word. And when I damn near died in Vietnam and came back, it was Shelly who met me at the airport with a bottle of champagne, Shelly who took me aside at my Aunt Esther's memorial and advised me to go to school again. Go to Berkeley, he said. It's your kind of place. Which I'm grateful for, because that's how I met Loretta. I don't know what I would've done without her.

But all this is beside the point. Or no, the point is that Shelly and I go way back. We were kids together, and now, hard to believe, we're two old men together, a couple of genuine *alte katchkes,* if you know what I'm saying. And here I am, after all these years, sitting across from him at a rickety table in the Farmers Market, the sun streaming down, me with a plate of hummus and falafel and a club soda, him with a Mexican beer and a cheeseburger. In his seventy years, Shelly's gotten fat and bald. He's had several cancerous moles removed from his face, and he's had three wives, each one of whom left him, and probably no longer speak to him. But nothing's changed; he hasn't stopped giving advice. *You should hang out with us, sometime,* he says now. *With who?* I say. *Clue me in, Shelly. These days, it seems like all we ever do is go to funerals.* He says, *you know me, Amos. I'm not a religious man. What's God ever done for me? All I care about is community. Community, pure and simple.* And then he explains to me that he and his friends have put together a little club. Very informal. No pressure whatsoever. They call themselves The Jews Who Eat. Funny name, huh? Hell, half of them aren't even Jewish. And even the ones who are, they're behind in their dues, let's put it that way. But still, they're like my own family, and all they wanna do is meet and talk and shoot the shit. And eat, of course. It's like being backstage on opening night. *Everybody's happy,* he says. *I can tell you're not ready to throw in the towel yet. You're not that old. You want another shot at happiness, nu? So come.* He clutches my hand like he's a used car salesman sealing the deal.

After a speech like that, you can't say no flat out, so I wag my head diplomatically from side to side. I tell him okay, maybe. I'll sleep on it. But the more I do, the more I wonder just where Shelly's sage advice is going to land me next. Maybe I've known him too long. Or maybe I'm just extra careful now about who I call a friend. Part of being a good detective, I've decided, is you always keep at least one card face down on the table. If everyone knows what you have, well, brother, you don't have anything.

CHAPTER 1

The crumpled corpse at the bottom of the big green dumpster looked familiar. I'd seen her before, but it took a minute or two before I remembered where. Then it hit me. The homeless lady I passed every week on my walk around the neighborhood. Sure. The one missing half her teeth. The one with the purple scarf draped over her head, always napping at the bus stop on 3rd. The one who broke into a happy little soft-shoe once when I handed her a dollar. That one.

"So she's local?" Lieutenant Malloy asks.

"About as local as they come," I say.

"You don't remember her name, by any chance, do you?"

"She never told me her name. We didn't talk a lot. All she had was a cardboard sign. 'Homeless people matter,' I think it said."

Bill Malloy folds his arms together. "That's swell," he says. These days, every time we see each other it's because somebody on his beat turns up dead. We try to socialize, sure, but the truth is, we're different. Maybe it's a cultural thing, I dunno. Still, here we are. It's the middle of February. There are probably only three people in Los Angeles who can remember the last time it rained. Right now, the sun is shining, the temperature is climbing, and we're standing around in this godforsaken alley, the Lieutenant and me. Murder is about the only thing that binds us together. That, and luck. My bad luck to be taking my usual morning stroll and walk right into a full-blown crime scene. We peer down into the dumpster one more time. A trio of flies have started buzzing lazily above her bare neck, landing, taking off, landing again. Waiting maybe to see if she reacts, which she doesn't. Malloy turns his head. He nods to the forensics guys in their silver minivan; they should go ahead and do whatever it is they do.

"Who found her?" I ask.

"Barista from the coffee bar came out this morning to toss in a couple of bags from last night. Nice kid. Teenager. This is her first real job. Scared the living shit out of her."

"I can imagine. Not the way you want to start off your Monday, huh?"

He doesn't respond, but the wheels are turning inside. Malloy is, beyond a doubt, the most decent cop I've ever met. Just seeing that poor Black woman lying there in the garbage is going to send him to the medicine cabinet. Not now maybe, but later.

"How'd she die?"

"Dunno," he says. His voice is flat. He tugs absentmindedly at his tie. It's an old pale blue silk thing with tiny sailboats crisscrossing back and forth. Bill's the only man I know who collects ties. Now that I think about it, he's practically the only one I know who wears them anymore. "Looks like someone went after her head with a hammer," he says, "but I'll leave that to the scientists. Whoever he was, he didn't like her, that's for sure."

A pair of deputies are quietly spooling out the yellow plastic tape, making a perimeter, and there are three black-and-white cruisers parked at one end with their blinkers going. On Beverly Boulevard, a handful of curious pedestrians have stopped to watch, but only for a minute. A police photographer is perched on an eight-foot aluminum ladder, snapping away at the dumpster from all angles. Malloy and I meander down the alley in the other direction. Even as he's talking, I see his eyes scanning the gritty pavement back and forth, hoping, maybe praying, for clues.

"This won't be easy," he says after a minute. "No motive, no witnesses. Hell, we don't even have the victim's name. Almost like it didn't even happen."

"You'd like it better that way, I'm sure," I say, and when he gives me a startled look, I add, "if it never happened."

"I would. Whenever I see something like this, it makes me wish I'd never given up drinking."

I pat him on the shoulder. After years of sobriety I'm sure he's not about to fall off the wagon. Not over this. He's got that talk about the Higher Power memorized. Still, the impulse is always there, isn't it? "Well, they didn't go after her for her money, we know that much."

"You can't rule that out, either. Another homeless Joe might have looked at her, seen something in that shopping cart he wanted. Who knows what goes on with these crazy people? They fight over crumbs half the time."

We pause in front of the old lady's rusty cart. There's a metal tag that indicates it came from Ralph's originally. Probably the one down on Wilshire and Hauser, not that it makes any difference. Inside the cart are piles of moldy old clothes in white plastic trash bags. Shoes and sweaters and sweatpants. Some of them folded neatly together, the rest just shoved in pell-mell. All things a veteran of the great urban outdoors would cherish.

"I'm kinda glad you walked in on us, Amos. I hope this"—he points to the contents of the dumpster—"doesn't ruin the rest of your day. I hope you don't mind."

It's a strange thing to say to me, really. I've been in a fog for so long. What happens now when you wake up all alone every day. "Mind? Are you kidding? This is exactly the kind of case I need."

"Well, it's not your case. Not strictly speaking. Forget about it."

"No, no, of course not, I realize that. It's a police matter. Only I happen to know a little bit about her. I also know the neighborhood. And besides, Bill—this retirement thing?—between you and me, I'd rather be dead."

"Don't say that, old man. You'll be there soon enough as it is."

"True. But for now, a body in a dumpster—you know what? I'm not gonna lie to you, it's exciting."

"Really?" I can tell by the tone in his voice that I've offended some part of his Catholic soul.

"Well, not exciting, maybe that's the wrong word."

"So what's the right word?"

I shrug. "I'm drawn to it, I guess. Some people, they look at evil and they run the other way."

"As they should," he says.

"With me, hey, it gives me a reason to get up in the morning."

Malloy chuckles, shakes his head. "You're a sick puppy," he says. "But okay, then, have at it. But just remember: This is a homeless person. Nobody cares. I mean that, Amos."

I tell him I'll snoop around, see what I can dig up, get back to him.

"Fact is," he says, "we're gonna need help here. If we ever picked her up for anything, we might have her fingerprints on file. For now, the neighborhood angle is all we've got."

We shake hands. "Not entirely. You've also got the best Jewish detective in Los Angeles helping you out," I say. "Or at least the oldest."

*   *   *

Before I wander back to my apartment at Park La Brea, I find a nice shady seat on a low cinder block wall in front of Wells Fargo. I take out my cell phone and punch in my new friend Mara's number. She'll be up by now. "You'll never guess what I've seen this morning," is how I begin.

"Please don't make me guess," she says. "I'm too sleepy."

"A corpse," I say. "A corpse in a dumpster."

"Oh my God," she says. Now she's wide awake.

Then I tell her about my encounter with Lieutenant Malloy and the poor battered woman in the alley. I tell her she has no name and almost no face and the cops don't know where to begin. "They can take pictures of her forever," I say, "they can shoot until they run out of film, it won't matter."

"Why not?"

"Because," I say, paraphrasing Malloy's words, "no one cares about street people."

"Not so," she replies. "You do. I do."

"Okay, well, maybe we're the exception, then. But nobody else."

Once I get back to my apartment, I plop down on the couch and take a twenty-minute nap. At my age, that's all I really need to snap back. Then I put my shoes on again, swallow a small glass of iced coffee, readjust my Dodgers cap, make sure I have my keys, and close the door behind me.

I trudge west again toward CBS and the Fairfax District, sharing the sidewalk with joggers in bright Day-Glo shorts and a young woman pushing a baby carriage. There's a newsstand near Whole Foods. Jamal is behind the counter as usual, restocking the shelves and selling cigarettes and lottery tickets. He's a wiry, fast-talking guy. Deep, dark, furtive eyes that go all the way down to his soul, and he wears a little white cotton cap that looks like a yarmulke, only bigger. The magazine business is slow, he tells me. No one reads anymore. No one cares which movie star is sleeping with which other movie star. Or if they do, they're reading about it on Twitter.

"Maybe you should just sell lottery tickets," I say. "Everyone wants to be rich."

"Yes," he goes, "that's America in a fucking nutshell."

Jamal doesn't gamble. He hates gamblers. He's told me more than once he thinks they're fools, but in his mind, that's a separate discussion. It has little to do with running a business. He's willing to take their money if they want to throw it away on a lottery ticket. He and his wife came here a dozen years ago from Ramallah. They had nothing. Now he has a small tract house in Studio City and a mortgage and a used Toyota minivan that he just paid off last month. He's worked here at the newsstand all that time, and lately he's been talking to Rick Sherman, the absentee owner, about buying him out. He thinks it's laughable, or at least ironic, that Rick, who is Jewish, was willing to hire him to work at the shop, and even more ironic that now he's on the verge of taking over.

"This wouldn't happen in Israel," he says. "Believe me, they despise us there. But here, in California, Jews and Muslims, we get along just fine. Religion? Who cares? That's what I love about this place. Anything's possible."

I'd like to stand around with Jamal and explore what a great country this is, how naïve we are and how much Jews and Palestinians really have in common. I would, but he hasn't learned the value of punctuation. He's the sort of guy who will go on forever if I don't jump right in and change the subject.

"You know that old Black lady who wanders up and down 3rd all the time? The homeless one who's always parking her shopping cart near the bus stops so she can sleep?"

"How would I know such a person?" he asks. "Does she buy magazines? Does she smoke cigarettes?"

I give him a look. "I'm afraid she doesn't do anything anymore, Jamal. She's dead."

"Ah. This is sad. And what is her name?"

"That's what I was hoping you knew."

He scratches the back of his head, readjusts his yarmulke. "I think I know who you are speaking of," he says, "but she never came into my shop. For that, I am thankful, naturally. Her cart was always full of old clothes. You should talk to the folks at Ross. Or maybe the Goodwill on Beverly."

I thank him. Before I go, I buy myself a lottery ticket. "I know I'm not going to win," I say, as the machine spits it out and he hands it over. "So skip the lecture. For a buck, you can dream, right?"

"Of course," he agrees. "You will never win. But you're right. This is the only reason to buy a ticket. For the dream." And as I go out the door, he can't resist adding what he thinks is another meaningless American phrase: "Good luck."

*   *   *

Gretchen, the manager at Ross Dress for Less, is a stout, quirky woman in her thirties. She's the kind of person who's always trying to lose weight, the kind many people look at and automatically feel sorry for, the kind you could make up sad stories about if you saw her sitting on a park bench at noon, eating her low-fat cottage cheese and diet Pepsi. What went wrong with her life. How she came to work at Ross. If you cared enough, that's what you'd do. She has eight different silver rings on her fingers and she seems to favor the color black. Today it's black pants and a charcoal blouse, covered by a long black cardigan sweater. Beneath the glass desktop in her cramped office she has put together a collage of poodle pictures. Dozens and dozens of white fluffy poodles. Or maybe it's just one white fluffy poodle at different times or in different poses, I can't tell.

I ask her about the homeless lady and right away she knows who I mean.

"Oh, that would be Delia," she says. She plays with her rings as she speaks. Turns them over, takes them off, tries them out on other fingers. Some rings don't work because the fingers are too pudgy. She doesn't look at me directly. She touches her hands again. The rings are her friends. "I don't know her last name. She's just such a character, you know. There but for the grace of God? She's always out front when I come to work. Sits on the bench every morning, singing and humming to herself, waiting for the bus. Never gets on, though."

"No," I say. "She'd have to leave her shopping cart behind. That wouldn't do."

"Come to think of it, I haven't seen her around," Gretchen says. And all at once her radar kicks in. "Is she okay?"

"Actually," I say, "they found her over in the alley nearby. I'm afraid she's dead."

"Oh dear," says Gretchen. "Oh, dear me." Her face turns pale and she bites her lower lip. "I—I didn't know." She stares at her hands and touches her rings again, one at a time.

"Of course not," I say. "How could you?" I thank her, stand up, and lay my business card down on her desk, just in case anything else about Delia comes to mind. I have lots of business cards. Too many, in fact. I worry that my business cards will end up in a landfill someday and people will talk about what a great waste of paper it was.

Outside it's starting to cloud over. Not cold or anything, but the weatherman this morning on channel 5 said there was a slim chance of rain, which in L.A. means there's really no chance at all. I head back toward the Whole Foods parking lot. Guillermo, the short leathery guy who sells fresh papayas and mangoes and guava juice out of his cart, waves at me. I ask him about Delia.

"I see her, for sure. I know who she is," he says. "*La vieja.* The old lady, *si.*"

"What else do you know about her, Guillermo? Did she have any friends? Did she have a last name?"

"She liked fresh mango. She could speak a little Spanish, a few words."

I give him my card. "Anything you can think of," I say, "just let me know. Or tell the police."

"You work for *la policia?*" he asks, suddenly a little uneasy. And all at once it dawns on me that Guillermo is probably here illegally, like half the town, and I probably should have kept my big mouth shut about the cops.

"I'm helping them out, that's all."

"If I remember anything, *señor,* I will tell you." He gives me a solemn look. I nod, and buy myself a small plastic cup of mango juice for the road.

*   *   *

Murder isn't what it used to be. In the old days, when I was a working stiff, if somebody killed somebody else, they had a damn good reason. You were screwing another man's wife, or you got fired from the factory, the only job you ever knew, and you said something when you shouldn't have, and suddenly it was the end of the line. Or maybe you robbed a jewelry store, and you didn't mean to kill anybody, but the clerk decided to be a hero and the gun went off. That's the way it used to be. There were whys and wherefores, or at least palatable excuses. You were jealous. You were desperate. You were wronged. You were enraged or temporarily insane. That's what the jury heard. That's the kind of argument a sharp defense attorney, like a four-star chef, could whip up in a bowl, could ramble on about in court forever. Now what you get is a poor woman—no rhyme or reason—just stuffed into a dumpster. Thrown away like yesterday's coffee. How's that for a metaphor?

As I step out of the elevator I run into my next-door neighbor, Mr. Wu. He's been in this building longer than anyone, which wouldn't be hard, since everyone is always moving in and out. Everybody except me and him, it seems. He is a short, quiet, balding man. I don't think I've ever seen him without suspenders and a bow tie.

"Good afternoon, Mr. Parisman," he says.

"Afternoon, Mr. Wu." In all the time we've known each other, it's never gone beyond that. As I put my key in the lock and twist the knob, it strikes me that I don't even know his first name. Just Wu. Old Mr. Wu in apartment 9H.

I call Lieutenant Malloy on his cell, tell him we're pretty sure the woman's first name is Delia, and also that she spoke some Spanish, which I think is kind of unusual.

"That would make sense," he says. "We've been picking through all the junk in her cart. A lot of Mexican clothing items there. Sandals and serapes, other stuff. Makes you stop and think."

"About what?"

"About what's really valuable in life."

Bill and I have had this conversation before, I realize. As he gets closer to retirement, he's starting to sound more and more like the priest his mother back in Chicago always wanted him to be. "Maybe you could send me a list, when you're done cataloging everything. It might help."

"I could. But really, the only other curiosity she owned was an old beat-up hymnal. It was tucked away inside a sweater. You know, holy roller songs. 'Oh What a Friend We Have in Jesus'."

"I'm familiar with the genre, Bill."

"Yeah, well, what's interesting is there's an address printed on the inside cover: property of the Eternal Light of Christ."

"Where is it?"

"Good question. It used to be on Sunset near Cahuenga or Cherokee. I vaguely remember it. One of those storefront churches. But that was so many years ago, before they started redeveloping everything and putting in those big box guys. I'm sure it's long gone. The rent alone would have sent them packing."

"Well, I guess I could still check it out. It's a long shot, but still, maybe worth a visit."

"You could, if you like. I'm gonna send Jason and Remo there to see what's what, so you don't have to. You're not being paid, Amos, remember that."

"I haven't been paid in some time, Bill. It's the story of my life."

CHAPTER 2

A couple days later, I run into Shelly outside of Amoeba Records. He says he's there to pick up an Edith Piaf CD for his latest girlfriend, Simone. Says she talked his ear off about Edith Piaf. What a gorgeous voice she had, what a miserable life she led. "You can't do better than that, I guess," is what he says. Then he shows me a picture of Simone, who really is a knockout. How Shelly managed to score with her is beyond my comprehension.

We wander around Amoeba together. It's a huge warehouse with concrete flooring and young kids sporting sneakers and tattoos and provocative T-shirts. And that's the help; I'm not talking about the customers. We go back to the jazz and old-timers section in the rear where they have the folks from our era and before. Bud Powell and Tito Puente and Sidney Bechet. I tell him about the murder case I'm working on. I don't tell him too much, just the basics. How Malloy called me in because I know the neighborhood and he's stumped. Shelly's fingers are flipping through the stacks of female vocalists, barely noticing the titles, and when I stop talking, he turns in my direction.

"Somebody paying you?" he asks.

"No, man," I say, "I'm doing this for myself. It's a good deed. A *mitzvah*."

"Huh," is all he says, and goes back to flipping.

"What's the matter?" I say. "You don't believe in mitzvahs?"

"Did you know this woman?" he asks. "The one who died?"

"We saw each other on the street," I say. "From time to time I gave her some money. Just a few bucks. But I never learned her name, that's as far as it went."

"A total stranger, then."

"You might say." I start to rummage through the section on Django Reinhardt. I have practically everything he ever recorded. Still, you never know. "But also a fellow human being."

"Huh," he says again. "You're an impressive fellow, Amos."

"Why's that?"

"Why? Because nobody in this country works for free. That's just a bald fact. Something I've learned in life. There's always an angle."

I grin. "Well, believe me, cousin, nothing would make me happier than to get paid for doing this, but at this point, I don't think that's gonna happen."

I spot a Django Reinhardt album that was new to me. A few minutes later we're standing at the checkout counter, and he takes it out of my hands and gives it to the clerk, along with the Edith Piaf CD he found. Then he throws down his Visa card. "Here, *boychik*," he says, "I'm buying today. Consider yourself on the payroll."

"Shelly," I say, "you don't have to do that."

"I don't want you working for nothing," he says. There's an adamance in his voice, as though I've tapped into a real nerve.

"So now what?" I ask. "I'm working for a song?"

"Something like that," he says.

*   *   *

As often as I can. That's what I tell folks when they ask me about Loretta. I go see her as often as I can. In the beginning it was every day. I was the loyal husband, the dutiful postman with his sack of mail. I delivered, every day, come hell or high water. But of course, it's not nearly enough. And I'm not talking about her, it's me.

When you live alone, the way I do, on the ninth floor in an old, drafty, unloved place like this, believe me, after a while, you start to mumble to yourself. Things fall apart. To ward off the silence, you whistle and you hum, you say all kinds of dumb stuff. You wonder how long a man can live on peanut butter and black coffee. Or if the last note Miles Davis ever made on that trumpet of his still exists somewhere in deep space. You ask yourself questions, and then you go ahead and answer them. Sometimes what's said makes sense, but not always. In the end, the questions don't matter much, you realize, so how can anyone care about the answers? Just words. And even as you say them, you grow awful tired of your own voice. The sad truth is that without Loretta around, every time I open my mouth, all I want to do is sob.

So I get in my Honda and drive out to the facility on Olympic whenever I can. Not a bad neighborhood, really. Two- and three-story pink stucco apartments everywhere you look. The usual spindly palm trees towering overhead and young people coming and going all the time like it's a revolving door, like there's no tomorrow, but that's what young people do in this town. They come in, chock full of energy, wise beyond their years. They just wrote a script and all they need now is someone at Netflix to read it. Or they want to direct. Or they just graduated from this fly-by-night acting school in Omaha and here they are in L.A. It's going to happen for them, sooner or later. And meanwhile they meet some tall dark creature online or at a club, and boom, the next thing you know, they've coupled up. And no one even mentions syphilis anymore, can you imagine?

They call it Olympic Terrace, and from the outside, you can't tell it's a nursing home at all, which, I must say, I like. You have to pretend; or let me put it another way: I've learned to pretend. Because if she were in her right mind, a nursing home would be the last place on earth Loretta would choose to be. And of course, under any other circumstance it'd be absolutely the last place I'd want her to be. So no, this isn't a nursing home, it's a hotel, a romantic hideaway she's decided she wants to live in for the rest of her days. There are lots of large potted plants on the ground floor, and the walls are different shades of pastel—lilac and ginger and ivory. The tall louvered windows on the second floor have spectacular views of the city. Best of all, they've done something remarkable with the aroma; it's like they're burning sandalwood incense nearby. At any rate, it doesn't smell like Lysol, which always makes me gag.

This afternoon she's flat on her back, sleeping, and I lean over and plant a light kiss on her forehead. "Hello, angel," I say. "Remember me?"

"Mmmm," she says, "I remember you." Then her eyes flutter open, and for a second she looks mildly surprised. "Amos," she says, "where have you been?"

I smile. It's a good day when she knows my name, that's the way I figure it. Even if she forgets later on, it doesn't matter. For now, for this moment, we're having ourselves a good day.

We usually spend around an hour together. She can't handle much more than that, and neither can I, frankly. I tell her what I'm up to, how I went grocery shopping, what vegetables I bought, or which new case I'm working on. Sometimes, if the litigation is too boring or too gruesome, I skip it. I ramble on instead about a cat burglar I once knew in Beverly Hills, or a missing woman I hunted down years ago in Bakersfield. Once in a while, if I'm between jobs, I'll make up a brand-new case and tell her that's what's on my plate now. It doesn't need to be the truth, I reckon, just entertaining. She doesn't care.

And when I see her eyes are drooping, or that she's starting to yawn, or act restless, that's my cue, that's when I push myself out of the chair and make for the exit. It always breaks my heart to be there, and it breaks my heart just as much to leave, but I've come to the conclusion there's no other way.

She's in room 212. Go down the hallway and take a sharp left and you'll see room 226. That's where Gus lives, if you can call it living. Gus Worthington is Mara's husband. He's a gentle old guy—frail, white haired, liver spots on his forehead. On a good day he weighs maybe a hundred twenty pounds. Light blue vacant eyes that stare right through you. In the two years I've known him, Gus hasn't said a single word to me. Which is curious, because Mara occupies so much of my time these days, you'd think he'd at least be a tiny bit jealous.

"Hey, Gus," I wave at him. "You know me? Amos? Amos Parisman? Yeah, we've met before. Many times, in fact."

Gus doesn't move a muscle. Just stares, and wets his thin lips every so often. He doesn't seem to feel the need to speak to anyone. The newly made bed next to his is empty. It used to belong to Peter Wang, but Mr. Wang passed away in his sleep three nights ago. Arrangements are already being made, I hear, for another occupant, so silent Gus won't be lonely much longer. The head of his bed is raised up slightly to allow him to look at the television hanging from the wall if he chooses to, but even if he weren't so inert he'd still have no idea how to work the remote control. Mr. Wang used to talk to himself constantly in Chinese; now that he's gone, the nurses leave the TV on all afternoon. They say it's to give Gus the illusion of company. Today he's watching, or not watching, a soap opera with the sound turned down to be almost inaudible.

*   *   *

Mara owns a small apartment up on Creston Drive in the Hollywood Hills. It has a spectacular view of the city, and according to the Armenian realtor who sold it to her, it used to be a trysting place for Bette Davis or Errol Flynn. *One of those fancy film people*, he said, only he wasn't exactly sure who. I think that was all she really needed to hear. Price was not an issue. Thanks to Gus, Mara has money to burn. And she has a much bigger house in San Marino where she and Gus lived for many years. It's still there, a Spanish-style mansion just a stone's throw from the Huntington Gardens. Once a week or so she goes back and walks through all the rooms, inspecting things. I don't think she cares about it, but she does it for Gus, in his honor. He was always after her: "Make sure the housekeeper and the Mexicans who mow the lawn aren't robbing us blind." Such a sweet man, Gus. Those were practically the last words he ever said. So she rolls her eyes and checks. The house is immaculate. The lawns and the hedges are clipped and trimmed to perfection. Mostly she prefers to be in the little place in the hills now; it's quiet, and much closer to where Gus is, and of course, it works out fine for me, too.

I let myself in with the extra key she gave me. "Hey," I say. "I missed you today. I thought you'd be down there with Gus."

"I dropped by around eleven. Everyone was sleeping. I got bored and left. Timing is everything, I hear." She smiles and gives me a short, intense kiss that seems to imply something more might be in the offing. She's been sipping red wine and reading her *New Yorker* this afternoon. The half-empty bottle on the table is a Malbec from Argentina. I can taste it, now that I think about it.

We hold hands and wander out to the balcony, where there's a padded couch and a bunch of potted plants. Young people might think that older folks don't know the first thing about love, or that they might have known once but somehow forgot. They look at old people and roll their eyes. How could they ever be as passionate as we are? As smart? As full of life? But it's not true. In fact, the older I get, the more I realize how much I've grown as a man, and in particular, as a lover of women. I may not be quite as capable as before, I tell Mara sometimes when we're lying in bed and gazing at the stars. Sometimes the machinery goes haywire, but my intention is magnificent. She laughs when I say things like that.

Mostly what we do is kiss, and touch each other. And once in a while, we progress far beyond that, but not often. I think we'd like to, mind you, if it weren't so goddamn exhausting. Today, on the couch, it's kissing and snuggling. She closes her eyes and presses herself into my neck. "I want to take a little nap now," she says. "Don't you move."

I sit there. The Los Angeles skyline is spread out in the distance. It's a beautiful day. You can see all the way to Mount Baldy, which is where Loretta and I once spent a weekend trudging around in the snow, ruining our shoes. I stroke Mara's hair, and I think that if she only knew, Loretta would approve of this. She wouldn't judge me harshly, that's for sure. She'd want me to be happy; that's what our love was always all about. And if our situation were reversed I would want the same for her. That's what I tell myself, anyway.

Later on, we team up to make dinner. Mara's a terrific cook; she doesn't need me, but she likes it when I stand beside her chopping the tips off of string beans or mincing onions. I tell her some more about the little bit I know about Delia and the sad way her life ended.

"Doesn't sound like she had much of a life to begin with," Mara says. She shakes her head. "I mean, living on the street, everything you own in a shopping cart, it's gotta be terrifying, especially for a woman. It has to make you crazy after a while." She pats the chicken parts dry with a paper towel and coats them with kosher salt.

"I guess so," I say. "Although she always put on a happy face when I talked to her."

"You were probably one of the three people in L.A. she wasn't threatened by," Mara says. "Kindness can be disarming sometimes."

"It didn't get her off the street, that's the tragedy. I couldn't give her enough to alter her circumstance. All I did was help keep her in burritos and beer."

*   *   *

After supper, she wraps a shawl around her shoulders and we return to our spot on the couch. I have a glass of wine in my hand, so does Mara. She's a far more serious drinker than I've ever been. I only do it to be sociable. One glass is plenty. The air is clear and cool, and a few of the bigger stars have started to emerge. Although we can't quite hear it, a tiny police helicopter down below is tracing out a perpetual circle near the Capitol Records Building.

Just then her phone rings. It's her granddaughter, Violet, calling from school, wanting to be sure Grandma will be there tomorrow afternoon. "Of course, honey," Mara says. "Three o'clock? The usual corner?"

Violet is fifteen years old. She has dark, curly hair. Her body is just beginning to take on the contours of womanhood. She has a bra; maybe it's a training bra, I don't know about such things, but she can be moody and irritated at the drop of a hat. She goes to a small private school in Claremont called Foxboro. No boys allowed. All the girls wear dark green skirts and pressed white blouses. Patent leather shoes. Way out of my league, but then I went to Hollywood High, what do I know? Foxboro might be fantastic. It's where they teach them the importance of geometry and how to speak French like a diplomat and what's valuable, or at least memorable, about Western civilization. Violet lives at the school during the week. She eats in the cafeteria and showers in the dormitory at night. At four o'clock every Monday and Wednesday afternoon she sees a therapist for an hour. This has been going on for nearly three years, and in that time Violet has made progress. That's what I hear. She's no longer afraid of the dark. She doesn't get sudden, mysterious stomach aches. She's stopped having panic attacks in shopping malls and other crowded places. She has real friends now, a structure in her life. But this costs a fortune of course, and Mara pays for all of it. She's been paying for it ever since her daughter Meghan overdosed in the backseat of a stolen Chevy in Highland Park. *Somebody has to take care of her*, she told the people at the Department of Social Services. *Who better than her grandmother?*

She turns off the phone and slips back into a carefully composed amorous position on the couch. "Do you want to come out with me to pick her up?" she asks. "We can make an adventure of it."

I consider that idea. I'm fond of Violet, although I've only met her a few times, but I'm not so sure she likes me back. That may be because I'm a male. Or because she's a smart girl and has figured out that I'm quietly *shtupping* her grandma. "I dunno," I say. "I mean, I do have a few other things to do, you know."

"Such as?"

"Such as that corpse I saw this morning. I need to follow up on that, dontcha think? The poor old woman in the dumpster? The throwaway?"

"She's not going anywhere," Mara says, which sounds cruel and indifferent, and we both know that wasn't her intent. Mara is high-minded; she's never cruel and indifferent, except occasionally, when she's had too much to drink. Then it's easy. Then the words just slide off her tongue. She takes another gulp of wine. "And besides, they're not paying you, are they."

"No, and neither are you."

"Okay, okay, don't get yourself all knotted up. I thought it might be fun. You know, a little drive to Claremont. Just the two of us."

"Three, if you count Violet."

We're silent for a time after that, both of us convinced. I'm not wrong. She's not wrong. Nothing to be done. And I know just how deeply Mara feels about Meghan. I know that the wound never heals. Not really. That she blames herself. That it's her fault her daughter started running with the wrong crowd and one dark thing led to another, and before you know it, it was too late.

"I should have said something," she whispers now in the deepening darkness. It's almost as if I were reading her mind. "I should have intervened. Meghan would still be here, she'd still be alive if I'd said something."

"Is that what you think?"

"I don't know. Yes. No. Maybe. But of course I didn't. I didn't say a word. I was silent. Why? What was I thinking?"

"She was all grown up. You can't control them once they leave home. And you were lost. You didn't know what to do."

"I had no idea, Amos. But that wasn't it."

"What then?"

"I was silent. I was silent because—because that's the way I was raised. Because I didn't know how to be heroic. I was all alone. Gus was already going in and out of the hospital. A revolving door. I had no one to talk to. And Meghan, sweet Meghan. She had no control, either. One day she woke and there she was, strung out.

That's the truth. At the end she was like—she wasn't much more than a rag, you know, one of those filthy dolls they shoot out of a cannon."

"You need to let go of this stuff, Mara," I say. "Give it a rest."

But she's not listening to me. Another voice inside of her has taken over and wants to finish. "It wasn't the heroin that killed her. No, not the heroin. It was me. Me. I let her go. I stood there and watched, and she drifted away."

I put my arms around Mara and hold her tight. "I'm sorry," I tell her. Sometimes there's no other answer. Sometimes that's all you can do, just say you're sorry, over and over again.

CHAPTER 3

A round midnight, I make up my mind to leave Mara's and
drive back to my place at Park La Brea. She's stopped weeping, and all the wine she's put away has finally begun to slow dance
around in her brain. Before she married Mr. Worthington, her last
name was Blumenthal. A shy girl from a small, backwater town in
New Jersey. What she liked best then was to lose herself in books.
That was her passion. Books were always far more stimulating than
boys. I don't imagine she was much of a *shicker* back then, either.
Or let me put it another way: I can count on one hand the number
of Jews I know who hang out in bars. A drink once in a while,
okay. It's nice to be sociable. But we rarely lose control. That's how
we are. And you can make that double for Jewish women. They
frown on that kind of blowsy behavior, so she must have picked up
the habit later, much later, at Yale, when she started rubbing shoulders with the outside world. Just my humble detective's opinion.

When her eyes close at last, and her breathing becomes more
even, I half-lift her, half-drag her into the bedroom and tuck her
in. I'm getting too old for this kind of thing, but somehow I manage. She has a luxurious queen-size bed, with white silk sheets and
a satin coverlet, and a killer view of Hollywood. I draw the blinds.
No point in disturbing that. I sit on the edge of the bed staring for
a while, wondering what might have been if I had met her before I
hitched my star to Loretta long ago. Then I stand up. *Time to shove*

off, Parisman. It won't matter if you're still there in the morning. It's not like you're the only love of her life. That would be Gus. Maybe that's why she married him. And besides, *boychik*, your career's just taken a turn for the better. You've got a case to solve. Your cousin's paying you and you're working for what? A song.

The next morning I get up early. The air is clear and brilliant; the sun is just peeking over the faraway mountains to the east. One of those impossibly beautiful, picture-postcard days they used to write tunes about in the twenties, when they wanted more tourists to pack up and move to Southern California. Or maybe not move but just be envious of. All that sunshine in February while we're knee-deep in snow. It ain't fair, ma. Oh well. I shower and shave. I sort quickly through the newspaper, throw out the sports and business sections, pick up a pen and try my hand at the crossword puzzle. Today, I'm better than usual. Either that or I'm awful lucky. Then, as I'm finishing my toast and a second cup of coffee, just like that, a new idea is born. Delia's been around these parts for years. The cops may not know her, but that doesn't mean squat. She's no mystery to someone. I take the elevator down to the mezzanine and out the door. It's only a couple of blocks to the 3rd Street bus stop, a place I know well. I pace around, studying the cigarette butts and other bits of trash on the ground for fifteen minutes before the Number 16 rattles up to the curb. The doors open. I climb aboard, ready to drop my change in the metal box—the kindness they extend to seniors like me—and off we go lumbering toward downtown.

My driver's name is Miss Jean. She's a sturdy Black woman in her mid-fifties, a workhorse who, as long as I can remember, has never once applied makeup or lipstick to her face. She came out here from Oklahoma when she was a girl, but the twang has never left her voice. She's been driving this bus for the last ten years.

"Miss Jean," I say, "a good morning to you."

"Mr. Amos," she replies.

Instead of taking a seat, I hang onto the closest handrail. The Number 16 is nearly empty at this point, but it starts filling up once we get to Western. Miss Jean has a mass of gray kinky hair and a small gold cross around her neck. It's the only hint of jewelry in her world, though I'm sure she never thinks of it that way. No sir, that would be blasphemy. Her deep brown, watery eyes tolerate no nonsense of any kind. She wears leather gloves and keeps her hands always sliding around on the steering wheel so she can smooth her way through traffic.

"I have a question for you," I say after we're moving again.

She's looking straight ahead, but I can see she's listening.

"I'm hoping you can tell me something about the homeless lady that's always sitting there at Gardner or across from Nordstrom's. Sometimes when I run into her, she has a purple scarf wrapped around her head."

"The one who just sits and sits? Never gets on?"

"That would be her."

"She's a tragedy, that woman. As I live and breathe. Yeah, I guess I know who you mean. Why?"

"You wouldn't happen to recall her name, would you?"

"I never talked with her, not directly. I've got a bus to drive. And she was always waving me on. You know. But my passengers did."

"So they knew who she was."

Miss Jean nods. "Folks call her Delia, I believe. Delia—Delia—Delia Martinez, maybe. Delia Montes, something like that. She married a Mexican, I heard one time. Long gone, of course. Not that I blame him."

A gaggle of people get on at La Brea—three young Korean girls in jeans with sunglasses and buds in their ears, also a Rastafarian guy in a faded orange T-shirt with dreads halfway down his back and high top sneakers, plus a couple of hefty Latinas with tote bags hanging from their shoulders and small children clutching at their skirts.

When we're underway again, she says, "Why do you care about her?"

"Oh, I used to give her money from time to time. Just trying to help out. But I haven't seen her in a while and now I guess I'm a little worried."

She nods and, in the same moment, makes an unexpectedly wide arc around a heedless kid flying along on a fancy red Italian bike. I hang on tight. I decide not to tell Miss Jean about Delia and how they found her in the dumpster yesterday. *Leave it alone, Parisman. What good will it do?* She still has seven hours left on the clock, and she probably knows all there is and more about man's inhumanity to man.

*   *   *

I get off at Western, wave goodbye to Miss Jean, and hike four short blocks south to Wilshire. The Metro station at the corner opened a few years ago, and they're working on extending it out to all parts of town, but that will take time, not something I have a lot left of anymore. Still, I never thought I'd see it get this far. I take the escalator below ground, and while I'm waiting in the vacant underground for the train I call my buddy, Omar Villasenor, to see if he's free for lunch.

"Okay, but this time it's my treat, old man," he says. "You're always buying me lunch. It's not right."

"Why isn't it right?" I want to know.

"Well, for one thing, I'm working these days, and last I heard, you're not."

"Wrong, Omar. I've got myself a job."

"Really! That's wonderful. Are they paying you?"

"Is that all you care about? Money?"

"So they're not paying you. That settles it, Amos. Lunch is on me."

An hour later, I get off at Chinatown and walk over to Nick's Café on 6th. Omar said he might be a little late, so I take a stool at the counter, order an iced tea, and look around. Nick's is a greasy spoon that started in 1948. They've erected a motley statue of a pink pig out front, because pork is what they do best. They've made a few improvements, but not so you'd notice. Stubbornness has been turned into a virtue here. It can be hard to find a parking space, and even after all these years, they still only take cash. No credit cards to draw in the tourists. The deeper truth is, though, I don't think they care if you find them or not. I like that. There's a make-shift plastic tent outside for those who want to dine al fresco, and a smattering of chairs and tables, but most folks prefer to crowd around the old U-shaped counter. The plywood walls are covered with framed drawings and news clips and testimonials from the past; no one pays them any mind. Cops eat here, so do firefighters and single dads who maybe only have their kids on the weekends. People come for the cheap food and the camaraderie. They come to lose themselves in the time warp, and to watch the waiters and busboys in red shirts hustle and sweat, carrying big platters of ham and eggs or pastrami burritos or sandwiches, refilling water glasses, pouring hot chocolate, and wiping down the counter. It's like a carnival, only no one's dancing or tossing darts at balloons; the joy all comes from watching them work.

"Hey, *vato*, how've you been?" Omar throws a big arm around my shoulder and takes a seat beside me.

"I've been," I say. "Not sure anymore if I will be, but Lord knows I've been." Omar gives me a huge Oaxacan grin and starts thumbing through the enormous plastic menu. He's almost a foot taller than me, so I'm always looking up at him. In fact, he used to be a wrestler when I first got to know him. Sometimes he'd do it for money, and other times he'd do it because somebody insulted his mother or looked at him cross-eyed. That was their misfortune. I call him a wrestler, understand, but that covers a wide array of skills. Let's just say he never killed anybody in the ring, not that I know of. Occasionally he'd find himself in a bind with the cops in Boyle Heights, and once a couple of rookies tried to pin a rape charge on him, but after I showed them the error of their ways, they finally let him go. In the last few years he's been my right-hand man. Whenever I need more muscle than I naturally possess, or whenever my rational mind kicks in and I realize I'm very likely to die without a bodyguard, that's when I pick up the phone and call Omar. Last year, we cracked a murder case at Shir Emmet, the

big orthodox shul down on La Brea. Right after that, he thought
he'd turn over a whole new leaf and become a cop. That surprised
both me and Lieutenant Malloy, but we did what we could to get
him into the program. He lasted all of six weeks before he got into
a fight with his superiors and walked off.

"I know it's lunch," he says now, "but they make a terrific hash
and eggs. You ever try it?"

"I think I've tried everything they make here, Omar, except
maybe the chorizo. You have to have a cast-iron stomach for that.
Either that," I say, "or you have to be twenty years old and not give
a flying fig what happens to you."

The waiter comes at us, and I order a tuna melt with a side
of coleslaw. He looks at me, not with judgment in his eyes, but
unsure. Why would you come to Nick's and not order something
with pork in it? Then he shrugs, writes down the hash and eggs
Omar wants, and heads back to the kitchen.

We shoot the breeze for a while. He asks about Loretta. I ask about
Lourdes, his new bride. He takes out a photo from his wallet. She's a
thing of beauty, with dark, lustrous curls. And her English is coming
right along. They're working on starting a family, he tells me. "Yeah
well," I say, "don't work too hard, you'll give yourself a backache." We
both laugh. Then he launches into an old familiar speech. How I saved
his life that time, remember when? And how, growing up in Mexico,
he never had a father, not really, and that it was from watching the way
I lived that he finally decided he could do the same thing, he could be
a success. And that's why he started his own detective agency.

"So how's it going?" I ask. "I know it's a hotbed of crime where
you live, but who has the money to hire somebody these days?"

"You'd be surprised, amigo, you really would. I have to charge a
lot less than they do in Beverly Hills, of course. But the same shit
goes on everywhere. And you know something? The cases are there
if you're willing. Plenty of cases. In fact, I've set up a special sliding
scale for my friends and neighbors in Boyle Heights."

"If you only speak Spanish, you pay what you can. Is that how
it goes?"

"Not quite," he says, "but no one ever gets turned away. Carlos and Ramon help me now; we're building up a satisfied customer base *poco a poco*."

I shake my head in amazement. "Well, good luck, man. That's wonderful. On second thought, maybe I should go to work for you."

"You could, only I couldn't pay you what you're worth."

"No one can, Omar. That's why I don't charge anymore."

He laughs. "You know what the problem is? You're too funny to be a detective. This is a serious business. The people who come to me—they're worried or scared shitless. They forgot how to laugh a long time ago."

"So?"

"So you can't be too happy, man. You have to listen and nod and pretend like you're feeling their pain. If you're too happy, they walk out the door. That's what I've come to realize."

I sip my iced tea. "You know something, Omar? You're right. It's a serious business." Then I tell him about the corpse in the dumpster, and how Malloy asked me to help.

"That's kind of strange right there, don't you think?"

"What?"

"Well, that he's asking for your help. I mean, I went through the training, man. That's not standard operating procedure. They have their ways. They don't like to take their dirty laundry outside."

"Malloy doesn't care about that stuff," I say. "I know him. He's his own man. He just wants to get to the bottom of this thing."

"Maybe so. But you know what I'm saying. They may come around to asking the public for help. Sooner or later, okay, sure. But not immediately. How long has she been dead? One day? Two days?"

I hold up my hand for him to stop. "We're old friends. I know the neighborhood. And honestly, he has nothing to go on. No motive, no suspect. Not even a name for the victim."

"Okay, I see your point." He clears his throat. "But that's not the way cops work."

"Actually, I may have found out her name. Although even that is a crap shoot. Delia Martinez maybe, or Delia Montes. Delia who was married to a Mexican once upon a time. Guy whose last name starts with M. Or who knows, maybe some other letter."

"Sorry, amigo, you're not ringing any bells."

"No, I said it was a crap shoot."

Our food arrives and we both dive in. "It seems as though someone clubbed her a few times with a blunt instrument," I say, "which would have been sufficient to kill her. But what's strange is that he made a special effort to deposit her in the dumpster."

"Why's that so strange?" Omar says. "You kill someone. The first thing you always want to do after that is get rid of the body. That's how it's done."

"No," I say, "I mean yes, normally, you're right. But it doesn't compute. Not in this case."

"You're losing me, man."

"All right. Think about this. It happened at night. In an alley. There was hardly any light. Obviously nobody saw it happen. He could have just left her there. They would have found her in the morning, either way. Why bother to lift her up and toss her in the dumpster?"

Omar puts down his fork. "Maybe she was already in the dumpster. Maybe, you know, she was crawling around in there, looking for something to eat, when somebody came along and whacked her."

"That's possible, I suppose. But she was a pretty decrepit old lady. I don't think she'd have the strength to climb into a big old metal dumpster. I'm not even sure I could do it anymore."

"You used to do that?" he asks.

"No. Of course not. But you see what I'm getting at."

"All right. So the killer put her in the dumpster. And you wanna know why?"

"I do."

"Simple," Omar says. "He put her in the dumpster because he was going to cover the body with more garbage. He was hoping she'd just get carted off and compacted with everything else."

"Right. Exactly. But the body wasn't covered. She was just all sprawled out on top of the trash. All you had to do was raise the lid, and there she was."

"Well, maybe that's what he meant to do. Cover her up. And maybe something happened—a car came roaring down the alley, and, I don't know, he panicked and ran."

"Maybe," I say. "But if that was the plan, why didn't he complete it? I mean, picking her up and throwing her in is the hard part, wouldn't you agree? I couldn't manage that."

"So her killer works out at the gym. It happens."

"Maybe. Or two people killed her and tossed her in. That would be easier, but that also alters the scenario."

"What do you mean?"

"Well, if one person kills her, it might signal a crime of passion. Or some kind of random mental breakdown. A homeless man attacks a homeless woman in a rage, for instance. That's what the police seem to be tilting toward."

"And more than one?"

"Two people is different. Two people suggests a plot. That they thought about it ahead of time, talked it over. That there was a motive, an opportunity, a reason."

"Still, someone—some very strong guy—could have just tossed her in. I agree with you, it's trouble, but how much did she weigh?"

"That's a damn good question. I don't really know. She was pretty much skin and bones. Just looking at the body I'd guess a hundred, hundred and ten, somewhere in that range."

Omar stares straight at me. "I think the cops are probably right about this, Amos."

"You do?"

"Yeah, I do. I've known you too long. And you know what? You think too hard. You make everything too complicated. That's how you are. If you ask me, this is just another one of those stupid, senseless street crimes they're never going to solve. Not unless they track down all her other homeless friends."

I've stopped eating my sandwich now. "I like what you said before, Omar. That the killer threw her in there because he meant to cover up the body and let the garbage men complete the task. That makes sense."

"Yes, it does." He smiles, motions to the waiter for more coffee.

"But even if a car came by as you say, and he got scared and ran away, he could always come back an hour or two later, couldn't he? When the coast was clear?"

"I dunno, I guess so."

"He could have come back. He could have even brought a few trash bags back with him, opened the dumpster and covered the body. At that point, he wouldn't be doing anything wrong. It's not a crime. No one would ever accuse you of murder if all you're doing is tossing in some trash at midnight, would they?"

"So what are you saying? I don't get it."

"I'm saying that there was probably a good reason they didn't try to conceal the body. I'm saying that whoever did this, they meant to put her in the dumpster. Not only that, they meant for her to be found in the dumpster. That was the point of the murder. To make a statement. To let people like her know that they're no better than garbage. To terrorize them."

"And what makes you think they're not already terrified, man? And besides, what the hell can they do about it? Find a nicer bridge to sleep under? Check into a four-star hotel?" Omar's whole body is tightening up. He shakes his head. "Like I said, Amos, you think too hard. I'll bet you twenty bucks that if they ever find the *pendejo* who did this, it'll be because of something simple. She had a bottle he wanted. Or some food stamps. Or they got into a shouting match and she lost control and told him to go fuck himself. Twenty bucks says that's what this is all about."

"Gee, I hope you're right," I say. "I like it when there's a simple answer to these cases. In the meantime, at least, I have something to keep me busy, huh? That's a good thing."

"I guess," Omar says, and grins. "I wouldn't want you bumbling around in a dark alley with nothing to do."

CHAPTER 4

After lunch, Omar gives me a lift back to Park La Brea so I can pick up my car and go out to see Loretta. When I get there, the door to her room is ajar, and I hear giggling and laughter. Carmen, the woman who used to care for her at home, is visiting. She's wearing a pink shawl and is holding a big blue photo album, showing Loretta pictures of her family back in Miami. I love Carmen. She has a huge heart and a natural talent for cheering up Loretta.

"Hope I'm not interrupting things," I say, walking in. Carmen hugs me. I hug her back and bend down and kiss Loretta. The aides have restyled my wife's hair this morning. She has new bright red fingernails and color in her cheeks. "You look like you're going to a ball tonight," I tell her. "Who's your date?"

"You!" she says, pointing at me. Her eyes beam. This thought has made her supremely happy.

I've seen the photo album many times before; it's something Carmen put together before she left Miami and came to Los Angeles years ago. Loretta has seen it, too, but each time Carmen turns a page, she finds something new and inexplicably wonderful. I only wish I could see it through my wife's eyes. We ooh and we aah at the color snapshots of Cuban refugees. "These are my people," Carmen says with pride. "*Mi tía. Mis tíos. Mi familia.*" Chubby men and women laughing and dancing in someone's backyard patio. A distinguished, scholarly gentleman with spectacles and a trim white beard pontificating from a wooden rocking chair. Three macho guys in undershirts, sweating, mugging for the camera, playing dominos and puffing happily on cigars, as if this is their idea of heaven. It goes on and on. A newborn baby. A soccer match. A pair of five-year-old girls in yellow sundresses grinning atop their new Christmas tricycles.

After an hour, Loretta begins to fade. She lets her head sink back into the pillows and her eyes drift toward the wall. Carmen and I look at each other.

"I need to go home now," she says. "*Mi esposo*, my husband, Antonio, will be back soon and he likes to eat early. You know how men are."

"I know how men are," Loretta repeats. But she's hardly awake now, she's just saying this to move things along, so Carmen and I can walk out the door and leave her alone so she can take a nap.

I give her a kiss on the cheek goodbye and I hug Carmen one more time. She feels warm and sad and weary. Coming to see Loretta is hard on her, too.

"*Hasta luego*, señor Amos," she says. "*Tien un buen día.*"

"*Egualmente*," I say. "You, too, Carmen."

*   *   *

Down the hall in room 226, Gus Worthington has also nodded off for the afternoon. I look in on him just so I can report back to Mara when I see her tonight. His eyes are closed. A little drool is seeping out of the corner of his mouth. The bed next to his is still empty and pristine, and the television on the opposite wall is happily promoting cheaper car insurance for everyone. As I head for the stairs, my cell phone rings. It's Malloy.

"We've found another one," he says. His voice is even, balanced, like he's a referee, like he's measuring every word before he pronounces it out loud, as though it might make a difference. "A guy in the parking lot of the lighting store on 2nd and La Brea."

"In a dumpster?"

"Not in, but right beside one. And whoever killed him probably used the same hammer as before, looks like."

"Jesus," I say. "You want me to come over? I'm not far away. Maybe I know who he is, too."

"Oh, we already know who he is," Bill says. "Louis Charles McFee. He made it easy. He had a wallet with a social security card and an old driver's license and some other little papers tucked away. Even had eight bucks in cash."

"So we can rule out robbery, then," I say.

"Maybe," says Malloy. "At least in this instance. But the way he died, the blows to the head—seems just like our friend Delia. So who the hell knows?"

"Tell me, Bill," I ask, "you have any idea how much this Louis McFee weighs?"

"Weighs?" He's startled by the question. "Well, I'm looking right at him. He's pretty tall and he had a lot of clothes on. More clothes than he needed for the kind of weather we're having. But I dunno, I'd put him at a hundred eighty, two hundred. Why?"

"Omar and I were talking at lunch. And it came to me. Maybe there are no accidents here. Maybe Delia was meant to be found in the dumpster. That it was deliberate, you know. Part of some elaborate hate crime."

"Somebody hated her, sure," Malloy says.

"And she was light enough that two people—maybe even one person—could lift her up and toss her in without that much effort."

"Maybe."

"But this McFee fellow, he might be too heavy for that."

"So they left him on the ground. Is that where you're heading with this?"

"It still sends a message though, doesn't it?"

Malloy doesn't say anything. I doubt he even wants to consider this idea. Not that it's impossible. He knows what hate crimes look like. It was a hate crime that got him promoted a few years back. Picture in the *L.A. Times* and everything. William P. Malloy, the one who busted a whole gang of skinheads—bored, pimply kids on their Harleys, rolling in from Palmdale to see what kind of Friday-night trouble they could find on Sunset Boulevard. Back then, of course, it was obvious: They were prowling for gays and transvestites to beat up. Anyone who even waved hello, that was enough.

"I wish this were that simple, Amos," he says finally. "Trouble is, how can you call it a hate crime when the truth is, nobody likes them?"

"God likes them, is what I hear. God loves them."

"Yeah well, God's love plus five bucks will buy you a parking space too. But you know what I'm saying. They're not just another group. They're about as popular as termites. You can't lump the homeless in together with Muslims or Blacks or gays."

"So where would you lump them?" I ask.

"I don't know," he says. I can hear the torment in his voice, the opinions shifting inside of him. "They smell bad. They're crazy. They spread disease. They leave their shit everywhere. I'm not defending the thug who did this, but you tell me, who's going to miss Louis McFee when he doesn't show up at the soup kitchen tomorrow morning? Who?"

"You're right. Nobody will care. But the good news is, it's not your job to figure out which life has value and which one doesn't. You don't have to judge."

"Thanks, Amos. I guess I needed to hear that."

"When you get promoted to God, then okay. Right now, remember, you're just a cop. A question like that? That's above your pay grade."

He kind of laughs. We talk some more about what they know about the latest case. Malloy ticks off the bare bones: Louis Charles McFee, born in Texas. Graduated high school in Odessa. Drafted into the Army, served one tour in Vietnam around the same time I was there. Infantry at first, then he found a cushier gig in the motor pool, nothing heroic. Came back, worked six years in a steel plant in Fontana. Met and married Jane Alexander McFee. No children. Married, divorced, laid off. Or maybe he was married, laid off, then divorced; that part isn't clear. Public intoxication. A DUI. An assault and battery, later dropped. A restraining order issued on behalf of one Jane Alexander McFee. Three years in Solano State Prison for a couple of botched burglaries in San Bernardino.

"All right," I tell Bill, when he stops to clear his throat. "I think we both knew he wasn't a Boy Scout. Any idea how he ended up in Hollywood?"

"It's the land of dreams," Malloy says. Then, "No, we have no clue. Maybe he knew someone once who offered him a bed when he got out. Maybe it was just warmer than anyplace else. If you're gonna sleep on the sidewalk, that's the kind of thing you think about."

I thank him, tell him I'm going to make the rounds and check into any connection between Delia and McFee. Maybe they knew each other, I say.

"You can do that," he sighs. "And while you're at it, let me know how many angels can dance on the head of a pin, will ya?"

"Consider it done," I say.

*   *   *

Mara calls later on that afternoon to tell me she's brought Violet back to the house on Creston Drive. Also, she's run out of wine. Would I care to join them for dinner? Of course I care. That's all I do, is care.

By the time I get there the sun is setting, and Violet has changed out of her uniform. Now she looks like almost any ordinary twelve-year-old girl. She's barefoot and she's wearing tan shorts and a pale blue halter-top. "Hi," I say, coming through the door, but she pointedly ignores me, which is perhaps understandable, since she's sprawled out on the couch, head down, eating from the plastic bowl of potato chips in front of her and simultaneously sending messages with her thumbs to alien creatures on her iPhone.

"Hi there," I say again, louder this time, with more determination.

"I said hi," she mumbles.

"Well, you may have thought it," I say. "Actually, I think you probably texted it to someone."

She looks up, offers me half a smile. "Well, I meant to say hi, Amos. I'm sooo sorry." The eyes roll, and her head dips again, and just like that, she's lost in cyberspace.

An hour later, Mara and I are standing in the kitchen, loading the last few plates and bowls into the dishwasher. Violet is back on the living room couch, watching a British cop show on public television. TV isn't allowed in the dorms at Foxboro; it's one of the few things they're strict about. No TV and no boys, so whenever she lands at Grandma's, this is her secret indulgence. I've sat through a couple of these shows before. And they're instructive in their way, if you can hear well enough to get past their accents. I've never been able to, but still, it's nice any time you're in Cornwall or the Midlands, isn't it? They serve a lovely tea, and the trains run on time, and everyone— the vicar and the maid and the chief inspector—is so fucking polite. What could possibly go wrong? Oh right, there's been a murder. I glance down at my watch and tell Mara I think under the circumstances maybe I ought to be shoving off.

"So soon?" she says.

"Well, you don't really want me sleeping over, do you? I mean, what about Violet?"

She dries her hands on her apron. "She's not blind. I expect Violet already believes we have something more than a normal platonic friendship," she says. "But you're right, Amos. We should tread carefully. For her sake. And for my own as well. I don't want her to think less of me."

"Come on, now," I say, "she adores you. You're all she has. You rescued her, you pulled her out of the abyss."

"She's a work in progress," Mara shrugs her shoulders. "I wouldn't call her rescued. Not just yet."

*   *   *

I sat next to Betsy Rollands in my ninth-grade government class. She was a tall, busty, talkative girl with big, piercing green eyes and brown, silky hair that she let me run my fingers through at will.

Somehow, she had chosen me. I was the love of her life; I found that out much later, not that it mattered. I was really no match for anyone in those days, and I was too gawky and innocent to know what she wanted from me. Whatever it was, I couldn't reciprocate. She used to rip out sheets of paper from her three-ring binder and pass me notes. Carefully folded up notes with questions. Are you free tonight? You understand the homework assignment? What do you really think about the Beatles? I tried to answer her. But no matter what I wrote back, the questions continued. Girls were a mystery I couldn't solve to save my life. Even after my mother sat me down at the kitchen table and explained how Betsy Rollands felt about me, and how sweet it would be if I asked her to the prom, I still didn't get it. Maybe I just wasn't ready. Wait. Scratch that. I know I wasn't ready. Her affections and her notes, everything she did sailed right over my head. Anyway, even though it didn't work out romantically between us, what's good is we've stayed friends all these years. And even though it's after nine, I tap in her number and she answers on the second ring.

"You still up?"

"Of course I'm up," she says. "I'm working on a piece for the *Atlantic*. Besides, who the hell can sleep at our age?"

"Well, I just hope the *Atlantic* pays better than the *L.A. Times*," I say.

"Fuck the *Times*," she says. Betsy still has a few leftover feelings about her former employer. Of course she would. Anyone would. How many nights have I sat around with her and listened to her rant in that gloomy little neon bar on Sunset? Hell, I can almost recite her indictment of the *Times* by heart. How it used to be a great institution, but now they're just a pack of myopic brown-nosers; frat boys who don't give two good shits about writing anymore, or the truth, or—God forbid—justice, no sir. Never mind all that. It's a brave new fucking world, that's what they say when the guard finally comes to escort you out of the building. That's supposed to console you after twenty years of service. Want to know what they care about now, Amos? The one thing? They care about their wallets.

"Yes, of course," I say now. "You're right, I agree. Fuck the *Times*. But that's not why I called. You see, I have this problem."

"That's the only time you ever call me, when you have a problem." There's a silence. Is she still in love with me? I wonder. Even now? Then, "Okay," she says. "So spit it out."

That's when I tell her about poor old Delia, and poor old Louis McFee. I tell her about the dumpster, and the flies, but I leave out the other nasty parts. Still, Betsy is a veteran reporter, I figure. She can read between the lines.

"So what would you like from me?" she asks when I finish. "You're the detective, remember? At least you used to be."

"There's a part of me that thinks these aren't random killings, Betsy. I mean, I suppose they could be. But my gut tells me no."

"Your gut could be wrong, you know. You ever consider that?"

"Sure, sure. But it's kind of like modern art. Once you start to see a pattern in what looks like chaos, or even if you're just imagining a pattern, it's hard to go back to chaos."

"Okay. I'll buy that. So you imagine there's a pattern. Then what?"

"Then, obviously, you need to test it out. See if the pattern holds up in a wider context."

There's another pause. "Let's cut to the chase, Amos. It's nearly ten, and I've got this piece to do and—"

"Yeah," I say, "that's why I called. You've done lots of stories about the homeless problem here. I read your stuff, Betsy. It was smart. Well-researched. And I know you have friends out there who are social workers—churchy people—people who actually go down to Skid Row and talk to them, counsel them, bring them blankets and tents and bottles of water."

"That was years ago," she says. "And it's pretty grueling work, even if you're a Christian. People volunteer, but then they see what they're really up against. They get tired. They burn out, they move on to other, more glamorous things. Voter registration is a very popular pastime, I've discovered. Especially if you're liberal and don't want to get your hands dirty. Know what I mean?"

"I guess so. But if you just could point me toward a few names, I'd take it from there."

"Names. You want names. Let's see. Well, I would probably start with Lemuel Carter at the Rescue Mission downtown. He's still there, I'm sure. That's his life's work. He knows the homeless scene as well as anyone, and even though the victims were living on your streets, not downtown, they probably passed through Skid Row. Tell him hi for me, will you? And Father Jack at Our Lady of Good Counsel up toward Hollywood. He's done a lot of outreach for the homeless. Either one of them might remember those people in the dumpster. A picture would help, of course."

"I don't think a picture *would* help, actually." That's when I decide there's nothing to be done, and so I mention the business about the hammer to Betsy.

She doesn't speak for a while. "Try Lemuel or Father Jack," she says again. "That's all I can think of for now. But as soon as I finish this story, I'll shake the trees and see if anything else falls out."

"Thanks, Betsy," I say. "You're the best, I love you."

"A little late," she says, hanging up.

CHAPTER 5

Omar calls the next day. Something he saw in the paper got him excited.

"You read the newspaper?" I ask. "Since when?"

"Since I started the agency," he says. "I figured I ought to start." He pauses, and for a moment it flicks across my mind that I might have unknowingly offended him. *You're an expert at that, Parisman, putting your foot in your mouth.*

"It may not pan out," he says then, "it may be a dead end, but still, I thought you ought to know. There's a get-together tomorrow night at the Episcopal church over on Wilton. The Mid-City Merchants Association is having a public meeting. They want to talk about the homeless problem, what can be done."

"That's probably always on their agenda," I tell him. "Merchants love to bitch and moan."

"Yeah, but I was thinking maybe this time they might talk about homeless people getting murdered in their neighborhood lately. How bad it is for business and all."

"That's exactly what they will say. It's bad for business. And that'll be the end of it."

"You never know," Omar says. "When you sit behind a counter all day long, I mean, you're right there on the ground floor. You hear things, you can't help but see what's going on."

"I'll grant you that."

"And maybe these guys have ideas. They all want to solve this problem, don't they?"

"Which translates to what?"

"Jesus, I don't know, man. I've never owned a store. I'm just thinking on my feet, the way you taught me. Maybe they'd be willing to pool some of their spare cash together. I'll tell you, if it was my livelihood, I'd be putting spy cameras wherever I could drill a hole. Every goddamn alley in town should have one, that's what I think."

"Every alley! Businessmen don't think beyond their own four walls, Omar. They have enough *tsuris,* problems, just making payroll each month. And even if they could spot a killer—an elaborate camera system like that? Come on. Only the government has that kind of money. I'm sure they'd much rather just rent a yellow school bus, grab those wretches up off the sidewalk, and dump them all in the desert. That would be their ideal solution. That's something they'd get behind."

"So you don't want to go?"

"I didn't say that. Of course I'll go. You're right. Someone might have a bright idea. Hell, the killer himself might be sitting there in the church, you never know."

"There you go again," says Omar. "You're thinking too hard."

*　　*　　*

I put in a quick call to Our Lady of Good Counsel, which is located up on the grittier edge of Hollywood. Father Jack, the woman at the desk informs me, left the church. It's been almost three years.

"You mind telling me why?"

Her voice gets decidedly stiffer. "Um, he wanted to leave," she says finally. "He's living in Seattle now. I believe it's Seattle. Or maybe not. Somewhere near there. That's what I heard. With his . . . with his partner."

"You don't have a phone number for him, do you?"

"We have no number here, no, I'm sorry. As I said, he's no longer with the church. You understand."

"I do. Thanks, anyway."

I decide to skip my usual afternoon with Loretta, and instead drive down to the Rescue Mission on San Pedro. It's a large, pastel, two-story barn of a building with little, if any, personality. It might have been a warehouse or a munitions plant in the forties when they first slapped it together. The cinder block walls are drab and solid, and when I look closely, dozens of people have scrawled earnest messages on them with permanent markers and crayons. It's a bit like what you might see in a dilapidated public men's room, except there are no stupid sexual innuendoes, no infantile cartoons of breasts and penises. No, this is more like a poor man's post office. A Wailing Wall for the homeless. There are names and addresses, phone numbers. There are pleas for help from someone named Tucson Ned, notes from a woman called Gabriella P. Love in a large, loopy handwriting scratched at odd angles, and poignant prayers to Jesus and to the Virgin of Guadalupe. About the only hostile thing on the wall is an inscrutable gang sign, spray-painted in purple to the right of the main entrance. No one at the Rescue Mission has bothered to scrub any of this off. Maybe they haven't noticed. Or maybe they thought about scrubbing it off, and then decided to just let the wall revert to the community they're supposed to serve. Which makes sense, I guess.

There's a reception desk once you pass through the double glass doors. It's staffed by two young, powerful-looking men and two equally intimidating young women, Three Blacks and one Latina, all of them clad in long-sleeve green shirts with the Rescue Mission logo on it. They're filling out forms and typing into laptop computers. I get in line behind a grizzled white man with shoulder-length hair. He's wearing blue jeans and no belt, and work boots almost as old as he is. The work boots aren't tied, either, which he doesn't seem to care about. Also, he's clutching a small suitcase in his arms, pressing it to his chest as though it were an infant. When I look over his shoulder I realize that the handle is broken.

The grizzled man stands there for nearly ten minutes, mumbling to them under his breath. There's something slightly frantic about him. His hands never leave the suitcase. Then the young Latina puts down her clipboard and smiles. She stands up, pushes her chair back and signals for him to follow her down the hallway.

"I'm looking for Lemuel Carter," I say to one of the guys when it's my turn at last.

"He's in room 10C," he tells me, pointing vaguely with his arm in the opposite direction of the Latina. "You have an appointment?"

"No," I say, "just a couple of questions. He's not expecting me, but we don't need to talk long."

"Everybody says that," the young man says. He shakes his head. He's supremely confident in himself, the way I was once, the way all young men are at that age. "You can't spend less than an hour with Mr. Carter," he says. "He likes to talk, you know. That's just how he is."

"A nickel says you're wrong," I tell him as I walk away.

The door to his office is open. I knock just the same.

"Come in, come in, come in."

Lemuel Carter must be in his seventies. He has a large, nearly bald head, and a substantial belly, which he doesn't bother to hide. He has pearly white teeth, a clipped white moustache and an equally well-tended white beard. He is also quite possibly the blackest man I've ever seen.

He points to a padded chair where he'd like me to be. "And what can I do for you, young fella?"

I give him a grin. "I'm probably not much younger than you are," I say. "But okay, I'll take that as a compliment."

He laughs. "Compliment? Hell, it's the truth. Ain't no compliment."

I hand him my business card. "I don't know whether you've heard the news, Mr. Carter. There've been two murders in the last few days, both of them homeless."

He sits up in his chair. You can see the muscles in his face tighten. "No, I hadn't heard. Not at all. Was it in the paper this morning?"

"Maybe," I say. "But I sorta doubt it. If there's another one, people will start to notice. They weren't living around your place, but nonetheless I expect the LAPD will be calling on you soon. They don't like it when things get out of control."

"No."

"On the other hand, they don't have much to go on at the moment."

"I expect they'd feel a whole lot better if it was a movie star," he says. "A homeless man? Not a priority in this town." There's no cynicism in his voice. It's just a fact.

"Not all cops see it that way. Some cops—"

"Yes, well." He stares at my card again, then glances up. "Of course, you probably already know that folks on the street don't live so long, anyway."

"I didn't," I say, "but sure, it stands to reason."

"Street people—my people—don't always make it much past sixty. Crystal meth. Crack cocaine. Heroin. Alcohol. And I haven't said a word about exposure. You wouldn't think a cold night in Los Angeles would kill you. You'd be surprised."

I nod. "So I won't waste your time, Mr. Carter. I'm just trying to find what I can about the victims."

"And who were they?"

"Well, the man was named Louis McFee. He was sixty-seven. And the woman—I couldn't give you her exact age, but her first name—we think—was Delia. And the last name might have been Montes, or something Mexican sounding. She was African American, though. Used to hang out on 3rd near the Farmers Market. Waited at the bus stop all day long. Never got on."

He squints up at the ceiling. "I can't say I know her. Not offhand. You have a recent photograph?"

"Whoever killed her and McFee did a pretty thorough job on their faces. Looks like he took a hammer to them, although we don't know what he used, actually. So no, I'm sorry, I don't have a recent photo. And if I did, you wouldn't want to see it."

He leans forward, grabs a pen, and makes a few notes. Then he stops and taps his fingers pensively on the desk. "Okay, let me look into this, Mr. Parisman. It may take a few days, but we can go back through our records. One of them, or maybe both of them, might have been guests here at the Mission before they headed west to your neck of the woods. We've been in business a long time."

"Over a hundred years, I'm told."

"That's right. I'll let you know." He glances again at my card. "One more thing," he says. "Just so I get this straight: you're not with the law, are you?"

"No."

"So somebody's paying you to look into this?"

"No, Lemuel, I wish to God they were. This one's on my own dime."

"Because?"

"Because I need to keep busy. Because even though I'm an old man, people tell me I'm still pretty good at what I do. I like hearing that."

He nods. "And even a poor, homeless stranger deserves justice in this world," he says. "Isn't that what you Jews believe? You *are* Jewish, aren't you? Parisman?"

"Isn't everyone?"

"No," he says adamantly. "Some of us are Black."

"Oh golly, I hadn't noticed."

He chuckles then. "Jews and Black folks. When it comes right down to it, somewhere along the continuum, we're all just slaves, ain't we?"

"We've spent some time in Egypt. It wasn't pleasant."

"Like Georgia and Alabama," he says.

I stare into his dark brown, compassionate eyes, and it's easy to see why a guy like him would feel right at home here. This is ground zero, after all. It can only get better.

I stand up, shake hands, and thank him. As I'm leaving, something else pops into my head. "Oh, I almost forgot. Betsy Rollands made me promise to say hello."

"You know Betsy?"

"She was in love with me in high school."

"My, my."

"And I was too stupid to love her back."

*   *   *

A quick check of the internet tells me that the Eternal Light of Christ Church, the place Delia got her hymnal from, still exists. Not on Sunset anymore, but there's an address on Rosewood near Fairfax High. I drive over there to take a look. What I find is an old storefront in the last strip mall that hasn't been gentrified; there's a tarot reader on one side and a South Indian greasy spoon on the other. The space I'm interested in used to be a hair salon, maybe, or a very large barbershop. Now it's kind of a theater. The curtains are drawn across the front, but not entirely. You can see that someone has set up a couple dozen wooden folding chairs, and on the low stage in front there's a podium draped in a purple cloth, with a microphone stand beside it. Behind the podium, against the white wall at the rear of the building, is a large crude golden cross. It's just a little bit smaller than what the Romans used on Jesus, and at first you figure it must weigh a ton, but then the more you stare at it, the more you realize it's probably Styrofoam, a cheap trick. Still, impressive. I try the door, which is locked, but a taped cardboard sign at eye level says that services are every Sunday and Friday nights at seven p.m., and that all men and women with Christian hearts are welcome. There's also a phone number and a note below saying that in the event of an emergency, or if you need immediate spiritual assistance, you should call Reverend Jimmy Archibald. I write down the number in my notepad and punch it into my phone.

He doesn't answer right away. In fact, just when I'm about to hang up, he comes on the line. I tell him my name, what I do for a living, and that I'm standing in front of his church. Also, I very much need to talk with him.

"Is this urgent?" he wants to know. His voice is smooth, mellow, almost other-worldly, as if I just interrupted some astral travel plans of his. That's one explanation. Or maybe it's simpler than that. Maybe he was just sitting around on a couch, exhaling a joint, when the phone rang and broke into his dreams.

"What do you mean, urgent?" I ask.

"Well, is this a spiritual emergency. Are you troubled, my son?"

"Mr. Archibald, I believe a member of your congregation might have been murdered," I say. "What would you call that?"

He doesn't know what to say to that remark, except to suggest that perhaps we ought to meet in person. An hour later, I'm sitting waiting for him at Bludso's Bar & Que on La Brea south of Melrose.

I'm there ahead of time. I'm almost always ahead of time, it's part of my nature. Hate to be late. He hasn't told me what he looks like, so that could be a problem, I think, but probably not. I'm sitting there with the rhythm and blues music pumping relentlessly through the ceiling. I've got my chin in my hand and I'm sipping an iced tea, checking out the brisket on the menu. Then I spot a Camry stop and do a deft parallel parking job right in front. The glass door opens and he waltzes in. That's him, there's no question.

The Reverend Jimmy Archibald is a wiry Black man in his forties with wide, red-framed glasses. He was calmer on the phone than he is now in the flesh. He's wearing a nice blue cotton sport coat, his dress shirt is open at the neck, and he's got on fancy loafers that for sure didn't come from Pay Less. I nod to him and he pulls up a chair.

"So, Mr. Parisman, is it?" He grabs a menu, opens it, closes it with hardly a glance. "I'm hungry, are you?"

"They make a good brisket here," I say. "That's what I'm having. You should, too. Unless you're a vegetarian."

"No," he says, "not a vegetarian. Okay, that's a good idea. I'll have the same." He waves at the waiter, who steps forward and jots down our order.

Then he turns back to me. "I can't tell you how upsetting your phone call was," he begins. He unfolds his napkin and gently centers it on his lap. He's fussy, I think. Or maybe he just cares an awful lot about his clothes. "Are you sure this was one of my congregants?"

I pass him my business card. "The police think she spent time at your church. They found an old hymnal with her things, but it was from years ago. When you guys were up on Sunset."

He examines the card and sets it down on the placemat. "I see. So who is this poor woman?"

"That's what we're all trying to figure out, Reverend. She was homeless. A Black lady, maybe fifty or sixty years old. But there was nothing to identify her. No papers, no driver's license. Just the hymnal. I checked around the neighborhood. Some folks knew a little bit about her. Thought her name might be Delia. Thought she might have been married to a Mexican once upon a time."

He plays with his knife and fork. "Delia. Delia. That is familiar, I have to say."

"I know you have a fine church there on Rosewood, but I thought—I was hoping maybe you'd have a record of your clientele."

He smiles. "People who come to my church don't always have names, Mr. Parisman. You have to understand. The folks I minister to are like dust. They don't belong anywhere. They're broken, lost. And even if they have names, what they'd really like to do is forget them. Start over, you know. That's how bad things are."

The food arrives, which is a blessing, since I was beginning to think this was another blind alley. He might remember Delia, and then again, he might not. And what would he remember? Who knows? That she smelled bad? That she liked to sing hymns about Jesus? And since Delia probably had nothing to do with Louis McFee, except for the fact that the same blunt instrument was likely used on both of them, where does that leave you, Parisman? Right back at square one, that's where.

Just as I'm finishing mopping up my plate, another thought occurs to me. "Tell me, Reverend, if you don't mind my asking, just how do you make a living doing what you do?"

"Excuse me?"

"Well, you told me the people who come to see you, they're dust. They have nothing. And yet, here you are, you're renting that place on Rosewood with the chairs and the Styrofoam cross. You're pretty well dressed. You drive a nice car. You must be doing something right."

"I'm not a full-time preacher, Mr. Parisman. I believe in helping my fellow man, that's how my mother raised me in Biloxi. I believe in the Lord, but I also sell real estate. That's what's kept me afloat. The folks who come to my church? You know what? They're hurting. Many of them are crazy. You don't want to be crazy. Not here, not in L.A. He pulls out his wallet and hands me a blue-and-gold business card. "If you're ever in the market, just let me know."

"Thanks," I say. The check arrives, and he reaches for it ostentatiously.

We stand up and shake hands. "If you can remember anything about Delia, maybe you'll give me a call, okay?"

"Absolutely," he says. "I'll do that. As God is my witness."

CHAPTER 6

Even though he stumbled onto it in the first place, I almost have to get down on my knees and beg Omar to tag along with me to the Mid-City Merchants Association meeting the next night. *You might be onto something.* That's what I say to him. *It's worth checking out.*

"I fuckin' hate things like that, man," he says. "I can't tell you what it does to me inside. Those fat gringos, those empty suits, talking and smiling and joking around. Like they own the whole goddamn world."

"Well, they sorta do."

"Not for much longer," he warns. These are just the bitter words of an impatient young man, I think. I get it. He quit trying to be a cop last year and went into the detective business for himself, but Omar Villasenor is still walking around town with a considerable chip on his shoulder. He doesn't like it when doors are slammed in his face. He gets livid when people—especially white people—tell him no, you can't do that. And except for me and Lourdes, his new bride, he doesn't take anyone else's suggestions. Which, ordinarily, would spell trouble.

Omar is strong and fast, and there's no one I'd rather have beside me if a fight breaks out, but what I admire most about him is that he has a foreigner's ear. He may not know the definition of every word, but he knows how to listen; he hears what's underneath all the gibberish thrown at him. Whenever Omar comes up with a response, it's always pure; he didn't just reach in and grab it out of the same giant cookie jar. He waits. He listens with his heart. That's why I want him to come with me.

"You're right," I tell him. "Someday, when you and Lourdes and your cousins have made a million more babies, and they've all grown up and registered to vote, it'll be different. You'll own the world then. You can tell all the white folks to go to hell. But right now, I need you at that meeting. Please, man, come on. Do it for me."

"Okay," he says. "For you, *vato*, I'll be there. But I'm not getting dressed up, you hear me?"

"A pair of pants will do just fine," I tell him.

*   *   *

Other than the metal cross and the abstract, wooden Jesus looking down from the wall behind him, there's nothing spiritual about Amory Blevins. Quite the opposite. The president of the Mid-City Merchants Association is a well-suited, well-fed, square-jawed man with red, puffy cheeks. I hate him already, and he hasn't even opened his mouth. I've seen fire hydrants with more charisma. His smile is forced. While he waits for everyone to take their seats and get settled, his eyes constantly shift all around the chapel; he keeps touching his head and pushing his blond hair back with his free hand, trying to mash it down, which is kind of odd, since he doesn't have that much to begin with. No tie, but an American flag is pinned prominently to the lapel of his crisp blue blazer, right next to his heart. The all-American boy. Ever since my days in the military, I've had a thing about grown men who get too cuddly with flags. Men in ballparks who stand up and sing the national anthem at the top of their lungs. Men in bars, drunks, who tell you that if you don't like it here, buddy, then you should leave. I'm trying to get past it, but it's not me. Amory Blevins, though, owns all of that.

He paces around near the altar, a microphone in his hand. He checks his notes one last time, squints up at the chandeliers high overhead. The room grows blessedly silent.

"When I was in college," he says, "years ago, I majored in mathematics. Numbers meant a lot to me back then. Numbers were real. Numbers pointed to the truth. So, if I may tonight, I'd like to start out by giving you some real numbers to think about." His hand makes a small, explanatory arc. "Tonight, tens of thousands are sleeping on our streets," he says. "Tens of thousands without easy access to a toilet, who don't shower, who may no longer remember what it's like to eat a simple home-cooked meal." He pauses to let the gravity of his words sink in.

"Some of these folks are ill; some carry communicable diseases. Some are drug addicts, or alcoholics. And, ladies and gentlemen, I don't think I have to tell you because you already know—most of them are spiritually lost, and more than a few of them are just plain crazy." Another pause. I wonder how long he worked on this speech, polishing the words. And what, I wonder, is Omar hearing, right beside me?

There are maybe seventy-five or eighty people in the chapel of the Episcopal church, which is a warm, bright, welcoming space. For decades, this building has been used for all kinds of political speeches—civil rights, anti-war rallies, grape boycotts, women's issues, gay pride, immigration, raising the minimum wage. The people who worship here are seasoned hands at this sort of talk. They recycle; they eat organic. They no longer own stock in tobacco or oil companies, and as best they can, they always want to do what's right. Omar and I are seated near the aisle, about halfway back in the wooden pews. I look around. Most of the folks who came out tonight are elderly couples. A lot of white hair and canes and walkers. And the front rows are crowded with earnest men and women leaning forward to better hear what he has to say.

He spits out another round of statistics: the rising cost of security guards in shopping malls, the number of homeless individuals they estimate have moved into the Miracle Mile District just in the past year, the amount of trash they produce, and the pressure their presence is putting on local businesses. One couple shrugs. They get up, fiddle with their overcoats, and head for the exit. Blevins keeps talking, but out of the corner of his eye he watches them until the door creaks closed behind them. "The Mid-City Merchants Association is committed to solving this problem," he says. "Believe it or not, there was a time when it didn't exist. And that time can come again, ladies and gentlemen, that is, if we all pull together."

The audience looks doubtful. They start whispering among themselves. As if these are just the kind of empty words you'd expect from the Mid-City Merchants Association. Then Blevins taps the microphone for silence. He says he doesn't want to go around scaring anyone, but since they live here, there's something else they ought to know. "The situation in our community has lately turned even more dire," he warns. And that's when he tells them about the bodies.

"Some of you may have already heard rumors. How all of a sudden homeless people are winding up dead in our alleys. It hasn't made the nightly news yet, but I can assure you, it will. The Los Angeles Police Department notified us yesterday afternoon. Two people have died so far in the past week. Just a few blocks from this church. Two murders, with too much in common to be coincidental. We have a serial killer, in other words, right here in our neighborhood. The LAPD is hunting for him, of course, and they're hoping that our local merchants, who are out there every day, can assist them."

An old coot near the back of the chapel raises his hand. "Didn't I just hear you say homeless people were a big problem? It sounds like somebody's finally figured out how to get rid of them."

"Oh, shut up, Bruce!" The woman seated next to him turns red with embarrassment. "How can you even think such a stupid thing? And in church, my God!"

Other people in the pews around him turn their heads. No one speaks, but they stare long and hard. This is not what they think.

This is not part of the Episcopal church. Blevins taps the microphone again. "No one here condones murder," he says. "Americans
don't act like that. No matter what our circumstances, at the end
of the day, we are all God's children."

Everyone shakes their heads. Are they being sanctimonious? Or
are they too sharp to be conned? I get the distinct feeling that
nobody here thinks of himself as a child of God. Bruce and his
wife can be heard muttering back and forth, but now that the
president of the Mid-City Merchants Association has put them in
their place, no one pays them any regard. Other hands go up, and
there are random questions from the floor about the circumstances
of the murders, where they happened, and what can be done.

"I think we have to let the police take charge of this," Amory
Blevins says. "If any of you have information, however, I would
direct it to them. But the association believes all of us can play a
constructive role. Make no mistake, this is an emergency. These
are not isolated incidents. Whoever is committing these crimes
can easily strike again, and when he does, other homeless folks
around here will be at risk."

A hand shoots up a few rows in front of me. "Isn't the city or
county already providing aid for these people?"

"They're counting them, mostly. Looking into providing more
restrooms and building more housing. That's nice. But that's not
going to cut it."

The audience begins to murmur, but Blevins presses on. "Look,
we don't pretend to have all the answers. But we do have a plan for
our area. We've made arrangements with an experienced team of
social workers. These folks have agreed to fan out into the streets,
find the homeless, identify them, warn them about what's going
on, and hopefully convince them to take advantage of the available
shelters in our town. It's a big effort, and they can't be expected
to work for free, naturally. So tonight, I'm here with my beggar's
cup. Tomorrow night, I'll be making the same appeal at the Shir
Emmet Synagogue down on La Brea. And on and on, until we
raise the funds to pay for their services."

This sparks a lot of heated conversation in the crowd. A short, scholarly gentleman with horn-rimmed glasses and a dismissive look on his face stands up and folds his arms. "So tell me, just how do you propose to get these folks to accept your offer? There's no law that says they have to seek shelter, is there? What if they don't want to move? What if they like their shopping carts and their grubby little squares of sidewalk? What then?"

Blevins raises his hands in consternation. "It's true. We can't make them move to a safer place. But as Christians, as Americans, as friends and neighbors, we've got to try. They're being murdered, for Pete's sake. We should at least offer them a reasonable alternative."

"Didn't you just tell us they were crazy?" shouts a woman's high, insistent voice a few pews back. "How can you reason with people who're nuts?"

"Look," Blevins replies. "We're facing a hard choice here. This could easily turn into an epidemic of murder. You may have gotten used to stepping over people sleeping on the street. But let me ask you this: how will you feel next week or next month when you're stepping over dead bodies instead?"

Some couples shake their heads and start to leave. More hands go up with questions. "I think that before you come to us," says one old woman in tinted glasses who is confined to a wheelchair, "maybe the Hollywood merchants should all get together and foot the bill themselves. I don't know about you, but I'm just getting by on social security. I mean, take a good look around you. Sure, we care, but it's not like we're made of money!"

This produces scattered applause.

"What I'm talking about is a very short-term solution," Blevins says, his voice rising. His face looks contorted. These are clearly not the choppy seas he anticipated. "We're trying to buy time, that's all. The association has voted to fund a third of the cost. We have a small crew already on the job. And we fully expect the police will catch this killer soon. We're hoping they take him off the street tomorrow. Maybe they will. Maybe that will fix the problem. But there's no guarantee. Who knows when this will end?"

"No!" shouts Bruce from the rear again. He has stood up and now he's pointing his finger, jabbing the air like an accusing prosecutor. "You don't know anything. This could go on for months, years even! Where's the money for that supposed to come from? I say, leave it to the cops. It's their goddamn problem."

Omar nudges me. "Sounds like this guy Bruce might be your killer right there," he whispers. "He doesn't give a flying fuck what happens."

I nod. "He's a troublemaker, you got that right."

Now a significant portion of the audience has risen from their pews and are making tentative moves toward the doors. Amory Blevins keeps at it. He has a silver bucket in his free hand, the kind of thing you usually keep champagne in. He's talking about small individual contributions, that no amount of money is too small. Also, there is a sign-up sheet on the side table for others who wish to donate at a later date. Some ladies are looking earnestly at their husbands, and a few—not many—are pulling out their wallets and lining up, taking him up on his offer.

Bruce, and the woman I assume is his long-suffering wife, shuffle out the back. We tag along behind. Bruce's hands are jammed down in his front pockets, like he's trying to keep them warm, or maybe he's afraid if he takes them out, they'll just naturally form into fists. He's a tall, angular man in worn cowboy boots and an oversized, red-checkered hunting jacket. He has long, gray, unkempt hair, and he walks with a limp, which the wife is careful to slow down for so that they stay more or less together. She's still chiding him about his obnoxious behavior, but he's unresponsive, just looks straight on toward the exit sign; maybe that's the kind of marriage they have. Or maybe he's just simmering in his own angry world.

In the parking lot, they climb into a tan Toyota pickup. The motor comes alive, purrs. Both of them reach for cigarettes. The smoke drifts out the windows while they talk. The woman is nowhere near finished with what she has to say. Omar and I stand just out of view. There are patches of rust on the wheel wells, I notice, and Bruce has stuck a few choice bumper stickers onto his rear fender. WHEN GUNS ARE OUTLAWED, ONLY CRIMINALS WILL HAVE GUNS. And right next to that: ABORTION = MURDER, followed by KEEP WORKING. MILLIONS ON WELFARE DEPEND ON YOU. Finally, in the far-right corner there's a small reddish circle with the words AYN RAND UNDERGROUND coiled insidiously like a black snake inside. "That's one I've never seen before," I tell Omar.

"Me neither," he says. "Who the hell is Ayn Rand? How'd he get his own underground? Isn't that like a subway?"

"Ayn Rand is a she," I tell him. "She was a writer. Some Republicans seem to favor her these days. All those self-made men, the ones who can't stand it when anyone tells them what to do."

"You ever read her books?"

"I tried, Omar. I really did. *Atlas Shrugged. The Fountainhead. Anthem.* You know what? For somebody like me who wants to heal the planet, for an old Jewish socialist—she's tough."

"What do you mean?"

"Well, it's not just bad ideas. Everyone has a bad idea now and then. It's bad writing. Bad characters. Characters just pasted on. Characters just mouthing words. Half the time I felt like I was wading through mud."

"Hmm. And you're the smartest man I know."

Bruce guns the engine. The muffler is too loud. It's not going to fall off tomorrow maybe, but there's no mistaking it, it rattles the way mufflers do that need serious adjustment. He makes a sharp right at the corner and the Toyota disappears into the unholy dark.

"Which makes me wonder," he says as we head slowly back toward our own cars. "If you had so much trouble reading those books, how the hell could a fool like that Bruce do it?"

"That's a question," I say.

CHAPTER 7

Like those ancient glaciers up in Alaska, the library in my ninth-floor apartment has been shrinking steadily over the last year. There was a time when we had books stacked in every corner of the house, even in the bathroom. Now it's downright pitiful. Three shelves, that's all. How can it be? Whoever said that you could reduce the wisdom of the world whenever you felt like it? How can you call yourself a Jew? How does a person not want to read anymore? These are the whips I use to beat myself with.

I slide my finger across the spines. Some paperbacks are so old they've started to yellow. Pages are bent at the corners from that time when I didn't believe in bookmarks, and there are only a handful of hardbacks, all of them with torn jackets.

I don't know what was the matter with me (*okay, Parisman, that's a bald-faced lie*), but when it came time to move Loretta to that place down on Olympic, a dam broke inside my heart. That's really the only way to describe it. I was overwhelmed. I was drowning. And the next day, after I spent the night alone tossing and turning in bed, with her scent still lingering on the pillows, I picked up the phone and gave nearly all our books away. It was that easy. *I don't want any cash or credit,* I told Maurice, the genial old bookseller who showed up at the door. *Please, just take whatever you want. Take it away.*

Looking back, it's not a coincidence, what I did. There are no coincidences, isn't that how therapists always put it? It's all *beshert*, meant to be. So what would a therapist say? That we used to own hundreds of books, she and I. It was the currency we traded in, our own private fortune. Once I remember thinking it was really the most romantic and satisfying aspect of our life together—just banging around bookstores at odd hours, finding novels to tote home and read to one another in bed, on the couch, at the dinner table. Reading was how we loved each other.

I'm staring, bleary-eyed, at the thirty or forty precious titles left on my shelves now, and even though they say there's no such thing as a stupid question, here I am, asking one. *Did you really give away those Ayn Rand books? Of course you did. Long ago. Why would you even bother to buy that tripe in the first place?*

It's five-thirty in the morning. Still dark out, and for the moment at least, Los Angeles is mercifully silent. I'm padding around in my underwear. I'm barefoot and unshaven, and the bones in my body ache in unison. Too late to go back to sleep, too early to call anyone. Bill Malloy will be in bed at this hour, and even if he were awake, he wouldn't get what I'm talking about; he knows as much about Ayn Rand as Omar.

I flick on the kitchen light, watch a tiny cockroach skate across the floor and disappear under the sink where he lives with his friends. I make myself a pot of strong coffee, toss a couple slices of sourdough bread in the toaster. The newspaper, by some miracle, is waiting outside my door, way ahead of schedule. I tuck it under my arm, and with my coffee in one hand and my toast in the other, I settle down at the table where Loretta and I shared so many breakfasts. I vow, as I do each morning, not to be in a rush. *No, Parisman, you can't rush this life. Everything will unfold as it was meant to be. Beshert.*

As I'm sipping my coffee, my mind keeps turning back to last night at the church, and how much Bruce's outburst colored the whole event. I'd like to believe that I get a rough-cut guy like Bruce. I've run into his type before, just not here in L.A. If you drove over the grapevine to Buttonwillow or Bakersfield, or if you stepped on the gas and went as far as Wyoming or Idaho, you'd meet plenty of folks like that. Out there, on the treeless plain, Bruce and his philosophy makes perfect sense. What doesn't fit, I think, is that Ayn Rand bumper sticker. Omar's right about that. So while I'm sitting here, trying not to rush things and waiting for the sun to rise, I pull out my computer and look it up.

The Ayn Rand Underground has a website and a phone number and an address in Studio City. I scroll through their blog. It's filled with text, but there are many pictures of happy, white twenty-somethings standing around, sampling shrimp appetizers and laughing at garden parties. Ayn Rand, of course, is also a major presence. Sepia photographs of her and selected quotes from her books line the margins. Whoever cobbled it together talks about freedom and selfishness and egoism, but you get the feeling that it's just jargon, that he doesn't know what the hell he's talking about. I'd bet a nickel on that. He likes her, sure, he's a fan, but Ayn Rand could just as easily be the name of another indie band he's infatuated with.

Another thing that tips me off: the Underground isn't a full-fledged hustle. They have a few choice things for sale: buttons, bumper stickers like the one Bruce has on his truck, tote bags, and baseball caps, but they're not pushing expensive stuff—no textbooks and correspondence courses and weekend symposiums. No one's making a living out of this. In the end, it's just a rant, a smug, self-contained club in Studio City, some young nerdy guy with time on his hands, mouthing off and smiling at his face in the mirror. I jot down the address in my notepad. Maybe it's worth a visit, but probably not. Bruce may be an idiot, but he's an unlikely killer. Or if he does kill things, at least he eats them afterwards.

*   *   *

Just as I finish brushing my teeth, the phone rings. It's Lemuel Carter.

"I'm sorry to call you so early this morning, Mr. Parisman. I hope I'm not disturbing you."

"Not at all, Mr. Carter."

"Please, just call me Lemuel. My father was Mr. Carter."

"Okay, then, Lemuel."

"Yes, well, I've been going over our records here at the Mission as I promised, and it seems you're right, we did have a Mr. McFee as a guest a while back."

"When would that be?"

"Oh, he came through last June. Even signed up for the program. We put him down for a bed, three square meals, counseling, showers, and haircuts—the works."

"And how long did that last?"

"Two months." There's a pause. "But that's not so unusual, you know. The first time a person ever starts down the road to Jesus, well, it can be long and difficult. They've been through so much. They often lose their way."

"I imagine so," I say. "Tell me this, Lemuel. Someone there must have had an initial interview with him, right? Sat down, took his personal history?"

"Oh, yes. We always do that. That's automatic. If you're going to have a stranger in your house, sleeping beside you, well, you don't want any surprises, now do you? You wanna know as much as you can."

"Great," I say. "Now, my next question. Can I read that history? It's not top secret, is it?"

"Well," he says, "under ordinary circumstances, it would be. Even a poor man has a right to privacy. But seeing as how he's passed, and, as you say, it's now a criminal matter, seeing all that, we might be able to bend the rules."

"You don't have to do it just for me, Lemuel. I don't count. The police, on the other hand, that's another story. They'll be interested in whatever you got."

"I'm sure. But you can come down and take a look if you like. I'll keep my eyes shut."

"I don't want to get you in trouble," I say.

"Young man," he sighs, "I've been in trouble most all my life. Why should I stop now?"

*   *   *

As I'm pulling onto the street, I call Malloy to fill him in. "Maybe you should send Jason and Remo down to the Rescue Mission this afternoon with a warrant for those papers. Mr. Carter will probably let you copy them anyway, but you're going to need them under lock and key eventually."

"Not if we don't find the killer," Malloy says. "Then it's just paper, isn't it?"

I also tell him about my lunch with the Reverend Jimmy Archibald, and what a weird guy he seems. "Maybe it's just the combination of Christianity and real estate," I say. "I mean, I understand. You can't make a living ministering to the poor. That storefront church of his is nothing. Less than nothing. Just a bunch of folding chairs and a Styrofoam cross. But then he's got this slick business card. And he's dressed to the nines."

"That's not so strange to me," Malloy says. "Religion, real estate—to people like that, it's all just one giant hustle. Doesn't matter what they're selling."

"Yeah well, he said he's going to see if he can find out anything about Delia, but between you and me, I doubt I'll ever hear from him again. Seemed like I was hardly a blip on his radar."

"No, probably not."

It's not what he says exactly, but there's an odd trepidation, a shakiness in between the silences of Malloy's replies, like somehow he's in over his head, like even with twenty years on the force, a voice inside is telling him it's not enough this time. "You sound kinda down, Bill."

"Do I?"

"Yes, you do. Want to talk about it?"

"Since when did you take up psychiatry, Dr. Parisman?" That's always his first response, to punch back.

"Oh, I've been at this a long time. It pays about as well as detective work, by the way."

"Well, let's not bother about my moods. I am down, if you want to know. In fact, every time I drive past a street person, I think: there he is, he's next. But I appreciate all the free legwork you're putting in. It helps. I'm just worried we're sitting on our hands and we haven't seen the end of it. This maniac's going to strike again, I can feel it."

"It takes time to crack things like this," I say. "You know that. You just have to keep digging." I'm stopped at the light on Normandie. "Oh, did you get a chance to interview McFee's ex-wife?"

"Jason and Remo did. She's in Tarzana now. Works as a house cleaner. Not a bad woman. Just trying to move on with her life, you know. She has a live-in boyfriend and he's got a couple of kids. She gets to play mom every other weekend."

"What'd she have to add about McFee?"

"That he was a drunk. That he had a mean streak. That when he drank too much, the mean streak would flare up. She didn't care for that, somehow."

"I don't suppose she was sorry what happened to him, then."

"She didn't cry, if that's what you mean. She didn't seem surprised, either. Said he had it coming. That's what Remo wrote down."

"What about her boyfriend? He have an alibi?"

"The boyfriend's a trucker. He was halfway up I-5, coming back from Sacramento, when they found McFee. I also don't believe she told him much about her marital troubles, so no, we can rule him out."

I finish up with Malloy and hang up. I don't tell him about my late-night conversation with Betsy Rollands. I don't tell him about the meeting at the Episcopal church with Bruce of the Back Woods and Amory Blevins of the Mid-City Merchants Association. Those are roads not taken. Probably roads that go nowhere, too.

CHAPTER 8

In the half hour or so it takes me to drive downtown and find a safe parking lot, Lemuel Carter has been having second thoughts. Now he's all about discretion. He suggests we take the McFee file a few blocks away to the Nickel Diner on South Main. "It'd be more prudent if we had ourselves some privacy," he says, sliding the manila folder deftly into his leather briefcase and clicking it shut. "And besides, man, this time of day, my stomach just naturally commences to growl."

The Nickel Diner is cozy. A diamond in the rough, is what I'd say, if I were a restaurant critic. The biscuits are great, and they do amazing things with ham and eggs. It also doesn't hurt that the prices haven't changed much since the Market crashed in '29.

Carter is in a buoyant mood, which may be on account of the sausage and biscuits and coffee he's putting away at a prodigious rate. He talks to me while I'm going over the report. "Now, I spoke with Abel Casselli, he's the one who did the writeup back in June. You see his signature right there at the top right-hand corner? Abel's a pro. Ain't nothin' gets by him."

"And just what do you mean by nothing?"

"Well, Mr. Parisman, I don't know how much face-to-face experience you have with homeless folks."

"Not a lot. I see them every day. But they don't let them past the gate at Park La Brea."

"Then please allow an old hand like me to teach you. People have these ideas—they'll see a homeless man walking along and it scares them. Like he's some kind of time bomb, like he's a creature from another planet, you know." He smiles slightly at his own description. "I've seen people turn right around and cross the street sometimes to avoid them."

"If they were from another planet, that might be a smart idea."

"It's about expectations," Lemuel says. "When you see something strange, or you meet someone who's unpredictable, what do you do?"

"Take a step back?"

"Exactly. The whole world disapproves of them. The world thinks homeless folks are ignorant and crazy, but they're not. Well, some are crazy, okay, but they're not stupid. Not at all. No sir, they can't afford to be.

"They're unlucky," I add. I take a sip of coffee. "And I don't care how tough you are. A run of bad luck will do anyone in."

"That's so," he says.

"When I was a kid," I say, "there was a woman in my neighborhood. Sweet lady. Mary Jo Baldwin. Worked for a dentist down on Wilshire. She seemed fine. Capable, I mean. But then her husband left her for another woman. Took every penny and disappeared. Which must have really slammed her. And she got into the habit of stopping at the liquor store on her way home from work, tucking a bottle away in her purse, you know, just to ease the pain. She might have survived, I guess, but then the dentist got sued for malpractice. Closed his office. That's what did it. That job was all she had."

He looks into my eyes and nods again. "But it doesn't end there, my friend. When you live out on the pavement day after day, when everything you own is flung in a shopping cart, and you curl up every night under a bridge or in an alley, with rats and lice and damp, you learn things. Lots of things. Your brain is half scared to death, and you, you're wide awake. The wheels keep spinning around, even when you finally sleep. And what you learn most of all is to be careful."

"Sounds like good advice for everyone," I say.

Lemuel ignores me. He's got a speech to make. "It's not that they're dishonest," he says, "no." He brushes a few errant biscuit crumbs away from his beard. "In fact, a homeless man is maybe the most honest soul on earth. But out there on the street, words can kill you. You don't ever tell a stranger what's really on your mind. It's like prison. You know what I'm saying? If you wanna survive, well, as long as you can, you keep your mouth shut."

"All right," I say. "I'll buy that."

"But see, when they come to the Mission, that all has to change. We need them to make a clean slate of their lives. Tell us everything about you. That's the way we start out. Tell us the facts. We know you ain't perfect, brother, otherwise you wouldn't be here."

I stop making the effort to read Abel Casselli's cramped hand-written field notes and look up. "Okay, Lemuel, so what was on Louis McFee's slate?"

"You don't wanna read it yourself?"

"I want to show it to my friends at police headquarters."

He chuckles, pulls the report gently out of my hands. "They can take what they want, long as they have a warrant. But here, let me walk you through it, son." His finger slides down the first page. "Louis McFee was born in Arizona near Flagstaff. He's been in and out of trouble. No mother. Brought up in fits and starts by James, his father, when he was sober, which wasn't often, and by his aunt in Albuquerque, whenever the father was in the tank."

"His father taught him to drink? Is that how he learned?"

"Funny, how we choose our heroes, isn't it?" Lemuel shakes his head. "His father taught him everything he knew. Taught him to fight. Taught him how to get kicked out of school. When you're sixteen years old and not in school, what do you do?"

"You tell me."

"I don't have to," he says. "You know the answer. Seems like just about every door you open at that age is trouble. In and out of trouble, yes sir. And that followed him around his whole life. Mostly because he couldn't help drinking, but for other reasons, too."

"Such as?"

Lemuel's finger slides wistfully further down the page. "Let's see, now. He told Abel about his days in the military, some hard times he had in Vietnam. A village they had to burn once. That couldn't have done too much for his character. Know what I'm saying?"

"Anything else?"

"Well, he had a temper, of course. And when you add alcohol and crack to that—and Lord only knows what he left out—you can't help but get yourself a bad mix. We don't need to bother with the criminal reports, do we, Mr. Parisman? He had a past, let's leave it there. No doubt your friends downtown are aware of that."

I nod. "But here's what I don't get, Lemuel. Louis McFee made a decision. He chose to come down here and lean on Jesus with you. That's good news, right? Abel must have found that encouraging."

"Abel's heard everything before. He's like a piano player in a whorehouse." Lemuel tamps the grease off his lips with a napkin. "Besides, this wasn't the first place McFee came to for help. He made the rounds before he ended up here. He went to Good Counsel and to the Quaker House and to the Eternal Light of Christ—"

"That hole in the wall by Fairfax High? He went there, too?"

"That's what it says. What difference does that make?"

"It's just that Delia, the other woman who was murdered, she might have spent time there, too. It's a coincidence, that's all. But in my line of work, coincidences count for a lot."

Lemuel Carter frowns. "In my line of work, it just shows how bad the poor man felt. He was at the end of his rope. You go from place to place, all the time looking for a home and not finding any."

"So tell me this. You say McFee stuck around here for a couple of months. He was clean, part of the program, did everything you told him to. What happened then? Why'd he disappear?"

He flips to the very last page in the folder, shakes his head, closes it and lays it down flat on the table. "You want me to speculate? Okay. People are fragile. But they're also complicated, that's what I've learned. Says here he got into a shouting match with one of our counselors the day before he left. He wanted a different bed and there were none available at the time. That might have set him off, I suppose."

"That's all it took?"

"Maybe. But he might have been fixing to go, anyway. Sometimes when you're on the path, you get anxious. You're doing everything you can, that's what you believe, and you want to skip right ahead, talk to the Man Himself. But the truth is, you can't." Lemuel's eyes are beaming at me now. "It's always one step at a time, even if you can see where you're going. Especially if you can see."

The waitress comes by and I signal her for a check. "Here," I say, "let me treat you, Lemuel. You've been very helpful."

He doesn't protest too vigorously. "I'm not sure about that. Sounds like this report just confirms every bad thing you already thought about him." he says.

"I just thought he should have had more chances in life," I say. "That didn't happen."

Lemuel smiles. "No, it didn't. But he's skipped on ahead to Jesus now. Skipped on ahead. He got what he wanted. So I imagine everything will be just fine."

*   *   *

Mara meets me downstairs at the Olympic Terrace at eleven. The sun is streaming in. She's a little overdressed, I think, like she just rushed in from a meeting with her lawyer, but what do I know. "I'm glad you could come early," she says in a hushed tone. "Gus isn't well."

"He hasn't been well for a while."

"No, you don't understand. He stopped breathing this morning. Just stopped altogether. Luckily, a nurse was in the room when it happened. They put him on oxygen right away. Now the color's back in his face, but I don't know. I really don't. When I look at him now, I think: he could die any minute."

We walk up the stairs. Mara grabs my hand, something she's never done before, not in public anyway. When we get to room 226, we see two nurses fussing over her husband. One blonde and one Latina. He's got a clear plastic tube up his nose, and a large gray oxygen tank next to the bed. He's more alert than usual, I notice; his blue eyes are drifting from side to side. All the female attention he's getting must be lifting his spirits, if nothing else. The blonde is adjusting the angle of his bed, and the Latina is filling out a chart.

Mara leans over and kisses him lightly on the cheek. "You gave me such a scare," she says to him.

He looks at her and sort of lifts his free hand cavalierly, as if to say, well, what the hell can I do? That seems to be the extent of their bond together these days. She tells him how he makes her feel, and he offers some cryptic gesture or facial expression in return. I shouldn't criticize. What I have with Loretta isn't all that much better.

We spend another fifteen minutes or so in the room. The nurses finally leave, and when they do, Mara leans forward and starts to mumble to him quietly. It's a soft, soothing stream of words about what she's up to, a lullaby of sorts. How over the weekend she took Violet to a new Vietnamese restaurant and some art museums, how yes, she knows, he probably wouldn't have cared for the art. Too modern for you, darling. Violet, on the other hand . . .

I wander down the hall and poke my head in to check on my wife, but she's fast asleep. I kiss her forehead and straighten the blankets around her. She jiggles slightly. A strange grin moves across her face. I don't know what she's dreaming about, but whatever it is, I'm envious.

* * *

In the late afternoon we return to Mara's place on Creston Drive. The light is already beginning to fade. She parks her Lexus in the garage and I pull in right behind her. I watch as she climbs out, straightens her skirt, reaches for her purse. There's an urgency about her. In the entryway she kicks off her pumps. She flips on the air conditioner, draws me into the bedroom, and starts to carefully unbutton her blouse. "Here," she says, "come on, help me with this. I'm too hot."

What's a grown man supposed to do? I help her. First with the blouse, then the bra, which is a dark, lacy French thing that probably cost a fortune. She drops it on the carpet. Then, in a single motion she steps out of her skirt and pulls me close. "I need you, Amos. I need you to be with me."

We kiss, a slow, lingering union that ends up toppling us both onto her bed. She tugs at my belt. Her hands and mouth are all over me. This isn't what I expected after our trip to the nursing home. She put on a good face when she was standing next to the oxygen tank with Gus, but still I remember how terrified she looked; I thought she might want to sit now with a glass of red wine and talk, or maybe not say anything, just sit and shake and have a good cry. But God knows I'm delighted, happy to be wrong. And here we are in the shadows, wrestling, my fingers sliding ever so gingerly above her knee and across her thigh, inching toward that inevitable place. She is waiting for me, I know, but she can hardly contain herself. Her eyes are closed, and we're speaking in tongues, touching one another in the old familiar ways, luxuriating in her silk sheets. Are we really so different? Aren't we all made of the same desperate material? Yes, we are.

CHAPTER 9

I haven't breathed a word to Shelly yet about Mara and what's going on between us, not because I don't love him or trust him (I do, sorta), and not because we have any mutual relatives still alive, anyone in our prudish universe who'd be offended if they only knew (we don't). No, the folks we cared about—my parents, his parents, brothers, sisters, aunts and uncles—they've all moved on, all found lovely, permanent spots for themselves in Jewish cemeteries on the East Coast or up and down the great state of California. Where they are, it's quiet. The grass is always green, always mowed, the sun is always shining. They're free. Now it's just the two of us; we're the only family we have left. Which you'd think would make things simpler. I want things to be simple, I do. And more than that, I want an honest meeting of the minds, but somehow, whenever we get together, it doesn't work out that way. We go for a barefoot walk in the warm sand near Santa Monica, or we sit for an hour at a greasy taco joint on Sunset. That's the extent of our relationship. He always has ideas, crazy schemes he dreams up in the middle of the night. Or just irritable things, things that weigh him down, things he's frantic to get off his chest. The latest suit his last wife's lawyer is bringing. What his new doctor thinks about his prostate. I listen, and the more he talks, the less room there is for me.

Shelly and I were close as kids; we lived a few doors away from one another. We played basketball in the same public park on weekends. He was older than me and much taller, but I was faster on my feet. I could always get around him, always drive inside and score. We went to the same Hebrew school, rode the same bus to the same summer camp in Ojai. Does history count? That's what I wanna know. Because he contributed to it mightily. It was Shelly who offered me a cigarette when I was twelve, Shelly who showed me my first *Playboy* centerfold, Shelly who taught me the ins and outs of playing poker, Shelly who could recite in graphic detail what teenage boys and girls did together in the back seats of cars. That kind of information means something, I think; it may not be wisdom, but still, it's a map. I owe that much to Shelly. He did that for me. He gave me a map to follow. I don't have to tell him about Mara, though. And I won't.

*   *   *

It's after eleven, and Mara and I are curled up together. We haven't moved more than an inch or two in hours, and now she's asleep. Me, I don't seem to be able to do that anymore—the new pills I take interfere—and anyway, I'm too wound up inside. I'm staring at all the red and yellow and blue Hollywood lights beyond the balcony below, watching them blink and vanish, blink and vanish, trying to remember which building is which, trying to locate streets and places in the dark. I think more about Shelly, what went wrong, and then I wonder if I was maybe too rash when I crossed that guy Bruce off my list of suspects. Maybe I should reconsider. I could always put on a tie and go to the next meeting of the Ayn Rand Underground. Studio City's just over the hill. And whoever hammered those people has to be a psychopath, doesn't he? Yes, he does. A loner. Someone with twisted, stone-age opinions. Someone who thinks just like Bruce. It's an absolute long shot, of course. So what else is new?

That's when my cell phone rings. I pick it up quick, which means I have to move my arm, which makes Mara stir. She lifts her head and shudders, opens one eye briefly, and settles back down again into her pillow.

"Hey," Malloy says, "you're still awake. I'm glad I caught you."

"Some folks would be apologizing about now," I say. "Have you looked at your watch?"

"I don't work nine to five," he says. That's as close as he's going to come to an apology, I can tell.

"So what can I do for you, Lieutenant?"

There's a muffled pause on the other end. He's talking to someone, giving instructions maybe. Then, a minute later, he comes back on the line. "We've got another body, Amos. Mexican woman, looks like. Think you can get over here?"

"Where's here?"

"Beverly near Stanley. There's a maternity shop next to a little motel."

I sit up, rub my cheeks and forehead. "Okay, sure, I'm on my way," I say. I slide out of bed and get dressed in the dark as quietly as I can manage. Mara hasn't moved. Her breathing is steady; the pillow is her best friend. And she won't be surprised to see me gone in the morning. Once she even made a joke about it. I was her ghost, she said. Her darling ghost. As I step into the stillness of the narrow, empty street, I promise myself I'll call her later and explain everything.

Twenty minutes later I'm standing with Malloy in front of a maternity shop. The police have cordoned off the whole area. There are black-and-whites at every corner, and a crew of technicians is setting up some bright lighting to flood the entire block. Lee's Babyland has somehow been turned into the star of this gruesome scene. Its display window features five pregnant pastel-colored mannequins, their arms raised in various bizarre angles. They all have short, black, clipped wigs. Their heads are tilted and their eyes are subtly Asian. They all have that serene, faraway look that suggests everything's been figured out. There's money in the bank. Food in the fridge, and all the kids are getting straight As. None of them are very fat. None of them are sweating or straining. None of them look anything like the pregnant women I've known in my life.

Facedown on the pavement outside the shop lies a half-naked woman in tight black running pants with her arms splayed out, her head half-twisted oddly in our direction. Jason and Remo are squatting down on their haunches, poking all around her. I figure she might be between thirty and forty, but that's hard to know. Someone has torn the blouse right off her back. Her bra is undone, and there's a dark clot of blood below her left shoulder. Her hair, which is thick and uncombed, has started to mat. Her left hand seems to be reaching out for the empty cardboard Starbucks cup a few inches away.

"So what do we have?" I ask Malloy.

"Don't know yet," he says. "We found a shopping cart full of someone's precious things right there. That's why I called you, Amos. At first, I thought for sure it was another homeless killing. I mean, it is. We've got another body. And it's not far from the others. But the longer I stand here, well, it's a puzzle. This one looks a lot different than the other two."

"You mean, because she was shot?"

"That's one thing. So maybe that says we have a brand-new killer on our hands."

"But why would he leave a shopping cart behind?"

"I dunno," says Malloy. "Maybe it has nothing to do with this. Or maybe he read about the other killings in the paper."

"A copycat."

"Maybe."

"Or maybe it's the same killer, and now he's decided to step up his game. Maybe he just got tired of hitting street people with a hammer."

"That could be. And you know what else rubs me raw about this?"

"What?"

"Well, look around you," Malloy says. "Look at the context. Where are we? Look at the cars zipping by. It's like, this guy didn't give a fuck where she died. He killed her right out here in the open. That's bold. What if there was a clerk in one of these stores? Or a janitor, working late? He was taking a chance, is what I'm saying. Anybody could have seen this happen. The last two, at least, they were both tucked away in dark alleys."

"So he's changed his style. Maybe he's daring you to catch him. Is that really a problem? I'd call that an opportunity."

"Sure," Malloy says, jamming his hands into his pockets. "I appreciate that. The bolder he gets, the easier for us. Problem is, it also looks like our killer might have wanted her for other reasons."

We both turn back toward the body. The print blouse she had on was torn from the nape of the neck down. The bra, a skimpy yellow thing, is dangling off her shoulders, and lying flat on the pavement, half her right breast is exposed. She was a pretty attractive woman, I think. Which makes me wonder if she really was a street person. Street walker, more likely. Or someone trying out for the job. Her hands seem soft and smooth. Too soft, maybe. Her fingernails are painted a delicate pink. In the surreal glare of the police lights, it seems like she might have lipstick on and maybe even a touch of eye shadow.

"How many homeless women you know wear makeup, Lieutenant?"

He nods. "I noticed, too," he says. "Except for the shopping cart, she seems a little too upscale."

"And it doesn't seem all that sexual to me," I say. "Looks like he might have reached for her. Looks like she tried to get away and he grabbed her and tore her blouse. Okay. But then he shot her. You don't shoot somebody you mean to rape, at least not until afterwards."

Malloy nods. "And you don't usually try to attack someone on a busy street corner, either."

"No, you don't," I chime in. "Not unless you're crazy."

"Still, he did reach for the blouse. And the bra is unhooked. Did he do that before he shot her, or afterwards?"

"Or did she reach in and do it herself?"

"Another possibility, yeah. Maybe there was some transaction going on. Whatever. That's gotta mean something."

"I don't know, Bill. Are you even sure the shopping cart is hers? People leave that crap lying around everywhere these days, who knows who it belongs to?"

"They're checking for fingerprints. If she's been pushing it around, they'll know pretty quick."

"Did she have a wallet or a purse? Any ID?" I glance down at her again, shake my head. "I think you're right. This one is just so different from the other two."

At that moment Jason taps Malloy on the shoulder and hands him a woman's light blue fanny pack. "Check this out, boss. It was thrown into the shopping cart with all the other crap." he says. "Maybe that's why it took so long to find."

Malloy holds it to the light and zips it open. He pulls out a small wad of twenty-dollar bills, a California driver's license, three keys on a metal chain, a small can of mace, a pharmacy vial with some white capsules inside, a couple of condoms, and a Visa card. Except for the license, he hands everything, one by one, to Jason, who puts it neatly into a crime bag for further analysis. He studies the photo on the license, glances down at the corpse to double check, then back at me. "Well, to answer your question, apparently her name was Maria Carlotta Ruiz. She would have been thirty-two next month. Lived on Cesar Chavez, in Boyle Heights. I'm sure we'll find out a whole lot more about the poor woman when we drive over there."

"Boyle Heights is a ways from here."

"Yeah, but we're not that far from the Metro. She could have used public transportation."

"Maybe she drove. I'll bet you there's a car around here somewhere that belongs to her."

"Maybe. But I didn't see anything that looks like a car key in her bag, did you?"

"No," I say, "granted. But what if her killer is also a car thief?"

Malloy rolls his eyes, like he's had enough, like I'm being a *nudnik* now and why don't I just shut up. "I'm just going to go over there and talk to her family."

"You want me to come along with you?"

"You can if you want, but for now it seems like this one isn't much related to the homeless murders."

"No," I say. "Probably not. Not unless our killer made a mistake."

"Meaning what?"

"Meaning maybe he went after her because he caught sight of her near the shopping cart. Because he thought she was a street person."

"Well," Malloy says sadly, "then she was just an attractive girl, in the wrong place at the wrong time."

I tell him goodbye, ask him to please let me know whatever he learns about Maria Carlotta Ruiz. Me, I have a more personal source of information, but I'm not going to bother him until he's had a good night's sleep.

*　　*　　*

Next morning at nine, I show up at Omar's office. It's on the second floor of a quiet, nondescript stucco building on 1st Street in Boyle Heights, the kind of antiseptic commercial space a contractor threw together without wondering, or caring really, what would ever become of it. There's an all-night drugstore, a bar, and a *lavanderia* across the street, and squad cars come and go at regular intervals from the Hollenbeck station just three blocks away. The first floor, which is closed and locked up tight this time of day, belongs to a bail bondsman named Emilio Cardozo. Actually, Emilio Cardozo & Son, so I guess that means the old man has made a decent go of things and now presumably wants to pass it on. He has posted an emergency telephone number on the thick glass door. And taped to the same glass door there's a small blue plastic arrow that points me up a narrow staircase to the Villasenor Investigative Service.

"You want to go out to breakfast—again?" That's the first thing Omar says when he sees me open the door, followed quickly by a devilish grin.

"No, I came here because I need a detective."

We're the only ones in his office. There are three desks. His other two employees won't be in until noon. He can't afford to pay them to work full-time, not yet. *But soon, you just wait.* Above the coffeemaker on the wall behind him is a large oil painting he toted back from his honeymoon in Oaxaca—a band of street musicians standing in the sunlight. An old couple is dancing on the cobblestones in the foreground, and the crowd around them, it seems, is swept up in some glorious motion; you can make out who they are by the instruments they're holding—the drum, the trumpet, the accordion, the guitar. You see it all plainly, but still it's a blur, an erotic tornado—as though the music has somehow managed to levitate them, lift them into the most joyous space imaginable.

"That's a great painting," I say, pointing to it. "Who did that?"

"Beats me, man. I don't think it's signed. I picked it up for fifty bucks at a gallery there. Every time I see it, you know, it makes me glad."

His desk is well arranged. He's got a laptop and a phone and a printer and a couple of nice new metal filing cabinets. There's also a small framed photograph of him and Lourdes on their wedding day, their arms wrapped tightly around each other, clearly in love. And the window near where he's sitting lets him take in all the colorful street life below. He gets up now and adjusts the blinds. "That's the only trouble with this damn place," he says, "sometimes it's too bright. What can you do?"

"You've got a good life, Omar. Don't knock it."

"Oh, believe me, I know." He produces two ceramic cups and pours coffee for both of us. "So, you don't want breakfast. Then what?"

"I'm still on the trail of those homeless murders, Omar. It's beginning to look like a plague."

He takes a short sip of coffee. "Last time we talked it was two, right?"

"Make it three now."

"And what do we know about the third?"

"That's why I'm here. It was a Boyle Heights girl. Also, as it happens, about the same age as you. Her name was Maria Carlotta Ruiz. Ring any bells?"

Omar gives me a startled look. "Maria? Maria Ruiz? Shit, man, we went to high school together. I used to bang around with her brother, Jesús."

"Great. So what can you tell me about her?"

He scratches his head. "Tell you? There's not much to tell. She was like a lot of girls I knew back then. Liked to party, have a good time. Jesús told me her mother had her heart set on her going to college. Maria was the smart one in the family, but Jesús said she never cared, one way or the other. She liked fast cars. She liked boys. Not me, but other boys. We lost track of one another. Like I say, I was closer to Jesús."

"Well maybe we can go talk to him."

Omar doesn't speak right away. He's trying hard to absorb what I've just told him, to brush it off like it's all in a day's work. "Who knows if we can even find him, man. He's become kind of a shadow around these parts. I invited him to my wedding. He never showed. What does that tell you?"

"I don't know. What else can you remember, Omar? Not about Jesús—about Maria."

"What else. What else. Maria Ruiz." He heaves a sigh. "Oh, yeah, well, after high school she sorta lost her way. Just went off, you know. She hung out with a couple of unpleasant guys for a while."

"Unpleasant in what way?"

For a moment, he tugs absentmindedly at his ear, as though that could somehow elicit an answer. "I'm thinking they were dope dealers, something like that. But hey, man, a lot of people were selling back then. It was like normal. Or almost normal. That was how you paid the rent. It was how you stayed alive, sometimes."

"So if it was normal, where did the unpleasantness come in?"

Omar pauses. "They were doing more than weed, these guys. They were ambitious, the way I remember. They were always branching out."

"Doing what?"

"Well, one of them's not doing anything anymore. Pablo got snuffed in the middle of a heroin war last year."

"I see. And his friend?"

"Julio? Julio is still around somewhere. He's not into drugs anymore, I understand. The last time I saw him, he was busy building up a little harem for himself."

"That would seem to fit," I say.

"What do you mean?"

"Well, Maria Ruiz was an attractive girl. They found her on Beverly, near a motel that gets some questionable characters. It was late at night. Not the best chemistry in the world for her."

"No, not exactly."

I take a sip of coffee. It's already starting to get cold. "Looks like somebody ripped off her blouse, and when she tried to get away, he shot her in the back. She had money on her, too. She had some pills, some condoms. What's that tell you?"

"*Entonces una puta.*" Omar picks up a brand-new yellow pencil from a cup on his desk, twirls it idly around. "Yeah, I suppose that could be." He blinks once or twice, shakes his head. It seems like he's in pain and it's probably my fault. "She liked to party," he mutters again.

Neither of us speak for a while. Mariachi music is blaring from a radio down the block. A parked car, I think, some kids maybe with too much time on their hands. Or a taco truck. Whatever it is, it's too loud. Outside on the street a bus squeals to a halt below and the doors slide open with a sigh. Then it rumbles off. The noise fades.

"This isn't the same as those other two," Omar says. "How'd you ever get involved?"

"Malloy found a shopping cart nearby and called me right away. He thought maybe it belonged to her. An honest mistake, I guess."

"Have the cops told her mother yet?"

I look at Omar. Now I can see the pain clearly in his eyes. "Oh, I'm sure she's been told. They've probably gone through the whole house by now."

"I know the mother," he says. "She would have had no idea, man. Not one fucking clue." He shakes his head again, frowns. "This will break her heart. You know that, don't you? This will fucking kill her."

CHAPTER 10

Betsy Rollands calls me while I'm stuck in a traffic jam on Sunset coming back from Boyle Heights. As soon as I can, I pull over next to a car wash. "What do you know?" I say.

"I know a lot," she comes right back. "You could say it was nice of you to call."

"All right," I say. "You win. You're nice to call. You're also beautiful. Now tell me something useful, Betsy. I'm at sea."

"Okay," she says. "Did you ever meet with Lemuel Carter at the Rescue Mission?"

"I did. We went out to breakfast. And he read me the file on Louis McFee. I don't know that these folks have anything to link them together, but I'm learning a lot about life on the street. It ain't pretty."

"Good. And did you see the piece in the paper about the Mid-City Merchants and the meeting at the Episcopal church?"

"I'm way ahead of you, dear. Omar and I even went to the meeting. What a fucking zoo that turned into."

"I'm sure," she says. "Now tell me this: Was Amory Blevins there? A little fat guy in a suit? Did he put the squeeze on them for money?"

"Yeah, of course. He had this terrific idea. Get them off the street before they get killed. Trouble was, he was asking the folks in the church to pay for it."

"You're so perceptive, Amos. I just wanted to warn you about him: he's an awful man. The purest of slime. I've known him a long time. I wish we'd never met." Then she proceeds to tell me the many capers he's been into—the fraud, the bankruptcies, the check kiting, the loan sharking—she has a whole file on Mr. Blevins, it appears. This is his first venture into using homeless people as a business opportunity, she says, but still, you might want to call him out on it.

"He's not a killer, is he, Betsy?"

"No," she says, "I doubt it. He might hire someone to do it—I'd buy that, but he doesn't have the balls. Besides, he doesn't pay attention to anyone else in the universe besides Amory Blevins. The way he sees it, nobody ever rises to his level. Why should he take a chance and kill them? That would sully himself. Ruin his afternoon. He's just a con artist."

"A con artist with a past, I suspect."

"Yeah, I guess. The Mid-City Merchants Association is real, though. It doesn't do much besides argue with the city about parking requirements and liquor licenses. How Amory got elected president, I'll never understand."

"Sounds like nobody except you ever checked him out."

"Could be. I know what he's done, and the cops might have an old list of complaints, but even so, he's slick enough these days they'll probably never lay a finger on him. Not unless they have help."

"So what would you like me to do?" I ask.

"I don't know," she says. "Maybe just remind him he can't get away with it. Not anymore. Tell him it's over. Tell him that your old friend Betsy Rollands is still keeping her baleful eye on him. If he thinks I'm lying, tell him I still have the documents."

"Okay, I will," I say. "What's the worst that can happen?"

*   *   *

The Mid-City Merchants is on Melrose near Fairfax. It's a little off my beaten path, but since I owe Betsy Rollands a favor, I drive up there. There's a raw juice bar next door and a convenient all-day parking lot on the other side, manned by a long-haired, handsome Iranian fellow in a white sports jacket and sneakers. He hasn't shaved in days, which I understand is the look everyone's after. Like you're too rich or too famous to care. I toss him the keys to my old beat-up Honda, tell him I'll be back in a few. He winks at me, says, "That's okay, boss, for a few minutes it's five bucks."

"Whatever," I say.

The office is quiet. There are several unwatered, half-dead plants in clay pots and some framed black and white photos of Hollywood back in the Golden Age. Buster Keaton hanging from a tall building. The Keystone Kops. Laurel and Hardy. Not much about the Melrose area. Who knows? Maybe there wasn't much around here back then. The receptionist desk is vacant. In a clear glass cubicle at the rear sits Amory Blevins. He's just finished talking to someone on the phone as I walk in. "I'm sorry," he says, looking up, a little startled that someone has entered his space unannounced. "I was about to go to lunch. We usually don't see anybody between twelve and one. Did Diana make an appointment for you? I don't know how many times I've told her not to do that." He pushes his chair away from the desk and rises.

"No, no," I tell him, "Diana's innocent."

"All right," he says. "Then maybe you could come back in an hour, say, and schedule something with her. I'm free about two or two-thirty."

"Actually, Mr. Blevins," I say, handing him my card, "I was at your talk the other night at the Episcopal church."

"Yes, well that didn't go so well, now did it." He looks briefly at the card, then tucks it nonchalantly into his shirt pocket. I'm guessing he's not too impressed by private detectives, maybe they're a dime a dozen, maybe they drop by all the time.

"You tried," I say. "And it was a noble idea, reaching out to the spiritual community. Not what I would ever expect from a group like yours."

"What do you mean?"

"Well, let's be honest. Businessmen look after their own interests first. That's how they stay on business. I'm not saying they can't be nice, but they don't usually make alliances with the Little Sisters of the Poor."

Blevins sighs, plops back down in his chair. I take the one on the opposite side of the desk, even though he hasn't offered. He shakes his head, pulls out my card, reads it over once again, sets it squarely in front of him. "Okay, Mr. Parisman, private detective, so what can I do for you? Make it quick, shall we? I've got to be somewhere in ten minutes."

I take out my cardboard notepad and a ballpoint pen. "Fine, then maybe you can tell me just who you hired to coax all those ornery street people into shelters. That would be the first item. Also, I'd like to know what you're paying them. That's a big job. Fifty to a hundred thousand, right? Wasn't that the number you were tossing around?"

"That was an estimate," he says. "And that's for all of L.A. We're just concentrating on our area. We have far fewer, obviously."

"Still, for all those people I see every day on the street, you're gonna need a bunch of social workers. Isn't that true?"

He looks baffled. "I don't understand," he says. "What's your angle? What're you investigating? The murders? Or me? I haven't done anything wrong. I'm just trying to help. I don't want to see any more people die. Is that so terrible? Why are you looking at me?"

"We're all trying to help, Mr. Blevins. But I was listening to what you said the other night, and it struck me that the Mid-City Merchants is kinda late to the party."

"I don't know what you're talking about."

"Let's put it this way," I say. "I think before you start skimming those old folks at the Episcopal church, and the Jewish temple, and all those other places on your speaking tour, you might want to talk with some real Christians."

"Real Christians?"

"Down at the Rescue Mission. See, they're already doing what you claim you want to do. And they're not charging a penny."

He frowns. "Look, I'm only trying to stop the fucking blood-bath," he says. "It's horrible for them, there's no denying. But more than that, it's also a disaster for the business community. Guess what? No one seems to want to set foot in those stores all of a sudden. What're those merchants supposed to do? How are they gonna pay the rent? They've been in a panic ever since that last body turned up over on 2nd."

"You're a little behind the curve," I say. "What about the one on Beverly last night? Or haven't you heard about her yet?"

He seems genuinely shocked when I say this. His whole body seems to wince at the news. I drum my fingers on his desk, and I realize again how smart Betsy Rollands is. He's no killer, just a con. And not even a clever con at that.

"Who died last night? Do they know her name?"

"It'll be in the paper by tomorrow. Name was Maria Carlotta Ruiz. Only she's different from the other two. You wanna know why?"

He bites his lower lip, nods. I'm not sure he wants more details, really, but he needs to hear them, if only to make him feel some compassion for another human being.

"The cops don't think she was a street person. They did at first, but now that they've had time to mull it over, it looks like she was trying her hand at being a prostitute."

"Really."

"She was young. In her early thirties. Whoever killed her ripped off her blouse first. Then maybe she got scared and tried to run away. Then he shot her. Pretty close range."

"I see. And this happened, you say, on Beverly?"

"Yeah, near Stanley. In front of a maternity shop. Lee's Baby-land. Maybe you've seen it. Kind of spooky, all those mannequins staring out the window, and her just lying there."

"No," he mumbles, "never heard of it. They must not be members."

"No, probably not, but it's not a total loss, is it?"

"Huh?"

"I mean you can still use Maria Ruiz. There's one more body for your epidemic, and it's still in your turf. You can still call her a street person if you like. Maybe she'll help you raise some dough."

I get up then. I don't care who he's hired or how much he says he's going to pay them. Shit, I doubt he's hired anyone. Why on earth should he? And he's not going to tell me anything useful, either, because he doesn't know anything. And because Betsy is right: in the end, this is all about him. He's sitting there, staring at me like one of those mannequins in the window last night. Only they were better looking.

"You should go get your lunch now, Mr. Blevins. Eat something. You'll feel better afterwards. Oh, and I've got a message from an old friend of yours."

"Who's that?"

"Betsy Rollands. She told me to tell you that you can't get away with it. Not anymore. That she's got her eye on you. Not only that, she still has the documents. What documents would those be, do you suppose?"

"I have no idea what she's talking about," he says.

"That's good," I say. "Then it won't matter to you when she lets the cops have a peek at them."

He frowns, puts up his hands in mock surrender. "Okay, Mr. Parisman, I lied. Betsy Rollands and I had some dealings, it's true, but it was years ago. I've changed my ways. I read the Bible now. Jesus has taught me a lot. You might tell her that the next time you see her."

"I will," I say. "But if I know Betsy, I doubt she's going to believe you. Actually, she told me not to believe you."

"Really?"

"More than that. She said you were slime. Not exactly a compliment in my book."

Blevins chuckles to himself. "You know something? When she first met me, it's true, I was slime."

"But now you've seen the light, huh?"

"Now I'm older. I've seen things I wish I hadn't. Now I'm trying to turn things around. You've gotta believe me."

"Well, Amory, the truth is, it doesn't much matter what I believe, does it? You say you want to take these people off the streets, get them out of harm's way. That's fine. All I'm saying is, be very careful. If this is another scam, you can be sure it's not going to end well. Not for you, at least."

I turn on my heel and walk out the door.

CHAPTER 11

Omar calls, asks to meet me on Beverly, says he wants to revisit the crime scene.

"Why?" I say. "It's not your case. Somebody hire you?"

"No," he says. "No, man, it's not like that. But I had a long talk with Maria's mother last night. Sat there in the living room. You won't believe how awful she feels. Hasn't stopped crying in days. She's a sweet old lady. We sat and she held my hands in her lap and every once in a while her shoulders would start shaking. It was hard. Finally I told her I know I can't bring her little girl back, but I said I'd do whatever I can to find this motherfucker. I didn't use that word in front of her, of course. But she understood. I promised I'd find him, Amos. So there you go, now it's personal. Maybe we can work together, huh?"

"Sure," I tell him. "I'll be there in half an hour."

I park at a meter three blocks away, push a couple of quarters in the slot until the damn thing starts blinking green, and walk over. I don't know why, but I was still expecting to see her body sprawled out on the pavement. I have an indelible picture in my mind, but of course the cops have long since swept everything up and carted her off to that cold room of theirs in the basement for further examination. That's what we do these days. We prefer our history neat and pain free. No muss, no fuss.

Now, a short, stocky, middle-aged man in sunglasses is smoking a cigarette and talking rapidly into his cell phone. He's pacing back and forth, back and forth, right where her body should be. There is no blood, no torn blouse, no coffee cup, no shopping cart full of rags. It's all benign. The slightly plump mannequins at Lee's Babyland look exactly as they did the other night. They stare eternally at each other, or past each other; they gesture in silence to no one in particular. After all, it's not about them; it's about their chic pastel pantsuits. The pizzeria next door is doing a brisk lunch business. People are coming and going on the sidewalk again. It's another day in Los Angeles. We should all be this happy.

"They cleaned it up nice," I say to Omar, who's been prowling around the perimeter. I point to where the cell-phone man is standing. "That's where they found her. Face down. Her blouse half ripped off."

"Looks like the only ones who saw anything were the window dummies," Omar says.

I nod. We both look down and scan the ground for a while, but it's just out of old habit really, not because we think we'll find a shell casing or a matchbook or anything useful.

"They interviewed all the businesses around here?" Omar asks.

"They did. Nobody was open when it happened, except the motel, but the desk clerk said she didn't know her."

"When was that?"

"Malloy thought the time of death was probably somewhere around ten, eleven. Couple out on a late date found the body and called it in."

Omar takes a long, wistful gander at the mannequins. "And there's no security camera here?"

"People don't usually steal maternity clothes, amigo. It's just not done, you know what I mean?"

He smiles. "You're funny." He walks around the back of the buildings where they keep the trash, and a few moments later, returns to where I'm standing. His cell phone rings. He pulls it out, and there's a long, lively stream of Spanish. Too intricate for me; I can tell it's one of his employees on the other end, that's about all.

"Anything to report?" I ask when he slips the phone back in his pants.

"No," he says. "My man, Carlos, has been going around, talking to her old high school friends. See if they have any dirt."

"And?"

"So far, they don't. Carlos thinks they do, but it'll take time to pry it out of them. They're scared."

"What about her mother?" I ask. "Did she say anything more about who Maria was hanging out with before she died?"

Omar shakes his head. "I don't think she could even guess what kind of a life Maria was leading. I mean, she's from the old country. A village outside of Merida. Still doesn't speak English. They were in two different worlds, really."

"And Julio? The harem builder?"

"I've got my man, Ramon, hunting for him. He knows Boyle Heights as well as me. But if she was one of Julio's girls, he's probably planning to disappear for a while. That's my guess. He has family near Guadalajara. This would be a good time for him to hop on a bus, then sit back in a hammock somewhere until all this blows over."

"Which leaves us precisely nowhere, doesn't it?"

"Maybe," Omar says. "But I've been thinking about what you told me the other day at Nick's."

"What did I tell you?"

"You know, man. That theory of yours. Whoever's doing these killings, he's got some kind of personal axe to grind, trying to send the world a message."

"You didn't care for that idea before, Omar. Now it appeals to you? Why?"

"If it were just homeless people he was killing, like the first two, I'd still argue that it's one of their own. But when you add in Maria, that doesn't make sense."

"How come?"

"Well, first, he didn't bother to take that wad of twenties she had. He didn't take anything. A street person would do that automatically."

"Maybe it was too well hidden," I say. "Or maybe he just panicked and ran when the gun went off."

Omar shakes his head. "That's number two. The gun. I'll bet there aren't six homeless people in L.A. who even own a gun."

"They probably should," I say.

"No," he says, emphatically, "no, they shouldn't. You get stopped by the man and they frisk you and find a gun, guess what? You're going to prison. They're gonna nail you for something, it doesn't matter what, believe me. Half the time, they don't even need to find a gun on you. It could be jaywalking."

We're strolling down Beverly now, toward Fairfax. I tell him Malloy thinks Maria's murder doesn't belong with the others, that we're fooling ourselves by lumping them all together; maybe it was just a trick gone bad.

"Is that what you think, too?" He stares down at me, his eyes are shifting back and forth, and I can see he's not easy with this case, that it's eating at him in a way that makes it tough to move forward. I've been there before. This isn't a job like any other. Malloy's right, it's not nine to five. It's relentless. And if you're going to do it well, you not only have to work your ass off, you also have to step back every now and then. Give yourself a chance to breathe. Close your eyes and collect your thoughts, even if they're crazy, even if they make no sense at all.

"I'm waiting for the fingerprint guys to finish looking at the shopping cart," I say. "But if her prints are on the cart, then yeah, somehow these cases are linked. Meanwhile, I'm like you, Omar. I'm at sea."

*   *   *

That afternoon, I check back in with Mara on Creston Drive. She's spent the whole morning with Gus. Now she's propped up on the couch, barefoot, with a half glass of white wine on the coffee table beside her. She's let her hair down, and there's a *New Yorker* in her lap, but this seems to me like a grand indulgence; she's really too worn out to read.

"So how's the patient?" I ask, plopping down in the easy chair facing her.

She smiles. "The patient? Better today. They took him off the oxygen, and he's eating again. Not a lot, but that's not so important.

He was never much of an eater, even in the old days. We'd go out to a restaurant sometimes and he'd leave most of it on the plate. I never understood that. The nurse was just thrilled he's got color in his face again."

"Yeah, well, that's a plus. You have to be thankful, even for small improvements."

She nods, reaches forward for her wine, takes a long, slow, judicious sip and sets it back down again. "I ran into Dr. Flynn afterwards, Amos. He was down on the first floor, making the rounds."

"And?"

"And he told me what he thought." She wets her lips. "He doesn't expect Gus has a great deal of time left on this earth. He says this last episode is probably a precursor of things to come."

"Ah. Did he say how long?"

"No. No, nothing like that. He's a sweet man." She brushes the hair away from her face. "A sweet man. Generous with his time. We just talked, and he explained how he pictured it would go for him. The way it goes for most of us. I mean, it's not like I was surprised by anything he said."

"No, you wouldn't be."

"It's just that when someone—someone in authority finally says it, well, you pay attention, don't you. It's out in the open. You can't just leave it sitting around in the back of your mind. He said he's going to die. Now you know. It's official." Mara lifts the *New Yorker* off her lap and flings it unceremoniously with one hand across the room. It makes a strange fluttering bird-like sound before it lands at my feet. Then she leans back into the pillows and starts to cry.

*   *   *

In the morning she leaves right after breakfast to commune again with Gus. I tell her I'll be over there later. Then I pour myself a second cup of black coffee, pick up the phone in the kitchen, and call Malloy. He's not so depressed anymore. In fact, he sounds both happy and bewildered at the same time.

Maria Ruiz's prints were on the shopping cart, he tells me. No doubt about it.

"But you saw what she had in her bag. The keys. The Visa card. Those twenties. She was anything but homeless," I say. "I don't get it."

"Here's something else you won't get," he says. "All that crap in the shopping cart? It's not hers."

"What are you saying?"

"We went through it pretty thoroughly. The clothes in there wouldn't fit her in a million years. Way too big. Jason thinks she— or somebody—maybe found it in an alley a few blocks away and rolled it over to Beverly and Stanley. Or they liberated a cart from Trader Joe's and filled it themselves. Any way you slice it, that's the only logical explanation."

"Weird," I say.

"You're telling me. And beyond the clothes, there's other stuff in there. None of it seems to match with her."

"Like what?"

"Oh, a long list. Food coupons. A stack of girlie magazines bound up in twine. Someone's old record collection from the fifties. Dean Martin and Bobby V. Soda cans. Different sizes of shoes. Even some men's shoes. It was a complete hodgepodge."

"Nothing that would point to somebody's name, though."

"Nope."

"You know what, Bill? You're gonna think I've lost my marbles, but it sounds to me as if this was intentional."

"What? The murder? I'm sure that was intentional, yeah."

"No, not the murder. Well, maybe the murder, but certainly the cart."

"The cart?"

"Yeah, you called it a complete hodgepodge."

"It was."

I hold my hand flat just above the rim of the coffee mug, watch the heat escape between my fingers. "Right. Now, think about this: if you were a homeless person, pushing a shopping cart around all day and night, what would you want to be in there?"

"I dunno, what?"

"Well, you're camping, aren't you? You'd want warm clothes and a blanket or two, some food. Maybe a toothbrush and a comb. You'd want whatever you think you need to survive."

"Okay, I'm with you."

"And even more important—you'd want things as light as possible. You'd never carry around both men's and women's shoes. Or record collections. Or girlie magazines. You couldn't spare the room. You wouldn't want the weight."

"So what's your idea?"

"I'm guessing here. But just imagine our killer came along, he found an empty shopping cart, then he threw together a whole bunch of junk—old clothes, soda cans, whatever—anything to make it look like a homeless person's treasure."

"Now why the hell would you do that? What's the point?"

"Fishing?"

"Okay, you and I wouldn't be attracted to it, we'd probably walk right by. But a street person, a scavenger, someone who lives by his wits alone—who knows what they'd do?"

"But that still doesn't explain Maria's fingerprints. If she was out there trolling for a good time, that's the last thing she'd want to touch. She wouldn't go near a shopping cart full of crap."

"No. No, you're right. Not unless it was part of the transaction."

"You're losing me, Amos."

"Okay. Okay, how about this? What if she met a man there near the maternity shop. It's late at night. He wants to party. He looks decent, and he's showing her cash. She says 'fine.' Then he says wait, he has a couple of little favors he'd like her to do before they really get down to business."

"And what would that be?"

"Well, first he gives her twenty bucks and has her undo her bra. Then maybe he points to the shopping cart, says it would make him so very glad if she were to push it around the corner into the alley. Maybe he says he'll toss in an extra fifty if she does."

"I don't know, Amos. I expect most professional women I've met would shy away from someone who acts like that."

"Understood. But she's young, remember? She's new at this. And he's already paid to see her tits. So maybe she thinks, what's the big deal? This is not so kinky. I can handle this, too."

"Okay. I'm listening."

"And so she agrees and starts to push the cart toward the alley. That explains the fingerprints."

"Right, but then what?"

"Then? Then something goes haywire. Whatever he says next freaks her out. Or he pulls a gun. Or he grabs her ass. We'll never get the answer to that. But she tries to run the other way. That seems clear. She runs. He catches up, rips her blouse, shoots her. The end."

Malloy is silent for a minute. "Maybe, I dunno. If you're right about this, then, yeah, we ought to be looking a little bit harder at that shopping cart."

"Who knows, right? Maybe our killer made a mistake. Maybe he left something useful behind in all that mess."

"It's an idea."

Malloy still seems hesitant when I finally hang up. Ten minutes later I'm sitting in my Honda. I've rolled open the windows and I'm dropping down the narrow, windy lanes of the Hollywood Hills. I slow down at each blind curve, past million-dollar enclaves where the white walls are festooned with Spanish tile and bougainvillea. Birds are singing, and because this is California, jacaranda trees have already started to bloom overhead. Pairs of young, bronzed, bare-chested, and, almost certainly, gay men are running some private marathon of their own, and individual starlets in tight shorts and tank tops are also out in the late morning air, tugging at their perfectly coifed little dogs. *At this moment*, I think, *I'm about as far away from the unpleasant lives of those people in the gutter as I can possibly be. I'm with the rich and famous.* The maidens on the street are self-assured; they're smiling as if they're rehearsing the speech they plan to make someday when they win an Oscar. They couldn't do it alone, after all; so many have helped them get to this point. Their mother, their father. Their boyfriend. Their agent who never quit on them. And that's okay. In fact, for now at least, it's just fine.

CHAPTER 12

You don't meet anyone by chance in this city. That's just how it is, one of those hard facts you learn to live with. Maybe it was different long ago, before the oil companies tore up the trolley tracks. And who knows, maybe it'll be different again, when the Metro finally goes everywhere, not that I'll still be around to see it.

After an hour or two at the Olympic Terrace, after I've paid my respects to Loretta and held hands quietly with Mara while she whispered sweet nothings in Gus's ear, something antsy wells up inside me and I need to get away. Loretta's fast asleep. Gus doesn't know I exist, and Mara—Mara who is wise beyond her years—understands. I get in my car and drive up Fairfax. I'm not sure where I'm going. I head east on Melrose, then go north on Vermont.

There's a wonderful barn of a bookstore near Franklin that Loretta and I used to prowl around in years ago. It was called Chatterton's back then. The owner was a sweetheart of a guy with a gambling problem. Now it's Skylight Books. It has new owners, and they use computers instead of cash registers, but who cares? It's the same place it always was. I'm drifting down the aisles, thinking I should go ahead and grab a copy of *Atlas Shrugged*, even if it's awful, just to support them and to confirm every dark thought I ever had about Ayn Rand. *Take it home, read the first three pages, Parisman, then you can put it back on your shelf and never look at it again. Money well spent.*

"What in God's name are you doing here?" Betsy Rollands's voice is unmistakable behind me. I spin around and she hugs me.

"Business," I say. "You know the killer I'm looking for? He might be a fan of Ayn Rand, believe it or not. I gave all my copies away."

"As well you should," she says. "Although I hear she's been making a comeback among the fascists."

We wander around, picking books up, making little comments. Betsy, who lives three blocks away on Berendo, has read far more than I ever will, but only biography and history. She thinks that's the fastest way to get to the truth.

We're in the poetry aisle, and I'm on my haunches, admiring their collection of Gary Snyder, when she touches my shoulder and tells me about the reward. "Did you read that bit in the paper this morning? The Merchants Association is on a spending spree. They're coughing up twenty-five grand to pay for social workers to get people off the streets at night and another twenty-five for information on the Hatchet Man. That's what they're calling him, which I think is a ridiculous name."

"Especially since it was probably a hammer," I say.

"Exactly. I hate that kind of lurid usage."

"Fifty grand. That's a nice piece of change. Amory Blevins must have hit the jackpot at one of his church socials."

"I don't think so," she says. "They don't make that kind of money going door to door. This came from outside. The paper said it was an anonymous donation."

"Well, great. When I finally nab that guy it'll be worth my while."

She frowns. "And here I thought you were a detective. Aren't you curious about where all that dough's coming from?"

"Does it matter? The only thing it says to me is that someone else in this world has a moral compass. And a wallet to match. Nothing wrong with that."

"Amos," she says. "I've been covering this stuff for years. I know how it works. When a child disappears, they put her face on a poster. Neighbors walk around in the woods with flashlights.

When something happens to a celebrity, there's a reward. Remember Patty Hearst? Remember the Lindbergh baby?"

"The Lindbergh baby was a little before my time," I say. "But I get your point."

"No, you don't," she says. "Those people were special. They were famous. Or even if they weren't famous, they were innocent and vulnerable. No one gives a good goddamn about the homeless. They just want them to go away. So what you should be asking—if you were a real detective—is how come somebody's suddenly willing to pay big bucks to find this killer? Does that make any sense?"

"Well, at least they're not offering that kind of money to kill them, are they?"

"No," she says. "They're not there yet. But that may not be far away."

I shrug. "There are so many people in this world, Betsy. Thank God not all of them are cynical like you."

She beams at me, and all of a sudden I'm staring into the green eyes of the same Betsy Rollands who tried to steal me away back in government class. "I guess that's what I've always loved about you, Amos. You act tough, but in the end, you know what? You can't help it; you're a hopeless romantic." She hugs me then, and I catch a whiff of the fragrance she's wearing. And I know that if the situation were different, if we were young and if and if and if . . . that things could go in an entirely different direction between us.

"So what would you say if this old romantic treated you to lunch?" I ask when we separate.

"Oh, I can be bought."

*   *   *

There's a decent Thai place a block down. There used to be an Italian bar and pastry joint called Sarno's nearby, back when Loretta and I first came to town; it was all glass and dark panels, and it was open late and people came in dressed to the nines from parties and movie openings. They'd crowd around the baby grand they had there, and some woman in a fur coat who could barely stand up would lean on it and belt out "Volare" or an aria from *Carmen*. That was then. Now, it's all a blur. Sarno's is dead. The piano's gone, the walls in the Thai place are stark white, and the best thing on the menu is pumpkin curried shrimp.

The waitress brings our plates and a ceramic pot of tea, and Betsy tells me about some of our old high school friends she's still in touch with. There aren't many. Most of them have died or disappeared into gated communities. I mention my cousin Shelly. She remembers him because he had a serious crush on her and she would never go out with him.

"Why not?"

She pauses a moment and grins. "I was saving myself for you, Amos. Somebody must have told you that."

"Actually, my mother said something to that effect. She tried to make the case for you. But I was a little too slow on the uptake, I guess."

"Yes, you were. Timing is everything, huh?"

I give her a nod. "You should have taken up with Shelly."

She gives me a derisive look. "But he was so much older."

"Not anymore," I say. "I mean, I'm not suggesting you date him now. He's already burned through three wives and a shitload of alimony. He's been through a lot. But he's starting to mellow. Says all he cares about now is friends and family. Community, that's his schtick these days. Which is amazing, because all he used to care about was money."

"No, that's not quite true," Betsy says. She sips her tea. "In high school, all he cared about was getting into my pants."

"He told you that?"

"He didn't have to tell me," she says. "I'm smart, remember?"

*   *   *

Omar has good news. He's located Julio, and he asks if I'd like to come with him to have a little chat. We meet at the corner of Glendale Boulevard and Perlita Avenue in Atwater Village. I haven't been back here in ages. Atwater is just a mile or so east of Griffith Park, but slightly gritty and down-at-the-heels. People slept here and worked downtown. Now, the artists and the more moneyed millennials have discovered it. You can tell. Vintage clothing shops have sprung up, along with Cuban restaurants and hip bakeries. Most of the bungalows have been repainted and some folks are adding second stories. A few years ago you could rent something simple here and it wouldn't cost you an arm and a leg like everywhere else. No more.

I get in Omar's car, which, like mine, dates back to the last century. Unlike mine, however, his is immaculate inside. It's a souped-up black Camaro with padded leather seats and an orange racing stripe. We go a few blocks down Perlita. It's a nice, wide, sunny street with palm trees and squat California houses from the thirties and forties. Two little girls in shorts are tossing a blue Frisbee back and forth across the street, and a shirtless man is leaning over the open hood of his old Ford Mustang. We pull up in front of a small, square, unremarkable residence. There are iron bars on all the windows, but otherwise it's just a quaint, white house with a dark green, wooden door and Spanish tile on the roof.

"How'd he end up here?" I ask.

"People know too much about him in Boyle Heights," Omar says. "Not here, though. This neighborhood's quiet. Easy to blend into. Also, he can still be back in the *barrio* in a few minutes. Just hop on the freeway."

We climb out. I stay by the curb, but Omar saunters right up to the front, tries the knob, peeks in the little window above the door, and returns. The place is set back from the street, and whoever owns it has been systematically uprooting the front lawn. One day soon it'll be a garden of colored gravel swirling around a few large desolate rocks. Not my style, but also not out of step with the drought-tolerant neighborhood. And at least he's got a vision. That's my first thought. My second thought is maybe he's just spending a whole lot of money trying to save on his water bill.

There's a long driveway to the left. Omar waves me toward it and we walk down together.

Julio Dominguez slouches in his silver Cadillac facing us. The motor is purring and his hand is hanging out the open window with a cigarette. Some sort of *ranchera* music is playing very faintly on the radio. We approach the driver's side and he nods to Omar. Me, he ignores. Or no, he doesn't ignore me. He gives me a quick once over and thinks he knows what he sees. He's a slender, handsome fellow. Lavender shirt, tan sport coat and shades. That's the first thing I notice. Also, he's got long, dark hair that reaches down to his shoulders, high cheekbones, and a thin, manicured mustache. There's something Indian about the way he looks sitting there, and something—to me, at least—unreadable. He and Omar go back and forth in Spanish, and then Omar wags his head at me, tells him who I am, I guess, and the conversation abruptly shifts into English.

"Too damn bad about Maria Carlotta," Omar says.

"Yeah man, I heard," Julio says. "That was terrible. Shouldn't happen to anyone." He takes a contemplative drag on his cigarette. Then he blows the smoke toward the rear-view mirror, puts his hand back out the window, and lets the filtered remnant drop onto the pavement. It's still burning.

I step forward and quietly crush it under my shoe. "We're trying to find out who did it, Julio. Like you say, it shouldn't happen to anyone."

Julio gives me a bitter, mocking look. He has a practiced indifference about him. Maybe it wasn't always that way, but now, it's who he is. "And why do you care, man? You a cop?"

Omar jumps in. "He's a detective, Julio. He saved my life. He's the one I told you about, kept me out of the slammer when those pigs tried to set me up. *Recuerda?*"

Julio nods. "Yeah, sure, I remember. Your guardian angel." Then he does something that surprises me. He reaches across and puts out his right hand for me to shake. "Hey, nice to meet you. *Encantado.*"

"Same here," I say. His hand is cool to the touch. I don't know what he and Omar have already discussed, but I figure I may as well start at the beginning. "So Omar tells me you might have had some kind of professional relationship with Maria. That right?"

He pauses before he opens his mouth. "She worked for me now and then," he says. "We knew each other a long time, you know. We were friends. I never pushed her into anything."

"No, of course not," I say. I reach into my jacket and fish out my cardboard notepad and pen. "But she worked for you. She was one of your girls."

"We never put it like that," he goes. "I'd give her ideas, places she could hang out if she wanted to meet guys. She enjoyed herself."

"And you helped her out?"

He nods. "Sometimes I'd make arrangements in advance, sometimes not. She'd come back the next day, we'd split the money."

"So on the night she was murdered, did you make any . . . arrangements?"

"No, not that night. She was on her own."

"And beyond making suggestions," I say, "what was your role?"

"What are you talking about, man? My role?"

"Well, if you didn't push her into anything, then what did you do?"

He pulls his shades off, and I can see the contempt racing around his eyes. "I took care of her, man. If she had a problem with a client, anything at all, she came to me. I'd make sure it wasn't a problem anymore. That's what I do for all my ladies. They know that."

I shake my head. "Well, it looks like you kinda dropped the ball with her, Julio."

He doesn't respond. Then, after a few seconds he lights up another cigarette and pushes the smoke defiantly through his nose. He doesn't show his anger, not easily, anyway.

"Tell me," I press on, "was that the first time Maria ever worked that spot on Beverly?"

"She had a few spots she liked. That was one of them."

"And when she met clients there, where would they usually go to finish the transaction?"

"Depends," Julio says. He works the cigarette around with his fingers. "Sometimes a guy'd pull up in a pickup truck and she'd get in. If it was a suit, that'd be different. She'd usually take them to a motel right there."

"So Maria had been there before. She ever mention the regulars she saw? Any names?"

Julio stares at me. He rolls his eyes. "Yeah," he says, "I have a ton of names in my Rolodex. A to Z. But I'm sure they're all bogus. Nobody ever tells you the truth in this business. Why the fuck would they?"

Omar asks him the name of the motel on Beverly, and at first Julio says he can't remember. Then he shrugs, pulls a card from his wallet and offers it up. "Here," he says, "it won't do you any good."

"Thanks," Omar says. He tucks it in his hip pocket. "We'll be in touch, okay?" He gives Julio his business card. "I know you want to find this *pendejo* as much as we do," he says. "So if you think of anything—"

"You'll be the first to know," says Julio. He takes a long, deep pull on his cigarette.

Then we both step to one side. He puts his shades back on, adjusts the mirrors, and rolls smoothly down the driveway.

CHAPTER 13

The Dunes Motel on Beverly near Curson is what they call a budget inn, but in this part of L.A. all that means is it's a bit cheaper than the rest of them. The color scheme is tan and beige, very neutral and serene, with a few potted cacti and desert trappings. We go through the thick glass door and up to the modest front desk. A sturdy, buttoned-down man in a dark suit and tie is filling out a form. His plastic name tag reads Paco. "Gentlemen," he says, looking up.

Omar tells him in Spanish why we're here, and all at once his demeanor changes. "You should maybe talk to the night manager," he says. "He'd know more about this issue than me. Since I got married, you know"—he tries to smile, as if that fact serves as a blanket excuse—"I don't work nights anymore."

I pull out a photograph, it's a copy I got from Malloy of Maria's California driver's license. It doesn't do her justice, but it's good enough. "Does she look familiar, Paco? Maybe she was here on one of those nights when you were still working."

He pulls out a pair of glasses, puts them on, studies it. "Yeah," he says, after a while, "yeah, she's been here. But like I say, you should talk to Jaime. He's the concierge in the evenings. He'll be here"—he glances at his watch—"in about two more hours."

We tell him thanks, and head back to the parking lot.

"There's no point wasting our time with these people," I say. "What can they tell us? That she came in with a few different men?

They won't know them. And even if they did, what difference does it make? It's like Julio said, nobody tells the truth in this business."

We're standing in the open air with our hands in our pockets. The sun is low in the sky, and a light breeze has kicked up out of nowhere. Besides my shabby Honda Civic and his ancient Camaro, every other car in the lot is clean, classy; any one of them probably costs more than Omar will ever make in a year. "You're right," he says, glancing around. "I don't think we're gonna find our murderer among the screenwriters who live around here." He tosses his keys up high with his right hand, catches them deftly with his left. Then the other way around. "Mexican juggling," he says.

Before we go our separate ways, he tells me he's going to go back tomorrow and have another talk with Julio. "I know he wants to find this guy," he says. "If nothing else, Maria was producing. He doesn't like it when someone comes along and steals his money."

"No, I don't reckon he would."

"He's got people, other people he knows who can go through the neighborhood, ask some questions, maybe ask them in a more forceful way than you or I would want to. I think that's what this may take, in the end."

"Just let me know what you come up with," I say. "The cops may have qualms, but I don't care how you get it."

*   *   *

Before I climb out of the car on Creston Drive, I call Malloy to fill him in on what we learned from Julio. I don't expect him to be impressed; admittedly, it's not much. But I also want him to know that we're pressing on, that we're not giving up. Most of all, I want him to keep talking to me, keep swapping information.

He likes what I tell him, it turns out. "We were going to try to find her pimp," he says, "but now you've done it for us. That's terrific."

"Well, it wasn't me, Bill. Omar tracked him down. But I don't suggest you talk with him. That's a bad idea. It'll spook him and he'll run."

"Not if we bring him in. It's hard to run when you're behind bars."

"Yeah, but the thing is, right now he wants to help. You don't want to jeopardize that, do you?"

There was a silence over the phone. "Well, since you're bringing him along. I'll let it slide for now. I see your point."

Then he tells me they found the cartridge from the murder weapon, and now they think they know what kind of gun he used.

"Let me guess. A 9mm something."

"Bingo," Malloy says.

"I own one of those myself, Bill," I say. "Nice old German Glock 9mm. Maybe I'm the one you're looking for."

"I wish it were that simple."

"Did you find anything useful in the shopping cart? That's really what I wanna know."

"Well, one thing, maybe," Malloy says. "A long shot. Remember how I said there was a stack of girlie magazines?"

"I do."

"Well, the guy who owned them had a subscription. His address was tacked right onto the bottom."

"And?"

"His name was Borquist. Arthur T. Retired mechanic. Lives over on Crenshaw. Jason and Remo went to see him. Said he got rid of those things months ago. His wife finally gave him an ultimatum. Either grow up or find someone else to do your laundry."

"So he tossed them. Why's that interesting?"

"Thing is, he wasn't gonna toss them. Not at first. He's a penny pincher. He tied them in a bundle with twine and took them down to Phil's Book Alley near Pershing Square. They were old, he said, *Playboy*s from the sixties. Thought they might be worth something."

"And were they?"

"Nah. The guy at Phil's told him there's a glut of that stuff. And besides, it's all on the internet now for free. Who's gonna pay anymore?"

"Well, I'm sure there must be collectors out there."

"A few," Malloy says. "But this stuff was in such ratty condition. They told him to just forget it."

"You're losing me, Bill. Why is this important?"

"It may not be. But as Borquist was headed out, another fella stopped him at the door, asked to look at what he had. Borquist let him see, the man whipped out his wallet and gave him five bucks for the whole stack. Kept the twine and everything."

"Really! Now that's interesting. I don't suppose Mr. Borquist remembers anything about this guy, does he?"

"Not much. He was glad to have the money, of course. And a little surprised. He told Remo it was a colored guy, well dressed. That was his description. A 'colored' guy. Nice slacks and shoes, he said. Like he was a ladies' man. Like he didn't seem to belong in a place like Phil's."

"Nothing else about what he looked like?"

"Remo tried to pump him. All he said was that all colored men looked the same to him. How's that for an enlightened viewpoint?"

"And the clerk at Phil's? He didn't know him, either, right?"

"People in places like that don't make a habit of recognizing their customers," Malloy says. "They're just moving paper around. If they're watching anything at all, it's the clock."

"So a well-dressed Black man bought the magazines," I say. "We don't know how old. We don't know how tall. We don't know how much he weighs. We probably don't even know if he was well dressed. I mean, does Borquist have any idea what it means to be fashionable these days?"

"Good point," Malloy says. "Still, it's something."

*   *   *

Mara seems upbeat tonight. "Gus is getting stronger," she announces. She's slicing zucchini as I come into the kitchen. "I thought this week might be the end, but today he had a lot more color in his cheeks. He's eating. He's smiling at me. A girl can't ask for more than that, can she?"

"How old is Gus?" I ask. I wrap my arms around her waist. She leans back, brushes a kiss by my cheek.

"He'll be eighty-five next April," she says, turning back to the zucchini on the cutting board. "That's twenty years older than me, if you're counting."

"Who's counting?"

"You're not counting?"

"No. I'm just thinking you're fooling yourself. Which is understandable."

She sets down the chopping knife, mops her hands quietly on her apron, and turns to me. "I know he's dying, Amos, I do. I'm not stupid. But I want the time he has left to be . . . pleasant. And if that means fussing over him and pretending he has some nice red in his cheeks, well, what difference does it make?"

*   *   *

After dinner, we take a bottle of Chilean wine and a couple of glasses and settle down on the couch. We haven't spent much time together in the last few days. I tell her how I've been making myself crazy, running around in circles with Omar, talking to Maria Carlotta's pimp.

"But I don't get it," she says. "What would killing a young girl—a prostitute, okay—have to do with the homeless murders? I mean, is there a connection? Did he use a hammer?"

"No," I say. "He shot her in the back. And there might have been some kind of sexual trade going on. That's different. The location is different. The weapon is definitely different. But the thing is, they found a shopping cart full of weird stuff nearby."

"Yeah. So?"

"The cart had Maria's prints all over it."

"But she wasn't homeless, right? Now I really don't get it."

"She wasn't homeless. And the only way I figure it makes any sense is that her killer asked her to roll that cart somewhere, as if she were."

"So she must have known him. Sounds like they talked things over beforehand."

"Maybe she just met him. That's what we think. Maybe she was just starting to get acquainted," I say.

Mara sips her wine. "All seems a little far-fetched, if you ask me," she says. "Still, you can't argue with fingerprints."

"No, but you wonder how they got there."

We pour ourselves a second glass of wine. Mara slips her sandals off. Outside, a gorgeous, fat, yellow moon is rising slowly over the city. She tells me how her week's been, how, after spending time with Gus, she's been going through their investments, selling off some stock and redirecting the money toward charitable purposes.

"Lots of money?"

"It's more than I'll ever need. And I've already set aside a trust fund for Violet. She's the only one who could use it. Now she'll never have to worry."

"Hey, what about me?"

"You! You're gonna die long before I ever do. I'll tell you what, honey—I'll throw you a real first-class funeral. You'll like it."

I nod. "Just make sure there's plenty of food, okay? And an open bar. I hate funerals where they skimp on refreshments."

"Okay."

"Also music. I want a jazz trio. Or a *klezmer* band. You know, something hot, something with some bounce to it."

"You want people dancing at your funeral? Really? Is that the idea?" She stifles a laugh.

"I don't care what they do," I say. "They can dance. They can weep. They can sit in their wheelchairs. Whatever. I won't be there." I finish what's left of the wine in my glass. I don't know how much I've had, but already I'm feeling slightly out of control. "Oh, and one last thing: no matter what, don't forget to invite my cousin, Shelly, okay?"

"Shelly?"

"Yeah, we've known each other forever. Shelly brought me up. He'd feel terrible, he missed my funeral."

CHAPTER 14

I'm skimming through the sports pages the next day, which—because it's February—has nothing but basketball. I used to play in high school, but the truth is, I was never much good. Also, it never made sense to me. Two points here, two points there. Throw the ball, bounce the ball. You run around and sweat for a whole hour and then at the end, it's just one shot maybe that decides everything. Where's the justice? Why bother? I'm working myself into a slow boil over this idiocy when the phone rings.

It's Reverend Archibald. "I haven't forgotten you, Mr. Parisman. I said I'd try to help. I hope you'll forgive me, but it's taken me a while to go through my list of parishioners."

"That's all right, Reverend. I'm glad you called."

"Yes, well, that woman you were asking about—"

"Delia?"

"Delia. I checked an old list I found in a drawer. Her full name is—was—Delia Montero. I'm pretty sure that's who you're talking about. I haven't had any contact with her in years. She used to attend our services occasionally when we were up on Sunset. That's how long ago it was. Before we lost our lease."

"How well did you know her?"

"Know her? I wouldn't say I knew her at all, really. I mean, we said hello, we prayed together, we sang praises to the Lord. That kind of thing. She enjoyed singing, I remember that."

"And what about her husband? He ever come around? Did she even have one?"

"I really couldn't say."

"And was she homeless when she came to see you?"

"Again, it's been years. Maybe, maybe not."

"So what do you have for me, beyond her last name?"

There's an awkward pause at the other end. "Ah, yes," he says. "She did have a friend here at our church. Another woman. Daisy Cooper."

"That's great. Daisy Cooper. I'd love to meet her."

"Of course. Unfortunately, Ms. Cooper moved away last month. Not far, though. I believe she's living with her daughter in Highland Park. She can't drive, and she doesn't get out as much as she used to. She was special. If you like, I can put you in touch with her."

"That'd be swell."

He gives me a phone number and an address, which I dutifully jot down.

"I'd call her first," he says. "She's at that age when she doesn't care for surprises. Not anymore."

*   *   *

Daisy Cooper turns out to be a gracious, proper, lively Black lady in her eighties. She's glad I called. She tells me that her parents named her in honor of Eleanor Roosevelt. Eleanor is her real name, but she was Daisy from the day she could walk. Ain't that something? And before I can venture an answer, she says she'd be delighted to have Omar and I over for tea that afternoon.

"My daughter asked me to stay here," she says, as we settle down on her flowered couch, "right after I fell down in my apartment and broke my collarbone. She thought it would be safer to have someone around, you know, who could pick me up off the floor. Someone with muscles."

We chuckle. "You seem perfectly capable," I tell her.

"Oh, I am, I am, but you'll never convince my Naomi."

There's a large pepper tree out front, from which someone has hung a set of metal chimes. Every few seconds, when there's even a hint of a breeze, the chimes tinkle. It's a charming but slightly oppressive living room. That's what I think, anyway, and I can't imagine what's going on in Omar's head. I'm sure he feels out of place here, but I'm hoping he'll ask questions, things maybe I'd never think of. Sometimes two different minds rub together, and out of that comes a spark, then a fire.

Her daughter collects little ceramic antique figurines; English lords and ladies decked out for the ball. Everywhere you look—on the mantel, on the end tables—there are dozens of them staring at you. I feel like Gulliver surrounded by Lilliputians.

Daisy bustles about, humming to herself, shifting the teapot and the cups around on a tray and setting a plate of sugar cookies out in front of us. Did we take milk? Or would we prefer lemon? Some people use lemon. These are the questions she frets over.

Finally, we start talking about Delia Montero.

"I haven't seen her in such a long time," she says. "Not since I moved away. Have you?"

"Well, that's really why we're here," I say. "I'm afraid I have some sad news. Your old friend Delia is dead."

"Oh," she says, almost matter-of-factly. Her expression remains the same. It's not that she has no feelings about this, I think; it's more like at her stage of life, that's the usual report, isn't it? Delia has died. So sad. "Is the tea too strong?" she wants to know now.

"No, ma'am," Omar mumbles. "No, not at all. The tea's just fine."

"Good," she says. "I'm never sure how much to put in the pot. I suppose I should measure it out, but somehow I always forget."

I lean forward on the couch. "Can you tell me a little bit about Delia?" I ask. "What was she like?"

Daisy takes a bite from a sugar cookie and sets the remainder back on her plate. "Well, she was always living on the edge," she says. "That was nothing new. She used to work in a café downtown making tacos and burritos, that kind of thing. That's where she learned Spanish."

"And probably where she met her husband."

"Maybe," she says. "He wasn't in the picture by then. I never heard her say a word about him."

"Where was she living when you knew her?" Omar asks.

She wags her head, unsure. "She had friends. They let her stay on their front porch, or they had a spare room for her now and then."

"You know their names, these friends?"

"No. I never met them. Friends would give her rides to church. Drop her off. Pick her up. She was always moving. Mostly, though, she spent time on the street. That was hard, but she made the best of it. You understand, I never saw her during the week, only on Fridays and Sundays when we went to church."

"And going to church—that must have been a high point in her life. She looked forward to that, huh?"

"Oh yes, I'd say so. It was a haven. The only time she could relax, be herself, you know. The only time when she wasn't feeling judged."

"And Reverend Jimmy was good to her?"

"Yes. That man was a saint. And"—she lowers her voice—"I expect he had a soft spot for her."

"How's that?"

"Oh, little things. He'd bring her up on the stage and put his arm around her. She'd be shy, sometimes she didn't want to say anything at all, but he'd coax her, just lean in and whisper some sweet thing in her ear, and finally she'd testify about how good it was to know Jesus. What peace He brought her, even living like she did. You believe that?"

"I do."

"And once in a while, somebody'd walk through the door with a guitar or a tambourine."

"And?"

"And that changed everything, don't you see? Then we'd have a little band. And Jimmy would have her sing gospel tunes from the hymnal. She had a voice, that girl. Everyone would join in, of course, but Delia—Delia could hit those high notes. She was always the star."

I sip my tea. "Tell me, Daisy. Did Reverend Jimmy or anyone there at the church ever make an effort to solve Delia's living situation?"

"No," she shakes her head. "That wasn't possible, really."

"Why not?"

"Well, for one thing, Delia wasn't the only homeless one in the congregation. You've seen the church? Of course you have. Not much to look at. Bare bones. And folks there were just as close to the edge as she was. We had problems. Drinking and drugs. So many things. Like all the world's trouble just landed on our doorstep. That's what Reverend Jimmy used to say."

"Not a bad description."

"It's true. I thought about that a lot. I was better off than so many folks, but all I had was my social security. Back then I was living in a single room. No car or anything. I used to walk to get groceries, walk to the church. As a group we didn't have the means to help anybody. Not really."

Omar stands up and stretches. He's not good with tea and cookies and small talk. I give him a look. He shrugs, rolls his eyes, and sits back down again.

"How many years did you go to Reverend Jimmy's?" I ask. "Sounds like both you and Delia found a home there."

"Lots of people felt at home there. He had a way about him." She raises her teacup to drink, then thinks better of it and sets it down before it touches her lips. "Don't get me wrong: I know I'm in a better place now. I'm grateful for that. I don't have to worry about my next meal or if I'll have a roof over my head tomorrow. I'm not alone, but that doesn't mean I don't miss it sometimes. I do."

"What do you miss most, Daisy?"

"The fellowship," she says after a moment's reflection. "Even though I only saw them twice a week for a few hours, we were friends. We knew each other's pain." She nods to herself. "We knew what a struggle it was to get by. I struggled, Delia struggled, lots of folks struggled in different ways. That's just how it was. It didn't matter."

"Why not?" Omar asks.

"Because we all stood together. You know what I mean? We stood together, and we got through it."

*   *   *

I leave Ms. Cooper my card and thank her several times for her tea and hospitality. As we're walking down the front path it strikes me that I never once told her we were detectives. Would that have mattered? Would she have been more talkative?

Omar and I sit for a while in my Honda with the windows rolled down. The chimes in the pepper tree are tinkling. Across the street there's a chubby old guy in shorts and a USC sweatshirt. He's bending over, yanking at the ripcord of his lawn mower. His face is turning red. Finally the damn thing roars to life. The old guy smiles, then the engine coughs, shudders a few times and stops altogether. Nothing to be done. "Fuck!" the man says. He gives it a sharp kick and turns to go back inside.

"So, what do you think, Omar?"

"What do I think about what? What the old lady said? Not much. Sounds about like every other storefront church I've ever heard of. People stand around talking about Jesus. How good He is. Makes me sick, if you wanna know the truth."

"Why?"

"Because it's such a fucking con. They don't need to come to Jesus, they need a bowl of soup. They need a bath."

"Granted. But they also need friendship. Daisy's right. Especially when they can't get a bowl of soup or a bath. Friendship counts."

I turn the key in the ignition and pull out onto the street. Highland Park used to be an unpleasant neck of the woods. Cheap, but dangerous. You ended up in Highland Park if you couldn't find anything else. Mara's daughter ended up here. There were Chicano gangs and graffiti and drug dealers. Maybe all that's still around, I don't know, I don't come this way often, but now—today, at least— it feels decent. I pass a white ice cream truck with a bunch of scruffy kids huddled around, yelling, laughing. I could live here, I think.

I'm on the Pasadena Freeway headed back to Hollywood when it dawns on me. "There's something about the timeline that doesn't fit," I say.

"What are you talking about?"

"Well, Daisy Cooper was going on and on about what a star Delia was at that storefront church on Rosewood. How much it meant for her to come there. How Reverend Jimmy brought her up on the stage, put his arms around her, all that."

"Yeah, so what?"

"And she seemed pretty sure of herself, didn't she? I mean, she's an old lady, but she's still got all her marbles."

"Yeah, you could say that. Put her up on the witness stand, I'd believe her."

"Then somebody isn't telling the truth."

"Huh?" Omar looks at me blankly.

"This morning when the Reverend Archibald called, he said he'd thought about it, he checked an old list, and he barely remembered knowing someone named Delia Montero. Not only that, he said it was years ago, from the time when the church was on Sunset. Before they lost their lease, he said."

"So?"

"So Daisy remembers her as a regular at the place on Rosewood. Daisy never went to the one on Sunset. She had no car. She walked everywhere."

Omar shakes his head. "That doesn't seem like such a big deal to me," he says. "People's memories are shot full of holes. Swiss cheese. You know that."

"Right. But this is different. The Reverend called me out of the blue to tell me he'd tracked down Delia Montero. Somebody he vaguely knew long ago."

"Sounds to me like he was doing you a good deed," Omar says. "Now you want to turn around and call him a liar?"

"I like it when things add up. He didn't have to call me back."

"No."

"In fact, I didn't expect he would. And you're right: memories are slippery sometimes. But then, lo and behold, he came up with her name. And not only that: her friend's name, too. Even gave me her phone number."

"He was doing you a favor."

"Maybe."

Omar sighs. "You have a goddamn funny way of showing gratitude, Amos. Remind me not to give you any more birthday presents, okay?"

"I don't have that many more birthdays to go," I say. "Save your money."

CHAPTER 15

The next morning I drive back to the Mid-City Merchants to chat with Amory Blevins. The same tall, dark, handsome Iranian is patrolling the parking lot next door. He takes my car keys just as nonchalantly as before, and I go inside.

I spot Blevins talking on the telephone in his cubicle, but before I can walk on through, the receptionist jumps to her feet.

"Do you have an appointment?" She's a smart, rakish woman in a short maroon skirt and a white blouse. Not more than twenty-six, I think, and this job is clearly just a way station on her way to the White House.

"You must be Diana," I say.

"How did you know that?" she asks.

"Oh, I'm sorry. Amory told me all about you the other day. I think you were at lunch. I had to defend your honor. Silly man, he's so insecure, he thought you'd abandoned him."

"Are you in his book? He knows you're coming?"

Just then, Blevins looks up from his desk, sees me, and frowns. I smile and wave. "He does now. Just tell him Amos Parisman's back. I won't take much of his precious time."

She turns in his direction, and a moment later, he nods reluctantly for me to come in. "You've got exactly five minutes, Parisman." His voice is flat, guarded. "Say what you like."

"Thanks," I tell him. "First of all, I want to apologize for the other day."

"Apologize?"

"Yeah, I came in like gangbusters and told you what I thought of you. Actually, I was just following up on what Betsy Rollands thought of you."

"Oh."

"She still thinks that, by the way."

"Thinks what?"

"That you're a miserable, lying piece of shit. Or words to that effect. But you know Betsy. She doesn't mince words. And I don't think I've ever seen her change her mind."

"And you have?" He looks cautiously hopeful.

"I'm like you, Amory. I believe in redemption, I give people a second chance. Maybe she had you nailed once, but near as I can tell, you're doing the right thing with this homeless problem. And I want to thank you."

"You must have heard about the reward and the money for the social workers, then."

"I did."

"That was a real windfall. We were never going to get anything done, just going around hat-in-hand to all the churches and synagogues. Now it looks like we don't have to."

"No, you don't. And that's a real blessing. But you still have one little problem on the table."

"I do? What?"

"Well, you've got this money, and I assume you're going to do the proper thing. Twenty-five for the social workers, and twenty-five for the reward, right?"

"Right. It's all being handled. Very transparent. You can tell Betsy when you talk to her next time."

"Oh, I will. But here's the thing: that's a lot of money, and reporters are going to wonder—I'm sure some are already wondering—where it comes from."

"I can't tell you that," he says. "Not now, at least. The donor wants to be anonymous."

"But if and when we catch this sonofabitch, then we'll find out?

Is that what you're saying?"

He nods.

"I mean, it's very generous of course, but you and I both know that nobody puts up that kind of money on a lark. If it's Patty Hearst, fine. If it's the Lindbergh baby, fine. A homeless person? Not so much."

"I understand," he says. "Believe me, we plan to disclose the donor when the proper time comes."

"Thanks," I say. "That's all I wanted to hear."

*   *   *

An hour later I get a call from Malloy to meet him right away in the back alley at Vista and Beverly. "We've got another one," he says.

This time the body's lying head-first in a shallow dumpster behind a family diner. I lean in. The stench is already pretty fierce. I cover my nose and mouth. His hands are splayed out in front of him. It's as though he were in the middle of a swan dive. The dumpster is nearly empty, with just a few white plastic sacks of garbage strewn around. One of them looks almost like he was using it as a pillow to sleep on, only he wasn't asleep, and the sack is streaked with blood from his battered head. He's a short, thin Black man. He could be anywhere from fifteen to fifty (from this angle it's hard to tell) and believe me, I'm not getting any closer. He's wearing a faded orange sweatshirt, high-top sneakers, and blue jeans that are torn at the knees. The jeans haven't been washed in years. I look down at his hands. They're flat on the floor of the dumpster and they're clenched. Was he making them into fists at the moment of his death?

I pull back and take a breath. Malloy is pacing the alley a few yards away. His eyes scan the ground. Remo and Jason are both talking on cell phones, and there are four squad cars with their lights flashing nearby. Both ends of the street have been blocked off and eight police officers are standing around with their hands on their belts. The forensics van has just pulled up. A cameraman, the same one on the ladder a couple weeks ago taking shots of Delia Montero, climbs out of his car. He nods at Malloy.

"Another day at the office, huh?" I say to Bill as we shake hands. "This must be getting old."

"Our guy has gone back to using a hammer again," Malloy says. He rubs his forehead.

"Also tossing them into the dumpster if they're light enough," I say. "At least he's thorough most of the time."

The lieutenant ignores my sick humor. "We know who this one is, Amos. That's the good news. Busboy from the diner says he called himself Lincoln."

"No last name?"

"We haven't touched the body yet. And his shopping cart—if he had one—is missing. I'm thinking he has some ID. It'll turn up."

"And what else did the busboy have to offer?"

"They were friends, I guess. This Lincoln treated the alley like he owned it."

"Meaning?"

"He kept it clean, made sure there was no broken glass, no cans or trash. He'd show up late, but regularly, two or three nights a week, and just camp. The busboy used to sneak him out leftovers sometimes. Said he felt sorry for him."

We walk back down the alley. The camera guy is positioning his aluminum ladder for the best angle. "You mind if I have a word with the busboy, Bill?"

"Why? You think we missed something?" Then, a moment later, he relents. "Sure, go ahead. He's that one in the apron talking to Remo."

I nod and go over. Remo sees me coming and takes a long, apprehensive look at Malloy, who waves him away.

The busboy's name is Kyle. He's got half a dozen tattoos on both his arms. His neck is also similarly adorned, and I bet if he removed his shirt and pants there'd be more. A tall, gangly kid with deep-set eyes and long, dark hair that he keeps gathered in a ponytail. I ask him what he does when he's not a busboy.

"I'm in a band," he says. His face lights up when he says this. "Bass. A bunch of guys I live with in Eagle Rock. We're about to launch our album. I mean, we're ready to record, but first we need to scrape up the cash. You know how it is."

"Oh, I do." I pull my cardboard notepad out of my jacket and click my pen ready. "I used to play guitar in a quartet, you know. It was a long, long time ago. Parties, weddings, sometimes a bar gig. We were just covering the standards back then. Django Reinhardt. Charlie Christian. Monk, of course."

"I've heard of Monk. Not the others, though. He was a piano player, right?"

"Something like that." I ask him if he wouldn't mind going over what he told Lieutenant Malloy, and he tells me how he was helping prep for the lunch crowd and he went outside to smoke a cigarette and there was poor Lincoln lying in the dumpster. Quite a shock.

"I heard you two were buddies."

"We used to talk, yeah. I would bring him leftovers from the kitchen if he was hungry. He was hungry all the time." He wags his head like he's trying to get a kink out of his neck. "Funny, though. No matter what I gave him, he'd only eat half."

"What'd he do with the rest?"

"Stuffed it in his backpack. Save it for later. You never know when you'll be hungry again. That's what he said."

"What else did you guys talk about—I mean, besides food?"

"This and that. He told me how he came to L.A. from Chicago. Told me about his family. Alcohol fucked him up there. He had no control. Cost him his job, cost him everything. What he said."

"Alcohol doesn't care where you are," I say.

"That's true. Anyway, he couldn't keep a job in Chicago, and when his money ran out, he started living in his car. It was one thing after another. The cops towed his car away. After that he kinda turned into a gypsy. But he couldn't live on the street, either. Didn't have a clue. It's a cold city. I've never been there, that's just what I've heard."

"So how often did Lincoln come to this alley to spend the night?"

Kyle runs his tongue over his lips while he thinks it through. "He was here during the week. I never saw him around on weekends."

"Did he say where he hung out then?"

"Yeah. There was some church he liked. I forget where it was. He said he felt safe there. Nobody bugged him. I mean, I guess they wanted him to accept Jesus, but they all do, don't they?"

"Usually Jesus is on the menu, I agree. But if you're homeless, that's a small price to pay."

Kyle folds his arms. "I'm going to write a song about him," he says. "He didn't have to die that way. Nobody should die that way." He shivers slightly, shakes his head. "At least he'll have a song, huh? That's something."

*   *   *

Malloy has a different look on his face when I come back from my chat with Kyle. He's still not smiling, but now at least, he's energized. "We've found what we're looking for," he says. "Down at the bottom of the dumpster." With his thumb and forefinger he holds up a clear plastic bag. There's a claw hammer floating inside. It weighs maybe a pound, and the head seems encrusted with a brownish goo. "Guess he dropped it and wasn't up to crawling around in the muck with Lincoln to get it back."

"That's one possibility," I say. "But it's more likely he was trying to make double sure Lincoln was dead."

"What do you mean?"

"Nothing. Just that he was following through, is my guess. He was probably trying to clock him a few more times, and he got a little overexcited and the hammer slipped out of his hand. Remember, he had to toss him in first."

"Good point," Malloy says. "In any case, we've got a possible weapon. That'll help. I doubt we'll be able to take any prints off it, but maybe. You know anything about hammers?"

"Nothing. Loretta always told me I was all thumbs when it came to manual work."

"Well, I'd say this looks pretty run-of-the-mill, but we might be able to trace it. The forensics guys are gonna be pleased."

"They'll be up late, that's for sure."

Jason steps into our circle. He asks Malloy whether they should run a computer check on Kyle.

"Why?" Malloy wants to know.

"Because he found the body. Because he looks suspicious. Because I don't like his tattoos."

"That's no reason," Malloy says. "Don't be a fucking idiot. Not now, okay?"

Jason nods, takes the plastic sack with the hammer inside, and heads back to the white van where they're assembling evidence.

*   *   *

I spend the rest of the afternoon hours with Loretta. The nurses put her in a wheelchair and roll her into the elevator and down, so we can take advantage of their sunlit gardens. When she's outside in the fresh air she seems to suddenly come alive. She's animated and cheery, practically her old self again.

"This homeless murder thing just keeps going round and round," I say. I'm talking to her, but she's studying the succulents and the flowering cacti, and I'm not sure she's listening that closely. Still, I need to get this stuff off my chest, and I figure if I keep it on an even keel and sanitized, well, she can stand to hear a little bit. "You know what's strange, honey? We never get any closer to the killer. They found another poor fellow this morning, and maybe even the murder weapon. But I don't think it makes any difference at all."

"They're already dead," she says then, wagging her head. "People with no homes. Already dead."

"Well, now, Loretta, that's got to be about the most cynical thing you've ever said," I tell her. A breeze is coming up. I spin the wheelchair around to go back inside. "And not only that—you're probably right."

*   *   *

Gus is fast asleep in room 226. I just poke my head in for a quick minute. There's a vase full of red roses on the sill across from him. As far as I know, Gus doesn't care about flowers, no more than most men do, but I'm sure Mara thought it would cheer up some part of his brain to see them. The beige shades are drawn and the television is off, but the oxygen tank is still there at the ready next to his pillow, just in case.

The light is fading as I get into my Honda. I go up Rossmore, a lovely narrow tree-lined avenue with elegant apartments on either side, until it turns abruptly into Vine. Vine is wider, but you'd never call it elegant. Maybe it used to be, once upon a time. Now there are potholes, and it's a hodgepodge of car washes, pizza shacks, and Thai takeout; even a stodgy Armenian church that looks left over from a Soviet movie. It's rush hour, and there are more than a few anxious drivers weaving in and out on the road. Everyone wants to go home. I take it slow. Eventually the light turns green at Franklin and I start climbing Gower to where it winds gently like one of Gus's long-stemmed roses into Temple Hill and on up to Creston Drive.

I turn the key in the lock. Mara's lying on the couch staring pensively up at the ceiling and listening to an old recording of Pablo Casals. Whenever she starts playing cello music I know she's got something on her mind. "My life is about to change, Amos," she says.

"So what else is new?"

"No, you don't understand. Gus is dying. And before long, Violet will graduate and be off to college."

"So?"

"She'll leave, and everything I've known, everything I've relied on for years, the whole nest, will be gone."

"Does that scare you?"

"Yes. No. I don't know. It makes me wonder what the hell is real anymore, that's all."

"Hey, welcome to my world."

Suddenly she sits up, smiles, pats the empty space beside her. "Come here. I need a hug."

We cling to one another for a while, which feels good. Our bodies seem to fit together seamlessly. Then she shudders and starts to cry, nothing anguished and wrenching, just a few soft nostalgic tears trickling down her cheeks, kind of like she's remembering romantic times she had with Gus: drinking champagne in Paris or Rome, or God knows where, wonderful times she'll never have again. The old music is playing in her head. That's what makes her sad.

"We should move in together," she says finally as we separate. "I've decided. That would help me out a lot. I wouldn't be so moody."

"Gee, Mara, I dunno."

"What do you mean?"

"You living in sin with an old married man?" I give her a quizzical look. "What would the neighbors think?"

"I don't care. Fuck the neighbors." She leans into my neck again. "Wait. Don't you want to live with me? Am I so terrible?"

"Part of me does. Part of me would like nothing better. But—"

"But what?"

"But there's another part of me that's still married to Loretta. You know how long we've been together? I don't have to tell you. You understand, I know you do."

She's silent for a long time. "Of course," she says. "We can go on like this. It's fine, really. I just thought—"

"We both need to let go of things, Mara. We both need to let go and move on. And it'll happen." I pull her close. "Believe me."

CHAPTER 16

The next morning I'm bending over Loretta to give her a kiss goodbye when the door squeaks open and Omar walks in. "I thought I'd find you here," he says.

I put my finger straight up to my lips. Loretta's just now fallen asleep. "C'mon," I whisper, "let's talk outside."

In the hallway a nurse in a pale blue uniform ambles by and nods hello to me. I've met her before. Her name is Patsy. She's usually behind the desk at the station, but today she's pushing a metal wagon on wheels that's filled with little green vials. Right behind her in the opposite direction, a young, buxom orderly with streaks of purple in her otherwise blond hair swings by us with a set of X-rays under her arm. Omar waits until everything's quiet before he opens his mouth.

"I've got something," he starts. "Yesterday I talked to Julio again."

"And?"

"He's still unhappy about what happened to Maria. More than unhappy, man, he's out for blood. He wants answers."

"Hey, join the club." We've walked down the hall to where it turns into a kind of solarium; there are large potted plants all around and simple, gray, leather couches to sit on, light streaming in from overhead. We find a couch away from the other guests.

"So what did he have to offer?"

Omar's eyes scan the hall before he opens his mouth. "Maria's friend, Tita, came to see him the other night."

"She part of Julio's collection?"

Omar nods. "Like Maria. You know, she works from time to time. Anyway, they were close. And Tita told him there was a regular client of hers, this guy who'd meet her down at 3rd. Not always, but once a week, once a month. It all depended."

"So?"

"Maria told Tita he was weird. That he wasn't like the others. He didn't just want to fuck. That he was always wanting her to do weird stuff besides."

"Like what?"

"Like he'd bring her strange clothes to wear. Nothing racy. Stuff that a much older woman might put on. As if she were gonna work in an office. Or a schoolteacher maybe. And once he asked if he could tie her up."

"A lot of these guys are weird, Omar. You know that. So he was weird. Did he ever hurt her?"

"Tita didn't say anything about that. But she told Julio that Maria was afraid of him."

There's a sudden itch behind my left ear. I don't get it often, only when things don't add up. And the only way to calm it down, I've found, besides scratching at my scalp, is to start asking serious questions. "Why didn't Maria tell Julio herself? Isn't he supposed to protect her? And this client, if he's so scary, why didn't she just find herself another corner to work from?"

Omar shrugs. "I guess we'll never know the answer to that one. Maybe his money was too good. Anyway, I know it doesn't sound like much, but I have a name for you. Tita said Maria called him Hayden."

"Hayden? That's it? No other name to go with?"

"That's it. And of course, like Julio said, everyone lies in that business, so maybe it's just an alias. But I don't think so."

"Okay, fine. Hayden, then."

"Here's the other thing, Amos. Tita described him to Julio. And

Julio told me. According to Tita, he was a smooth, well-dressed Black dude. Sound familiar?"

"Sounds like the guy who bought the *Playboy*s at Phil's Book Alley, yeah."

"That's the first thing I thought." Omar smiles. "Now do you see where I'm going with this?"

"So maybe the shopping cart was part of this Hayden's elaborate fantasy. Maybe we're finally starting to zero in on our suspect."

We get to our feet and take the elevator down to the first floor and out toward the parking lot. "Of course," Omar pauses now and leans back against the hood of his shiny black Camaro, "this is nothing we can take to the bank."

"Not yet."

"We gotta be careful, you know. I mean, there are thousands of smooth, well-dressed Black men in L.A."

"At least."

"And maybe that guy Borquist, the one who sold him the *Playboy*s, maybe he wasn't the sharpest pencil in the box. Who knows what he was remembering?"

"Exactly," I say. "The mind plays tricks."

"On the other hand, if Tita's telling the truth, and if I had to bet—"

"On the other hand," I say, "you're right. Odds are, there probably isn't more than one or two well-dressed Black men in L.A. named Hayden. It's a big town, but still."

*   *   *

At three o'clock that same afternoon, I'm crouched across from Lieutenant Malloy in his office, an old sweat-stained Dodger cap in my lap, waiting while he finishes up with someone on the phone. I don't like seeing him here on the fourth floor; it's a pain in the *tuchus* to get downtown any day of the week, and unless you ride the bus, which I didn't, parking's impossible. Anyway, I'm here. I look around. Women in pantsuits control certain desks. The one nearest Malloy has an impressive square glass vase filled with pink and purple chrysanthemums. *Maybe it's her birthday. Or maybe she has a boyfriend who's mad about her. Or maybe they've had a terrible fight and now the poor slob wants to make up for it.* These are the things that run through my mind while I'm waiting, probably none of which are true. The women are busy studying screens and typing on keyboards. A few of them seem to be talking to themselves, but I know they aren't. Men in white dress shirts and ties walk around from one computer terminal to another; some of them have guns strapped on, and some carry manila folders. I once worked in an antiseptic place like this. Not for long, thank God. But there were days, I remember, when it was exciting. When it all made sense. Now, as Malloy sets the phone down in its cradle and meets my eyes, I'm grateful those days are behind me.

"Amos," he says, extending a hand, "what brings you to our little wonderland? You have news?" There's a heap of official papers in front of him, reports and case files and other details he needs to think about. But not now. He pushes it aside.

"Maybe," I say. "I've been talking with Omar. He's signed onto this project, you know, ever since Maria Ruiz was gunned down. It's personal with him."

Malloy raises his eyebrows, ever so slightly. "I thought we agreed that Maria's killer was not the same guy as the one with the hammer."

"He didn't use a hammer, but now we're thinking yeah, he might be the same guy."

"That'd be terrific," Malloy says. "So whatcha got?"

I tell him what we learned from Julio's girl, Tita. About the smooth, well-dressed Black man on 3rd. The one Maria was afraid of. Hayden.

Malloy nods. He taps his fingers on the desktop like he's waiting impatiently for me to fill in the next blank.

"So don't you see? That fits perfectly with what Borquist told us," I say. "The Black guy who bought the magazines? Maria called him Hayden. She was afraid of him. Isn't that news?"

"Maybe," Malloy says. "Maybe so." He takes his pen and writes Hayden down on a pad of paper. "Is that his first name, you think, or his last?"

"I dunno."

"Or is that even his real name? Hayden. Seems like we're clutching at straws."

"What else do you have?" I say. Maybe it's the heat, or maybe it's because I'm tired and haven't had my afternoon nap, but this kind of bureaucratic inertia gets on my nerves. Sometimes I admire Malloy's meticulous style. Not now, though. We don't have the luxury, I think. "Come on, Lieutenant, people are dying. And I might have just given you your first solid lead."

"And on behalf of the LAPD, I thank you." Like a beggar, he holds out his open hand. "But what do you expect us to do with this information?"

"Well, for starters, I suggest you run some sort of computer check on Black men in California named Hayden. See what falls out of the tree. That shouldn't be very taxing."

"Okay, we can do that." He scrawls a neat little heart over Hayden. "You know, you might be a wee bit too enthralled with modern technology. Me, I wouldn't be so hopeful."

"I'm not hopeful, Bill. I'm persistent."

He smiles. "You sure as hell are." He picks up the pile of papers he'd just pushed away a few minutes before. "Now, is there anything else?"

I lean back in my chair. "Well, yeah. I was sorta wondering what more you learned about our latest corpse, Lincoln."

Malloy shrugs. He sifts through his paper pile until he finds the pale blue one he's after. "This is the lab report. There's nothing useful on the hammer we found," he says. "It was clean, apart from the victim's blood. That could mean our fellow was fastidious and put gloves on before he went to work, but it's neither here nor there. The hammer itself is pretty common, you can buy one at any hardware store in town."

"And Lincoln?"

He pulls a thin manila folder out from right underneath and starts to flip through it. "Lincoln's story matched up with what that busboy told us. We found a wallet on him. Lincoln James Greer. No known address in L.A. He had a little black leather notebook with some names and phone numbers, most of them family members in the Chicago area. We contacted them."

"And?"

"Nobody wanted to talk about him. It's like they were hoping never to hear his name again. Even his own parents had kind of given up on him, if you can believe that."

"He must have been trouble."

"You're telling me. Anyway, he came out from Chicago, stayed at the Y for a while, did odd jobs here and there. When he was sober at least. Autopsy showed he'd been doing a real number on his liver with all the booze."

"Anybody in L.A. know him besides Kyle? Any friends?"

Malloy shakes his head. "His last employer was a guy named Jasper Cawley. He hired him last month to do clean up at his frame shop over on Fountain, *schlep* boxes and shelves around. They were doing a remodel and ran out of day labor."

"How long'd that last?"

"Three days. Two, really. He didn't show up on the third day. That was that."

"What'd you mean, that was that?"

"That was that, he fired him."

I nod.

"If it's any comfort to you, Cawley said he hated to let him go."

"How come?"

"Cawley thought he was a nice guy. Thought he had a big heart. And an open mind. If it weren't for the drinking, he might have crawled his way out of his situation. That's what he told Jason and Remo, anyway. A shame."

"Cawley didn't say anything else, did he?"

"Like what?"

"Oh, I don't know," I say. "He was a young man, he must have been doing something to fill all those hours when he wasn't working or drinking. Kyle said Lincoln never came around on the weekends, that there was some church or other place he hung out at. What about that?"

"That never came up," Malloy says. "When you're pushing a broom around, or lugging sheetrock off a truck with strangers, that's not exactly when you bring up Jesus."

*   *   *

As I'm heading down the stone steps from police headquarters and wondering where the hell I left my car, another thought occurs to me. The sun is low in the sky. And it's Friday, which means that the Eternal Light of Christ Church will be opening its doors soon. I call Mara, tell her I'll be late coming home, just so she won't worry about me. She's not at all worried, it turns out—she's stuck in traffic on the 210 freeway heading to Claremont. Violet is waiting for her, pacing around on the front lawn at Foxboro. *Violet wants to spend some quality time with Grandpa Gus before it's too late*, she says. *Really?* I think. There's a pause on the line. *Well, maybe she doesn't want to*, Mara continues. *But she needs to. That's the plan.*

Because it's rush hour, it takes me longer than I thought to get from headquarters to the storefront church on Rosewood, and another half hour before I spot a place to park.

The lights are on inside. I look down at my watch. It's not due to open for another hour, but I step forward and knock anyway—you never know.

After a moment, someone flips the bolt on the door and I'm looking at Reverend Archibald. He's still wearing those same wide red-framed glasses, but now he's also sporting a shiny white-and-purple robe that almost touches the floor. You can't see his shoes, and it gives the impression that he's floating somehow. I extend my hand. "Reverend Archibald, you remember me? Amos Parisman."

"Oh yes, yes, of course, the detective. Please, come in." He leads me into the church, which has maybe thirty wooden folding chairs facing the podium. The gold Styrofoam cross is in place against the wall, and there's a stack of Bibles with red covers on the stage. The Reverend picks up a few. "I was just going to lay these out on the chairs. You never know how many will show up," he says, smiling, "and we don't have enough to go around, so if there's a crowd, well, they'll just have to share, won't they."

"Here," I say, grabbing another stack, "let me help you." We go down the rows distributing the Bibles, one for every two or three chairs.

"I keep meaning to buy more." he says. "Problem is, I'd rather not pay out of my own pocket."

"But you could. It's not like you don't have the money."

"Oh I could, certainly. It's the principle of the thing. I'm already paying the rent and utilities on this place. And this is supposed to be a church, after all. A group effort. That's all I want. But given my congregation, it'll be a cold day in August before that ever happens."

We sit down next to one another in the front row. He closes his eyes, then opens them again and stares at me. He probably never expected to see me again, and now he's perplexed. "Are you here for the service tonight? You're early, you know."

I shake my head. "No, I'm still working these homeless murders, Reverend."

"Right. So have you made any progress? Did you speak with Daisy Cooper? Did she help you?"

"I did. What a delightful old lady."

"Yes, I was very sad when her daughter uprooted her like that. But we can't be in charge of everyone's life, can we? And she's in a better circumstance now."

"She is, but she said she misses the church. Misses you, in particular."

"Well, that's very kind of her."

"Yes, she couldn't say enough about how generous you were with everyone. Particularly with Delia. How you'd bring her up on the stage sometimes, put your arm around her, make her feel loved."

"I try to do that with everyone, Mr. Parisman."

"Sometimes, she said, there'd be music. Somebody would show up with a guitar, you know."

"Yeah, that's happened before. Whenever I can, I like to make a party out of it. Music is another road to God."

I finish scratching the itch behind my ear, turn my head to one side, and give him a look. "There's something that doesn't quite work though, Reverend."

"What's that?"

"Well, remember when we spoke on the phone, you told me you hadn't had any contact with Delia in years. That you knew her vaguely from the first church you had on Sunset."

"That's true."

"But Daisy seemed to know her only from here. Daisy said she hadn't seen Delia in a few months, not since she moved away. Months, not years. So one of you must be confused."

He listens intently, his brow furrowing as though he's trying to process exactly what I'm getting at. "Ah," he says then, "you know what? She's right. I don't keep good track of who comes and goes here, and the place on Sunset, I have to tell you, was not much different than this. Now that I think about it, Delia was never at the Sunset church. That was another woman. She's the one I haven't seen in years. Her name was Dora, I believe. Or Donna maybe."

I nod. "Good, good, that clears that up, at least. Although Delia had an old hymn book with the Sunset address on it."

"Those hymn books moved here about the same time we did. I'll bet I still have some with the old address." He gets to his feet and starts to adjust the microphone at the podium. "I don't really need this," he says. "My voice is loud enough to fill the whole room, but once in a while when someone else gets up to testify, especially a woman, you want her to feel . . . empowered."

There are two other empty folding chairs on the stage. "Are you thinking there's gonna be music tonight, Reverend?"

"Who knows?" he says. "It certainly changes the atmosphere if we have musicians up on the stage. There's one old fellow named

Jack who plays a mean guitar. He told me he'd be back again tonight, but I learned a long time ago not to count on folks. If they come, they come."

I get up and smile. "Well, I don't want to be taking up too much of your time," I say as I turn to go.

"Why don't you stay?" he asks in a hushed tone. I get the feeling he really means it; he's not just trying to be Christian and sociable. But then the old unwanted Jew in me kicks in, and I can't help it, suddenly I'm back on the basketball court at my junior high, trading punches with Larry Burch, who's in the ninth grade. He's calling me a dirty kike, yelling that I killed his Lord. Even as I'm staring now at Jimmy Archibald, I'm reliving just what it felt like half a century ago when my right hand surprised Larry's stupid adolescent face, and he stopped speaking and his nose started spurting blood all down his uniform and onto the waxy floor. I remember not caring whether I hurt him or not. I remember that it was a big game that evening and wondering whether the coach would make me mop the floor for what I'd done.

"Some other time maybe. I'd like that. I bet you put on a great show."

"I try, Mr. Parisman. It's what I do."

"No, you also sell real estate as I recall."

"That's just for money. This is my calling. This is what the Lord wants for me. You understand the difference."

"I guess. Say, I know this is out of left field, but you don't happen to know a homeless guy—skinny, African American—goes by the name of Lincoln, do you?"

"Lincoln. Lincoln. No, I can't rightly say I do." He smiles. "Coming from the South, I suspect I'd remember a name as distinguished as that."

"That's okay. It was kind of a long shot." I shake his hand. "Well, thank you for your time. I'll be on my way."

"Wait." He reaches out then and touches my shoulder. I turn around. "This man, this Lincoln. Is he another one of your victims?"

I nod.

Jimmy Archibald shakes his head. "That's what I thought. Well, it won't bring him back, but I'll be sure to include him in our prayers this evening."

"Thanks."

A moment later I'm outside with my hands jammed in my pockets, studying all the cracks in the sidewalk. A cool, devilish wind has spun up out of nowhere. The sun is about to set, and the traffic along Fairfax is getting relentless. People are tired. It's Friday night, they just want to forget their troubles, go home, kick off their shoes, and bust open a cold beer. Probably what Jason and Remo and most of the LAPD are doing about now. Hell, what I'd like to be doing myself.

CHAPTER 17

Mara and Violet and I spend several sessions that weekend with Gus, who has slowed down considerably. Mara brings him more flowers and an armful of magazines he used to read in the olden days. She plumps up his pillows, adjusts the angle of the bed, and jokes about how he's smitten with Bettina, the voluptuous new nurse on the floor.

Violet isn't nearly so involved, but then she's just a kid, and it's true: she has barely known her grandfather when he wasn't ill. Mostly she sits in dutiful silence or communes with the screen on her iPhone. But then, Sunday afternoon, when it's time to leave, she finally screws up her courage. She takes hold of his bony, blue-veined hand, smiles, and launches into a French folk song she recently learned at school. *"Au Bois de mon Coeur."* In the Woods of My Heart. She has a high, thin voice; it's like a breeze blowing through a clutch of reeds in a pond, and Mara and I applaud afterwards. Who can gauge what's going on in Gus's mind? He might be listening; he might know more than all of us put together. He has some lingering drool on his chin that Mara wipes away, and his eyes scan from side to side in bewilderment. Or is that joy?

Around midnight, on Sunday, the phone rings. Violet is back at Foxboro and both of us are fast asleep. Mara takes the phone, listens for a while, blinks, nods, says yes, yes, she understands, yes, of course, thanks for letting us know, tomorrow, yes, that's good, I appreciate it, and hangs up.

"What?" I ask.

"Gus died," she whispers. "They tucked him in for the night. The orderly said he looked all right. And then, ten minutes later Bettina came by to check. That's how fast it happened. They wanted me to know." She lies back in the bed.

"Shall we get dressed and go down there?"

"No," she says. "There's no point."

We lay there for a while, and I think I can hear her weeping. "Mara, honey, are you all right?"

"I'm fine," she says. "Really. He had a great life. We had a great life together. At least until the last few years. And he didn't suffer much at the end. No pain. He even got to hear Violet sing. You can't ask for more than that."

She pushes closer to me in bed. I can smell her perfume and feel the steady warmth coming off her body. Ordinarily I might reach for her, but not tonight. Instead, I stroke her hair, which always seems to soothe her.

"I have something to tell you, Amos," she says all at once.

"Now? Isn't it a little late to start a discussion?"

"Just shut up and listen to me, okay?"

"Okay."

"I don't want there to be any secrets between us. It wouldn't be right. And now that Gus is gone, well, there's no reason." She rolls over, faces me in the dark. "You know how suspicious you are of Amory Blevins and the Mid-City Merchants Association?"

"Amory Blevins? Amory Blevins? That's what you want to talk about? Not Gus?"

"No. Listen to me. I need to tell you that it was me. I'm the one who put up the $50,000 reward. I mean, my lawyer did."

"You put up the money? Why? I don't get it."

"Because I wanted to help you find the killer. Because I'm sure you will one of these days. Because I see how hard you work, and the truth is, I don't want you to work for free."

"You don't need to do that, Mara."

"No, of course I don't. I know that. I did it to help you. I see what a tough case this is, and I thought, for that kind of money, someone might just step out of the shadows and say something, give up a name or an address. Isn't that how it works?"

"If someone knew something, yes, they might be tempted. It's not a bad idea."

"Good. Then you approve?"

I stop smoothing her hair. My hand slides down to her cheek. "Look, the reward is fine. I mean, it is what it is. But so far, all it's done is generate a lot of free publicity for Blevins and his crew. I should take you to meet my friend Betsy Rollands, let her tell you what she knows about him. You'd probably want a refund."

"What I want is for you to catch this maniac. Then we can get on with our life."

"This *is* my life, Mara. This case. This is what keeps the wheels turning inside me. People used to hire me for stuff like this, once upon a time, but the fact is, I don't need to be paid. Not anymore. Does that sound naïve?"

"If Gus were still alive, he'd have other words, even less complimentary."

"What about you?"

She pauses before she speaks. "I think you're an honorable man, Amos Parisman. An honorable man who I've had the great misfortune of falling in love with."

"You could do worse," I say.

*   *   *

She's already made all the funeral arrangements. I should have known. When I ask about it the next morning over breakfast, she says that Gus is being cremated. No ceremony, nothing. "It's what he wanted," she says. "He even wrote it into his will. Believe me, honey, I tried to talk him out of it. I told him Jews don't do that sort of thing. He said, 'Do I look Jewish?'"

"What did you tell him?"

"I couldn't lie," she says. "I said no, not even remotely."

"And what was his response?"

"Word for word? 'So okay, then. Just spread my ashes someplace nice.'"

"For a millionaire," I say, "he was pretty aloof about death. Most big *machers* I've ever known like their wives to put on a gala when their time comes."

She shrugs. "Oh, I'll probably have a memorial service for him later on. But maybe I'll wait until the fall. We can do it at the house in San Marino. All his old business chums will want to drop by. They'll pay their respects, get sloshed and tell a few sordid tales."

"What about his family? Is there anyone left?"

"He has a younger sister who's still around. I haven't told Zoe yet. I will, as soon as I settle on a date. She won't show up in any case."

"Really? It's her brother."

"You don't understand. Zoe's a real New England horror story, you know, the ones with gray wool suits and sensible black shoes. She's lived north of Boston most of her life. I don't know how mobile she is anymore. They weren't close. And now it's too late."

"Well, sure, it's too late for him, but—"

"No, it's too late, period. There's no reason to try to open that door now. Let me put it this way, Amos. I saw her exactly once—on the day we were married." She takes a long, deliberate sip of coffee before she continues. "And that's only because Gus paid for her plane ticket."

*   *   *

The next day I'm sitting in a swivel chair in Omar's office in beautiful downtown Boyle Heights. My feet are crossed and planted on his desk, which I wouldn't ordinarily do since it's rude, but my feet are tired, and Omar says he wants me comfortable for the presentation he's about to make. He's pinned a blown-up map of the

Wilshire District on the far wall. Carlos and Ramon, Omar's associates, are standing behind me. I can smell their cigarette smoke as it drifts upward toward the ceiling.

"I've been going over the geography of the murders," he begins. "And if you count Maria Ruiz along with the other three homeless victims, you'll notice something interesting." He takes a ruler and points to a red X near Beverly and Fairfax. "Here, in a dumpster in the alley, is where they discovered Delia Montero. And here, on 2nd and La Brea, right next to a dumpster, we found Louis McFee." The ruler drifts to the left. "And over here—Beverly near Stanley—is where Maria was gunned down and the bogus shopping cart was found."

"We know all this, man," says Ramon. He stubs out his cigarette in an ashtray. "What's your point?"

"Let me finish," Omar says. "And finally, here behind the restaurant on Vista and Beverly, in a dumpster again, is where they found Lincoln Greer."

"So?" says Carlos.

"So all these murders are walking distance from one another. Now why would you think that is?"

"I have no fucking idea," says Carlos.

"Could be a lot of reasons," I say. "It could be that the killer lives somewhere within that nexus of killings. Maybe he owns a house there. That he has an elevated sense of moral worth, and he's killing these folks to clean up his neighborhood, so to speak."

"You mean he has a twisted sense of worth, don't you?" Ramon says.

"I was trying to keep it light," I say. I take my feet down from the desk and stare back at him. "I think we all agree this fellow's a whack job." I watch everyone's head nod up and down. "But there's all kinds of crazy, isn't there?"

"I guess," Carlos says. He's frowning now as he takes another drag on his cigarette. Carlos is an evidence guy, I can tell. He likes to see things up close; instead, I'm dragging him deeper and deeper into the psychological weeds. That makes him uncomfortable.

"And I'd even be willing to bet you that he thinks he has a green light," I say, "somewhere in the back of his mind, he thinks God wants him to eradicate these folks."

"Are you saying he's hearing voices?" Ramon asks. "Is that what you're talking about?"

"Possibly," I say. "Or maybe there's a political element here. Who knows? He could be stealing a page from Hitler. Getting rid of the Jews was always a winning slogan in Germany. Maybe this guy—on a smaller scale, of course—is just acting out how the rest of America really feels about prostitutes and homeless people."

Omar drops his ruler unceremoniously onto his desk. The sharp clattering noise startles us; everyone turns in his direction. "Look," he says, "we can keep going round and round about this guy's profile. But I put this map together because it said something to me about where we're most likely to find him. All of these crime sites are close. And Amos might be right—maybe he lives in the neighborhood—but there has to be a reason they're near each other. They're connected that way."

"And if you toss out Maria," Ramon says, "they're connected another way, too."

"How's that?" I ask.

"Well, all three of these street people went to church. It was a part of their lives, maybe a major part. Delia and that guy Louis McFee both spent time at that storefront church near Fairfax High. We know that. And that busboy said Lincoln also vanished on the weekends. Why? Maybe so he could go to church."

"We don't know which church, though," Carlos says.

"No," I say, "but it was always on the weekends, and that's the only time when the Eternal Light of Christ is open for business."

"So are ninety percent of the other churches," Omar says. "That's not gonna narrow the field. Besides, if I had no roof over my head and if I didn't know where my next meal was coming from, hell, I'd look for a church, too. That's just common sense."

Carlos and Ramon glance at their watches and say they have to shove off because they have a meeting in the next half hour with Maria Carlotta's mother. She wants to show them some things she found in her daughter's room. It's probably nothing, Omar thinks, which is why he's sending Carlos and Ramon. Probably just some sentimental trinket, but you never know.

After they leave, I turn to Omar. "That Ramon's a sharp cookie. He might have figured something out, in spite of himself," I say.

"Meaning what?"

"Well, I've been wondering myself about the churches they attend. I mean, church is where you make friends, right? Isn't that what it's all about?"

"I dunno. It's been a long time since I set foot in a church."

"Well, maybe you should try it. I hear the Reverend Jimmy Archibald puts on a great show at the Eternal Light."

*   *   *

On the off chance that Ramon may have tumbled onto something significant, I drive out to Highland Park to chat once more with Daisy Cooper. She's surprised to see me, but she lets me in and sits me down at the living room table while she rummages around making tea in the kitchen.

After a few minutes she emerges with an old silver tray in her hands. "I'm afraid I don't have any cookies or pastries to offer you. My daughter was going to the grocery store this afternoon—"

"That's all right. You don't have to entertain me. In fact, I don't even need the tea."

"No, no, I insist, young man." She places a sweet, steaming porcelain cup in front of me. She smiles benignly. "Now, then, here we are. What was it you came about?"

"I came back to test your memory, Daisy."

"Oh, dear," she says. "That old thing."

"No, no," I say, "your memory's been spectacular so far."

"Well, I was never very good at tests, you know. I failed algebra back in high school. I just could never understand what they were talking about. Always trying to find X. 'What's X?' I asked the teacher. Why would anyone ever want to do that?"

"Good question," I tell her. "What'd your teacher say?"

"I don't remember," she says. "It's been so long. I think the whole class laughed at me." She blows on her tea cup, lifts it gingerly to her mouth, then sets it down. "To this day, though, I still wonder what that damned X is good for."

I ask her if she's had a chance to go back to Reverend Jimmy's church yet, and she says no, not yet. Her daughter has promised to take her one of these days, but when she gets home after work on Friday nights she's tired; she's been on her feet all day and she doesn't want to go out again and face the traffic. "And Sunday," she says, "well, that's the only day of the week she can catch up on laundry and cleaning. I don't want to bother her then. Sunday's supposed to be a day of rest, after all."

I nod. Then I ask her what I really came for. "Did you ever remember meeting a fellow at Reverend Jimmy's named Lincoln?" I ask. "Lincoln Greer?" I pull out a copy of his driver's license that Malloy gave me and push it across the table.

Daisy picks up the paper and stares at it. "Lincoln. People called him Linc, I believe. Yes, that's him. He was a charmer. Always willing to help, always so polite. One night, when I stayed later than I should, he even insisted on walking me home. I told him it wasn't necessary, but he said we have to look out for each other, that's what Christians do."

"So Linc was a regular there."

"Regular? Well, I can't say that. He showed up. He wasn't as regular as Delia, that's for sure. But people knew him."

"He didn't talk to you about his personal life, did he? Where he came from. Why he came out to California."

She shakes her head. "We had little conversations, but I don't remember what they were about. I'm sorry."

"That's okay. That you remember him at all is important." I lean forward. "You told me last time I was here that lots of folks at Reverend Jimmy's had troubles."

"Yes. He seemed to draw particularly from the downtrodden. That's what he called them. I remember him saying once that God has special chairs at his table for the downtrodden."

"He said that?"

"Oh yes. Jimmy would bring them up onto the stage sometimes, ask them to testify. It was good. It cleared the air."

"And did Lincoln ever testify?"

"I expect he did, yes."

"So did you know that he had a serious problem with alcohol?"

The tea has cooled enough now that Daisy feels it's safe to drink. She takes a tentative sip. "You're speaking of him in the past tense, Mr. Parisman. Does that mean he's cured?"

"No, Daisy, I'm afraid that means he's dead."

"Oh," she says. "That's too bad. I liked that man."

*   *   *

His nutritionist has warned him against it, but Bill Malloy has a sudden rebellious hankering for a hot pastrami on rye, so we meet at Canter's. It's only a little after five and it's the middle of the week, which means finding a table will be easy. I see him sitting in a padded booth in the corner and come over.

Moira hands me a menu. "You having what he's having?" she asks. She's been here for years, like everyone else, and time has taken a toll on the way she walks, but she still can pull a laugh out of thin air.

"Look at me, Moira, I've had what he's been having all my life. I think it's about time I quit, don't you?"

"Am I a doctor?" she asks. "I say eat what you want. Life's short."

I glance at the menu, fold it shut and hand it back to her. "In that case, give me the cheese blintzes and a cup of coffee."

"Cheese blintzes," she says, writing it down. "Cup of coffee."

"Right."

"Not the pastrami like him."

"No, pastrami will give me heartburn. Who needs heartburn?"

"You shouldn't have the coffee, then, either. It's too late in the day. Coffee will keep you up all night. How about I bring you some nice decaf?"

"Fine," I say. "Blintzes and decaf. Whatever."

Bill glares at her and shakes his head.

"I'm just looking out for you," Moira mutters as she walks away.

"Is she always like that?" he asks when she's out of earshot.

"They know me here, Bill. We're family. The word is *mishpucha* in Yiddish. People who are *mishpucha* can say what they want to each other. I don't know if Irish Catholics have something similar."

"No, they don't," he says. "The only thing they have in common is that they hate the English." He loosens the knot of his tie. "And I'm not even sure about that anymore."

We trade pleasantries. His pastrami arrives, and right after that, my blintzes and decaf. He asks about Loretta, I say she's the same, that it's probably going to be like this for a long time, and I'm just trying to get used to it. Jessie, his wife, has a new drug for her arthritis, and it seems to be helping. He can't remember the name, though.

"Speaking of names, did your computers ever find out anything interesting about Hayden?"

"Yes and no," Malloy says. "There's no information on any African American in California named Hayden. It didn't seem to matter whether that was his first name or his last name. No Hayden in California. Not currently."

"So maybe it's a made-up name, like Julio suggested."

"Or maybe there is a Hayden here, and he's flying below the radar. That's harder to do, but possible, I guess."

"You said 'yes and no,' Bill. What do you mean?"

"Well, there were no Haydens in California. But when we went to the FBI's national database, we did find a tiny little something. Once upon a time, it turns out there was a Joe John Hayden."

"Oh yeah?" I put down my forkful of blintzes.

"I wouldn't get too excited if I were you."

"I'm not excited, just curious."

"Okay, whatever. He was a Black kid in Mississippi. Spent time in a mental lockup there. Thirty years ago."

"For what?" I say.

"It might be for nothing," Malloy says with a shrug. "I read the report. He was mouthing off in class, and they sent him to the principal, and things went south from there. Eugenia Foley was her name. All the teachers said she was a sweetheart. Anyway, she talked with him, and even she didn't like what he had to say."

"And?"

"And so they called the police. That's how they did things in Mississippi then. Anyway, he ended up in jail. And eventually a judge sent him to this place."

"So why do we care?"

"Why? Because this kid, this Joe John Hayden, escaped after three months, and the next day they found the principal's body in her bedroom. Someone did a number on her."

"He use a hammer?"

Malloy frowns. "No. She was raped and then strangled with a bra. Then, to top it off, whoever did it set the house on fire. They found her and the singed bra, but no fingerprints. I have a copy of the police report, you want it."

"And Hayden?"

"Disappeared."

"Huh. That's curious. I don't know what we can do with it, however."

"Me neither."

I sip my coffee. "You don't suppose these folks down in Mississippi have an old moldy photo of this kid, do you? Any intake records we could see, or—God forbid—prints?"

"The county lockup might. Emphasis on the *might*. We can ask. But remember—it's a small town in Mississippi. And it's been a long time."

"True."

"He's most likely dead, but if not, he's gonna look a whole lot different. And forget about prints. So far we haven't been able to pull anything useful from these murders."

"What about the shopping cart?"

"Oh yeah, I forgot about that. We have a few partials. But no match yet on who they belong to. Nothing definitive."

"But this is what we have, Bill. I think you should at least give it a try."

"You know what I think? I think I'd have a better chance of getting hit by a meteor. I mean, all we're going on is what Maria Ruiz allegedly—*allegedly*—told Tita. How do we know Tita didn't get the name wrong? How do we know she wasn't making it all up to score points with Julio? How do we know this man wasn't lying to Maria?"

"Those are good arguments."

"And even if it's all true," he continues, "even if there is a goofball named Hayden in L.A., and this Hayden was paying to screw Maria, what then? What then? All we've heard is that Maria thought he was weird. What the hell can you do with that?"

I stare at Bill Malloy for what feels like a lifetime, so long, in fact, that by the time I finally lift my cup of decaf to my lips again, it's gone cold. Everything he says stands to reason. "You're right," I say.

"You better believe I'm right." His jaws grind away on the last of the hot pastrami sandwich.

"But there's just one little thing."

"Oh yeah?" he says. "What?"

"Somebody killed Maria. Somebody she probably knew. And somebody who matched Hayden's description helped fill that shopping cart, the one with her fingerprints on it. Okay, it's not much to go on. But—"

"But what?"

"Just a question, Bill. You got any better ideas?"

CHAPTER 18

That night I'm back at my old, empty apartment in Park La Brea, poking around on my computer, searching for anything I can find about Mississippi and its historic approach to mental health—which, let me tell you, doesn't make me confident about the future of mankind. The phone rings. It's Shelly. He's calling to say he's arranged a special invitation for me to the next Jews Who Eat. It's this Saturday at noon at the Farmers Market. "Right by the falafel joint we ate at last month, you know the one I'm talking about, don't you, Amos?"

I tell him, "Thanks, but I'm not sure I can make it, I have this murder case I'm working on, you understand."

"Oh," he says, "you must be awful busy, *boychik*, I tried you on your landline I don't know how many times and you never once answered. Don't you have a goddamn message machine like the rest of the civilized world? Even at seven in the morning, nobody's home. What's up with that?"

I hear the hurt and suspicion in his voice, and in the silence that follows, I lie. I tell him, you know how it is, Shelly. I'm a lot younger than you. I'm still not quite through running around. Day and night, going to bars, checking out leads. What can I tell you? That seems to satisfy him for a moment. After that, he goes back to the Jews Who Eat, how it's only for an hour or two, no big deal, but still, if it's at all possible, I should make an effort to come. Why? I ask. Because, he goes, because there's someone he'd really like me to meet. Her name is Arlene Zimmer. She was friends with my second wife, he says. Her husband Phillip was a complete schmuck. She's divorced now, thank God, in her fifties. Likes Groucho Marx, wild about Larry David. I think you two would have a lot in common.

"Shelly," I say, after a pause, "have you forgotten about Loretta?"

"Not at all," he says, "not for a minute. I love Loretta. In fact, it's on account of Loretta that I even thought of you. I don't want you to be lonely, cousin. That's all. That's what this is about. Loretta wouldn't want you to be lonely, either. You know that, too."

"Thanks," I say. "I'll see if I can make it. Saturday's dimly possible. No promises, though."

"No, of course not," he says. "But if you can see your way clear, you'll try, right? That's all I ask."

"I'll try," I say. "And Shelly? One more thing, before I hang up. Listen to me. Just so you know, I'm not lonely. Really. I'm fine."

*   *   *

Next afternoon, Betsy Rollands calls and asks me to meet her at her favorite bar that evening. Says she has useful information. "Why don't you just tell me on the phone?" I say.

"Because I still like your company," she says. "And because sometimes a girl gets tired of buying her own liquor."

The Tiki Lounge is on Sunset, near Doheny. It's decorated with kitschy memorabilia from a bygone era, back when Hollywood was in the thrall of Hawaii. Plastic leis and a chorus line of ceramic hula girl statuettes behind the bar. The place is pretty dark overall, except for the far wall, where they've spotlighted a huge bamboo-framed black and white photo of Bob Hope and Bing Crosby on a romantic beach, grinning, coconut palms overhead. Crosby is holding a ukulele. Hope has that Casanova leer in his eye. As I walk in and take my seat at one of the empty red leatherette stools, I note that they're playing "Blue Hawaii" on a jukebox; the Elvis Presley version, naturally.

"That's my least favorite song in the world," I say to Betsy Rollands as she slides in next to me. "In fact, if I never hear 'Blue Hawaii' again it would be swell."

"I don't like it either," she says. She turns to the bartender. He's a round, even-tempered-looking fellow with pink cheeks and a receding hairline. "I'll have a single malt, Martin. I'm in that dark, smoky sort of mood." Then she points over to me with her thumb. "He will, too."

"Do you always make a habit of ordering drinks for strange men?" I ask.

"You're not so strange," she says. "Don't let it go to your head."

Martin lays down little paper coasters and places the drinks in front of us, then retreats to his cash register at the other end of the bar. "Blue Hawaii" has concluded, and now, instead of merciful silence, Don Ho, or someone just like him, has begun to croon.

Betsy sips her drink, puts it down. "While I was in between writing assignments, I thought it wouldn't hurt to do a little more research into our mutual friend. I hope you've been keeping track of him, Amos. He's a slippery son of a bitch."

"Well, I did find out where his reward money is coming from, if that's any help."

"You mean, he didn't steal it?"

"No, not at all. Someone just came along. Someone with more money than she knows what to do with. Just dumped it in his lap. Said here, find the killer."

"Really?" she said.

"You don't believe me? That kind of thing happens all the time in L.A. So many nice rich people."

"You don't happen to know her name, do you?"

"Oh, I know all about her, Betsy." I take a small sip of my malt and put it back on its paper pad. "But it's exactly like Amory said. For once he's being honest: she wants to remain anonymous."

"Did Amory bother to say why?"

"She told me why. She doesn't want people coming after her, left and right, asking for money. She also doesn't want any notoriety for this; she's only trying to move the needle any way she can."

"Hmm."

"I can tell you're doubtful. But you'll just have to trust me on this. Her motives are beyond reproach. And you can be damn sure her lawyer will see to it that Blevins doesn't abscond with a penny."

"So how did you get her name if she wanted to stay—"

"That's a long story," I say. "Amory didn't tell me. I'm not even sure he knows who the donor is. But it doesn't matter. Her money's not tainted. I don't know if it'll help find the murderer, but that's another subject."

She takes a long gulp of her drink and empties it. Then signals Martin for another round. "Okay then. Forget about the money. Maybe you're right about that. But did you hear the other news about Amory Blevins? That he has a lover?"

I shrug. "Should I care?"

"I don't know about care. But you might be interested, Amos. He's a married man. Two children. His wife works in a dentist's office in Westwood. Everything's very proper these days."

"Except that he has a lover."

"Not only that. A Black *male* lover."

"No kidding? And just how did you discover this juicy little tidbit?"

"I should have been a detective," she says.

I finish my drink. "And he has a name you're going to tell me, right? You're not sworn to secrecy like I am?"

She's silent for a time. It's like there's this adding machine calculating things in her head. Then she pulls a notebook out of her purse, scribbles something down a page, tears it off and pushes it over to me. "Jack Harper," she says. "Here's his address. He's got an apartment on Curson. I've known about him for a week or two."

I stuff it in my jacket pocket without looking at it. "I just have one question for you, Betsy."

"Only one?"

"For the moment. Why? Why do you think this is so important? Didn't you tell me yourself that Blevins wasn't a killer? That he didn't have the balls?"

"That's true, he doesn't. But his friend, Harper, does."

She's finished her second drink. I signal to Martin to pour her another. "Okay," I say, almost in a whisper. "Let's say, for argument's sake, you're right. Amory Blevins is sleeping with a man who's capable of murder."

"He is."

"Fine. But you and I both know that's not enough."

She bites her lower lip, and I realize I'm going to have to drag whatever she's thinking out of her. "So tell me, what possible reason could he have for doing these vile things?"

"I haven't worked that part out yet. Not completely. All I have is a theory."

"Well, let's hear it. Even if you're wrong, it'll be more than what the cops are chewing on."

She swirls her new drink around, studies the amber coloration as if that might offer some wisdom. "Okay," she says finally. "Amory Blevins is an ambitious man. You've seen how he operates. He's always wanted to go places, and he's never cared how he got there."

"Yeah? So what? That's the American way."

She rolls her eyes. "Before, it was little scams. Then he went off the radar for a couple of years. In fact, he's been clean for a long time."

"That's good, isn't it?"

"No," she says, her voice growing more impatient. "Don't you get it? He hasn't changed his spots. And now all of a sudden he's taken out papers. That's what tipped me off. He's planning to run for the open L.A. City Council seat. What I think is"—her voice drops to a whisper—"he's using these murders, and all the notoriety that comes his way, to get elected."

"And just how does he benefit?"

"Think about it," she says. "They can't be random, Amos. There's no way. They're a setup."

"You know this for a fact?"

"No. But there are just too many in the same area. And it's too regular, week after week. All in the same district where there's an election coming. What does that tell you?"

"I'm not sure it tells me much of anything," I say. "What's it tell you?"

"That there's a larger purpose behind them. That someone—someone like Amory—is getting set to seize on this and run with it."

I put my hand on her arm. It's meant to calm her down, but she pulls it back from me, and I realize I'm having the opposite effect. "Hold on, Betsy. Let's slow down a minute. I mean, I like a good conspiracy theory as well as the next fellow, but—"

"I'm just trying to help," she says.

We're both quiet then, like we just somehow stepped on each other's toes. The music shifts to slack-key guitar. It's still Hawaiian, but minus the cheesy lyrics.

"All right, let me see if I can read your mind," I say. "Amory wants to be on the city council and he needs an issue. Something he's uniquely qualified to take the lead on."

"Exactly."

"And you're thinking that this Harper fellow is—how shall we put it—that he's out there paving the way for Amory?"

"Campaigning with a vengeance," she says.

"And that he's doing all this on Amory's orders?"

"I don't know," she says, looking away. "I'm not in their bedroom. I don't know what they talk about."

"So where's your proof, dear girl? You told me Amory's no killer. And now you're saying that Jack Harper is. Is this just a warm fuzzy feeling, or what?"

"It's more than that. Harper has a violent past."

I nod. "Okay. But even if Amory is involved, how does that help him get elected? You think people will just vote for him out of fear?"

"No," she says. "People will vote for him because they see someone stepping up and advocating for the homeless. That's how he's going to frame this. I can see it already. It'll be his personal crusade. And I think these murders will continue right up until the election, and then, the minute he wins, you know what? They'll stop. It'll be a miracle. They won't find the killer, but Amory Blevins will be the one person around here who tried to get all those poor souls off the street. And he'll get the credit for it."

I swallow the last of my single malt. "Well, it's a nice, neat story, but you're going to have to fill in a whole lot of blanks before the cops will ever believe you."

"I'm aware," she says. "But at least I have someone with a plausible motive. Seems to me that's what's been eluding us so far."

"That's not true. Lieutenant Malloy told me—and this is a direct quote—'homeless people are about as popular as termites.' Everyone wants them gone, in other words."

"Fine. But no one would bother to go after them as systematically as this fellow is doing—not without a reason."

"You think Jack the Ripper had a good reason to kill all those prostitutes in London? Hitler had a reason?"

"Well, maybe reason is too strong a word. More like an excuse."

"I'll buy that, Betsy. But in the meantime, I hope you have something more on Jack Harper besides his romantic interest in Blevins."

She reaches for her purse, and pulls out her reporter's notebook. "I talked with my friends at the LAPD. They're not as high up the totem pole as Malloy, but they also don't mind breaking the rules to help me out."

"And they told you what, exactly?"

"That Jack Harper has done time for manslaughter. Also assault and armed robbery."

"Sounds like a nasty man," I say. "Also, it doesn't sound like someone Amory Blevins would ever want to date."

"No," she says. "They're an odd couple, no question."

"And that's another hole you'll have to fill before Malloy gives you the time of day."

Betsy slides off the stool, slings her big leather purse over her shoulder. "When you're on the trail of something, you have to go wherever the facts lead you. You know that better than most. And you're right—I can't account for what a wimp like Blevins and a thug like Harper see in one another."

She kisses me gently on the cheek. "But then I was never that smart when it came to love, was I?"

"It's not your fault, Betsy."

Martin, the bartender, lays a chit on the counter between us. Betsy slides it over to me. "Take care of this, will you, Amos? I'm still waiting to be paid from *The Atlantic*."

CHAPTER 19

I wake up the next day chewing on a pillow in my old bed at Park La Brea. I force my bare feet onto the rug and stumble into the kitchen to make toast and coffee. One by one, I unscrew the plastic caps on my prescription bottles and set the six different colored tablets I'm supposed to take every morning on the counter. Outside the window a dull fog is covering the hills. Usually you can see Griffith Park Observatory, but not today, not yet. Someone has tripped a car alarm in the parking lot down below, and African pop music wafts from a nearby apartment. I look around me. Just stuff, that's all I see. Worthless stuff we picked up on sale at Sears or IKEA or God knows where. The couch. Chairs. The oval breakfast table with the permanent scratch in the middle. This is our home, and I keep trying to find some meaning, but it's hard without Loretta here to light up the atmosphere. That's what she did. Hell, even the coffee tastes flat.

Like Malloy, I think I'd probably have a better chance of getting hit by a meteor, but since Betsy Rollands is a friend, and since she's got this bizarre (okay, clever) idea about Amory's secret life, and since I have help, I call Omar and tell him about Jack Harper. "Maybe you can put Ramon on it," I say. "Might make sense, just follow him around for a few days and nights, see what comes of it."

"Have you talked to Malloy yet?" he wants to know. "Why don't they do something? I've got just three guys in this whole fucking office."

I realize he's stretched thin, and offer to put in time myself, even though I'm getting a little old and rusty for the job. In the end, Omar relents. Fine, he says, he'll go along with the program. For Maria's sake. That's why he's doing it. And for her mother.

"You've got a good heart, amigo," is what I tell him, *"un buen corazon."*

"Skip the Spanish, man," he says, "you're giving me a headache." Then he hangs up.

After that, I call Lieutenant Malloy. He's in an agreeable mood for a change. "Sure, Amos, we could put a tail on him, but that costs the taxpayers. At the moment all your friend Betsy's come up with is a hunch. Last I heard, it's not illegal to run for office in this town. And it's not illegal to sleep with another man, either, not anymore."

"I get that, Bill. It's a hunch."

"And taxpayers don't pay for hunches."

"No, but they have a thing about murder, don't they?"

"Sure," he says. "And that's why I'll run Jack Harper through our fancy machines, I'll do that for you. It can't hurt. And if Omar can find out any more, so much the better."

*   *   *

I take a quick shower, shave, and get dressed. Then, a quiet comes over me, and before I leave, I open my sock drawer and rummage around until I find something cold, dark, and heavy. I haven't handled my Glock 9 in years. Now I fish it out, slide in the magazine, check the safety, and tuck it into the leather holster I've strapped on by my ribs. It feels a little tight, but that's because I've put on some weight. *There now, Parisman, it's official. You're armed and ready. Just like the olden days.*

I throw on my sport coat, grab a second piece of sourdough toast, and head for the elevator. Mr. Wu is coming toward me with a paper sack of groceries. We nod hello. As I climb into my Honda, I call the number on Reverend Jimmy's business card. A female voice answers. Mr. Archibald is just finishing up a meeting, she explains. Can you hold? Forever, I tell her. Thirty seconds later, Jimmy Archibald is on the phone.

"Mr. Parisman," he says. "I didn't expect to hear from you again. Not so soon at least."

"Well, you know how these things go, Reverend. It's what I do."

"No," he says, "actually I have no idea."

Jimmy Archibald didn't ask, but all of a sudden my mind goes into overdrive, and that's when I launch into my detective speech. What we really do. The big disclaimer. How Chandler and Hammett and all the rest of those movie monkeys got it wrong. How there's absolutely nothing romantic about it. No lurking behind potted palms in seedy hotels, no barroom brawls, no beautiful dames throwing themselves at us, no wild car chases down busy streets with guns blazing. "That's a load of horse excrement," I say.

I could go on like that for maybe five minutes, but then my heart starts to pound and I stop. There's a long pause at the other end. "So, what do you do?" he says finally, bewildered.

"I ask questions," I say. "And one question very often leads to another. I keep drilling down. In a way, Reverend, I think your work and mine aren't that different. We're both of us looking for the truth."

"Yes, well I'm sure there are similarities." He doesn't seem to want to continue this conversation. Maybe I shouldn't have called him at the office. Maybe that's what's behind the constraint.

I cut to the chase. "Thing is, I still have a few unanswered questions for you, Reverend. I wonder if—"

There's another muffled pause then as he speaks to someone nearby. I can't make out the words, but then all at once he's back. "I'm afraid I can't talk right now, Mr. Parisman. Some clients just arrived, and I need to show them a property. But what if we met later this afternoon? Coffee somewhere? Is that convenient?" He mentions an espresso place in Brentwood near Bundy. "I'll be finishing up with these folks around 2, I imagine. Do you want to get together at 2:30? That's the earliest I can make it."

"Sure," I say. "No problem."

*   *   *

I turn the key in the ignition and head for the address on Curson that Betsy gave me. I don't really expect I'll learn much from this exercise. Jack Harper is probably not home, or if he is, he's probably sound asleep, and I'm not about to knock on his door and try to borrow a cup of sugar.

I pull over across the street from a pleasant two-story stucco apartment building that dates from the eighties or nineties. Each of the upstairs apartments has a balcony, where residents have set out little barbecue grills and chaise lounges for sunbathing. One of them has a lavender and white beach towel hanging precariously over the edge. The building is a soft tan with dark orange molding around the windows and doors. It's as if the owner had some dream about old New Mexico and wanted to take you back in time. Three enormous sycamore trees dominate the front. The owner had nothing to do with that, I figure. They were there long before he came to town. I get out and walk toward the front to check the names on the bank of mailboxes. Trees this tall means there's a glorious sprinkling of shade all around. It also means the sidewalk is broken by their roots, and you have to watch out or you'll trip.

Harper is in number 12B. There's excess mail in his box. I fish a few pieces out of the metal slot, not that I'm about to plow through his private correspondence or anything. This is the USA, but you know, if it's right there for anyone to see, well, what are these eyes for? He's got a statement from the Bank of America, a cable bill, a Nordstrom's advertisement, and a long silver envelope from the Mid-City Merchants Association. Probably a love letter, I think. That Amory Blevins must really be smitten. And I admit, I'm tempted to take out my pen knife and pry it open, but then I see a young Asian woman in shorts and sandals coming out of her upstairs apartment and I stuff it all back.

She walks by me, nods, glances at her cell phone, turns left, and disappears down the back alley where the cars are parked.

I wait until she's gone, then I reach in and retrieve the letter. It takes just a second to open it with my blade. Inside, there's a short official letter from President Amory Blevins, thanking Mr. Jack Harper for his diligence in recruiting a team of professionals on such short notice to move the endangered street people to safety. And, along with the letter, the Mid-City Merchants have generously written him a check for $8,500.

"How sweet of them," I say. Then I fold it all up, seal the envelope with some homegrown saliva, and put it back where it came from.

I wait around in my car for a good hour. Nothing is going on in the apartment. A sleepy-eyed, bare-chested kid, the one who apparently left the beach towel dangling, comes out on the balcony to rescue it before it tumbles to the ground. A very pregnant red-haired woman with a baby in a stroller emerges from the court-yard, and, steering clear of the broken sidewalk, heads slowly up the block toward Santa Monica.

Omar calls to get more dope on Harper. "I mean, we don't even know what he looks like," Omar says. I tell him Malloy is working on it and when he sends it to me, I'll send it to him. Twenty minutes later, Ramon shows up, parks, and leans into my car window.

"You don't need to hang around, Parisman. Seems like Lieutenant Malloy is working with us. He sent over a nice snapshot of this guy, Harper. Sent his whole rap sheet along too, in fact. I can take it from here."

"I'm sure you can, Ramon. That's fine. Only don't get too close to him. Also, you probably don't even have to start shadowing him until after dark. None of the killings happened any earlier than nine. He's a night owl."

*   *   *

Inside Café Maxx it's cool and clean and airy, and the metal tables and dark wood chairs with their soft leather seats make you want to stay there forever. That's the point, I guess. Just sit back, nibble their pastries, sip the coffee, and let the world go by. There are no problems at Café Maxx, nothing that can't be solved by a little sugar and more caffeine.

I'm pretty wired by the time Reverend Archibald shows up. "Sorry," he says, "I didn't mean to be late. These clients wanted to see every inch of the house. And then they wanted to stand around and talk about it."

"Well, if they're going to spend their hard-earned money, you'd expect them to be thorough, wouldn't you?"

"If it were their money, yeah. That's the problem. They're just looking to buy houses for other folks so they can sell them six months from now. It's a game. The people they work for live in Texas. They'll never even see these places." He shakes his head.

I wait until he orders a cappuccino and has had a taste before I start asking what I want to know. "So Reverend," I say, "I went back and had another chat with Daisy Cooper."

"Ah yes." He plays with the sunglasses he's placed on the table. "A lovely woman. Also a lonely woman, I think. I'm glad you're able to spend time with her."

"I didn't do it out of compassion, Reverend. Business, you know."

"Of course. But I'm thinking about it from her perspective. When she lived closer, she had the church. It meant a lot to her."

"It still does, so she tells me. Who knows, maybe one day she'll get back to it."

"I hope so." He looks at me in earnest. "But you didn't want to speak about Daisy, did you?"

"No, not exactly. Except that I asked her about Lincoln."

"Lincoln."

"The latest guy I asked you about. They found him in a dumpster behind a restaurant. Lincoln James Greer. The one you couldn't remember."

"I'm sorry, Mr. Parisman. People come and go. I don't remember everyone. Not anymore. Half the time I don't even try to learn their names."

"That's okay. I understand. But I thought you'd like to know that Daisy remembered him well."

"I believe it."

I finish the last of my coffee and push the cup and saucer to one side. "So now I'm trying to piece this whole puzzle together. And one of the things that jumps out at me is this: there've been three homeless people killed around here in the past month. Delia Montero. Louis McFee. And now Lincoln Greer."

"Yes?"

"And, by coincidence, it seems, all three have spent time in your little storefront church."

"Does that surprise you?" he says. "Really? I mean, that's who my congregation is, for the most part—homeless, desperate people. If somebody was going around killing Jews in one small part of L.A., I'm sure you'd find that they all belong to the same temple."

I stare at him.

"I don't understand," he says finally. "What are you suggesting?"

"I'm not suggesting anything, Reverend. I guess what I want to do is ask you—and you can interpret this however you like—is there anyone in your congregation, anyone at all, who doesn't seem to fit? Somebody you notice maybe with an attitude toward street people? Somebody who sets himself apart?"

Jimmy Archibald thinks a minute, then shakes his head. "I can't honestly say," he replies. "I mean, except for a few souls, I don't have the time or the energy to get to know everyone who walks through the door. Most of them are hurting. And there may well be a bad apple in that crowd, but if he's there, I don't know him. I'm a weekend preacher, Mr. Parisman. I talk about Jesus. I tell folks how much good he's done for me. How happy I am to get to know him. Beyond that, I really couldn't tell you."

"Well, it was just a shot in the dark, really. Funny," I say, "you'd think with all the people this guy's butchered around here that we'd have more to go on. That he'd make a mistake. You know, leave us something behind. A fingerprint, or a toothpick with his DNA on it. Anything."

"Oh, he probably will," Reverend Jimmy says. "It's a matter of time before all these horrible things come to an end. You'll find him. You know why? Because whoever he is, I'm sure there's a part of him that really wants to be caught."

"You think so?"

"I don't think it, Mr. Parisman. I know it's true. God doesn't want his creatures to live in fear. That's not how it works."

In spite of his assurances, I'm at loose ends. I reach for a paper napkin and meticulously wipe the stray flakes from my chocolate croissant from the table. They're beautiful, I think, these glossy steel tables at the Café Maxx. Almost works of art. Jimmy Archibald watches me for a minute, then he sighs, slips on his sunglasses, gets to his feet, and takes two steps toward the door. "Oh, Reverend, before you go—"

He turns. "Yes?"

"Just one more question." I throw him a smile. "It's probably nothing."

"Another shot in the dark?"

"Exactly."

"Go ahead, then."

"Does the name Hayden mean anything to you?"

"Hayden?"

"Yeah, there's this other case that may or may not be linked to these homeless murders. We've never talked about it. A young woman named Maria. I'm trying to hunt down her killer, too."

"She was homeless?"

"No, she was just a poor kid trying to make a living."

"And how does this person relate to that?"

"Hayden was a man she dated sometimes. It was in the same neighborhood as these other killings. I don't know, I just thought, since all these folks attended your weekend get-togethers, maybe the name would ring a bell."

He takes off his sunglasses and reclaims his seat. His face has suddenly grown somber. "You know," he says, "there was a fellow named Hayden in our congregation. But it was some time ago.

He was hard to read. Never said anything. Never smiled. Never clapped his hands. Never joined in when folks started singing. Never dropped an offering on the plate when it came around. A hard man. I often wondered why he bothered to come."

"You wouldn't know where I could find him, would you?"

He shakes his head emphatically. "He's been gone a while, like I say. And I couldn't have told you much about him even when he was here."

"I see. Well, that's something, I guess. Glad I asked."

"Tell you the truth, Mr. Parisman, when he finally stopped showing up for services, it was a relief. I felt like a great stone had been lifted from my shoulders. I don't know how to describe it more than that."

CHAPTER 20

As I'm driving back to Park La Brea, the cell phone rings. It's Omar.

"There's good news and bad news," he says.

"I hate it when you start like that."

"Okay," he says at last. "I have bad news. Ramon tailed that Jack Harper fellow."

"And? Did anything come of it?"

"He got a short visit that evening from his boyfriend. He was gone by eight. After that, nothing."

"So what's so terrible?"

"Well," Omar says, "Ramon means well, you know, but he and Carlos are sorta green at this detective thing."

"Yeah."

"Well, Ramon told Carlos about Harper, and Carlos mentioned it in passing to Julio."

"He didn't."

"Yes, he did. And Julio—you know how he's out for blood over Maria? Well, Julio and his boys paid a visit to Jack Harper a little while ago."

"They didn't kill him, did they?"

"Not quite, but they beat him up pretty bad. Trashed his apartment, too."

"How do you know all this, Omar?"

"They bragged to Carlos about it afterwards. They also talked with Jack Harper. He said he didn't know anything about anyone named Maria, that he was gay, that he didn't give a fuck about women. I don't think they believed him when he said that. And besides—just between you and me—Julio's not so fond of gays. Anyway, that's the story."

I feel an itch at the back of my skull. "This isn't good. Malloy's not going to appreciate this."

"You don't have to tell him, do you? I mean, what's the point?"

"What's the point? What's the point? I finally come up with a lead in this case, somebody who lives in the neighborhood, who has a bad past and a plausible motive, and Julio and his goons go and beat the shit out of him. Malloy is looking into his record as we speak. Don't you see? The idea was to watch him, Omar, just watch and wait. Give him a chance to fuck up."

"I know," Omar says. "I get it, I'm sorry, man."

"Now he's a basket case. Is he in the hospital?"

"For sure. Carlos rushed down there just in time to watch the ambulance take him away. He followed them to Cedars-Sinai."

"Well, if he ever leaves the hospital, his days as a serial killer are over. That's if he was the killer. Now, we'll probably never know."

*   *   *

Malloy meets me at Harper's place on Curson less than an hour later. He's got a search warrant in his hip pocket, not that anyone's around to read it. He's also got Jason and Remo in tow. And a photographer, a young fellow named Fong. Fong has two cameras around his neck and a canvas bag on his shoulder. He's a model of efficiency, ready to start clicking away the minute he walks through the door.

We chat briefly with the manager, a tanned, earnest guy in his forties. "Call me Roger," he says. He shifts the beer can he's holding from his right hand to his left, so we can all shake good and proper. "Roger's my middle name, but what the heck—that's what

I go by." First thing I notice is his Midwestern accent. Minnesota? South Dakota? Somewhere. We climb the stairs and he lets us in with his master key. The second thing I see is that Roger's not married anymore; there's a pale band of skin on the fourth finger where the wedding ring used to be. What else? The brown hair is thin and receding at the top, he hasn't shaved in days, and even though it's not quite there yet, he's clearly working on a paunch. Hawaiian shirt, cargo shorts, flip flops. Put all that together, and I'm guessing his wife left him, he lost his real job, and now here he is, bewildered, but trying to settle into the grand routine of apartment management. Welcome to L.A.

"I didn't know Mr. Harper," he says. "I mean, I don't know any of these folks, to be honest. I just took over here the last week in January." He pauses to survey the chaos in the living room. His eyes widen. "Jeez," he says, "I didn't think people lived like this."

"People don't live like this," Jason corrects him. "Not unless other people come along and beat the shit out of them."

"I guess," he says. "Jeez."

He leaves us alone and retreats back downstairs to his own quarters.

Malloy turns to Jason and Remo. "Who called the ambulance?" he wants to know. "It obviously wasn't Roger."

"Nice lady in 14B," Remo says, looking down at his notes. "Frieda Weinstein. "She heard the ruckus, waited for it to stop, then came over. The door was open, that's what she told the dispatcher, anyway. She didn't want to intrude. Door was open, radio was on, and there he was. That's all we know so far."

"There's probably more she can tell you," Malloy says, and points across the hall with his thumb.

Jason and Remo nod, and shuffle out.

Fong has wandered into the bedroom, where he's busy snapping pictures.

"So what do you think?" I ask.

"What do I think? I'll tell you. I think Omar needs to find some new assistants. Or at least teach them to keep their fucking mouths shut. That's number one. Number two, I'd like to grab Julio and turn his face into oatmeal. Number three, I don't know, Amos. Number three, I was getting hopeful, but now it seems like we're right back where we started."

"Maybe not," I say. We walk around the detritus of the room, picking up papers, opening drawers, examining *tchotchkes* on his coffee table and the half dozen large art books on his shelf. "For one thing, if he was our guy, maybe he left something incriminating around here. A hammer. A pair of gloves. A hit list. Who knows, maybe you can link his DNA to one of the crime scenes."

"Possibly."

"And for another, after he's out of critical care, you can certainly grill him, see if he breaks. You could say you have witnesses. You could suggest he might end up behind bars again if he doesn't talk. He's tough, okay, but he won't fancy that idea. Also, you can put the screws to Amory Blevins right now."

"What'll that accomplish? Sounds like all Blevins has done so far is pay him for his services. And I'm not talking about his services in the bedroom."

"No, but the fact that you're onto them will make Amory nervous. He's got his happily married image to maintain. He's got plans. At a minimum you can end his political career."

"That's not what cops are paid for, Amos. Even if I agree with you, and I do, it's not my job."

"All right. You leave that part to me."

"You do whatever the hell you want," he says, frowning. "I just want the body count to stop. The sooner the better."

"Well, if he was our killer, he's out of business now, right? For the next six months, for sure. Hell, maybe forever. That's good news."

"Don't try to cheer me up," Malloy says as I head for the door. "And don't worry anymore about Harper. We'll keep our eye on him. He's not going anywhere."

*   *   *

Shelly calls me later that evening. At that moment I'm feeling low and lost, and just like that I give in to his nostalgic desire for community. Okay, fine, I tell him, you win, I'll meet you for the Jews Who Eat. Shelly's pleased, I can hear it in his voice. About time, *boychik*, he says, but I always knew you'd come around in the end. You know why? Because in the end, you're one of us, there's no denying. I tell him I wouldn't be so smug about that, and straight away he says sure, sure, whatever. But you're gonna have a good time, don't worry, you won't regret it. We're harmless, most of us. Then he starts talking about Arlene Zimmer again, how delightful she is, and she still has her figure, you know what I mean? I do, I say, I know just what you mean, and suddenly it's like we're hormonal teenagers again, hanging out in his upstairs bedroom with the surly James Dean poster, oohing and aahing over the preposterously beautiful models in his *Playboy* collection, turning the pages one by one. It's nice, I tell him, when a girl keeps her figure, but now I'm already thinking this is a big mistake. Not because of Loretta, Shelly's right about that. Loretta wouldn't care, she's moved on. But I can't do this to Mara.

"Shelly," I say all of a sudden, "you know something? This Saturday lunch is not going to work for me. I just checked my calendar and realized I have a couple people left to interview about these murders. It's literally life or death, man. I'm sorry."

"Life or death?" he says. "Life or death? Well, since you put it that way. I wouldn't want a tuna melt to get in the way of life or death."

*   *   *

Omar has a sheepish expression on his face when I walk through the door the following afternoon. The office is empty. He's got the overhead fan on, and his shirt sleeves are rolled up to his elbows, like he's just about to get down to work. There's a manila folder in front of him.

"Am I interrupting?" I say. The door squeals shut behind me.

"No way, man. It's only the two of us." He points me to a seat opposite his desk. "In fact, it may soon be only the two of us from now on."

"What do you mean?"

"I just fired Carlos, that's what I mean."

"Yeah, but you still have Ramon."

He wags his head. "Ramon's friends with Carlos. They go way back. He may be gone by the end of the week. Wouldn't surprise me." He flips open the manila folder. It's a stack of handwritten job applications, I see, maybe half a dozen in all. Each one has a black and white photo neatly paper clipped in the top right-hand corner.

"Carlos made a mistake," I say.

"No, man," says Omar. "It was me. My mistake. I should have trained them better before I gave them something like this. Told them they needed to be more discreet. Keep their mouths shut, you know."

"Everybody makes mistakes."

"Yeah, but this may have cost us the killer."

"You spoke with Malloy?"

He nods. "An hour ago. Right after that I told Carlos he had to go. We couldn't keep him."

"Did you tell him why?"

"Sure I did. He couldn't see it at first. He has lots of pride, you know. But in the end I think he understood." Omar pushes one of the applications away and glances at the one underneath.

"Good jobs are hard to come by. Especially for a kid from the *barrio*. Are you sure Ramon's gonna quit?"

He looks at me. "No. Ramon hasn't said a word. But he talked to Carlos. It's just a feeling. My intuition."

I ask him about Lourdes then, try to shift the mood a little, and as soon as I mention her name, he brightens up. Tells me she may be pregnant. It's not for sure yet, but she's late with her period, and that doesn't usually happen in her family. She's going to see the doctor next week.

The phone rings then. It's Ramon. I only hear half the conversation, and of course it's in rapid Spanish, but it sounds like
he wants to take a few days off to think about things. Not that
he's quitting, not yet. Omar is patient. He nods as he talks. His
voice goes soft.

"Ramon's a good man," he says after he hangs up. "He's trying
to see the big picture." And with that, Omar slips the job applications back inside the manila folder and closes it. "What do you say
we go have a drink?"

We walk three blocks through the glare to a bar called El Coy-
ote Azul. It's dark and cozy inside. If you're too tall, you have to
duck your head under a piñata just past the door, and there's happy
music coming out of a jukebox in the corner. We find a wooden
table and order a couple of Negro Modelos. The waitress brings us
chips and guacamole too, even though we haven't asked.

Omar seems more relaxed here. "This is my second office," he
confides in me. "You can talk to people here and they won't get
uptight. Not like that other place."

We nurse our beers and dip into the guacamole. There are a few
other souls perched on stools at the counter studying their drinks,
but it's still too early in the day. Another hour, I figure, before the
working stiffs shuffle in.

"You haven't seen any more of Julio, have you?" This is a sensi-
tive subject, I know. But the old detective in me feels like I have to
keep asking.

"Why do you want to know?" he says. "Hasn't he caused enough
trouble?"

"Of course," I say. "But think about it. Without Julio, we'd
never have met Tita."

"Yeah, so what?"

"Look, Omar, this is important: Tita told Julio about Maria and
Hayden. Maybe she didn't know it at the time, but she remembered that Maria thought he was weird. Hayden is an odd name
for a Black man, don't you think?"

"I don't know," he says.

"Trust me, it is. I've never met any. But then, just the other day, Archibald told me that he knew someone once named Hayden, along with the three other dead street people we're investigating. And guess what? They all belonged to his church at one time or another. Isn't that amazing? It's starting to line up."

"Congratulations, man. Now all you have to do is find him."

"Which won't be easy. In fact, it'll probably be harder now, because of all the mistakes that were made."

"You mean because Carlos told Julio?"

"That was one. But only because it triggered an even bigger one. Julio's boys didn't wait like they should have."

"No," Omar says, "that's not how he runs his business." He finishes his beer, signals the waitress for another. Did I want more? I put up my hand. No, *basta*, enough.

"So here's my latest theory: Carlos tells Julio, and Julio sends his goons over to Harper's apartment without thinking it through. Or thinking maybe he could end this problem the old-fashioned way and that would be that."

"But then they beat up the wrong guy," Omar says.

"Possibly," I say. "Harper *could* be Hayden, who knows? I mean, the names do sound alike, don't they? Maybe the Reverend got it wrong."

"Okay, sure."

"And from all I hear, Harper is a mean, nasty sonofabitch. And he's in bed with Amory Blevins, that puff face we went to see speak at the church last month."

I get a blank look.

"The president of the Mid-City Merchants Association. Remember him?"

"When you say in bed, what are you talking about?"

"I mean, in bed."

Omar rolls his eyes, takes a long swallow from his second bottle of beer. "You better have another one, too. This is beginning to sound like a long night."

CHAPTER 21

Malloy tells me he has a morning doctor's appointment on Brighton Way in Beverly Hills, so we agree to meet afterwards at Nate 'n Al's around the corner. Nate 'n Al's is another deli, and because it's in Beverly Hills, it's more upscale than Canter's. More expensive, too, but they give you more pastrami than you can possibly eat, and the waitresses aren't as world-weary. Rich people favor Nate 'n Al's, elderly men in loafers with no socks on; also, writers and movie directors and young buxom girls in shorts and sunglasses. What's not to like?

I'm waiting for him in a booth when he comes in. He's holding his right arm.

"What happened?" I ask.

"Oh, the usual," he says. "They took blood and the new nurse there couldn't find a decent vein, so she worked me over. I'll be okay." He plops down and sighs, glances at the menu in front of him.

"You want coffee?" I ask. "That's what I'm having. Also, matzo brei. I couldn't resist."

"What's that?"

"Fried matzo. Think of it as Jewish French toast. I'll let you taste it."

He nods. "First, I need some orange juice, Amos. Something cold and sweet."

I signal to the waitress and he orders.

Once we have our drinks and the matzo brei is in front of me I ask him about Harper.

"He still can't tell us much. Jason and Remo tried to get a statement from him at the hospital, but seeing as how his jaw is broken and wired shut, and he's pretty doped up, in a way it doesn't matter, does it?"

"What do you mean?"

"Well, Omar told us what happened. We're never going to be able to arrest anybody for it, so it's a dead end."

I take the extra plate they gave me and fork some matzo brei over. "Here, Bill, try this. It'll put hair on your chest."

He smiles, tastes it. "Not bad," he says. "Comfort food."

"Exactly. What I ate as a child."

He sips his orange juice. "We did search his apartment. That was interesting."

"Any blood-stained hammers lying around?"

"No. Just a bunch of gay magazines and some racy photos of his boyfriend, that guy, Amory what's-his-name."

"Blevins."

"Blevins, right. Naked shots of Blevins."

"Well, that's not a crime."

"Only among devout Catholics," he says. "And not all of them, either."

"But you're going to keep your eye on him, aren't you?" I ask. "I mean, when he finally goes home?"

"Oh sure," Malloy says. "Even all beat up, he's still the only suspect we've got." He leans forward. "We also looked deeper into Mr. Blevins, just for the hell of it. He's been on the edge of things, no real record. Just a lot of lawsuits and dropped charges. Smoke," he says, raising a cautionary finger, "but never a fire."

"That's him, all right. I don't think you have to worry much about him killing anybody."

Then I tell him about Reverend Jimmy's storefront church near Fairfax High. What a coincidence it was that all the victims plus someone named Hayden attended there at one time or another.

"So what are you saying?" he asks. "That they knew each other?"

"Maybe. Or that something happened at that church, and it set Hayden off."

"Something set Hayden off, that's for damn sure. Or Harper. Or whoever."

"But if it's confined to the church, that's good," I say. "Because only a few dozen people ever attend."

He gives me a blank look.

"Well, don't you see? It's not random. It means all the other street people—the ones who've never set foot in that church—they don't have to worry. Hayden is working from a much smaller pool."

"I can't tell you how relieved that makes me feel." He rolls his eyes and with his straw finishes the last of his orange juice.

The rest of the meal is small talk. He tells me about Jessie. About this cat she wants to adopt from the shelter, and how he's on the fence about it. Not that he hates animals, mind you. It's just one more thing to think about, and at his stage of life, he's tired of thinking. "Besides," he adds, "it's a black cat. Bad luck. Who goes looking for bad luck?"

I ask him if he's heard any news from the Mississippi Bureau of Mental Health.

He wags his head. "They're looking into it. There might still be a file on Mr. Hayden, but like I told you, it was a long time ago, and these things move around. Even the facility where they held him back then is history. They closed it down ten years ago. God knows what happened to the paperwork."

"Maybe they made duplicates?"

He shrugs. "It's Mississippi, Amos. Remember who you're dealing with."

*   *   *

That afternoon, I call Daisy Cooper. "It's Friday, Ms. Cooper. How'd you like to visit your old church over on Rosewood?"

"Oh," she says, "I'd love to. Only I have no way, you know, to get there."

"That's why I called," I say. "I'm feeling religious all of a sudden. It's Friday and I need a date."

"In that case, I'd be delighted." She says the meeting begins around seven, so I should pick her up by 5:30—"just so we won't be late, you know. I'll leave a note for my Naomi. She won't be home until later and I wouldn't want her to worry."

After I hang up with her I put in a call to the Reverend Jimmy, just to double-check the time and to make sure he really wouldn't mind having an old Jewish white guy in his midst.

"I told you you'd be welcome, didn't I?" he says.

"Yeah, you said that, but it's still kind of foreign territory for me."

"It's a house of worship," he says. "One's about the same as another in my experience."

"Not quite. I mean, we never gave it up for Jesus at my synagogue, as I remember. Just wasn't done, if you know what I mean."

"No, I guess not."

Then I mention I'm bringing Daisy along, that she's been missing it.

"That's very kind of you," he says.

"Oh, no, not at all. It's the least I can do. She's been so helpful in this investigation. I would never have gotten this far without her."

"Yes, well, she knew so many of the congregants. I'm not surprised."

*   *   *

I tell Mara not to expect me for dinner, then I spend a lot of time at Park La Brea trying on different pants and shirts and coats and staring at myself in the mirror. I don't want to be overdressed. On the other hand, I don't want to embarrass Daisy and look like I'm slumming, just because it's a poor community we're going to. I'd like to blend in, but given my complexion and the capacity of the building, that's unlikely. In the end, I choose the most conservative outfit in my closet—black slacks, a blue linen shirt Mara gave me, a black tie, and a black sports jacket. "You look like you're going to a funeral," I say to myself. Then, thinking I might get lucky and run into Hayden, I strap on my gun and head out the door.

Traffic is heavy, and by the time I finally turn onto Daisy's block in Highland Park, the sun is beginning to set. *We're going to have to hurry*, I think, *or we'll be late*. I pull up in front and start walking up the front path. As I reach the bottom porch step, I notice her door is slightly ajar, which is odd. Daisy's a trusting soul, and this neighborhood isn't as bad as where she came from. It's not smart, though. I take the steps two at a time and tap on the open door. "Hello? Daisy? Anybody home?"

Inside is nothing but silence. I take a tentative step in. "Hello," I call out, louder this time. Maybe she's in the bathroom freshening up, or upstairs. Maybe she was going to wait for me on the porch, which is why she opened the door in the first place. Maybe she just forgot something and went back to retrieve it.

I glance into the living room, the one with all the porcelain figurines. That's when I see her. She's leaning back on the sofa in a long white gown, her hands demurely in her lap, her eyes closed. There's no color in her cheeks. It's almost like she's praying, except for the dark red stains on her chest that run down to the floor, soaking the carpet. I walk over, bend down, put two fingers against her neck to check for a pulse. Nothing. Then I reach instinctively into my pocket, pull out my phone and dial 9-1-1. Even if an ambulance came in thirty seconds, I know it wouldn't matter. Still, you have to go through the motions.

Whoever shot her walked in through the front door. That doesn't explain much; Daisy would have welcomed Attila the Hun with a smile and cup of tea. And I'm standing there, pacing with my back to the windows, talking to the dispatcher. She wants to know if anyone else is hurt. What kind of injuries are you describing? Should she call the police? Just an ambulance? "An ambulance?!" I'm shouting. "An ambulance? I don't fucking know—the woman is dead, for chrissakes."

Then I hear the blast right behind me. A giant, sucking *whoomph!* Window glass shatters everywhere, glass sprays over my head and shoulders. Porcelain lords and ladies go flying, legless, headless. The mirror above the mantle breaks into a dozen jagged pieces. I drop the phone and hit the floor beside Daisy. My shirt soaks up some of her wet blood from the carpet. I yank out my gun and peer cautiously over the rim of the sofa and onto the street. Another blast drops me down beside her. Squealing tires as a car races off. Then silence.

I climb to my feet, creep slowly out to the porch. I crouch down, the gun dangling from my hand. A siren wails from far away. An ambulance. Or maybe a neighbor who called the cops. More than likely a neighbor. Maybe that crusty old coot across the street.

*   *   *

Two hours later I'm still around. Naomi has yet to come home; she's supposedly on the road and her phone's turned off, so she doesn't know about her mom. I'm sitting on the top porch step with Lieutenant Malloy. My shirt sleeves and my shoes are covered with Daisy's blood; when I run my hand through my hair, fine bits of glass and sheetrock sprinkle down like rain. LAPD from the Highland Park station are everywhere. They're very nice. Most of them have names like Cuevas and Ortiz and Herrera. There must be twenty cops here, cordoning things off, searching for clues, calling in to headquarters. Yellow crime tape rings the yard, and unless you can prove you live here, Daisy's street is closed to through traffic.

"I was taking her to church," I tell Malloy. "She was my date."

He nods. "Looks like you showed up a minute or two behind the killer," he says.

"She was still warm, yeah."

"And he must have spotted you from his car. That's why he started shooting."

"Maybe." I shake my head. "Although why didn't he just drive off? Why'd he need to blow the living room to hell with a shotgun? If all he wanted was Daisy, well, that was mission accomplished, right?"

"Good question," Malloy says.

We're silent for a while. Then Malloy turns to me. "You think she knew him? I mean, she let him in. There was no forced entry."

I shrug. "She let everyone in, Bill. She was a generous soul."

"A little too generous." He gets to his feet, offers me a hand up. "Here, old man. There's nothing more we can do. Let's leave this to the local constabulary."

I stand and glance down at my shoes, which look like I've been tramping through mud. "Don't you think I should stay and talk with her daughter? This is going to be like walking into hell for her."

"And just how do you plan on making it any easier?" he asks.

We stare at each other for a second. "You're right," I say. "You're right, the police know as much as I do."

I drive slowly back to Mara's place. It's only around eight and she's surprised to see me. "I thought you said you'd be at church," she says. Then she notices my shirt and shoes. "Amos, honey, what happened?"

"Someone shot Daisy Cooper just before I got there," I say. "She was sitting there all alone on the sofa. She had this strange, satisfied look on her face, like she'd just heard the most wonderful story."

"Was she dead?"

"Dead? Maybe. I don't know. Maybe she was still alive, but there was nothing I could do. She had no color, no pulse. And then, while I was calling for an ambulance, someone took a shot at me, too. Obviously, they missed."

Mara's embracing me now. "Look at you," she says, astonished and scared and thankful, all at the same time. "Look at you, my God."

CHAPTER 22

The next day my phone rings. It's Malloy, and he's in a better mood. "Guess what?" he says. "Mississippi came through for us. They found Hayden's file."

"Terrific," I say.

"More than that," he says. "Seems they took his fingerprints way back when. And we matched them to the partials we found on that shopping cart on Western. So we know for sure he's here in L.A., and he obviously had a hand in that murder, at least. Probably others, too."

"Yeah. Now, all we have to do is find him."

"That's why I called. I'm thinking of sending Jason and Remo around to have a serious talk with that Reverend Archibald. He's the only one who remembers him. Maybe he can give us some kind of physical description."

"Why don't you let me handle that, Bill? I know him. We've talked before. If he starts getting impromptu visits from the LAPD, well, you never know. He might not be so cooperative."

"What are you talking about?"

"He's a Black man, Lieutenant. He's careful, deliberate. He's someone who's pulled himself up by his bootstraps. He also works with poor folks and street people."

"So?"

"So they don't always have the tightest relationships with cops.

And Jason and Remo? I mean, it's your call, but they're not known for their bedside manner."

Malloy is momentarily silent. "Okay," he says at last, "okay, fine, you talk to him first. But stay in touch, huh? And try to remember, will you—you're a civilian, Amos. Keep your head down. Last night was a little too close for comfort."

"You're telling me."

*　　*　　*

"Goddamn," Omar says, when I recount what happened at Daisy's. This is about as close as he's going to get to feeling my pain. Then, he says, "Well, I guess that eliminates Jack Harper as a suspect. I mean, he's still in the hospital, right?"

"Sure. And even if he wasn't, he wouldn't be in any shape yet to drive, let alone fire a shotgun."

"No. But that still leaves Blevins," Omar says.

"Forget about him. Amory Blevins doesn't like getting his hands dirty," I say. Then I tell him what Malloy told me about the fingerprints from the Mississippi mental health folks, how they match the ones on the shopping cart.

Omar says we should get together with Maria's friend, Tita, see if she can help. "Tita quit working the street," he says. "After what happened to Maria, she's had a change of heart. She's back in school. Taking business classes at Cal State LA. I'll see if we can't meet her for coffee or something."

"Maybe you should talk to her by yourself," I say. "I mean, I don't want to spook her. What if she thinks I'm a cop?"

"It's okay," he says, "she's a big girl. She'll talk to both of us."

We meet at Los Compadres on Sunset. It's Omar's choice, not because of the food, which isn't bad—it's one of those old-fashioned Mexican joints only gringos go to—I think he really chose it because of the flaming margaritas and also because it's so dark no one would ever notice us. You almost need a flashlight to see the menu. Tita and Omar are sitting in a booth when I slide in beside her and shake her hand.

"Tita," Omar says, "this is Amos Parisman. The guy I told you about. My friend. He's trying to find out what happened to Maria."

"Nice . . . nice to meet you," she whispers.

She's a shy, slender girl in a simple flowered tank top and tight jeans. If I had to guess, I'd say she was twenty-five. She doesn't look at me directly. In fact, her dark eyes never stop scanning the room. Her hair is newly blond and cropped into a boyish cut, and she has a large black plastic purse that she keeps close by her side.

We order food and flaming margaritas. Tita's not very hungry, and she passes on a margarita in favor of an iced tea.

Omar dives right in, asks whether Maria talked about what Hayden looked like. "Anything physically weird about him? Was he tall? Short? Fat? Bald? Old?"

She frowns. "I don't remember that, no. Maybe he was in his forties or fifties, but it's just a guess. She never said."

"Did she ever mention where he lived," he asks, "or what he did for a living?"

She shakes her blond head. "I don't think they talked like that. If they did, she never said nothing. Most of the time, it was—you know—just business."

I lean forward. "Now, Tita, I know this may be hard for you, but it would help if you could tell us exactly what kind of—business—this Hayden usually had in mind."

She covers her mouth for a moment. "Okay," she says finally. "Okay, I will tell you. If it will take him off the street." She sips her iced tea and then she begins. "Sometimes," she says, "he'd meet her on the corner. They never had an arrangement, but he would come for her when he felt like it and he would take her by cab to a certain hotel on Wilshire. He would act like a perfect gentleman in the taxi, but then, the minute they got into the room, he would change."

"What do you mean?"

"Maria said he would yell at her and call her bad names and order her to take off all her clothes. He'd make her walk around on her hands and knees. He would stand there and have her touch his . . . his—you know—with her mouth and kiss it until it got very hard, and then he would grab her from behind. Sometimes he would grab her by the throat. His hands would leave marks on her. He would say all kinds of terrible things in her ear while he was doing this."

"What kinds of things?"

"She never told me the words, but it scared her. He wanted to kill her, that's what it seemed to her."

"And was the sex between them always like this? Did he ever ask for other things?"

She nods. "Sometimes he didn't want to touch her at all. Sometimes he brought a suitcase full of outfits for her to put on and parade around in."

"Sexy outfits?"

"No. Just clothes. Well, not ordinary clothes. Things like an old woman would wear. Nothing sexy. Many of them weren't so clean. They smelled, you know, stale. And most of the time, the clothes didn't even fit well, Maria told me. They were too large or too tight, and she looked awful in them, but still, he made her walk around in front of him."

"Nothing else?"

"What do you mean?"

"Well," I say, "sometimes men ask women to put on certain things and when they do, that's when they get excited."

"She didn't say nothing about that. She said all he did was look at her. It would have been better if that's what turned him on. But it never did. He just stared and stared at her. He told her not to talk. Not to smile. He told her to keep moving around. It made her crazy."

A few minutes later, Tita slips out of the booth and loops her purse over her shoulder. "I have to go," she says. "I have a test to study for. I'm sorry. I hope . . . I'm sorry."

Omar pulls out five twenties and puts it in her hand. "For talking with us, Tita. Here. *Gracias*. I know this isn't easy."

She takes the money without looking at it, stuffs it in her pocket. There's no reaction, no surprise, no what's this for? "I'm just trying to move on with my life. You know." That's all she says.

And then she's gone.

Omar looks at me. "Well, at least he's not your normal, run-of-the-mill pervert."

"Yeah, that's a real plus," I say.

The waiter comes by. Omar asks for a coffee and a flan for dessert. When he looks questioningly in my direction, I shake my head. "No," I say, "Too rich."

I watch while he eats, and we go over the events of Daisy Cooper's death once more. It's like shoveling sand at the beach; every once in a while, you never know when, something new turns up. A feather. A seashell. An old rusty dime.

"Daisy died because somebody wanted to shut her up. Maybe she could have told us something about Hayden. But what I still don't get," I tell him, "is why he bothered shooting at me. I mean, what was the point?"

Omar puts down his coffee. "To kill you, man. Is that so hard to understand? He was fucking trying to kill you."

"But he didn't know me, Omar. I was incidental. He didn't know I'd show up. He was after Daisy, and he got her. She let him in. He put two bullets in her chest. He shot her at close range. There was no doubt she was gone. And he was already back in his car, safe and sound. Why didn't he just drive off?"

"That's what you or I might do," Omar says. "But I think the folks back in Mississippi had him pegged from the start. He's *loco*."

*   *   *

After I leave Los Compadres, I get in the Honda, roll down the windows, and drive east on Sunset. The day has turned hazy; it's not smog exactly, but close enough to confirm the perennial bad rap about L.A. Not that I care. My mind is on Daisy Cooper and what I might have missed. I take the Pasadena Freeway back to Highland Park.

The yellow crime tape has come down from the perimeter around Daisy's house, and a carpenter has installed a fresh sheet of plywood across the front window. The police presence is gone, but as I unbuckle my seatbelt I notice a frowning guy in shorts and a Dodgers jersey staring at me from across the street. He's sitting on his front porch step with his fat arms folded and a cigarette in his hand. Why do I get the feeling he doesn't like me? Two doors down, there's a beige curtain ruffling gently to accommodate an old lady's keen observation. I wave to the man, and, to reassure him, I pull out my wallet and jiggle it in his direction. Of course, it's only my driver's license I'm flashing, but from this distance, I figure he'll think I'm a cop.

He nods and I walk confidently up the path. The wind chimes are tinkling; it's almost as if nothing has changed. I'm taking a chance that her daughter Naomi won't be home at this hour. You never know, but given that her mother has just been murdered it's pretty unlikely she'd go straight back to work. I wouldn't, at least. So I knock. After a moment, the door cracks open and I'm looking at a younger version of Daisy, a strong, middle-aged Black woman, her hair pulled back in a ponytail. There are bags under her eyes. She has clearly been weeping.

"You must be Naomi," I say. I hand her my business card. "Amos Parisman. I was going to take your mom to church the other day. I got here right after she was shot. I'm so sorry."

She nods, lets me in. "Right. They mentioned you were here. What is it you want?"

"Just to talk," I say. "If this is a bad time—"

She shakes her head. "There's no good time. But I'm afraid we can't sit in the living room. Not yet. It's still a mess."

"That's okay. No need to apologize."

"I'm not apologizing, Mr."—she looks at my card—"Mr. Parisman. I'm just heartsick." We go into the kitchen. There are a few dirty dishes waiting to be washed in the sink. On the table there's a white plastic tablecloth with pastel flowers on it, a pair of ceramic salt and pepper shakers and a blue plate with some cold, uneaten toast left over from the morning. She points me to a chair and takes one opposite. "I didn't get home until late." She wipes away a speck of dust from her eye. Or maybe it's a tear, I can't tell. "The cops stopped me at the corner. They weren't going to let me down the block. My own block. Can you believe that?" She smiles bitterly. "You never think about these things."

"No."

"One day you're fine. You get up in the morning, you brush your teeth, you've got a job to do, everything's rolling along like it should. And then," she says, "you come home. To this." She waves her arm dismissively. "You come home and your whole world's upside down."

"It happens," I say quietly. "Not usually all at once, but it happens."

"And now here I am trying to think about a funeral. I don't know anything about funerals. What Mom would have wanted. We never talked about that."

"No, not many people do."

"She was going to Heaven. She used to say that all the time. But that's as far as it ever went, you know. Just a phrase. Going to Heaven."

"Maybe you can talk to Reverend Archibald about arrangements," I say. "She trusted him. Maybe he can help with the funeral."

She turns and reaches behind her to pull a Kleenex from the box on the counter, puts it to her nose, and blows gently. "That's an idea," she says. "That's a good idea, yes. Thanks, maybe I'll call him."

"Or I can have him get in touch with you, if you like. I'm going to see him again before too long. He's lost a number of parishioners in the last month or so. Daisy was just the latest."

She stares at me long and hard. I've seen a lot of people grieve, and they touch on all the emotions they can think of before they come out the other end. That's the way it is. "Daisy"—she says now, her voice rising slowly in anger—"Daisy was not just the latest. She was my mother."

"Of course," I say. "She was my friend, too, Naomi. And I feel terrible I wasn't here . . . in time to save her."

She starts weeping again. Tiny tears at the edges of her eyes. "Is that why you came? To say you're sorry?"

"Partly. Because I didn't want you to feel so alone." I drum my fingers softly on the table. "And also because whoever shot your mother tried to kill me, too. I'd like to find out who he is. I'd like to bring him in."

She goes through another Kleenex, then looks up, a little more hopeful. Her nose is red, and her eyes are glistening, but clear.

We spend the afternoon looking at albums and reminiscing, what Daisy was like when she was younger, the early days of her marriage when they lived in a little house near Long Beach. Mr. Cooper, Naomi tells me, Alvin, Daisy's husband, was involved in the longshoreman's union. He had an eye for the ladies, her mother used to say whenever his name was mentioned, which wasn't often. There's a small gold-framed black-and-white wedding photo in Daisy's bedroom. She brings it out and shows it to me, then says, "That's the only piece of my father I have left, Mr. Parisman, and that was a long time ago. I can't remember much else about him. He moved out when I was seven. I don't know where he lives. I don't even know if he's alive or dead. I never saw him again."

I nod solemnly and lay the picture down on the kitchen table. "Do you think she had any enemies?" I ask.

"Enemies?" The question throws her. It's as if I'm suddenly speaking to her in Swedish.

"Okay. Not an enemy. Maybe someone who made her feel uncomfortable?"

"If she did, I never heard about it," Naomi says. "My mother was the gentlest soul on earth. She made friends everywhere she went. Everyone liked to talk with her. She would run into a poor man at the supermarket or in a parking lot—a total stranger—and twenty minutes later he'd be sitting right here in our parlor having tea."

"I understand. But she wasn't really here long enough to get to know many folks, was she?"

"No," Naomi admits. "I was beginning to introduce her to the neighborhood. When I had time, I mean. I took her to the used book sale at the library a couple of weeks ago, that kind of thing. But you're right, most of her friends go back to the church, when she lived near Fairfax."

I glance again at the framed wedding picture, then turn to Naomi directly. "I want you to think about this before you answer me," I say. "Did Daisy ever talk to you about someone at the church named Hayden? That name mean anything to you?"

"No, nothing. Why do you ask?"

"Oh," I say, "there was somebody who used to attend. That's what Reverend Jimmy said. A hard man. Never said anything. Never joined in the fun. I just thought your mom might have noticed him."

"She never told me about any Hayden. And she knew most everyone there. That's why it was so hard for her to move away, I think. They were her friends."

I tell Naomi to please count on me if she needs any help with anything at all. Then I walk out the front door, past the debris still in the living room. I pace up and down the sidewalk. The police have removed any ballistics evidence they could find, and things are pretty clean, but I go over it again anyway. It was dark when they were here poking around, and I don't want to cast any aspersions on the Highland Park officers, but you never know.

I'm still being watched by the guy in shorts and the Dodger jersey; he's like one of those garden gnomes, I think—rain or shine, he'll always be around. A couple of teenagers wander along, backpacks on their shoulders. They hold hands and pause and lean into one another and trade kisses every three or four steps. Then, afterwards, they turn back in my direction. I don't know whether they want me to notice that they're in love, or that they think I have no business looking at something so intimate and should ignore them.

I want to tell them I approve. I want to tell them they're too young to know what the hell they're getting into. I want to tell them I don't care. Somehow, all those things are true.

CHAPTER 23

The sun is fading into the Pacific when I pull into Creston Drive and park next to her Lexus. I let myself in and I notice something's different right away. And Mara has a mischievous look on her face. She takes me by the hand.

"What's up?" I ask, but she tugs me along. Then I see it. She's brought in a team of movers and they've cleared out the spare bedroom. In fact, it's completely bare: There's no more couch, or chairs; even the cute brass bed that Violet was using is gone. All that's left are the indentations in the beige rug.

"So what do you think?" she asks, as I walk around, giving it the once over.

"I don't know," I say. "What am I supposed to think?"

"You're supposed to think this would be a spectacular office for the world's oldest Jewish detective," she smiles.

I nod. "Oh, it would. You bet it would. But what about the space I already have at Park La Brea? The one I've lived in for years? That's not too shabby. And I can't be in two spaces at once, can I? Not unless I'm—you know—half-assed."

She squeezes me gently around the middle. "I sorta thought you might just want to give that one up. It costs money."

"So?"

"So I happen to know the landlady here. This one's rent-free." Then she touches my cheek. Her lips brush against mine and there's a faint taste of wine on her breath. "And when you consider the commute to see me, of course. It's so much shorter."

"Uh huh."

We hold hands and glide slowly into the living room. Part of me resonates with her proposal. It seems like the next logical step, and I'm mulling it over, giving it the proper respect it deserves. I'm quite fond of this woman, I tell myself, and she's being uncommonly generous. But another part of me, that ancient stubborn part, still can't make up its mind; that side is still tossing it around like a pancake. "What about Violet?" I ask. "Where's she going to sleep?"

"Violet? Violet can stay right here whenever she comes," she says, patting the couch as we settle into it. "We've talked it over and she's fine with the idea of you living here, Amos. I know she hasn't said much, but she likes you a lot. She thinks you're funny."

"Tell you what," I say. "I know what you're saying makes sense, but I haven't changed my address in donkey's years. I'd sorta want to tie this case up in a ribbon first before I do anything momentous like move in with you."

"Why are you so worried? It's not about Loretta, is it?"

"No. Loretta would approve."

"Then what?"

"It's not anything. Nothing at all." I hold my thoughts for a minute. If we're going to go forward with this, then she needs to hear the truth. "I'm really a simple person, Mara," I say as I wrap my arm around her.

"What's that mean?"

"That means I don't do two different things at once. I don't tell jokes and tap dance. I try, but I get in trouble when that happens."

She stares at me. "I don't believe you're simple at all. But if that's what you need to do, okay then, I'll wait." She kisses me again. "Just so you know," she whispers, "you don't have to worry, the rent's not going up anytime soon."

*   *   *

I don't make it down to the church until Sunday evening. I'm late because I can't find any decent parking nearby and end up in a lot five blocks away. By the time I get there the place is full and all the folding chairs are taken. Reverend Jimmy's up on the stage in his purple robe. The gold Styrofoam cross is shimmering, floating like a star in space right behind him, and folks are clapping their hands or shouting, or every now and then raising them high up in the air, which I guess is how they like to pray. The crowd is mostly Black and older, but there are also a few Latinos in pressed white long-sleeved shirts and jeans, the women in flowered dresses. There are even a couple of burly, unshaven white guys in baseball caps hunched in the corner.

The stage lights are on and Jimmy is sweating and pacing back and forth with the Bible. "The time is at hand," he says. "You've suffered long enough. The time is at hand." He puts the back of his hand to his head and closes his eyes as if thinking. Or maybe he's waiting for a message from on high. "Jesus knew it even then," he says. "You can't wait forever."

"No sir!" someone shouts agreeably in the front row.

"You can't wait forever. Not if you're suffering. Not if you're cold and all alone. Not if you're hungry."

"Amen!"

"Not if you're wanting and never getting. Not if you sleep in the dust. The Bible doesn't allow for that. No how. No way. No sir."

"No sir!" several people shout at once.

"The Bible tells us clearly. There's an end to your suffering. Let me say it again: there's an end to your suffering. An end to your pain." He scans the audience. His hand touches his heart. "I'm here to tell you. Believe me. Please, you gotta believe me. Oh, it may not come today. Or tomorrow. You can't mark it down." He wags his finger. "You can't put it on your calendar for next Wednesday, no."

"No, no way!" someone shouts.

"No, that's not the way it works," Jimmy says, shaking his head and smiling. "God wants you to come to Him, He loves you, but

He wants you to come at the proper time. At the time of his own choosing. And I know, I've prayed on this and I can tell just looking at you and hearing your stories week after week. God is eager, He's eager to have you join Him before too long."

"Praise Jesus."

"Yes," Jimmy says, "praise Jesus, that's correct. That's exactly right. Praise him. For just as Jesus was lifted up into His Father's merciful arms, so will you, my brothers and sisters. So will you. Just look at how you suffer! Are you any different than our Lord? Are you less deserving?"

"No!" comes a defiant shout near me.

Jimmy rifles through the Bible until he comes to the page he wants. "It's all here," he says. "In the Book of Romans it is written: 'We rejoice in our sufferings, knowing that suffering produces endurance, and endurance produces character, and character produces hope, and hope does not disappoint us, because God's love has been poured into our hearts through the Holy Spirit which has been given to us.'"

"Amen! Praise Jesus!"

Several people are on their feet now, clapping and shouting and hugging one another. The Reverend lifts his purple-robed arms in ecstasy. He motions to his right, and two dapper Black men drag a chair onto the stage next to him. One has an old battered guitar in his hand. He's wearing a Borsolino hat and silver sunglasses. The other has a perfectly bald head and a tambourine. The guitarist sits and starts to play. The bald one with the tambourine grabs the microphone and lays down a tap dance step of his own making. Not fast or slow, but a sweet, steady *click click* shuffle you can hear throughout the room. Then a sound rises up from deep within his chest. He's got a strong tenor voice. He's singing the blues, but it's all about Jesus. *Jesus won't never let you down. Jesus won't never let you down. No suh. No suh. Come to Jesus.* The audience joins in. They seem to know this tune and it lifts them, you can feel it. It really does lift them out of their pain.

I stand there waiting until nearly everyone has left. An old man in overalls and red high-top sneakers is shuffling around, slowly and systematically folding up the chairs in groups of three and four and stacking them against the wall. Reverend Jimmy sits on the rim of the stage. He's still wearing his purple robes. Now he's smoking a cigarette, however. He's chatting with a gorgeous light-skinned woman in a very tight brown and white dress that almost touches the floor. She might be thirty, I guess. And she's not part of the homeless crowd, that's for sure. She's got long dark hair and a face that could easily be in the movies. She'd been dancing a lot; as I come nearer she looks at me defensively, and daubs her forehead with a handkerchief from her little golden purse. This is my space, her look says; you don't belong here.

"That was quite a show you put on," I say to Reverend Jimmy, extending my hand.

"I'll be going now," she says to him.

He smiles diplomatically. "Okay," he says. He leans forward and gives her a hug. Nothing too romantic. "Okay, but don't be a stranger, you hear?"

"You know I won't." And we both watch her strut toward the door.

When it clicks shut, he turns to me. "Mr. Parisman," he says. "What a pleasure. But I'm a little confused. Weren't you going to be here last Friday?"

"I meant to," I say, "but something came up."

"Oh, what was that?"

"I was bringing Daisy Cooper, you remember. And I drove out to her house to pick her up, but when I got there, she was dead."

"Dead? Daisy?" He drops his still burning cigarette on the floor. His face, which had been calm and self-assured, now looked numb. "Oh, my God. Oh, my God, what happened?"

"Someone shot her, Reverend. I'm kind of surprised you hadn't heard. It was all over the ten o'clock news that night."

"No I—I wasn't listening to the news. I mean, I was here. It was Friday. No one notified me. Oh, my God. What—what a shame." He puts his hand over his mouth, then stiffens.

"Of course. There's no way you could know."

He bends over, holds his head in his hands for a moment, closes his eyes. "Jesus," he mumbles, "what's going on?"

"I wish I knew, Reverend. It looks to me like somebody has a chip on his shoulder."

"I'm sorry," he says. "I'm not following your words. Who has a chip—what are you saying?"

"Somebody's trying to kill off your congregation one person at a time. That's what it looks like."

He picks up the remains of his smoldering cigarette from the floor and takes a short, pensive drag on it. His eyes lock with mine. "Hayden," he says, finally. "That's the only person I can think of. He knew most everyone here. And like I said before, he was a difficult man. He might be angry enough. But still, you know, still it makes no sense."

"Not to you, maybe." I take out my notepad and pen. "I'd like to hear a little more about this Hayden fellow."

"Okay, sure. I'm happy to help if I can. What do you want to know?"

"Well," I say, "for starters, what's he look like?"

"Oh, he'd be about six feet tall, I guess, heavier than me."

"And how heavy would that be?"

The Reverend scratches his head. "I'm close to one-eighty. I imagine he'd be two-ten, two-twenty, thereabouts."

"Age?"

"Late forties, early fifties."

"Any identifying marks, scars, mannerisms, things like that?"

"It's been a while. I can't recall."

"Okay, then. Any idea where he might live? Did he ever mention a street or a bar or a neighborhood? Someplace he went to after work?"

The Reverend shakes his head. "That's a tough one. That would require an extensive conversation, and I don't believe he ever exchanged more than ten words with anyone here, me included."

"So if he never said anything, where'd you get the idea that he was angry?"

"A man doesn't have to say a word to show who he is underneath," Jimmy says. "Sometimes you can see it in his eyes. Sometimes all a man has to do is look at you a certain way. You know what I'm talking about, Mr. Parisman?"

I take a seat next to him on the edge of the stage. "About how long did you deal with this man, Reverend?"

He half laughs. "How long? Lord. He was here forever, it seemed."

"And he never spoke to anyone? Really?"

"No, I'm probably overstating it. But the truth is, the only one who knew even a little bit about him was Daisy Cooper."

"They talked?"

"Now and then. Daisy could get anyone to open up. She had a gift."

"I'll give you that." I stand up then, click my pen shut, and slip my notepad into my jacket pocket. "So he was here forever, and then one day, he just stopped showing up. Is that it?"

"Not quite. Something set him off the last time he was here."

"You wanna talk about it?"

He shrugs. "It must have been a year, a year and a half ago. I can't be sure exactly, but I was riffing about love and salvation the way I do, and I was revving the folks up. Nothing out of the ordinary, I don't think. But I mentioned a line from First Corinthians—maybe you're familiar. 'Love bears all things,' I said, 'believes all things, hopes all things, endures all things.' My people need to hear that message more than most, because you know, soon as I'm through talking, many of them will be out on the street looking for a safe place to sleep."

"And that's what upset him—those words?"

"Could be. Maybe. It was like he'd been listening and listening and now he'd heard enough. All I know is he stood up and told us we were damned. We were damned and there was nothing we could do about it, and everyone here was going straight to hell. That's what he said. Straight to hell. Then he stormed out and slammed the door shut behind him."

"Huh! That must have put a damper on things."

"For a few moments, yes. No one made a sound. But you have to realize," he continues, "Hayden was such a looming presence, he was so dark, so filled with judgment, that the minute he was gone you just felt better. Like all of a sudden you could breathe again. I guess that's the only way to explain it."

"And that was the last time you saw him?"

He nods. "And I hope never to see him again."

*   *   *

The next afternoon I drop by Lieutenant Malloy's office downtown. He's drinking coffee at his desk. Every once in a while, he peels off the silver from a roll of Tums and pops one in his mouth.

"That must taste dreadful," I say as I take a seat across from him.

"Not so bad," he goes. "You wash it down with the coffee and pretty soon you don't even notice."

"Right. I shoulda thought of that."

He wags his head, smiles. "Okay, it tastes bad. But what else can you do with the kind of heartburn I got?"

"I dunno, Bill. You talk to your doctor? Maybe it's more than just all the Mexican food you eat."

"I'm trying to cut down. It ain't easy." His phone rings then. "Yeah, Remo, whatcha got?" They talk for a while. Malloy jots a few things down on a pad in front of him. "Yeah, well," he says, "that's promising. Keep at it, okay? Let me know. Yeah, yeah, I'll be here. Thanks."

He hangs up the phone and we stare at each other.

"So? Any news?"

"Maybe. Remo and Jason have been nosing around the neighborhood in Highland Park, and they think they've got something on the car Daisy's murderer was driving."

"No kidding. What are we looking for?"

"Late model Hyundai or Honda. White or silver."

"That's a million cars in Los Angeles."

"Yes," he says, "that's true. Only this one has a sunroof."

"How did they figure that out?"

"Some old guy across the street pulled his curtain back, and he caught a fleeting glimpse of the shooter. He said he saw this Black man with his head and arms out the sunroof just as he let loose with a gun."

"He's sure it was a Black man?"

"It might have been. Black or Mexican. All he saw was the back of his head. That part he thought was Black."

"I mean, I'm not saying he's wrong, but that kind of eyewitness isn't worth much."

"It's what we've got."

"Exactly. But the light wasn't great, and he was across the street, and it all happened pretty fast."

"True," Malloy says. "But we still think his take on the vehicle is about right. A couple of newlyweds out walking down the street saw a muscle car taking off just after they heard some loud booms." He touches his fingertips together. "It fits."

"What about the shell casings? That tell you anything?"

"No. Nothing he couldn't have picked up at Walmart. It's just lucky you weren't killed is all."

*   *   *

That evening, my throat starts to ache and I can barely swallow, and by the next morning when Mara takes my temperature, I'm 102. "I thought you were healthy," she says as she plumps up my pillows and pulls at the sheets. "What am I doing, getting all tangled up with another sick guy?"

"Beats me," I mumble. Then as I try to get up, I have this sudden need to shave my face, but it's no use. I never get sick, which leads me to think that there was something toxic in that unagi sushi I picked up on sale at Ralphs. For the next four days, all I do is sleep and force myself to make it to the bathroom without falling down.

Saturday morning, my phone rings. My temperature is down, and for the first time in a while I have an appetite. "Omar," I say, "where have you been?"

"You won't believe this, Amos, but last night I went to church."

"You're right, I don't believe you. Aren't you the guy that said it was all a big con? That they need a bath, not Jesus?"

"Guilty as charged, *ese*. But I decided we weren't getting any closer just talking to Tita and Julio. What I really needed to do was focus on Mr. Hayden."

"So? Don't keep me in suspense."

"So I combed my hair and went down to Reverend Jimmy's place."

"He have a crowd?"

"Oh, yeah. He got them pretty excited, too. Talked about the Rapture. How all the good people would be getting on the train and going to heaven, and how bad ones, well, it wouldn't be pretty what happened to them."

"Never mind that, Omar. Did you talk to folks about Hayden? What'd they say?"

"That's why I'm calling," he says. "I must have asked ten people there in the audience, and not one of them knew this guy, Hayden. Never heard of him."

"Maybe you asked the wrong people. You didn't talk to everyone, did you?"

"No," he admits, "not everyone. I couldn't. But it was about a third of the audience, I guess. And I picked the old-timers."

"You mean the ones that looked like they might be street people?"

"Some, yeah. And others. You know, old, but respectable."

"Folks drop in and out of that place. Reverend Jimmy says he doesn't know half the people in the room."

"Still, I drew a blank. I got nothing, Amos. For a minute I thought I was in the wrong church."

I'm silent. "I don't know what to say, Omar. Maybe you came on too strong."

"No, man. I was smooth, I tell you. I wasn't being pushy. Not at all."

"Yeah," I say, "you were smooth. But you'd still be a stranger in their eyes, wouldn't you? Did you act like a cop?"

"I—I don't know."

"I mean, maybe they took one look and decided to keep their mouths shut. Maybe you scared them, Omar."

"I'm telling you they were friendly, most of them, they were pleased to talk to me, and they never heard of no Hayden."

CHAPTER 24

To celebrate feeling better, I take a drive over to Pasadena. My dad taught me how to drive in the Rose Bowl parking lot. He figured I couldn't kill anyone there, it was just wide-open spaces. And I still like to go back to Pasadena whenever I get nostalgic about him, or wistful, or just feel at loose ends, which is often nowadays. Pasadena always seems like another country to me, another golden vision of what California could be, should have been, if anyone had had any sense.

I'm on my way back home, crawling along at five miles an hour behind a yellow Dodge pickup filled with furniture tied every which way with ropes and bungee cords. That's when a new idea pops into my head. I turn left onto Melrose and make my way through the afternoon traffic to the lot next to the Mid-City Merchants Association. The same barely shaved, handsome Iranian future movie star nods hello to me as always. He peels off a ticket, waits to be paid. Today he's wearing a white sport coat, but underneath it's blue jeans, a pink polo shirt and polished cowboy boots. Someday I'm sure I'll see him on the silver screen.

"So. We meet again," he says. It sounds forced, this line, as if he's rehearsing it for a coming audition.

I hand him my five-dollar bill as I get out of the car. "Hey, what's your name?" I ask.

"Mohammed," he says. "Only I go by Mo. It's Mo for all my head shots."

"Well, Mo, I'm not really planning to stay," I tell him. "I just need a little pertinent information."

"From me?"

"If you know the answer, yeah. In fact, I'd rather not bother Mr. Blevins. Not if I don't have to."

"You don't have to. For twenty bucks I'll even put my thinking cap on."

"Good. My question is, what kind of car does Amory Blevins drive?"

"That's all you want? Really? That's simple." He points to the end of the row at an older tan Mercedes. "That's his, right there. Next to the fence."

"He never drives anything else?"

"I've been working here for four years, man. That's his car, trust me."

We walk over to the fence. I lean against the back window and look into the Mercedes. There's nothing interesting there. Just some trade magazines and a blond Barbie doll that's missing her right arm. The front of the car is no more fruitful. I notice a few CDs on the passenger seat. Italian operas, it looks like.

"You know Mr. Blevins is married, don't you?"

"I heard that, yeah," he says. "I think he has kids, too. But I've never laid eyes on them."

I pull a crisp twenty out of my wallet. "You ever see him with a friend? Younger Black guy? Kind of rough around the edges?"

He smiles patiently. It's as if he were expecting this question all along. "You're talking about Jack Harper? I guess I'm not supposed to know about them. But so what. That's the beautiful thing about this town. Romance is always in the air."

"So you knew they were lovers? They didn't try to conceal it?"

Mo wags his head from side to side. He is beyond cynicism. "You work here long enough and you keep your eyes open, well, you see what you see. It's a free country, huh?"

I hand him the twenty, which he takes without blinking and stuffs it into his jeans. "One more thing," I say. "This Jack Harper—you ever notice what kind of car he had?"

"I haven't seen him lately, but back when he was coming around, he had a little red Porsche."

"You positive?"

He nods. "I loved that car, man. It was a classic. Black leather interior. Very clean inside. He and Mr. Blevins would go racing off around lunch time and then come back a few hours later. Two or three times a week he'd drop by."

"Thanks, Mohammed," I say. "This really helps. I'll see you in the movies." I climb back in my Honda and turn the key.

"One of these days you will, my friend."

*   *   *

Omar and his bride live on Dacotah Street in Boyle Heights, just off of 4th. Every house on the block looks pretty much the same. His is the third from the corner. It's a sand-colored bungalow with a new tile roof and fresh blue trim around the windows. A spiked, dull-orange metal fence surrounds the whole property. Built in the thirties, I'm guessing, when nobody could afford to have kids, but still, they needed a roof over their heads. I pause at the gate. Some contractor has come through and done a little renovation since then. Added solar panels on the roof. Reset the bricks on the front path. *Real estate is how you make a killing in L.A.*, I think, *even here in Boyle Heights.* The front yard is barren because of the endless drought. No trees or shrubs, and whatever grass remains is brown and brittle.

I knock on the screen door. There's a clumping sound inside and then Omar appears and lets me in. We step into the living room and he points to the couch, which is secondhand and draped with a Mexican blanket. There's a TV on a mobile stand in the corner and a few wooden end tables. A ceiling fan is churning overhead. No pretense, but it's clean and quiet and lived in. I feel immediately at ease.

"You need coffee," he says.

"Always."

He vanishes into the kitchen. I hear him talking softly to Lourdes, then she comes in with a couple of steaming cups and sets them down in front of me. "Sugar?" she asks. "Milk? *Crema?*"

I've met Lourdes before, but mostly I remember her from their wedding reception. She's still shy around me, I don't know why. Maybe because she's working on her English, or because I remind her of her grandfather, or because Omar has said so many flattering things about me that I'm somehow in another league.

"No, Lourdes," I shake my head. "Black coffee is just fine. *Gracias.*"

She nods, beams at me, and heads back to the kitchen.

"God, she gets more beautiful every time I see her," I say.

Omar grins. "The truth is you'll never win her heart if you keep talking like a goddamn gringo."

"Just give me a few more years, Omar."

He sips his coffee. "Hell, you won't need to. She'll be teaching ESL classes by then."

I smile. He's right. Lourdes never went past the sixth grade in Mexico, but she's got more drive and intelligence than anyone I've ever met. And of course, it doesn't hurt that she's gorgeous.

"I've tried to put two and two together, Omar," I begin. "And guess what? It doesn't add up."

"Is that how you're gonna start out," Omar wants to know, "with a riddle? Can't you just fucking say what you mean?"

"I wish," I tell him. "But Jews don't think that way. It's never all black or white. Mostly we deal with nuance. Dissonance. That kind of thing."

"What's nuance?" he asks.

"Never mind," I say. "You remember how nobody at the church knew Mr. Hayden?"

"That's right," he says. "Not a soul."

"Yeah, okay. But that's the odd piece, Omar. That's what's been keeping me up late at night."

"How come?"

"Well," I say, "it doesn't jive with what Reverend Jimmy said. He remembered quite clearly the last scene he had with Hayden. Told me all about it. It was right there in the church. Hayden interrupted everything, started shouting in the middle of his sermon. Telling people they were damned, telling them they were going straight to hell. That there was nothing to be done about it. Now I'm no expert, but it seems to me Christians don't generally disagree with each other. Not in church at least. Not like Jews, anyway."

"No," Omar nods, "we like to get along. It's one big happy family when you're in church. That's why I dropped out, if you wanna know. Besides the fact that it was all a con. Plus I could hardly stay awake."

"Exactly," I say. "Which is why a performance like the one Hayden put on before he stormed out would have woken people up. There had to be somebody in that crowd you talked to who remembered it."

"And they didn't," Omar agrees. He sets his coffee cup down on the table in front of us. "Now I see what you mean. Two and two not adding up."

Neither of us speak for a bit. "So where do you plan on going with this?" he asks.

"I need to sit down and have another chat with Reverend Jimmy," I say. "He gave me all kinds of facts about Hayden, didn't he? Physical stuff. His age. Weight. How tall he was. I thought I could almost see him. Now, either he's lying, or he's crazy."

"He could be both," Omar goes. "Priests, people like that . . . you never know."

*　　*　　*

I'm laying the dinner plates down on the table when Malloy calls. He's in a positive frame of mind. I can hear the old reliable Irish cop in his voice again, the one who escorts little old ladies across the street, who coaxes kittens out of trees. "We got the report back from ballistics," he says. "Whoever killed Maria Ruiz used the same gun on Daisy Cooper. It's a match. And everything's pointing toward our friend Hayden."

"Except that Hayden doesn't exist," I say.

"What the hell do you mean?"

I tell him about Omar's undercover visit to Reverend Jimmy's church and all the questions he asked. And all the answers he never got. And I throw in the discussion I had with Reverend Jimmy about Hayden's last appearance there. All the hubbub Hayden caused. Or maybe didn't.

"Doesn't compute," Malloy says when I finish. "Something's out of whack."

"Agreed."

"I'm going to do a little research on Jimmy Archibald," Malloy tells me. "Don't you move in on him until we know who we're dealing with."

"Okay."

"I mean it, Amos. Don't crowd him. Just stay the hell away. Give me a few days."

"I don't want to lose him, Bill. Not now. Not if he's the one."

"I understand," he says. "And we'll keep an eye on him, believe me. But there's still plenty we don't know. All you've got is this disconnect between his memory of Hayden and Omar's man-in-the-street survey. That's fascinating, and it could be important, but it doesn't make him a killer. Not in my book."

"Yeah, but there's some sort of link, Bill. Admit it. You've got Hayden's—or somebody's—prints on that shopping cart, right? And the same gun was used on both Maria and Daisy."

"True."

"And here's something else: it was the Reverend who connected me with Daisy Cooper. He knew I was going over there to see her that night. We talked about it."

"Okay, but wasn't it also Reverend Jimmy who gave you Hayden's name in the first place? Told you all about this evil man?

Why would he do that if he knew it might lead back to him? No murderer in his right mind would do that."

"I never said he was in his right mind."

"Fine. So let's back up, then," Malloy says. "It could just be that he's crazy. Or that he has a wild imagination. Or a giant ego. I mean, think of it. People at your little storefront church are suddenly turning up dead, one after another. That's a big deal. Your church. How would you feel about that? You might be terrified. You might think you're next in line."

"That's not the way he's acting."

"No," Malloy says, "Maybe not. But then, he's a minister. A man of God. Maybe death doesn't scare him as much as it does other folks."

"I suppose so."

"And he also sells real estate. So that tells me he might be something of an opportunist. That he looks for angles."

"He is complicated," I say. "Sure."

"So maybe, if you're bent a certain way, well, who knows? In the back of your mind, you might think a little notoriety—even bad publicity like this—could boost your status."

"With who?"

"Damned if I know. Maybe he thinks this is all between him and God. That God put him in that church on Rosewood, and now God wants him to be in the middle of this storm. That this is His big fucking plan."

"You're giving God a helluva lot of credit, Bill."

"No, I'm not," he says. "I'm just trying to get inside somebody's head before I send Jason and Remo in there to break down his door and put the cuffs on. So far as I know, he's never harmed a fly. And this could all be perfectly innocent on his part." I tell Malloy okay, I promise to be a good boy scout, I won't go near Jimmy Archibald, not until I hear from him. Then, just as I'm about to say goodbye, he adds, "Oh yeah, and one last thing: Do me a favor, will you? Keep Omar and his wrecking crew the hell away from this. Let's just pretend this whole conversation between you and me never happened. I still have a bad taste in my mouth over what those gorillas did to Jack Harper."

"You bet," I say, but the phone has already gone dead in my hand.

"What was that all about?" Mara wants to know as I take my seat opposite her and she passes the vegetable terrine.

"That was Lieutenant Malloy thinking out loud."

"Sounds like he was chewing you out."

"He's a pro, Mara. In fact, I think he's about the best cop I've ever come across. But he has this little bee in his bonnet: he likes to do things on the up-and-up."

She wants to know what I'm talking about, and so I tell her again how Omar's man, Ramon, let Carlos know about Jack Harper, and how Carlos leaked it to Julio, and how Julio's boys drove over to Curson Avenue and took Harper apart, one gay limb at a time. I tell her these things in detail. I don't leave anything out, and when I finish talking I notice Mara has lost her appetite. She's staring at me numbly, and her knife and fork are still untouched in their original positions on her napkin. "So that's what he wanted to talk to you about?" she asks after a moment.

"Partly," I say. "The truth is, Harper is old news. He may even be out of the hospital by now. No, we were talking about another person of interest, and this time Malloy wanted to be sure I didn't tip off Omar."

"I see." She picks up her utensils and sets her napkin on her lap. "That person wouldn't be Amory Blevins, would he?"

"No," I say. "My old school chum, Betsy Rollands, had it right. Amory is a slimy opportunist, but he doesn't have the *chutzpah* to kill another human being. I suppose that's a redeeming feature, huh?"

"I'll talk with my attorney," Mara says. "See if he can't terminate the arrangement we made with Mr. Blevins."

"I don't know whether he can get your money back," I say.

"I don't know, either," she says. "But he's good at what he does. Maybe he can channel it so that it really does put people into shelters. That would be better. I just don't want a single dollar lining Amory's pockets."

"Well," I say, "Amory's not our murderer. I'm pretty sure of that."

"Because your friend said he's a wimp?"

"That, and because his car doesn't match the one the cops are looking for. The one that belonged to the guy in Highland Park who tried to kill me."

"So they think this is all the work of one man?"

"Seems to be." Then I explain how disappointed I am that we don't have Amory Blevins and Jack Harper to kick around anymore. That with those two, we at least had a plausible motive. "Power," I say, "that works for me. Amory Blevins wants power. I believe he wants to get himself elected to the city council and that he'd be more than willing to let his boyfriend kill people to advance his career. Any decent DA could make a splendid case, if only it were true."

"And now?"

"Now," I say, "that's all down the drain. We have no motive anymore. We're back to reading tea leaves. Unless . . . unless you count evil, of course."

"And you don't believe in evil?" she asks. This is a question we've never discussed before, although I can see by the way her brown eyes light up that it interests her. Maybe it's something she's thought about deeply. Maybe she was a student of Nietzsche. Maybe she was one of those people who latched onto evil the way some young girls fantasize about horses.

"In the Hitlerian sense, yes, I do," I tell her. "But really, how often do you ever meet someone that demented? And wouldn't you know him if you did?"

"I'm not sure," she replies. "I had an Uncle Phil once who I could never get close to. Every time he walked into our house the temperature seemed to drop. He scared me so much. He never touched me or anything, but I always had this sense—I just knew the way a child knows—that he was evil."

"And was he?"

She blinks. "Evil? Maybe. Maybe not. He died when I was seven. A heart attack, my mother told me. He was a smoker. Everybody was a smoker back then. I told my parents I couldn't go to the funeral. I pretended to be sick."

*   *   *

I take the whole next morning off to be with Loretta, wheeling her slowly through the tropical garden at Olympic Terrace. Before I left the house, I asked Mara if she wanted to tag along, but she said no, no, it's important that you spend time alone with your wife. The way she said it made me sad, but I knew she was right. I can't have it both ways. *There's the woman I love now and the woman I've always loved, and somehow, Parisman, it's a conundrum, but they're no longer one and the same. What can you do?*

Later, I wait outside her room in a plastic chair while two young Filipina nurses give her a shower and put on some fresh clothes and makeup. I can hear them talking to her in their singsong voices. Hard to know what they're saying. In fact, if it's really English I'd be astonished, but they're so cheery and comforting, the words themselves scarcely matter.

My phone rings.

"Mr. Parisman? It's Jimmy Archibald calling."

I sit up straight. "Reverend Jimmy. What can I do for you?"

There's a pause on the other end. "Well, something's come up. The truth is I have some disturbing information for you."

"What is it, Reverend?"

Another pause. When he comes back on, his voice is very subdued. "I'd rather not discuss it on the phone, if you don't mind. I'm leaving the church right now, and I have a couple of quick errands to run, but how about we meet somewhere in half an hour?" He wants me to go to this Southern fried chicken joint he knows down on Pico near 12th. Lettie's. It's not that far, he says, and we can have a bite there and talk.

"Okay, sure," I tell him. "I'll be there." After I hang up, it occurs to me that I just told Malloy I wouldn't put myself in Reverend Jimmy's proximity and now here I am again, proving myself a liar. *Oh well*, I think, *he asked to see me, didn't he? What can I do? Surely the Lieutenant will understand.*

The nurses open the door and let me in. Loretta looks radiant. She's sitting up in bed, smiling. They've put on some silvery eye shadow, I see. Her cheeks look rosier now than they did before, and her hair is washed and soft and fluffy. I tell her, I'm sorry, but I have to go. I'm on a case.

"I know," she says. She grabs my hands, bends down, kisses them. "You're going to catch the killer, right?"

"Right," I say. "And the minute I do that, I'll be back. I promise. You wait here, okay?"

*   *   *

I thought I'd be early as usual, but when I finally find a place to park and come through the smudgy glass doors at Lettie's, he's already sitting at a table in the corner, scanning a menu. This is a Black neighborhood, more or less, but when I see all the white people in their shorts and Birkenstocks at the counter lining up for takeout, I start to rethink that idea.

"They're known for their spicy chicken," he says, when he sees me looking at the line. "It's down home from Memphis. Jonathan Gold raved about this place. Now it's not a secret anymore."

I grab a chair and sit. "Never been to Memphis," I say. "But I'll give it a try."

He's wearing a tan sport coat with matching pants and a light reddish polo underneath. Not exactly ministerial, I think, but perfect for real estate and cruising L.A. I'm eager to get down to business, that's the way I'm wired, but not him. We dance around, trade small talk. He notices the simple gold ring on my finger and that leads somehow to a discussion of Loretta. I tell him we've been married a long time and lately she hasn't been well. I'm not going to give him more than that. He nods, says he'll include her in his prayers if that's okay. I say, sure, why not. He fiddles with his sunglasses, holds them up to the light. He waits until the waitress sets our food down on the table and leaves before he begins talking about anything important.

"I asked you here, Mr. Parisman, because you've been around a long time and you've probably seen more than your share of trouble. And I just didn't feel comfortable saying anything over the phone. Not at the church, anyway. There were other folks around, and . . . I don't know if any of them are involved, I can't be sure, but, well, maybe when I tell you, you'll understand."

"Tell me what?"

He tugs at his lower lip. Then he reaches into the side pocket of his sport coat and pulls out an envelope with his name scrawled in pencil on the outside. "I found this under the front door when I arrived," he says. He pushes it across the table. "Go ahead. Take a look."

The seal has been broken and stuck haphazardly back together. I pry it apart and take out a folded sheet of yellow legal paper. Someone with a cramped, angry hand has taken a pencil and written a rambling manifesto, it seems. At the top, the paper is titled, Just So You Know. *We have talked it through and we all agree that the end is near,* it begins. *And because our lives on this earth have been so very hard, and because you, Reverend Jimmy, have taught us about God, how God loves us as much as any Wall St. millionaire and doesn't want us to suffer, and because you always said the world that waits for us in Heaven is so much sweeter than this one, well then, we have no choice. We have to do what is necessary. That's why we have come together. You should know that we are not running away. None of us. We are not cowards. We hope our deaths, however they are achieved, will clear a bright path for the rest of humanity. We hope it will speed up the Rapture you promised. You always said it would come one day soon. We are sinners for sure but it doesn't matter anymore. It's like you said. When you are the hammer of God you can do no wrong. Soon we'll be together again in a much better place with no pain and*

no cold and no more suffering. Jesus will walk among us. We all agree
to make this happen. We have drawn lots to make it happen. Amen.

Right below this paragraph are a list of ten names. I recognize
the first three: Delia Montero, Louis McFee, Lincoln Greer. The
others I've never seen before.

"All right, so what does this tell you?"

"Well," the Reverend says, trying hard to keep his voice in
check, "don't you see? It's a pact. The Rapture isn't that way at
all, but they've got this twisted idea. They mean to kill each other
off, one at a time. That's what it tells me. And maybe because of
something I said. Just look at the names. The three at the top are
already gone. And the next one on the list is Glen Simon. That
is, if they go right down the list, I don't know." He's scared now,
I can hear it.

"What exactly did you tell them, Reverend? That they have to
die to get to Heaven? That it doesn't matter how it happens?"

He holds up his hands defensively. "I preached the Rapture, yes,
of course. How it will be at the End of Days. And with a group
like this, maybe I talked about it more than I should. Maybe they
didn't hear it right. Maybe they were drunk or stoned. But you've
got to understand, it doesn't matter what your circumstances are.
I don't condone, the Bible doesn't condone, Jesus himself would
never say something like . . ."

"Okay," I say, "so let's back up a minute. This thing"—I hold
the paper up as though offering it as evidence, then gently set it
back down—"this announcement or threat or whatever it is, just
appeared on your doorstep. That's all you know?"

"Right. Someone must have slipped it under the transom before
I came. They knew I would be there at three. I usually am."

"So presumably it was a member of your church. Someone on
the list, or at least someone known to you."

"I'd imagine."

"Okay. And he came along out of the blue. Slipped it under the
door. Then left."

"I'm guessing that's what happened, yes."

"All right," I say. I rub my chin. "But why would he do that? That's what I want to know."

"Huh?"

"You're a minister," I say. "A man of God. You counsel troubled people all the time, don't you? Well, here's a guy in trouble. He's got something enormous on his chest. So why wouldn't he come to you in person?"

Reverend Jimmy looks down at his plate. He hasn't touched his food, and now it's starting to get cold. "I have . . . I have no idea," he stammers. "He's probably scared out of his wits. I would be, too. Yes, I talk to folks about many issues. But murder? Murder and suicide? A death pact? No. No, never. That has no place in Christian teachings. I don't even know where to begin."

"Clearly, whoever dropped this off is still among the living," I say. "And if I had to bet"—my finger touches the names on the paper—"I'd say it was probably one of these folks here."

"Because?"

"Fear," I tell him. "Fear, pure and simple. In your words, he's scared out of his wits. Maybe he signed on once upon a time, maybe he even believed all that shit you talked about. But now that it's his turn to kill someone, or his turn to die, he's getting cold feet. That's how this letter arrived on your doorstep." I take a few bites of my spicy chicken breast. "Death has a way of focusing the mind, doesn't it?"

Reverend Jimmy braces his hands on the edge of the table. He looks at me as though I'm the only one who can save him. "You can see why I didn't want to breathe a word about this in the church, can't you?"

"I guess. But why would someone come to you? What do they think you can possibly do for them? That's what I still don't get."

"What do you mean?"

I take a long sip of my iced tea before continuing. "Well, if he really wanted the killings to stop, why wouldn't the fellow who brought you this just tip off the police? He could even erase his own name if he was worried, couldn't he?"

"He could, sure."

"So what's he after?" I ask. "Why does it matter that you know? Does he want you to intervene? Is he asking you to turn them in?"

Reverend Jimmy sighs. "I can't go to the cops with this, Mr. Parisman."

"Why the hell not?"

"Think of the consequences," he says. "They'll arrest the ones still on the list. Take them downtown. They'll get confessions out of them. You know they will. One way or another."

"Isn't that the point? Don't you want the killing to stop?"

"Of course," he says. "And maybe it's as you say. Maybe whoever passed me this note wants it to end, too. But if the police swoop down and arrest everyone, don't you see? That's not the only thing that will happen. That's also the end of my church. I don't want that." Now it's his turn to point to the paper. "And I don't believe they want it, either."

"No, they just want to die. And you would go right ahead and let them, wouldn't you?"

He sighs. In that moment, with the late afternoon sunlight streaming into the restaurant, his head tilts to one side in a sad, bewildered way. "I've never been any good at pretending to be God, Mr. Parisman. I can only do so much."

"And that doesn't include saving lives, I don't suppose. That's where you and I part company."

"Look," he says, "these people don't intend to stop. I know who they are. I know their pain. They're serious. They want this to go on."

"You're sure about that?"

"I am. The seven names left on that list? They've lived on the street so long they don't know up from down. They're beyond desperate. I believe them. God help me, but they're actually trying to induce the Rapture."

"Well, that's pretty fucking crazy," I say.

We stop talking for a minute. The natural noise of the restaurant, the clatter of knives and forks, the clink of glass, beer and soda bottles, the screeching of chairs and the orders for coleslaw and fries and chicken shouted from the counter into the overheated, yellow-tiled kitchen—all of that rushes in on us like water from an ancient, crumbling dam.

"So why did you tell me, then?" I ask. "You want me to take this piece of paper to the cops? Is that it? So you can absolve yourself? Be above it all? Go back to your precious little church and pray?"

Reverend Jimmy pulls himself wearily to his feet. "I'm going to do what God intended for me to do," he says. "I'm going to talk with them individually and in private. I'm going to listen and offer them hope. I need to try to understand, even though, as you say, it's crazy. I need to calm the storm if I can." He takes out his wallet and flings a twenty-dollar bill down on the table. "You do what you like with the list, Mr. Parisman. You may think of them as criminals. To me, they're still souls I'm trying to save."

CHAPTER 25

I'm one of the few guys I know on this planet—probably the only detective—who listens to what his body is telling him. Many women have mastered this art; men, not so much. And if they're men of a certain age, they either ignore it or try to tough it out. Men can be exceedingly stupid, let's get that out of the way. But when I get a twinge in my knee, I look up at the sky and start thinking it's going to rain, and nine times out of ten, it does. The same thing when somebody says something that doesn't logically fit together. It trips a silent alarm inside me, and I feel it. It's physical. Sometimes my ears turn red. Sometimes my stomach will tighten up. Once, I remember hearing a witness accuse an innocent man of murder. My mouth went dry and my heart started pounding faster than it should. I was terrified. It was the same feeling I got when I was a kid and I had to sit in front of a crowd of more than three people in my teacher's living room and play the piano.

Now I'm in the car and driving downtown to see Malloy. The written statement Jimmy Archibald gave me is on the passenger seat, and even though the light is fading and it's cool outside, I'm sweating. I stop at a red light and punch in Omar's number.

"This has just gotten a lot more complicated," I say. "Now we're talking a suicide pact to bring on the Rapture."

"Fucking religion," is Omar's response.

I tell him about my conversation with Reverend Jimmy and the list. "I guess now I have to take it down to Malloy. See if he can't prevent any more mayhem. That is, unless you have any better suggestions."

"Hell, Amos, I don't know. What's he gonna do? Is that piece of paper proof of anything?"

"No, but if the next man on the list suddenly turns up dead in a dumpster and we just sat on our hands, how would that look? This is above my pay grade, Omar."

"You're working for free, remember? Like me. Ten cents is above our pay grade."

That Omar is right makes me both happy and sad. I'd rather work for money, of course. On the other hand, I've seen too much dead meat in dumpsters lately, and it's getting harder and harder to dredge up a normal human emotion anymore. You revert to form. A corpse is a corpse; it doesn't matter where you find it. We stepped over them every day of the week in Vietnam. Just kept walking through the brush. What you had to do if you wanted to stay alive.

*   *   *

The fourth floor where Malloy works is quieter than usual. Most of the staff have already left for the day. A tall, Black, uniformed officer is talking to a couple of white plainclothes fellows as they put on their sport coats and yank off their ties. Vinnie and I are going to that bar down on Broadway, he says. It's a good place to catch the Lakers game. You wanna go with? The plainclothes guys glance at one another. I catch a little flicker of apprehension. Then they shrug their shoulders, nod. Hey, why not. They step around me as I walk past.

Malloy's corner is at the far end. He's all alone, filling out a report, looks like. The computer screens are shut down, and the papers on everyone else's desks are square and neat and tidy.

I pull up a chair in front of his desk, pull out the handwritten statement from my jacket and let it drop. "This is something you need to see."

He picks it up, adjusts his glasses. His lips move silently as he reads. "Where'd you get this?"

"Jimmy Archibald gave it to me about an hour ago."

"I thought I told you to stay away from him," Malloy says. He's not happy. "What the fuck are you trying to do? Are you and Omar out to blow this lead like you did with Harper? Is that what you want?"

"He came to me, Bill, I swear. He said somebody slipped this note under his door at the church and I was the first one he called. He was upset. I didn't call him."

"I'll bet." Malloy frowns and drums his fingers on the desk.

"So what do you think we should do?"

"What should we do? Hell, Amos, that's easy. We should go out right now and round up all of these people, assuming we can find them. We should bring them in and shine a light on them and grill them all night long if we have to until one of them cracks." He stabs the paper with his index finger. "But of course, the truth is we can't."

"How come?"

"Because this is just a piece of paper," he says. "We don't know who wrote it or why."

"No, you don't. But you can't discount it, can you?"

Malloy has always been one of those cops who lives and dies by the numbers. Now he gives me a cynical look. "I don't discount it, no. But it could just be a sick prank. Or a smoke screen. And unless we have some more information, it's not evidence of anything."

"You have the names of the first three victims."

"Any fool could put that together just reading the newspaper."

I sigh. "That's true enough. But what happens a few days from now, Bill?"

"What do you mean?"

"I mean if it's not a prank. If you're wrong. I mean when you find the next man on the list—Glen Simon, or whoever he is—in a dumpster with his head bashed in. How's that gonna make you feel?"

Malloy shakes his head. "There's nothing specific in this note," he says. "They don't say that tomorrow night we're going to knock off so-and-so." He reads it over quickly a second time. "Heck, even if this list is accurate, how do we know they're the ones involved in these killings? Could be there's another person out there—someone smart enough to leave his name off."

"That's possible."

"Look, I'm not buying the idea of a suicide club. Not yet. Not till I see something more convincing than this." He holds up the paper and lets it flutter onto his desk. "People don't go around collectively killing themselves."

"The hell they don't," I say. "What about Jonestown? What about Waco?"

"Those were different circumstances. Cults. Ruthless people. Everyone in those groups was being systematically brainwashed."

I bite my lip. "You know, Lieutenant, what you're describing doesn't sound all that different from organized religion."

"Okay," he says, "okay." His hand makes a feeble sweep at the air between us. "Maybe so. I sorta see what you're getting at. But this just seems so weird. So out of context."

"Why do you say that?" I ask. "These people are desperate. They've been living on the street for years. What do they have to lose?"

Malloy glances again at the written statement in front of him. He shakes his head. "Desperate families, yes. Husbands and wives, sometimes. I've seen murder and suicide combinations, sure. But not ten perfect strangers. I'm sorry, that's not how it usually works."

"Okay," I say, backing down. "I still thought you'd find it interesting. It's so out of left field. And like I said, it really shook the Reverend up when he read it."

Malloy leans back in his chair, laces his hands behind his head. In the glare of the overhead fluorescent lights his face resembles the surface of the moon. "I'm surprised he didn't contact us first."

"He was worried you'd pick them up, that's why. He said given the way things are between the police and the homeless, chances were pretty good that you'd get a confession out of them. Then pat yourselves on the back and go home."

"If they're the ones doing the murders, what's so wrong with that?"

"But, like you say, that paper isn't evidence."

"No, but along with a confession or two, it might be."

"Confessions can be produced, under the right circumstances. You know that as well as I do, Bill."

"Are you saying that we'd do something unethical?" He raises an eyebrow.

"Not you, no. But street people often get the short end of the night stick. If you brought them in, they might be treated fine. But they also might not see a lawyer as soon as other folks. They might have to wait around."

"Well, I'll think this over, Amos. But now, for the time being, anyway, I'm not bringing them in."

I get to my feet. I've done my duty. "No. And I understand why. But you ought to keep an eye on them, don't you think? There hasn't been a killing since Daisy Cooper."

"That's another reason to sit tight," he says. "Daisy Cooper wasn't on the list. Neither was Maria Ruiz."

"Exactly. Which probably means it's Glen Simon's turn. And soon."

CHAPTER 26

I leave the note sitting on the desk with the Lieutenant, but not before I've extracted a promise from him to put a tail out on Glen Simon—that is, if he can be located. "You have to go that far," I tell him. "Please, Bill, if you want to sleep at night."

Malloy nods glumly. He doesn't like being lectured. He has more than his share of Catholic guilt; it's his Achilles's heel. He knows it and I know it, and I only ever play that card in dire straits. In fact, he didn't promise me at all. What he said was, he'd look into it, which with someone as upright as Malloy is as good as a promise.

As I pull out of the underground parking lot, the sky has suddenly darkened. Rain is in the forecast, which means next to nothing in Los Angeles, but now clouds are overhead, and they're big and round and ominous, just like what the cute Chinese weather girl on channel 7 predicted. I roll down the window; it's at least ten degrees cooler than when I was last out on the street an hour ago. At a stoplight on Temple, I glance down at my phone, and on a whim I call Reverend Jimmy back. He picks up on the third ring.

"Reverend, it's Amos Parisman."

"I know," he says.

"Yes, of course," I tell him. Then I ask him if he has any idea where I could find Glen Simon.

"Well, I don't have an address for him," he says, "if that's what you mean. In fact, I haven't seen him at church for a while, which is troubling. But he likes to eat. And most days he goes to that big Unitarian church up on Santa Monica that hands out lunch bags. I'd look in that neighborhood. And even if he's not there, the folks there would probably be able to track him down. Say, if you find him before I do—"

"It won't be me. That's what cops are for, but I'll let him know you want to get together. That's what you were going to say, right?"

"You read my mind, Mr. Parisman. I need to have a serious talk with all those people about the Rapture. What it is, and what it ain't."

I thank him, then call Malloy back and convey this information.

"We've got a team on the way right now," he says.

"How're they gonna find him?" I ask. "Do they even know what he looks like?"

"Glen Simon?" he says. "Are you kidding me? Glen Simon has a rap sheet longer than my pool cue." Then he hangs up.

It's rush hour, and because it's starting to sprinkle, I decide to stay off the freeways and just meander. Eventually, I find my way to Echo Park and Sunset Boulevard. I head south, past the sad, gaudy pink-and-orange taco stands, the hole-in-the-wall thrift shops and leather boutiques, the honking cars, the hodgepodge of tarot readers and massage parlors and record stores where they insist that vinyl is making a comeback. At another red light on the corner of Temple I see a cluster of young men, laughing, yelling back and forth in Spanish. There's a dark energy about them. They're wearing sunglasses and baseball caps and they're all doing tricks with skateboards, one after another. Spinning and turning, bounding on and off the curb, past the limp, half-dead palms, dodging deftly in between the determined Latina women lugging plastic bags of groceries and pushing their baby carriages home.

The light changes and I drive on, past MacArthur Park, which, even though it's not yet dark, people have begun to evacuate. Some people, anyway, while for others, toting their soiled sleeping bags and overstuffed shopping carts, this is a final destination.

I don't know what to think about the conversation I just had with Malloy. Part of me thinks he's right—ten perfect strangers wouldn't get together to kill themselves, even if they really believed all that nonsense about the Rapture. I certainly wouldn't, of course, but maybe Jews have always placed a higher value on life than some other faiths. Okay, we killed ourselves at Masada, I remember reading in Hebrew school, but that was only to deny the Romans the pleasure.

On the other hand, there's the note and the names.

By the time I reach Creston Drive, raindrops as big as nickels are slamming down on my windshield. I've finally come to a reasonable idea of what this case is all about. I'm not saying I know who's behind it. But at least I know who I want to talk to. And I don't care what Malloy says.

*   *   *

Jimmy Archibald lives on the third floor of the Excelsior on Rossmore, just a few blocks from the Wilshire Country Club. It was once a very grand hotel in the twenties and thirties. Clark Gable and Olivia de Haviland and Edward G. Robinson used to drop by. The bar had a gorgeous countertop made of zinc, or so they said, and an extensive wine list, even during Prohibition. Upstairs, the bedrooms were spacious and quiet and well appointed. It was a place for assignations, as they used to say. In fact, before the War, lots of famous people passed through its portals, that is, until they suddenly stopped being famous, or got so drunk and disorderly that the liveried doorman tossed them out.

I step into the golden elevator, push the ancient black button. The doors take their sweet time closing, and the whole contraption trembles like an old woman as it ascends.

He knows I'm coming. We sit in his living room. He has a long, maroon L-shaped couch, which faces a huge television screen on the opposite wall. Fresh flowers in several vases. I've been in a lot of houses this pristine before, but they were always the handiwork of women.

"You run a very neat ship," I say as I sink into the couch and cross my legs. "I'm impressed."

"Thanks," he says. "It's a habit I've worked on for a long time. I didn't used to be so neat, believe me."

Did I want something to drink? Water? Coffee? Wine? Beer? I tell him no. I have a few questions, that's all.

"You know, Mr. Parisman," he says, "the police were just here yesterday morning. And that's what they said. We just have a few questions."

"Really?" I say. "How long did that run?"

"About an hour. There was a Mr. Jason and . . ."

"Remo. I know both of them."

"Yes," he says, "I imagine you do. They brought along the list of names I gave you."

"And what did you tell them?"

"I told them the same story I told you. Also, I gave them some ideas about where they could find the other seven people. They said they wanted to interview them. I said I hoped they didn't arrest them."

"I don't think they're going to do that," I tell him. "Arrest them for what?"

"Exactly. Just because their name is on a list?"

Reverend Jimmy asks me again if I don't care for something to drink. When I shake my head, he excuses himself and comes back with a mug of black coffee for himself.

"So," he says, taking a short sip. "What would you like to know?"

I pull out my cardboard notebook and a pen. "I'm confused, Reverend. There are a few inconsistencies that I'm losing sleep over. I'm hoping you can clear them up."

"Okay. Shoot."

"First, let's talk about Hayden. You said the last time you saw him was at your church."

"Yes."

"And that's when he caused a scene."

"Yes. It was a few years ago."

"Okay. But I sent one of my assistants to your service recently. And he talked to maybe a dozen members. And not a single one of them had any memory of Hayden. Or the incident."

"Which proves?"

I hold up my hand in consternation. "It's one of those he-said-she-said things, that's all. Let's put it this way: you'd think that if this Hayden had a meltdown in front of everyone and then stormed out, that somebody might remember. I would."

"It happened," he said. "It's a fact. I didn't make it up."

"That's the question, isn't it?"

Now he looks me coolly in the eye. "Not everybody's memory is the same, Mr. Parisman. Maybe your man didn't talk to the people who were there that night. We have a big turnover, you know. My audience changes a lot. There have been times when I didn't recognize anyone in the first three rows."

"It's possible," I say. "But from the way you described him, Hayden was like this looming evil presence. Larger than life."

"He was to me." He points to his chest. "To me. That was my first impression. That's what I always felt about him. But I don't claim to speak for other people, how they felt. They might have ignored him the whole time."

I put my notepad back in my pocket. "So who, besides you, has any recollection of Hayden?"

The Reverend sighs. "Well," he says, "probably the person who knew him best at that church was Daisy Cooper."

I shake my head. "That's not going to do me much good."

"I realize that," Jimmy Archibald says. "I'm sorry."

We stare at each other for a minute. I can hear the clock ticking in the next room. "You know what, Reverend Jimmy? I believe I will have something to drink after all."

We talk for another hour and in the end, he makes me lunch. Shrimp salad and a cup of homemade minestrone. He's a meticulous cook, but it's right in line with the way he keeps his apartment. I'm sure if I walked into his bedroom the pillowcases would be creased and ironed.

As I'm pulling away from the curb I spot a car across the street. Jason and Remo nod at me from inside. I nod back and put my foot on the gas. *Good to know that the cops are on the case*, I think. Although God knows what they'll get from following Jimmy Archibald around.

I head up Rossmore, which turns into Vine. It's when I take a hard right off Franklin onto Ivar and start climbing into the Hollywood Hills that I notice it's me they're tailing. They're trying to be clever and stay several cars back, but I wasn't born yesterday. I ignore them. I keep weaving slowly up to Creston Drive. Maybe Malloy's just being an old Irish mother, I think. Or maybe they want to be sure I arrive at my destination safe and sound. But then when I turn into the driveway, Malloy himself is waiting for me. He's leaning against a squad car with his arms folded resolutely.

"This isn't where you live," he says, as I climb out of the Honda.

"No, Lieutenant, you're right. This is where my girlfriend lives." I wasn't planning on saying that, but the minute I did, I felt so much better. It's like someone suddenly let the air out of a balloon that was stuck inside my chest. Also the fact that he's standing here waiting for me to show up—well, that tells me he's nobody's fool.

He shakes his head. "I thought you were a happily married man, Amos. I'm disappointed."

"I am a happily married man, Bill. Loretta's the love of my life. You know that."

"So you don't hold with any of that 'till death do us part' business?"

"I'll never walk away from her," I declare earnestly. "But the truth is, she's not there anymore. She hasn't been for some time. Do you realize—do you have any idea what that's like . . . living with a ghost?"

Malloy comes closer. He puts his arm on my shoulder. Jason and Remo are still planted in their car and out of earshot, but he lowers his voice anyway. "I'm not judging you, Amos. Believe me."

"I know." *Malloy's like an iceberg*, I think; there is so much going on beneath the surface that he never conveys; you can't see it, but you can't help but feel its presence.

"We tripped over"—he pulls out a paper from inside his jacket—"Mara Worthington's name a week ago. We were looking a little further into Amory Blevins and his boy toy. All that reward money she put up? Well, it raised some eyebrows."

"How'd you know it was her?"

"Amory told us, bless his heart. We leaned on him, just enough to make him sweat."

"And?"

"And he thought maybe if he was cooperative, we wouldn't say anything to his wife. He still wants a career in politics. Go figure."

"Sounds like Amory, all right."

"Then, ever since Omar tipped off his friend Julio and caused all that ruckus with Jack Harper, well, I thought it might be prudent to keep an eye on him, too."

"Omar?"

Malloy nods. "Omar led us to that nursing home on Olympic where Loretta's at, and that's where we spotted you and Mara holding hands. One thing just sorta led to another, you know."

"Small world. Okay, I get that. But Mara has no ulterior motive, Bill. She just wants to find the killer. And she has the money, so why not put it up?"

"Like I say, it's a lot of money. Especially to track down somebody who's killing street people. Makes you wonder, is all."

"So where are you headed, Bill? You wanna lock her up for being generous? Isn't that what rich folks are supposed to do? Give it away?"

"We're just touching all the bases. That's what we do at the LAPD."

I fish around in my pocket and come up with the front door key. "So come on in then, I'll introduce you."

"Thanks," he says. Then he turns and waves Jason and Remo away.

Mara's outside on the padded back deck, reading her *New Yorker* and sipping white wine with an ice cube in it. Even though it's February and it just rained the day before, she's wearing light blue cotton shorts, and her bare feet are propped up on the edge of the glass coffee table. Her toenails are bright red and she wriggles them immodestly in my direction.

"Honey, this is my old pal, Lieutenant Malloy. Bill, meet Mara."

She extends her hand and he reaches over the coffee table to shake it. "Can I offer you some refreshment, Lieutenant? Wine? Beer? We have all kinds."

"Oh no, Mrs. Worthington. I couldn't possibly. I'm on duty."

We both sit facing her. "All right. So what brings you here?" she asks.

"I'll come straight to the point," he says. "We understand you're the one who offered a reward for information about the guy who's killing homeless people in town."

"I'd like to find him," she says. "Wouldn't you?"

"Yeah, sure," he says, "but it's the money—"

"Oh, the money. Well, the truth is, I had my attorney give that money to Mr. Blevins because he was making such a public display about the problem and I thought a little extra publicity, well, it would light a fire under the investigation." Then she turns to me. "Also, I have to admit, I was hoping Amos would find whoever did this."

"Why's that?"

"He works very hard," she says. "I've hardly seen him all month. And I just feel bad about him working so hard for free. Am I being selfish?"

Malloy and I look at each other. Some male tribal wisdom passes silently between us. What can you do? The woman wants to spend her money on you. Money means nothing to her. If she could, she'd set it all on fire just to keep herself warm.

*   *   *

I walk him out a few minutes later. He pulls out a Marlboro, offers the pack to me, but I shake my head. "I thought you quit," I say.

"I'm working on it. I'm down to three a day. Next month it'll be history." His phone rings. He listens to it for a while. Occasionally he says yeah, uh huh, wonderful. Then he mumbles, "Thanks, Janette. See you back at the ranch," and hangs up.

"Well?" I ask.

"That was Janette."

"I figured."

"They just got through interviewing the seven other people on that list. Seems like Reverend Jimmy had it right. They are some kind of fucked-up suicide cult."

"So you got confessions?"

"Every one of them claims they were involved, yeah."

"That's gonna be a helluva trial, Bill."

"Why you say that?"

"Well, think about it. You'll have a packed crowd, plus seven batshit-crazy people raising their hands and testifying about the Rapture in front of a judge, who's probably an atheist, or at least pretty cynical. I don't know if they'll get a conviction, but one thing's for sure: the press will have a field day."

"Maybe so," he says. "But you know something? Murder is murder. And juries understand evidence. They do. That paper you gave me may not count for much, but we took their fingerprints, and they look like a possible match up with the victims. We also found a weapon. It's a crowbar, not a hatchet or a hammer. Which makes sense when you think how their heads were bashed in. It was tucked away in a rain boot in one of their tent houses up on the edge of Hollywood. Forensics is going over it just to be sure, but it's all falling into place."

"Finally."

"Yeah, right. Finally." Malloy takes a long, satisfied drag on his cigarette and blows the smoke off to the right. Then he tosses what's left of the butt onto the pavement and stubs it out with his shoe. "Hell," he says, "the way this is going, I may quit next week."

CHAPTER 27

Omar's hunched over the kitchen table. He's wearing a long-sleeve polo shirt, brushed jeans, a tan sport coat, and the boots he bought on his honeymoon in Oaxaca. He hasn't shaved in a day or two, and now he looks like every other soon-to-be-discovered actor in Hollywood. When I ask him about it, he says he's done this intentionally, in order to blend in. Shabby chic, you know. He's nursing a cup of black coffee. The coffee's hot, so he has to blow on it from time to time. Then wait.

We're back in my old apartment in Park La Brea. It's very early, especially for Omar. The sun is pouring through the slats, and if you lean over and squint your eyes at just the right angle, you can make out the L.A. skyline.

"You always make it too hot," he complains. "Didn't Loretta ever teach you to make coffee?"

"That's how I like it," I say. "Shoot me, kill me."

He blows on it again, takes a sip, sets the cup down. "Too damn hot."

He's here to talk about the new developments in the case. Also because I needed a change of clothes, and because it's quiet here, at least before 8 a.m., when the leaf blowers start up down below. "So to hear Malloy tell it, the police think they've done their job," I say. "They've got seven homeless people behind bars; seven typed up, signed confessions; three bodies. The killing spree is over. That's tomorrow's headline, anyway." I take a sip of coffee and pull away. Omar's right, it is too hot.

"And you don't think so."

"I dunno. I think they think it's solved. Part of it. But I still don't buy this Rapture cult. People don't usually agree to go around collectively killing themselves. I don't care how desperate they are, it's weird."

Omar nods. "But if it's a group effort, it's easier to throw them in the dumpster afterwards. Teamwork and all that."

"That doesn't explain why they left Louis McFee lying on the ground."

"Maybe," he says, "they only had one man do the job that night. Or maybe they sent two men, and they still couldn't lift him. He was heavy, remember? Or a dog barked, or they heard a siren, or they saw something that scared them off. Not everything has to fit a pattern, does it?"

"Okay. You're right. But even if they've stopped the street killings, what about Maria and Daisy? Their names weren't on the list. They weren't homeless. And they were shot, not clubbed to death. How can you put them in the same basket?"

"You can't," Omar agrees. "We're talking about two different killers, it looks like."

I ask him how his business is doing. "Not good," he says, avoiding my eyes. "In fact, I'm thinking about giving up my office to save some dough. I've got a lot on my plate these days. Lourdes may be pregnant, and I'm trying to figure things out. It's hard. Carlos is gone. I told Ramon I'd call him if I had any fill-in work for him, but now, man, it's just me. I am the detective agency."

"And you're one of the best in the business," I say. "You may not know it, but I do. And I've been around a while."

He looks up, smiles. "That's great, Amos. But it's the first of the month and I still need to pay the rent."

There are turning points in a man's life. Somebody says something, and suddenly the whole rest of your future snaps into focus. This is one of those moments, and I'm proud of myself. I don't hesitate. I make it clear to Omar that the reason this apartment is so empty looking is because it is; I don't really live here anymore. He knows about Mara, how we met at Olympic Terrace, that one thing led to another and now we're together, we're walking each other back home. But then I tell him the kicker: that Mara has more money than she'll ever spend and she wants to support me in my quaint pursuit of justice and the American way.

"Hey, man, that's great news," Omar says. "I'm happy for you."

"You don't have to be happy for me, Omar. This is about you, too."

"What are you talking about?" he asks.

"I'm talking about the two of us going into business. We can be partners, or, if that scares you, then you can work for me like in the olden days. Either way, I have cash now. That's what I'm talking about. It's up to you."

Omar takes a long, thoughtful gulp of his coffee. It's no longer too hot. "Ain't nothing scares me. But I don't want you paying me just because I'm down on my luck."

"I'd never do that," I say. "And besides, I know you, Omar. You make your own luck."

I make us both scrambled eggs, and we talk for the rest of the morning. In the end, the plan we come up with is simple enough. We'll work together as long as it lasts. Or until he finds something else.

*   *   *

Jimmy Archibald is less welcoming the second time I come to see him in his apartment. I don't know whether it's the short notice, or maybe because he said he had other things to do later that day; there was a closing in Brentwood and an open house he had to plan for in Ladera Heights. He's polite, but I can't help feeling he just wants me to say my piece and leave. It's after four; the windows of his living room are thrown open to let in the brisk air, and three stories down below on Rossmore you can hear the occasional horn and sense the grim anxiety starting to build in the rush hour traffic.

"What's all this about, Mr. Parisman?"

"I'll try to keep it brief, Reverend. I've been doing more research on this Hayden fellow you talked about."

"Have you, now?"

"Well, not me. The police. I asked them to look into it. It seemed like a real longshot, of course, but this case has been so baffling."

"So I've heard."

"Anyway, LAPD ran this name Hayden through their nifty computers. That netted nothing, *bupkis*, but then they went a step further and used a national database. That's when they hit pay dirt."

He does a sidelong glance down at his watch. "Yes," he says. "Continue."

"Thirty years ago there was someone named Hayden. A teenage boy in Mississippi. Joe John Hayden. And this Hayden got into trouble at his high school one afternoon. I don't know what he did, but he ended up in jail, and then eventually they put him in some sort of mental facility. This was a long time ago, mind you. I don't think it would happen today, but you never know."

"Some things never change," he says.

He seems curious, but not alarmed, by what I'm saying.

"Anyway, they let me look at the report they dug up from that time, and I wanted to go over it with you, if you don't mind. Just to see if it matches with what you know about the Hayden at your church."

"I've told you everything I know about Hayden, Mr. Parisman. I don't see how—"

"Could they be related?" I ask. "That's my question. I read these reports, Reverend. From the jail and from a therapist at the Mississippi mental-health facility and I thought, you know, it's not too far-fetched."

Reverend Jimmy sighs. He leans forward, cups his chin with his right palm. "Okay, then, let's hear what you have."

"Thanks," I say. I flip open the manila folder I've brought along, which contains a Xerox of the stuff Malloy dredged up in Mississippi. "So according to the therapist in Jackson, this Hayden lost his mother when he was eight. That's what set him off. His father did what he could, but you can understand. Anyway, after his mother died, the boy was always getting into trouble. He was upset, naturally." I look up from the folder. Jimmy Archibald is looking at me intently.

"Yes, I can understand."

"And then this incident happened in high school, and they sent him to the principal's office. The principal was a woman named Eugenia Foley."

"And?"

"And apparently she was well thought of, a conscientious woman. They sent Joe John to her office because he'd had run-ins before, and she and he had come to know each other. They even liked each other. That happens."

"And what did this Mrs. Foley do?"

"Miss Foley, actually. Usually, she'd talk with the boy and sooner or later he would calm down and she would send him back to class. That was the standard procedure."

"But not this time?"

"No. This time—again, I don't know what happened—but he was uncontrollable, and she ended up calling the authorities."

"I still don't see where you're going with this."

"All right," I say. "I know you're pressed for time, so I'll just cut to the chase. Three months after they put Hayden in the lockup, he escaped. I guess it wasn't one of those high-security places. And the next night, there was a fire at Miss Foley's house. When they finally got inside, they found her body."

"Oh no," he says. "What happened?"

"Someone strangled her, then torched the place."

"Someone like Hayden?"

"Well, there was no evidence. No fingerprints or anything. But . . . given the circumstances . . ."

"And they picked him up?"

I shake my head. "No, that's the thing. Somehow Hayden just vanished completely. It was like he fell off the earth. That is, until last month, when you maybe brought him up."

He looks at his watch again and stands. "The name could be a coincidence, don't you think? It's not that uncommon."

"No, you're right, Reverend. But the Hayden you talked about in your church and the kid from Jackson, Mississippi—they were both black, and they'd both be about the same age."

"So what? You look in any phone book in any big city. There's probably a hundred Haydens." He stands.

I close the manila folder and stand up as well. "I know you have to leave," I say. "But there's another coincidence I should mention. There was a murder a few weeks back on Beverly near Stanley."

"Another homeless person? I missed that in the newspaper."

"No," I say. "Her name was Maria Carlotta Ruiz. A lovely girl. She was thirty-four."

"So?"

"She wasn't homeless. She lived with her mother in Boyle Heights. I guess you could call her a street person, though. She was a prostitute."

He purses his lips and spreads his hands in consternation. He has very delicate, well-manicured hands. "And how does this relate?" he asks.

"She was killed just like Daisy Cooper. In fact, whoever shot Daisy also shot Maria. They're pretty sure of that."

"You're losing me, Mr. Parisman." He looks again at his watch. "And I have an appointment—"

"Sure, sure," I tell him, pointing him once more in the direction of the couch. "But just give me two more minutes, okay?"

He collapses again on the couch. He's had enough of me. I've put a monkey wrench in his afternoon. I can see it in his eyes. About now he's probably thinking he's missed his last chance to take the freeway. No matter which way he goes it'll be bumper to bumper. Maybe he's already planning to phone ahead as soon as I walk out the door. Tell his secretary something came up, see if she can reschedule.

I continue standing. The sole of my right foot starts itching slightly; I ignore it. And I don't quite know what I'm going to say next, but in some way it doesn't matter; I'm on a roll. *Is this what it's like to be Catholic?* I wonder. Because suddenly I feel like I want to confess; I haven't done anything wrong, and yet Reverend Jimmy is sitting there, and he seems like the best man, maybe the only man I can turn to. "See, right now the police are happy, they're jubilant because they've wrapped up the homeless murders. In their mind, that's it: that's the end of the story."

"And you're not?"

"Of course I am. But don't you get it? Daisy Cooper and this other woman, Maria? They're different. They don't fit the mold. That's what I'm working on now."

"And I wish you luck," he says.

"You wanna know what I think? About Hayden, the kid who killed that principal and then vanished? I'm guessing he's somewhere here in L.A. I'm guessing he's turned his life around in that time. On the surface, at least. Underneath though, it may be thirty years later, but he's still the same desperate, needy kid. Only now he's what—forty-five? And just like before, he's drawn, as that therapist in Mississippi said, to warm, compassionate women— people who can talk to him and touch him and mother him the way his own mother used to before she died."

"You should have been a psychiatrist," Jimmy Archibald says. "That could very well describe the Hayden that came to my church."

"That's what I'm thinking. You know what else I'm thinking? That something went wrong between him and Maria and then later on, with Daisy."

"I can't imagine," he says. "Daisy never had an unkind word for anyone."

"No," I say, "but who knows with a psycho like Hayden? I'm guessing he's some kind of time bomb. All you have to do is cross an invisible line. Could be perfectly innocuous. In any case, it wouldn't take much for him to feel betrayed the same way Miss Foley made him feel years ago."

"And so?" He's on the edge of the couch now, staring at me, waiting for an answer.

"And so he killed them," I say. "That's what I think."

He stands up again. "Anything's possible," he says. "But I never got to know Hayden, not the way those poor women apparently did. To me, he was a menacing face in the crowd. That's all. I never dared to reach out to him, not like Daisy. She was fearless."

He walks me to the door.

"Maybe he revealed a little too much about himself," I say. "I'm just speculating, of course. But in Hayden's mind, that might be reason enough to kill her."

Jimmy Archibald shrugs. He's worn out by everything that's happened. It's like he just wants it to go away. "Reasonable people don't commit murder," he says. "Reasonable people talk things over. Even if they disagree."

CHAPTER 28

I turn the key in my car and drive slowly up Vine toward Sunset. I'm still mulling over Jimmy Archibald's words. He's a smart man, a complicated man. I make myself a mental note to take a good look at the titles on his bookshelf the next time I go see him. All around me it's wall-to-wall cars. Young, self-assured men in sunglasses on the move, only now they have to sit there and wait for the light to change, like everyone else. On my tape deck Buffalo Springfield is twanging out that old reliable magic again. *There's something happening here. What it is ain't exactly clear.* Well, that's for damn sure, isn't it, Parisman.

Betsy Rollands asked me if I would meet her at the Tiki Lounge at five o'clock. She didn't say why, but then she rarely does. I don't get there until 5:30 and then parking is almost impossible. I push through the door, thinking if I were her I would have given up on me by now, but Betsy has a crocodile's hide. Besides, she's on intimate terms with the bartender and, I don't know why, but she seems to enjoy being surrounded by all this cheap Hawaiian paraphernalia. What can you do?

She's wearing a denim jacket and she's perched at the end of the bar, and by her posture and the color in her cheeks I'm guessing she's been there a while.

"Hey." I grab a stool next to hers.

She turns in my direction. "Hey yourself. You're late. I thought Jews were never late."

"We're not. Except when there's traffic."

She smiles, nods, and signals to the barman. "He'll have a beer, Martin. What do you have that's dark and furtive and German?"

Martin rattles off the list from memory, looks at me. Waits.

"How about Heineken?" I ask. "You got that?"

"Heineken's Dutch," he says. "But yeah, we got it, sure."

"Okay, then."

Betsy is working on something fancier, a Manhattan it looks like.

"I like Dutch beer better," I tell her. "Not that I have anything against the Germans."

She chuckles. "The hell you don't." She takes a final gulp and drains the glass, then holds her hand up for another. "I'm glad you came, Amos. I need someone to talk to. Especially tonight."

"How come?"

"Obviously," she says after a moment, "obviously you didn't hear the news." She reaches out, covers my hand with her own, as if to comfort me. "Do you even listen to the news, Amos?" She frowns and shakes her head. "I'll bet you don't."

"I do, sometimes. But only if I want to get depressed."

"Well, then, okay, I'll tell you the news. Our friend, Amory Blevins, held a news conference a couple of hours ago to let everyone know he's running for city council."

"Is that news? You told me that's what he was up to."

"No, you're right. It was how he did it. First, he said that in view of the arrests of those crazy street people, he was proud to be handing the $25,000 reward money to you."

"To me? Me? Why?"

"Because you turned them in to the cops. You're a hero, Amos. That's what the Mid-City Merchants think. Anyway, the check's in the mail."

I raise my beer glass. "Well, gosh. I'll drink to that."

"Then of course he said he had decided to run for city council. That Los Angeles needs someone like himself who's not afraid to step up to these big intractable social problems. Blah, blah, blah. He's throwing his hat in the ring. Blah, blah, blah."

I look at her hard. "And that's what's depressing you, Betsy? I don't get it."

She takes a short sip of her new drink. "No, that's not it. The thing is, I never realized how gifted a politician Amory would turn out to be. I thought he was slime. He is slime, but at least I had the goods on him. That's what I always figured. He would never be brave enough to cross that line, he'd never dare to put himself out there, not with what I know."

"And?"

"And I was wrong. Dead wrong. He called my bluff. Not only did he say he was running, he stood there in front of the cameras and admitted—in the next breath—that he was bisexual. Even said he's in a long-standing relationship with Jack Harper."

"But didn't I also hear that he was married?"

"Yes! Yes! That's what's so amazing. His wife was there, right next to him. I wasn't in the room, but one of my old colleagues told me they were holding hands. And according to him, his wife has agreed to stand by his side, come what may." She takes another swallow. "Come what fucking may."

"Doesn't sound much like a winning formula," I say. "Not to me."

"If this were Kansas or Nebraska, you'd be right. But in Hollywood, he's betting it gives him a boost. I can see that. Everyone else who's running is a bore by comparison. Not Amory Blevins. Now he's a flawed man, fighting the good fight. A sinner asking for redemption. An anti-hero. They love that kind of shit around here."

I lose track of the time, but I sit with her forever. What's really bugging her, I decide at last, is that journalism, the hard facts she's been so busy ferreting out all her life, don't amount to anything. In the end, Amory Blevins has just shrugged them off, which leaves her feeling pretty worthless. Not to mention drunk.

"You're too wasted to drive, Betsy," I say. "I'm taking you home."

She doesn't protest. I lay some crumpled bills on the counter for Martin, more than enough, apparently. She leans on my shoulder and we limp past the hula girl cut-outs and push our way sideways through the swinging doors into the night.

*   *   *

About an hour after I get back to Creston Drive, I'm sitting on the edge of the bed, half-naked, trying to fit my legs into pajamas, when the phone rings. It's Omar.

"I've been tailing him, Amos. He waited until dark to leave, but then he drove clear out to Santa Monica."

"Sometimes he does real estate out there, Omar."

"Maybe so, but not this time. This time he parked down at the beach and walked clear to the end of the pier."

"Really."

"I got as close as I could. I didn't want to spook him. I thought maybe he was going to meet someone, but he just stood there, staring out at the ocean. Then he took something lumpy from his pocket and heaved it as far as he could into the water."

"And then?"

"Then he turned around, walked right past me and back to his car. I figured he had to have seen me, but if he did, he didn't show it."

"Thanks, Omar. That's what I wanted to hear. Oh, by the way, partner, I'm giving you an early paycheck for all you've done."

"Huh?"

"Let's get together in the next few days. How does $25,000 sound to you?"

"Are you kidding?"

"No, I'm dead serious. You deserve it."

"Well, Jesus, I don't know what to say."

"You don't have to say anything. Just don't take your eyes off Jimmy Archibald, okay?"

"*No problema*," he says.

*   *   *

Mara arrives much later and kicks off her shoes. She's been shopping and she is delighted that the Mid-City Merchants are giving me the money. "He did the right thing," she says. "Although really, he should have talked more about you. That was the least he could have done. He barely mentioned your name. That pissed me off. I saw the whole thing on channel 5 this afternoon. It was all about him."

"Hey, I'm happy to be anonymous," I tell her. "Any detective worth his salt wants to stay in the shadows. That's how we make our living."

"I suppose," she says. "But I'm not voting for him. Even if it was me who ponied up the cash for this whole sordid business." She wags her head dismissively. "I just can't get past—well, you know."

"No, I don't."

"Yes, you do. I saw him standing there with his wife. She was all dolled up in a dark green suit. But she was holding his hand. *Holding his hand!* I can't imagine what was going through her mind. And he was going on and on about 'this other relationship'— that's how he spoke about it. This other relationship. As though it were—I don't know—a dental appointment or a book club he belonged to. Anyway, there's just something wrong about a man carrying on with another man—I mean I don't care about that— but not while he's married to a perfectly decent woman."

"And how's that any different than what we're doing?" I smile at her.

"Are you serious?"

"No. Yes. Maybe."

"I can't believe you said that," she says.

"Well, think about it. Gus is gone. You're a widow. And even though there's sadness—tell me if I'm wrong, but you seem more or less at peace. In my case, technically, Loretta and I—"

"In six months, Loretta won't know who you are, Amos. She's already sailing off into the sunset. The truth is, you're practically a widower right now. You know that." She reaches out across the bed and strokes my arm.

"Yeah. Yeah, you're right," I say. I pull back the covers. She drops her jacket on the rug and crawls in beside me. "Still," I whisper, "we've been together so many years. We've been through so much, and there are moments—they're few and far between now, but when I look at her, the connection—the link is still there, Mara. It doesn't just disappear. And I'm not even sure I want that. How can you want that? Her mind may be gone, but her heart's still beating. It's still her. She's still real to me. I can't let that go, can I?"

"No, you never let go," she agrees. "Never."

*   *   *

Lieutenant Malloy doesn't attend church, but he tries to go for a walk every Sunday morning down by the Los Angeles River. It's his way of taking time out, I guess. There's a footpath along the edge with sycamore trees and brush. The river was always something of a joke when I was growing up; teenagers used to come by after school to ride their bikes or turn tricks with their skateboards down the angled concrete embankments, and it was all fine and good until suddenly it rained. Then the catch basins filled up and kids who should have been home studying for a Spanish quiz instead got swept downriver.

That was then. Even now, it still doesn't usually have much in the way of water. In late summer, if you pick the right spot you can sometimes step across without getting your feet wet. I call him up and ask if he could stand a little company.

"Your company?" he asks.

"No, Bill, the President of the United States."

"I didn't vote for him," he says. "You'd be okay, though. Sure."

We walk together without speaking for maybe a quarter of a mile. I spot a small rabbit. He hears a frog.

"So I thought I'd take your temperature," I say finally. "I mean, you must be feeling pretty good with those seven homeless people locked up."

"Oh yeah," he says. "It's a weight off my shoulders, I'll tell you. And you know what? I think it's a weight off theirs, too."

I give him a look.

"No, really, Amos, I'm sure they're much happier being incarcerated. They had nothing. It got so bad they were willing to die.

That's what the DA will say. Now, look at them: they're sitting pretty. They can't lose."

"I don't follow you, Bill."

"No? Well, if we convict them and send them to death row, they're fine. If they get life without parole, which is likely, that's good, too. If somehow we find an insane asylum that'll take them, what do they care? The state of California has rescued them, you know what I'm saying? They're getting three squares a day. They've got clean clothes. They're getting showers and haircuts. They can work out with weights. Hell, if I didn't have something more noble to do, I'd probably cop to murder myself."

"You're a funny guy, Lieutenant. The LAPD could use more standup comedians like you."

"No, I'm serious."

"No, you're not."

I need to catch my breath, and we find a public bench to sit on. A young, wiry woman in peach leggings jogs by. She's like a gazelle. She's wearing sunglasses and a Dodgers baseball cap, and her expression tells me she's addicted to fitness and health, the same way I used to feel about hot pastrami, back in the day, before my doctor told me no.

"Of course, this case isn't over yet," I say. "There's still Maria Ruiz and Daisy Cooper. Somebody killed them, and it sure wasn't your Rapture Club."

"No," Malloy agrees. "We've hit a brick wall when it comes to them."

I ask him what he's found out about Jimmy Archibald.

"Not much," he says. "I sent Jason and Remo around to interview him. He was very cooperative. Made them sit down. Insisted that they have coffee and homemade pound cake. Remo likes pound cake."

"Never mind that," I say. "What'd they find out?"

"Nothing, really. Just background. Said he learned to minister when he was still a teenager. He ran away from home in Alabama, jumped a freight train, ended up at the Mission downtown."

"So he must know Lemuel Carter, then. That man's been there forever."

"I'm sure," Malloy says. "Anyway, they took him in, fed him, told him all about Jesus. Got him interested in books again. Even helped him find his first job in real estate. He says they saved his soul, plain and simple, and now he's made it his life's work to return the favor. That's where the little storefront church comes from."

"And you believe it?"

Malloy shrugs. "It fits, doesn't it? He's been preaching on his own dime for years. It's not what you'd call a moneymaker. What's not to believe?"

"I don't know. You may be right. It all fits. On the other hand, his name seems to come up with all the victims."

"Not Maria Ruiz."

"Well, yes, even with her, in a way. It was because of Maria that we found out about Hayden, and Jimmy Archibald remembered that there was a Hayden in his congregation."

"It doesn't matter," Malloy says. "Until something changes, as far as I'm concerned, Jimmy Archibald is not a suspect. I'd let it go, I was you."

We both stand up and continue walking. I ask him how Jessie is doing, and he tells me the new arthritis doctor in West Hollywood seems to be helping with her knees, but he costs a fucking fortune.

"Yeah, well."

At this point, ordinarily, he'd ask about Loretta. Not today. He glances down at me, and even though he's mum about it, I'm sure he's trying to juggle the two women in my life. I get it. He's not prudish or shallow, but he's always lived in a stark moral universe. Where he comes from, everything is understood. There are facts and traditions and rules, and good reasons for those rules. He likes it like that. He believes in marriage. He also believes in love, and doesn't want to pass judgment on an old friend. He'd never do that. But this is uncharted territory for him. *Me, too,* I want to say. *Me, too.*

*   *   *

Later that afternoon I drop in at the Rescue Mission on San Pedro. Lemuel Carter's in his office. His desk is a hodgepodge of papers and coffee mugs and leftover takeout containers with what looks like the remains of Chinese food.

"Bet you weren't expecting me, Lemuel."

"No, sir. You're a surprise. But at my age, just about everyone's a surprise." He laughs, points me to a chair. "You take it the way it comes, you know what I'm saying? The way it comes."

I nod. "There's one more person I need to ask you about. I hear you have his record. Fellow by the name of James Archibald."

"Reverend Jimmy?" His eyes light up. "He was one of our big success stories. But, good Lord, it's been years."

"I know. He and I have had a few conversations already. He's a remarkable gentleman. But I'd like to see what you thought of him when he came through."

"First the police, now you." Lemuel Carter reaches with difficulty for his phone. "Well, I suppose since they've already been and gone, it won't make no never mind if you see the same report."

"Thanks, Lemuel. I appreciate it. And I promise"—I lay my hand on my heart—"I won't leak it to the *L.A. Times*."

He lifts up the phone, puts in a call to the main desk. "Ain't nothing there to leak," he says after he hangs up. "He was just a poor kid, down on his luck. Still, it's personal. You don't want just to let that information run wild. Even if Reverend Jimmy doesn't care, it might lose me my job. You know."

A few minutes later one of the young, sturdy men in the green T-shirts knocks once and comes in. He lays a manila folder down on the corner of his desk, which is the only bare spot left.

Malloy was right, there isn't much new in the file, although young Jimmy Archibald was not very forthcoming about how or why he left his home in Alabama. There were some references to drunkenness and his father's occasional violent rages directed mostly at his mother, but the man who compiled the report—a Robert Mayhew—seemed less interested in the family dynamics and more in what the boy wanted to do with his newfound freedom in California.

"How old was he when he arrived at the Rescue Mission, Lemuel?"

"How old? I don't know. He was just an infant, I'd say. Sixteen, seventeen, maybe."

"So if he was a minor, why wasn't any effort made to send him back? What about his family? Did you contact them? Isn't that what you're supposed to do with runaways?"

Lemuel thumbs through the file, his old eyes stopping in places to read a specific paragraph. "He didn't want to go back, man," he says now. He hands me the folder. "That's what the report says. And besides, it didn't matter how old he was. There was no way we were going to send him back. Lots of kids are like that, you know. They come here hungry and scared. They're looking for help, but you tell them you're going to make them go home to someone who's maybe gonna beat the daylights out of them"—a frown—"that doesn't work so well. Five minutes later they're out the door."

CHAPTER 29

The next afternoon around four o'clock, I'm brewing myself a fresh pot of raspberry tea in the kitchen when Omar calls. "I think he's on the move, man."

"What do you mean?"

"Well, I've been watching him like a hawk ever since he was at that pier in Santa Monica. I'm sitting in the underground parking lot now, and he just came out with a big heavy suitcase. Threw it in the trunk. You don't do that unless you're going somewhere."

"Did he take off yet?"

"No," Omar says, "no, not yet. He went back inside the elevator. Maybe there's more to come, I don't know."

"Okay, fine," I tell him. "You just stick with him. But not too close, understand? Malloy and his people don't think he's the one, but I'm going to call them anyway. Maybe they'll change their tune if they hear this."

"Maybe. Okay, man, I gotta go."

"Oh, Omar," I say, "just one more thing. Call me back as soon as you've figured out where he's headed. I'll try to meet you there."

"Right."

"You have a gun?"

There's a silence over the phone. "Why you say that, man? You think I'm gonna go up against this guy without one? I'm not a cop. You think I'm stupid?"

"It's just a question, Omar. You're my partner. I like you. And remember: I still haven't paid you the money I owe."

"Meaning what?"

"Meaning I want you to stay alive long enough to collect, that's all."

"Don't worry about me. You go ahead and call the cops. I can take care of him if I have to."

I wait a moment, count to ten before I call Malloy. I don't have much to go on, I know he's going to treat me like a petulant child at best, or a thorn in his side at worst. He's already taken Jimmy Archibald off his list. So who am I to put him back on again?

"Malloy here."

"Bill, it's Amos. I thought you might be interested to hear that Reverend Archibald has packed his bags. He's heading out of town."

"Who told you this?"

"Omar. He just watched him heave a big suitcase into his trunk."

There is a short pause and I hear what sounds like a sniff or a sigh on the other end. "You're going to have to do a whole lot better than that, Amos. People travel all the time. Maybe he's got some real estate in Oregon. Maybe he's off to see his poor old mother. Maybe he has a girlfriend in Poughkeepsie. Who the fuck knows? You got a thousand reasons to leave town, most of them legal as far as I can tell."

"Well, yes," I say, "but if he drops off the radar now, doesn't that at least make you wonder?"

"I'm filled with wonder," he replies. "But like I said before, there's not a dime's worth of evidence against this guy."

"He had a link with all the victims," I say. "Even Maria Ruiz, since she was *shtupping* Hayden, and the Reverend said Hayden attended his church for a while."

"I've arrested a lot of people," says Malloy, "and more than a few of them turn up dead before their time. Does that make me the killer? Because we were acquainted? I don't think so."

"I know I'm skating here, Bill. There's no proof. But maybe somewhere inside his brain he has the same low opinion of street people that everyone else does. Maybe it was him who was trying to bring on the Rapture."

"That's a wonderful theory, Amos, except he also furnished you with the club's manifesto, didn't he? He handed you the fucking list. And we picked them up, and guess what? They confessed, didn't they?"

"Yes, but—"

"But nothing," Malloy says. "If you ask me, I'd say he's not just innocent, he's a damn good citizen. We could use more people like that."

There's no use arguing with Malloy when he gets this way. His facts will beat my feelings to a pulp every day of the week. "I hope you're right, Bill. But I still think it's an odd time to pull up stakes. He knows we've had him under a microscope. He knows his congregation needs him. And he told me himself he's worried about the church—whether it has any kind of future, whether it can still go on with all this publicity."

"You keep traipsing after him if you like, Amos. What I'm saying is, that after all he's been through, if now he feels like he's maybe entitled to a little getaway, who am I to get suspicious?"

"That's your personal view, right?"

"It is. And it's also the view of the whole Los Angeles Police Department."

I thank him and hang up. The raspberry tea has been sitting so long on the counter that now it's dark. I spoon the tea bag into the trash, raise the still smoky cup and take a small sip, add some honey, sip again, then set it back down. Wait, I tell myself. Tea always takes time to be tolerable. A minute or so later it occurs to me that I never said a word about Omar following him down to the Santa Monica pier and watching him throw something into the water. I start to punch in Malloy's number again, then stop. I know what he'll say. Is it a crime to toss something off a pier? Shall we bust him for littering? That's what he'll want to know. I can almost see the snarky look on his face. And I'll say, it all depends on what it is, doesn't it? And the conversation will go precisely nowhere.

Mara comes up behind me and wraps her bare arms around my chest. "I could only overhear half of what you were saying to the Lieutenant," she murmurs. "But I'm guessing it didn't go well."

"You got that right."

We settle ourselves on the couch. She rubs the top of my hand gently with her own. I pry off my shoes and socks, stuff my tired feet in among the pillows. She's been playing a Chopin recording all afternoon. I don't know my musicians—could be Horowitz, or maybe someone else sitting there at the piano. She has most of his recordings, not that it matters. In the stillness of the living room, with the golden half-light streaming in through the eucalyptus in the next yard, the notes are having a powerful narcotic effect. I could get used to this, I think. I could easily lay back and close my eyes, forget that this is the same world where a sweet old lady is gunned down in her parlor, the same world where it's normal for people to bed down on the sidewalk every night, the same world where young girls paint their faces and go out and offer themselves to whoever comes their way. My eyes start to close. Then they flick wide open and I sit up straight. I'm not about to forget.

*   *   *

My gun is still in its leather shoulder holster and hanging in the closet where I left it. I check the safety, then buckle it on and go back and lace up my shoes.

"Where to now?" Mara asks.

"I dunno," I say. "Malloy doesn't think it means much that Jimmy Archibald is leaving town. And he may be right. But there are just too many unexplained things about him."

"Such as?"

"Such as he ran away from home right about the same time this fellow Hayden did. He says he came from Alabama. Hayden was from Mississippi. I'm sure there's a difference, but still. Such as every murder victim is connected to him one way or another. Such as this Hayden seems to be a pretty unforgettable creature—those aren't my words, that's according to him—a real drama queen. And yet he's the only one in his church who remembers him. It's strange. And I haven't even begun to try to unpack all that crap about the Rapture."

Mara helps me into my sport coat. "I have to find you some better clothes," she says. "How old is this thing? Have you noticed there's a little tear at the elbow?"

"I never look at my elbows," I tell her. I head for the door. "Don't wait up for me," I say.

"You never answered my question," she says. "Where are you going?"

Fear is welling up in her voice. She's become attached, and now she's just starting to come to grips with what that means. "I'm going to try to meet up with Omar," I tell her. "He's tailing him. It's just a feeling, but since the cops won't lend a hand, well, I don't like the idea of him tackling this all alone."

"You be careful."

"Sure," I say. I lean in and kiss her quickly on the cheek. "And Malloy's probably right. Maybe he's just off visiting his mom, for all we know."

Then she says something I wasn't expecting. It stuns me because the truth is, I've heard it before, many times. It was what Loretta used to say whenever I strapped on my gun and walked out the door. "Call me when this is over, okay?"

"Sure," I say. "Sure. You better believe it."

*   *   *

My cell phone rings just as I come to the stop light at Melrose and Vine. "He's heading east on 3rd, Amos, toward downtown. We just passed Carondelet. He could have picked up the freeway at Vermont or Virgil, but he didn't. Only taking surface streets."

"Maybe he's worried about being followed, Omar. How far back are you?"

"Three cars. You don't have to worry, though, I'm being careful. And so far, he's not doing anything crazy. Not suddenly turning left then right. Just driving. If I were betting, I'd say he's going to Union Station."

"Well, if he is," I say, "he can't be in much of a hurry. Not if he's on 3rd at this time of day. Maybe the train's not leaving until tonight."

"Maybe we're getting ahead of ourselves," Omar cautions. "I just threw out that idea about the train station. I have no idea where he's going."

"You're starting to sound like Lieutenant Malloy."

"Just looking at what's in front of me, Amos. That's all."

A few minutes later he calls back again. Now Jimmy Archibald has turned onto Beaudry and then left over the Harbor Freeway. He's slowly plodding his way through the Financial District and Pershing Square. I know that part of town. It's crowded even when it's not. Rich and poor and everything in between. Everyone waiting for the light to change, everyone just wanting to go home and close their door before the darkness swallows them whole. Omar tells me they're moving at a snail's pace and he's having a hard time keeping the Reverend in sight.

"I'll meet you near Union Station, Omar. I'm on Beverly right now, but traffic's not bad. I'm guessing half an hour."

"If that's where he's going," he says, "then that's where we'll meet."

Forty minutes later I pull into Union Station. I find a parking spot within sight of the entrance. The curb is painted red. If I stick around more than fifteen minutes somebody in a uniform will come along and give me a ticket. I don't care, I say to myself. I kill the engine and call Omar. The sun is fading. On Olvera Street nearby, where the pueblo of Los Angeles began a few hundred years ago, the soft orange streetlamps are slowly coming to life. "Where the hell are you, man?"

"I'm inside. Your boy's in line at the counter right now buying a ticket. What do I do if he turns around and heads for a train? You want me to buy a ticket, too?"

"No. No, let's just sit tight and see what happens."

"Okay," says Omar. "That's good, because I didn't say nothing to Lourdes about taking a trip." The mention of his wife churns up all sorts of raw emotions in him. Without me saying a word he starts talking about how she made the best *carne asada* the other night, just how he likes it. Even better than his mother in Oaxaca, but he didn't tell her that because he didn't want her to get any fancy ideas about herself. Then, right in the middle of his dream of Lourdes, he stops. "He bought the ticket, Amos, looks like. He's putting something in his coat pocket now. And he's walking back out toward the entrance."

"I've got my eye on that. Maybe he's early. Maybe he's going back to his car to get his suitcase. Maybe his train doesn't board for a few more hours."

Omar says, "Or maybe he doesn't plan on boarding that train at all."

"Whatever," I tell him. "You just tag along. I'll keep you posted."

"*Que bueno.*"

A minute later I see his tall, distinct figure emerge from the elegant Spanish building. He's wearing a tan jacket and gray slacks. The same red-frame glasses as before. He strolls a few steps to the left and pauses under the clock tower, looks up, checks his wristwatch. Then he stands there with his hands jammed in his pockets and looks around in both directions. From where I'm sitting, it's hard to tell what's on his mind. Waiting for someone? He doesn't seem to be smiling. A cool breeze kicks up out of nowhere and he pulls his sport coat closer to his body. Then he steps off the curb and moves purposefully across the street. His car is parked in a handicapped spot, not that far from mine. I notice he doesn't stop to open the trunk where his suitcase is hidden. Instead he climbs in and revs the motor. When he pulls out into traffic on Alameda, I'm right there behind him. He's not paying attention to me; his eyes are focused straight ahead and he's heading for Chinatown. And when he gets to Hill, he turns north and gets on the Pasadena Freeway.

* * *

I've done my fair share of following people around. More than most, in fact. And it's a real pain in the *tuchus*, but you can't take any shortcuts in this business if you want to succeed. I remember one guy, he robbed a jewelry store in Beverly Hills. I had a bad feeling about him from the beginning. No proof, though. Then all of a sudden he got on a Greyhound, rode it all the way to Ohio. It took nearly three days, and I sat there in the rear, no luggage or anything, just the clothes on my back, dining on corn chips and Coca-Cola the whole time. Never took my eyes off him. And when he landed in Cincinnati I phoned the cops and they picked him up an hour later at his girlfriend's. He was just bringing her an engagement present. That's what he claimed when they put the cuffs on him. Twenty-carat diamond ring. Hey, what's wrong with that?

The Reverend seems to know his way around Pasadena. He cruises down Del Mar past all the well-appointed apartment houses, then takes a left at Lake Avenue. This is the fancy part of the city, or I should say, the fancier part, because a lot of Pasadena has recently gotten stylish. He goes by the banks and the brokerage firms, the art galleries, the department stores and steak houses, and I'm right there two or three cars back. Omar is behind me; I called him as soon as I was sure where we were going. Now, as the Reverend takes the onramp to the 210 East, I make up my mind to place one more call.

"Sorry to bother you on a Saturday night, Lieutenant. I know you always have big plans."

He's in a better mood than the last time we spoke. "Actually, Amos, Jess and I were just warming up the tuna casserole from yesterday. I like leftovers. Things taste better when you know what you're in for."

"That's all I ever eat," I tell him. Out of the corner of my eye I catch a brief glimpse of Omar in the fast lane. He waves. "So the reason I called is, I'm in Pasadena at the moment."

"That's terrific," he says. "Tell the Rose Queen hello for me."

"Well, if I could, sure. I'm on the 210 going east. I'll be in Pasadena for oh, possibly another six exits. Then who knows?"

"You shouldn't be talking to me on the phone, Amos. Not while you're driving sixty miles an hour. There's a law, I believe."

"Sorry. I couldn't help myself. I just thought this was important."

"Okay, fine, never mind. You're on the freeway. And you're shadowing Mr. Archibald, correct? Is that what this is about? Are we still hung up on him?"

"You know me, Bill. I get something stuck in my teeth, I have to pick at it."

"And here I thought we Irish were the stubborn ones. Can't hold a candle to the goddamn Jews." He pauses. I can almost see him shake his head in disbelief. "All right, so what do you have?"

"About an hour ago, Omar watched him buy a ticket down at Union Station."

"So?"

"So then, right after he bought it, he walked out the door and drove off."

"Hmm."

"That's all you have to say? 'Hmm?'"

"No. I'd add something to that. I'd say, it's suspicious."

Now it's my turn to be exasperated. "This afternoon, you had a million reasons for people to go on trips. Now, he buys a ticket and walks away without getting on the train, and you call it suspicious. C'mon, Bill. He's up to something."

Malloy doesn't speak for a while. "You're right," he says finally. "Of course you are. He could buy a ticket, think it over, and maybe change his mind. That works. But then he'd turn around and ask for his money back. Especially if he was still right there."

"Exactly. So why'd he buy the ticket, then?"

"Dunno," says Malloy. "What's your thought?"

"My opinion? To send us a message. He's worried he's about to be busted. He's worried, and he decided to run."

"And the ticket?"

"That's for us. That's a decoy. His name attached to a train that left the station for New York or Atlanta or God only knows. He figures if we're after him, we'd find that information soon enough."

"We would. And it would be only logical to assume he was on board."

"Anyone would think that," I agree. "Meanwhile, he's driving off into the night."

"Makes sense," Malloy says. His tone has turned resolute. "I'll have my people check out that ticket. Where are you now?"

"Let's see, I just passed the Rosemead exit. Omar is driving close by, and we're keeping him in sight, but this freeway goes on forever. I've got less than half a tank. Sooner or later I'm going to have to stop for gas."

"Well, as long as the two of you are in separate cars, you can probably manage that and still keep a fix on him. Stay in touch, though. If he gets anywhere close to Arizona or the Mexican border, I'd like to hear."

"That all you're going to do? Wait for him to skip out of the country?"

"No. I'll let the CHP in on where you're headed. I'll also see if I can't persuade a judge to execute a search warrant of his apartment, even if it is after office hours. Who knows? Maybe there's a matchup between his prints and Joe John Hayden's."

"Now you're talking," I say.

CHAPTER 30

We keep pace with him as he leaves the 210 for the 15 North. Just shy of Barstow he suddenly puts his foot down hard on the gas pedal and takes an off ramp into the desert. I'm the closest car behind him, maybe five hundred feet, and Omar's right in back of me. This time of night, and this far away from the lights of civilization, you don't expect any traffic, and sure enough, there is none. Which is bad, because now I think he's onto us. The silver Toyota comes to the bottom of a long, steep incline. There's a stop sign waiting there, but Archibald ignores it and veers to the left. We trail haplessly along. The road narrows. His car is faster than my old Honda. I make out what look like mountains looming in the east, but the landscape right around us seems mostly flat. With each curve in the highway my headlamps pick up a fresh mound of sand and clusters of rambling tumbleweed.

I pick up my cell phone. "This is trouble, Omar."

"You think he knows where he's going?"

"He might have, once upon a time. Not anymore, though. Now he's running away," I say. "We've spooked him."

"So now what?"

"I don't know. Just stay back, keep him in sight. He may try to turn off somewhere and kill his lights, hope we pass him. That's what I'd do if I were running."

"Not many spots you can do that around here," Omar says. "I'll bet if you saw this place in broad daylight you'd think it was a parking lot."

"I don't plan to be here when the sun comes up," I say. "In fact, I just hope he pulls over and we can have a nice friendly chat."

"If we scared him, it's not going to be friendly," Omar predicts.

Ten minutes later he does exactly that. There's a wide turn in the road, and beyond it an outcropping of large, jagged rocks. The rocks have been there a few million years; they must have impressed the early pioneers coming through here. Enough to build the road around them, anyway.

By the time we pull up, he has already parked the Toyota and crouched down among the larger ones. Our headlights illuminate the whole scene, but he can see us, too, so that makes us even.

I cut the motor and kill my lights, signaling to Omar that he should do the same. We both sit quietly for a moment. I release the safety on my gun, then crack open the door. "Mr. Archibald," I call out.

"Who are you?" he shouts back.

"It's Amos Parisman. You're a long way from home, Reverend." I look around, shake my head. "I mean, I don't think even Jesus would want to be caught in this wilderness."

"Parisman?" He seems surprised and more than a little confused. Did he think we were the police? Was he running from someone else?

"Yeah, it's me," I say. Now we're both in the semi-darkness. He can make out the cars, though. And without the headlights on he's just another blur sliding around among the rocks. "I wanted to talk with you. It was kind of important, but you drove off before that could happen."

"And you followed me all this way?"

"Me and my pal, Omar Villasenor. We did, yeah. Like I say, it was kind of important." I think about taking a step or two forward, away from the Honda, but then I decide no, let's wait. There's something eerie about having a conversation in the dark in the middle of a desert with someone you think just might be a murderer.

Omar gets out of his car and squats behind his door like me. His gun is drawn and he seems agitated. I don't know why, but I can tell the minute he opens his mouth he's going to play the bad cop, since I'm dancing around, being Mr. Nice Guy. "Why don't you come out with your hands up?" he says. His tone is cold, suspicious. "You don't have any more guns, do you? I saw you throw one off the pier in Santa Monica the other night. Was that what you used on Daisy and Maria?"

Jimmy Archibald seems to cough, or maybe laugh, it's hard to tell. "You're mistaken, I'm afraid. I didn't kill anybody. You have no proof."

"Well, we'll just see about that, won't we?" Omar says. "Wait until the divers find the gun. And believe me, they're out there right now. The water's not that deep. And they're good at their job. They'll find it."

"That wasn't a gun, Mr. Villasenor."

"Oh no?" he says. "So what the hell was it, then? You sure threw something into the water. Sure looked like a gun."

There's no answer for a moment. "Not a gun," he says at last. "A Bible." There's a sad clarity in his voice. He may have lied to me before, but this time it feels like the truth.

"Why would you want to do that, Reverend?" I ask him.

"Why? Because for so many years I've relied on the words in that book. It was my rock. It was all I thought I needed, really."

"A lot of folks have found comfort that way," I say.

"Yes, well, a lot of folks have let themselves be duped," he says. "And I came to a point in my life, I—I can't do that anymore."

"Is this about the homeless killings, Reverend?" I ask. "Nobody thinks you're involved in them."

"Oh, but I am, Mr. Parisman. I am. I didn't kill them, but I may as well have. My words, the sermons I preached, everything I told them led to their deaths. Absolutely. Doesn't that make me complicit?"

"I don't know," I say. "Not in a court of law."

Neither of us talk for a time. I look to my left and I see Omar still crouched behind the door of his Camaro. His gun is moving slowly, inch by inch across a level plane. He's cocked and ready, and he doesn't care for this lengthy conversation one bit. We're splitting hairs, trading philosophy in the night, and Omar's mind doesn't work like that. He's already sorted things out. There's a killer nestled in the rocks a hundred feet away. He's coiled like a spring and I can almost hear him thinking: what are we waiting for?

Then, just when it seems like neither one of us might ever say another word, the Reverend's voice interrupts the darkness. "My life has come full circle, Mr. Parisman. Full circle. It's been a long time, but I'm back where I started. It's amazing. And this may be hard for you to understand. I'm not . . . I'm not really the person you thought I was."

"You're not Jimmy Archibald. I've figured that much out already."

"No, you're quite right, I'm certainly not him. That was vanity on my part."

"So was there ever a James Archibald?"

"Oh yes," he says. "Jimmy Archibald was famous in certain parts. I met him one night in a rail yard in East Texas. Long ago, thirty years, maybe more." He stops, and when he starts again, it's as if he's just pulled the memory out of a sack. "Isn't it funny, Mr. Parisman, the way time twists things. How, if you wait long enough, even the least among us gets famous for something?"

"Who was he?"

"Archibald?" The question seems to float in the desert air. "Jimmy Archibald was a hobo. A nobody. A con. A toothless failure. No. No, let me amend that. He wasn't just a hobo. He was the king of the hobos. The kindest of men."

Omar and I exchange looks. I don't know how far he ever got in his police training, whether he studied the part about talking people into putting down their weapons and surrendering peacefully. I sorta doubt it.

"Took me under his wing," the Reverend is saying now. "Kept me alive. Kept me safe. I was running, and I came to him one night, all chewed up, and he nursed me back. Showed me how to live in the shadows. I could never repay him, you know. Not in a million years."

"No, those people are few and far between," I chime in. "You need people like that in your life. We all do."

"Yes. I wish to God he were still alive."

"So what happened?"

He doesn't respond immediately, but when he does, his tone shifts, becomes softer, almost wistful. "Same as happens to most of them. Jimmy was getting on. And he had a weakness. He liked to drink. In all the days and nights we spent together I never once saw him refuse a drink. You can understand that, surely."

"I can."

"It's a hard enough life as it is," Archibald says, "always being on the road, always glancing over your shoulder, running from the railroad bulls. Never knowing where your next meal is coming from."

"And when he died, you took his name. Is that right?"

"I wanted . . . I wanted to honor him, yes. I was just a kid. He'd carried me. He bore the weight. And my name was already dirt. They were looking for me. My picture was tacked up in the post office. Why not aspire to something more?"

Our conversation is getting more mellow now. I don't want to continue shouting back and forth in the dark like this indefinitely, and whatever he wants to talk about, it'll go far better if we're face to face. I take two tentative steps away from my car. "I'd like to talk to you in person, Jimmy, if you don't mind," I say. "I'm not an orator like you."

"Please stay where you are, Mr. Parisman."

"I didn't come here to hurt you," I say, "I just want to talk." Two more steps. Little by little we can make this happen.

A shot sings out and bounces off a rock to my right. I drop flat to the ground and start to crawl forward like they taught me in the

Marines. He can't see me slithering on my belly, but maybe he can hear my heart pounding away.

"So you kept the gun," Omar yells from behind now. "You should drop it. You hear me? Drop. It. Now. No sense getting yourself killed, Reverend."

"No, that's not true," he shouts back.

"What the hell are you talking about?" Omar yells. He doesn't understand. "You wanna die? Here? In the middle of fucking nowhere?"

"No," the man behind the rocks answers. His voice is quavering. "I don't want to die. It's Hayden. Hayden wants to die."

"Hayden?" I shout. "Tell me about him, Reverend. Why does he want to die?"

A queer sound comes now from behind the rocks. Like sniffling. Like a grown man weeping. "Hayden," he mumbles, "that Hayden, he did a bad thing. He was good for so many years, but then he lost control. I couldn't stop him. He . . . God help us, he killed those people. To cover his tracks. It was him, not me. Daisy Cooper. And Maria. Lovely Maria. Hayden talked too much. Even as a kid. He had such a big mouth. He had to go and tell them who he was. And now look. He has nothing more to live for. Nothing. It's Hayden. Hayden brought me to this spot."

I keep crawling forward to a safe resting place behind an enormous rock and level my Glock against a ledge. I can hear his voice. He's only about thirty feet away and I have a strong sense of where he is. All he has to do is fire again and I'll see the tiny flash. That might be enough.

"So shall we call you Joe John Hayden?" Omar asks. "That's who you really are, isn't it? Why hide behind the church? You threw the Bible into the sea. Jimmy Archibald would never do that. Hayden would. Isn't that who you are?" He's taunting him now, and it seems to be working. The Reverend Jimmy Archibald or Joe John Hayden or whoever he thinks he is now, crouching down in the brush, that person is breaking apart before our eyes.

"No! No! No!" he shouts. "Hayden's a killer! I'm—I'm a man of God. Please—you need to stop him."

"Okay," Omar says, trying his best to play along, "fine, we'll stop him. But first, first, let's get you to a safe place, huh? You just come out from there. You don't want to be around when we shoot Hayden."

"No, you're right, I don't."

Omar takes a small step away from his car door. "I'm going to help you get away from him, Reverend. But I need you to trust me. If you don't trust me I can't do anything. So listen carefully. The first thing I want you to do is put the gun down."

"I can't do that," he says. "I need the gun. I need it. That's the only thing that's stopping Hayden. You don't understand."

"Put the gun down," Omar repeats. "If you put it down nothing's going to happen, I promise. Put it down and just come out to where we can see you, okay? How about this? I'll meet you halfway." Then he steps away completely from his car and starts walking slowly, deliberately, toward the outcropping.

It's impossible to know what a man is really thinking in that terrible moment when he points a loaded pistol at another human being. Oh, there are all kinds of brilliant excuses they come up with in courtrooms later on. That's how lawyers earn a living. But when you dig down beneath the anger and the lust and the greed, when you hear the defendant say that he feared for his life, when all the clever nonsense is unpacked and dismissed, the honest answer—the only word that comes to me—is chaos. Chaos is the swamp, all we had in the beginning, what came before religion. Hell, that's why they invented religion. To keep chaos at bay. Chaos doesn't care. Chaos grabs you by the throat like a schoolyard bully. There's nothing you can do about it. You're going to die, pure and simple. Your whole world is suddenly dust. Every inch of your body knows this. And a gun doesn't grant you any power. If you're lucky, a gun just buys you a little time. It wards off chaos, that's all. That's what Jimmy Archibald or Joe John Hayden wants when he steps out from behind the rocks and opens fire on Omar. And that's what I want, too, a split second later, when I pull the trigger.

* * *

I'm guessing Malloy alerted the local cops. He must have, in fact, because a police helicopter arrives overhead not ten minutes later. Maybe they know where we are because of our cell phones. And just to make it easier, we turn on our headlights so they can land away from the rocks. They're busy administering first aid to Hayden, who is okay, but numb from the bullet that caught him in the thigh. "Just missed the femoral artery," the cop says. "You're one lucky SOB."

Four Highway Patrol cars descend on us, one after another, sirens on, red and blue lights blinking away. They climb out cautiously with their guns cocked and ready. Then an ambulance shows up from the Barstow Community Hospital. Hayden is flat on the ground. He keeps moaning and cursing and writhing around and telling everyone who'll listen that he's going to die, which, now that the EMTs are pumping him full of morphine, is not only false, it's almost laughable.

Omar's fine, thank God. The shots Hayden intended for him went clear past. One went through the windshield of his car, though. And that pisses him off, because there aren't many things in life he loves more than that car of his. "Man," he says, "man, it's a good thing you got him. I was about to unload my whole fucking clip."

"No," I say, "It's not a good thing. The only thing good is that it's over." I look at his car. "Can you drive that beast in that condition? What do you think?"

He examines it close up. "It didn't shatter. For sure, the crack's gonna grow, but it'll hold up until I get it back to a body shop in Boyle Heights. You better pay for it, though."

"You got a deal, Omar."

The CHP has other ideas. They've taken our statements and talked at length with Malloy on the phone. The sergeant, a burly, red-faced guy whose name tag says Lassetter, insists on holding onto the Camaro. That they need to recover the Reverend's bullet, which is lodged somewhere in the upholstery. Evidence, he says. And besides, no one can drive a vehicle with a smashed windshield. *Unsafe* is the word he uses several times.

"I don't give a damn, I just want to go home," Omar says. "I've had enough. And Lourdes is going to kill me when she hears about the Camaro."

*   *   *

We drive back to L.A. together. We don't talk; there's not much to talk about, actually. Somewhere around Claremont, I start to thank him for his courage, tell him it was brave of him, stepping out of the darkness. Then I backtrack. Well, maybe not brave, I say, maybe a little bit stupid, but you know, it turned out brave in the end. He looks at me, he gives me that old Aztec, hard-as-stone, thousand-yard stare, that I-can't-fucking-believe-you-said-that stare, and shakes his head.

When I get close to Pasadena I call Mara. "Just thought you'd like to hear. It's over," I say.

"Are you all right?"

I glance at Omar. His eyes are drooping and he's starting to doze off. "I'm tired," I tell her. "We're both tired, I guess. And I've been crawling around in the desert, which doesn't do much for my clothes. I probably smell terrible. But everything's fine, yeah. It's another day here in paradise."

CHAPTER 31

There's a story that La Parrilla, the old Mexican joint on Wilshire I go to now and then, was once one of Charlie Chaplin's homes. It ain't so. The truth is, the guy who developed it back in 1905 was named Charles Chapman, and some joker, maybe he was deaf in one ear, thought it belonged to Chaplin, and now, along with the clunky Mexican furniture and the ticky-tacky stuff hanging from the ceiling, there's all kinds of Chaplin memorabilia on the walls. I've always liked that tale, because it corresponds so closely with my own years as a detective. It's how the world works really: You want your life all laid out in a straight line, but you never know when things are going to take a sharp left. Which they always do. And for no good reason.

I'm sitting here with Mara. We're holding hands like teenagers under the table. The sun is shining. We're both nursing margaritas and working through a pile of fresh chips and salsa with Lieutenant Malloy, who's hunched across from us looking mournfully at an iced tea.

"Where's your cousin?" Mara wants to know. "It's almost one. Didn't you say 12:30?"

"He'll be along," I say. "Shelly likes to make an entrance. Hollywood's in his blood."

"Well, I'm on duty, I can't stick around here forever, especially for a prima donna," says Malloy.

"I understand, Bill. And I don't even care if you ever meet him, but I did want you to spend a little time with Mara. Get to know her." I smile in her direction.

"We've met before," he says. "Remember?" The look on his face says he's still not quite sure about us, our relationship. Sometimes I think the fact that William Malloy is an old-school, blue-eyed Irish Catholic is a wonderful thing. But it can also be an obstacle.

"Mara sees Loretta on a regular basis," I say, by way of reassurance. "They've become close friends."

"And Loretta . . . she knows?"

I nod. "She knows. Of course, she mostly forgets that she knows, but then we remind her and it's fine."

Malloy shakes his head, grins. "Well, I guess it's all right, then."

"At our age, Lieutenant," Mara jumps in, "being discreet doesn't pay many dividends. You have to take what the circumstance will allow. My Gus got to know Amos before he died. At least I think he did."

Malloy pushes a chip sideways around on his plate. "Hey, don't get me wrong," he says. "I'm not here to judge."

"No," I say, "but I can tell you have opinions."

"Which you'll notice I'm keeping to myself," he adds. He takes a chip in his mouth, crushes it, and turns to Mara. "Actually, I'll tell you the God's honest truth, I'm glad Amos has found a new friend in his life. I am. Otherwise, you know what? He'd be stuck with me. And I'm lousy company. Even my wife says so."

I ask him about the case against Archibald.

"It'll be some time before it goes to trial," he says. "He's got a decent lawyer, but given his history of flight risk the judge wants to keep him in the slammer. Better safe than sorry."

"He hasn't confessed, has he?"

"All depends who you're talking to," says Malloy. "If you're talking to Joe John Hayden, he's the killer of all of them, no question. If Jimmy Archibald shows up for the interrogation, well, that's another story."

"Sounds like they're building a good case for insanity."

"I'd be fine with that, frankly," Malloy says. "Not that I have any say-so. I mean, I know you got the reward for busting up the Rapture Club, but it was Archibald who gave you the list of names, right? We weren't going anywhere till that happened."

"It was also Archibald who killed Daisy Cooper and Maria Ruiz."

"Actually, it was Hayden," Malloy says. "I'm not saying Archibald's a saint, but he did help us. Or one of his personalities did, whatever his motivation." He raises a finger in the air. "And that manifesto? We've been comparing his handwriting, and it turns out he wrote it, not one of the street people. So what does that tell you?"

"I'm not sure," I say. "If he wrote it and put those names on it, then that was his hit list. Or alternatively, it was a helluva red herring he created."

"Right," says Malloy. "And then he handed that statement to you because he was counting on you to put an end to it. Not the usual impulse of a killer, I'd say."

"But you've got confessions from all the homeless people on that list," says Mara. "What about them?"

"Like I told Amos," Malloy says, "life on the street is so damn hard. It makes prison look inviting sometimes. Archibald—or Hayden, or whichever one wrote that list—he picked the most desperate folks in his church. He knew they'd confess to anything, anything at all, even something they didn't do, just to get to a safe place with three meals a day."

"You ever ask Archibald why he didn't just go to the police himself with that list?"

"As a matter of fact, we did. He said he was scared—claimed he was petrified. If he went to us, he said, those people would turn on him, make him their next victim. That's why he came up with that anonymous piece of paper, all that gibberish. It was an excuse, of course, something to buy himself a little distance with. It could have been any one of them who wrote that and slipped it under his door, after all. And he could always claim he never ratted on them, which is true; you did that."

"Clever fellow," I say.

"But what about Daisy and Maria?" asks Mara. "Isn't Archibald to blame for their deaths?"

Malloy sighs. "Yeah, sure, he's to blame, or rather his other self is. We've got his signed confession as Hayden. But we don't have much in the way of evidence. We don't have any weapon, for example."

"You don't?"

"Nope. There was no hardware at his apartment. Nothing in his car. Nothing registered in his name. He's pretty good at covering his tracks."

"You looked off the Santa Monica pier?" I ask.

"Of course," Malloy goes on. "We had our divers all over the place. And when he told you that it wasn't a gun, it was a Bible he threw in the water? Well, we found a Bible, sure enough. Even had his name on the inside cover. But no sign of a gun. Not yet."

"What about the gun he tried to kill us with out in the desert?"

"Now that, that's a different issue," Malloy says. "First of all, it's no match to the one that killed those women. Number two, his lawyer is suggesting his client felt threatened by you. It was night. You guys were following him into the middle of nowhere. He was confused. Afraid. Crazy. So afraid that he pulled off the road and tried to hide in the rocks. Told you not to come any closer."

"We were no threat to him, Bill."

"I know that, sure," he says. "And you know that. But a judge or a shrink might take it into consideration."

I shake my head. "I still don't get it. He was clearly on the run that night."

"Yes, but from who? From the police? From some maniac juiced up on the Bible? From voices inside his own head? How can we tell?"

I feel myself getting angry. "Didn't he say that the reason Hayden killed those people was because he talked too much? Isn't that an admission of something?"

"Hayden," Malloy says slowly under his breath, "Hayden will

admit to anything under the sun. I could solve every murder in L.A. if I just asked Hayden. Hell, he killed people that aren't even dead yet. He can't tell you how or why, but still."

"I see."

Malloy lays his hand down flat on the table. "Don't get me wrong. I'm not saying he didn't do it. All I'm saying is the court will take what we have and grind it into powder, and in the end, after the state has gone through a fortune, he'll spend years in a psychiatric lockup. That's the likely outcome. That's what we'll call justice."

"And that's the best you can do?" Mara wants to know. She's not happy. I'm not happy. Malloy probably isn't, either, but he's been through this many times before, and his face betrays no emotion.

"About the size of it," he says finally. He sips his iced tea for a moment. "No, wait, I take that back. We've done a damn good job, all in all. Far too many died, but with the Reverend's help, and with your help, Amos, we've kept even more homeless folks from dying. We've stopped the panic in the streets, and soon, God willing, we'll be putting one very sick individual away where he can do no more harm. And maybe, just maybe, there's a doctor there who can bring out the human being in him. That's where we're at. Not too shabby, in my opinion."

Malloy stands then. "I gotta shove off," he says. "Jason and Remo are waiting for me. Burglary last night down on La Cienega."

"You need my help?"

He grins at me and Mara, adjusts his tie. "Nah. You stay put. Eat your lunch. Good luck, you two."

He pushes through the wooden doors, and not thirty seconds later I see the large, stylish presence of my cousin Shelly ambling toward us. He's got a purple silk handkerchief in the breast pocket of his sport coat, and both of his arms extend in an exaggerated greeting. "*Boychik*," he says.

*   *   *

Shelly is a complicated guy. I watch him slide into the same seat Malloy just occupied a minute before. He smiles and jokes around with Mara, so glad to finally meet her at last. Grabs her hand, smothers it in both of his own. What a lucky lady she is, if she only knew how many gorgeous women have been lusting after Amos Parisman all these years. He winks at me as he says this. Opens the menu, closes the menu, cracks it open again. A few tiny beads of sweat dance around his forehead, and he's talking a mile a minute, something he does when he's nervous or unsure of his surroundings, which is most of the time. I notice how he wears his age and his heft and his clothes and his Jewish demeanor, every aspect ironed and accounted for. He's like an armored knight, primed for battle. There's something regal and also infinitely sad about him, though it's hard to put my finger on what it is exactly.

I watch him hold forth. He orders us all another round of margaritas while we go over the menu for lunch. This is the first time he's ever been here, can you believe that? Thought he'd been to every Mexican joint in L.A., but somehow he missed La Parrilla. Oh yeah, he says, and by the way, Amos, this lunch is on me. Just keep sitting on your wallet, don't even try to pay. Another wink at Mara. How often do I get the distinct pleasure of dining with my *mishpachah*, huh, my family? I'm all alone right now, but I've had three wives, just so you know. Three wives. Four sons, two lovely daughters. Last day of every month I write the checks. Did Amos here ever tell you how much family means to me? Did he ever mention me at all?

Shelly is spinning, I can tell. I'll never hear a word about it, but in the back of his mind he's secretly fuming. Somehow I betrayed him. I set him up. How could I be so silent? How is it he never knew a thing about Mara? All this time he was feeling so sorry for me, worried I'd drop dead someday all by myself on the ninth floor in Park La Brea, trying to fix me up with his ex-wives' friends, and here I was, doing just fine on my own.

Mara squeezes my hand. When Shelly goes off in search of the men's room, she leans over and kisses me on the neck. "I like him," she declares.

"You do?"

"Of course. He reminds me of people I grew up with back East. He's just another misplaced Old World Jew, is all. This town's full of them. What's not to love?"

"Well, I just wanted you to know what you were getting into. That's the kind of *mishegas* I come from."

"Show him some kindness, Amos. C'mon. You can do that. He's a wounded animal."

"Aren't we all," I say.

ACKNOWLEDGMENTS

Even though it has my name on it, I'm very aware that whatever I write is a collaborative effort. Many people helped me finish this book. Thank you to the staff of Readers' Books, for reading it early on, and for allowing me to fool around in my office writing fiction when I should have been out front selling it. Big thanks also to Colleen Dunn Bates, my former publisher, who helped edit and nail down L.A.'s shifting geography. Thanks to Ron Raley and Cheryl Howard for their narrative and linguistic expertise, and profound gratitude to Beth Hanson, whose level-headedness and compassion kept me sane during the pandemic. Without these folks around, it would never have happened. And of course, thanks to Lilla, my north star.

ABOUT THE AUTHOR

ANDY WEINBERGER is the author of *An Old Man's Game*, and a longtime bookseller, and founder/owner of Readers' Books in Sonoma, California. Born in New York, he grew up in the Los Angeles area and studied poetry and Chinese history at the University of New Mexico. He lives in Sonoma, where Readers' Books continues to thrive.